UNTIL OUR BLOOD IS DRY

Kit Habianic grew up in Caerphilly, Colwyn Bay and Cardiff. As a freelance journalist, she slept under the stars in the Western Sahara, chewed qat in the souqs of Yemen and sailed the backwaters of Kerala, purely for research purposes. Her journalism has appeared in *The Guardian*, *The Daily Mirror*, *The Times*, *Marie Claire* (US) and *Time Out* and in trade titles in Europe and the Middle East. Based in London, she processes copy for a business daily, all the while plotting new stories to write. Her short fiction has appeared in anthologies and literary magazines and made the shortlist for the Willesden Herald short story prize. *Until Our Blood is Dry* is her first novel.

UNTIL OUR BLOOD IS DRY

Kit Habianic

PARTHIAN

Parthian
The Old Surgery
Napier Street
Cardigan
SA43 1ED

www.parthianbooks.com

First published in 2014
© Kit Habianic 2014
All Rights Reserved

ISBN 978-1-909844-53-7

Editor: Susie Wild
Cover design by www.theundercard.co.uk
Front cover image © John Mason /
www.geologywales.co.uk
Typeset by Elaine Sharples
Printed and bound by Gomer Press, Llandysul, Wales

Published with the financial support of the Welsh Books
Council

For Jack and Marion. With love and thanks.

It is bitter to know that history
Fails to teach the present to be better than the past
For man was a slave in the morning of time
And a slave he remains to the last

Idris Davies, *Gwalia Deserta*

'Tributes are pouring in for a miner who died earlier this morning following an incident at a churchyard at Ystrad, a village on the South Wales coalfield.

'The dead man has been named as Gwyn Pritchard, 45, an overman at Blackthorn Colliery near Ystrad.

'Mr Pritchard was one of just three miners to have continued to work at nearby Blackthorn Colliery, breaking a strike that has halted the UK's coal production for nearly 12 months.

'In a statement released minutes ago, the National Coal Board paid tribute to the dead man. Area manager Adam Smith-Tudor described Mr Pritchard as "a solid family man who died defending his right to go to work at the pit he loved".

'South Wales police have made one arrest and say they are looking for a second person in connection with the incident. A police spokesman declined to confirm reports that the dead man was attacked by striking miners.'

Transcript, radio news broadcast,
9am, March 1, 1985

WINTER 1984

Mid-evening, and The Red Lion was empty. Gwyn Pritchard sat at his usual table in the lounge bar and sipped ale from his tankard. No music pounded from the jukebox in the main bar. There was no tobacco fug above the pool table. Not tonight. He twitched a faded chintz curtain, raised a nostril-full of dust, and stared out into the gloom. The north wind howled, vicious. At the bottom of Ystrad High Street, the pavement was pooled with light spilt from the windows of the Miners' Institute. His men were still in there, still stewing over the morning's accident, that bastard Dewi Power stirring up their grief, no doubt.

He dropped the curtain, turned his attention back to his pint. His fourth. But the beer wasn't doing what it should. Tonight, the more he drank, the more he ended up dwelling on it. The rescue workers trooping out of the wheel house to the courtyard. The stretcher covered with grime-streaked canvas.

Steve Red Lion plucked the last packet of peanuts from the poster pinned behind the bar to reveal a topless blonde in all her glory, tits like ice creams. He stared at her, damn as near dribbling. Gwyn caught the landlord's eye. Steve flushed pink from neck to pate and started polishing the optics, at a loss to know what to say.

'Cold out tonight, eh, Gwyn,' he tried.

'That piece'd keep a fellow warm.'

Time was, Mrs Steve ran the pub. A proper little dragon, barely the height of a bar stool but not afraid, come closing time, to grab a drunken collier by the collar, drag him outside and drop him on the pavement. There were no topless posters at The Red Lion when that one was around.

'I heard about Gabe, poor old bugger,' Steve said. 'Hit you hard, I'll bet.'

There it was. The image assaulted him again. Gabe Parry, face peaceful despite the broken-doll neck, the forehead flecked with bone and brain and clotted blood.

He shrugged. 'Seen a fair few deaths in my time. Won't be the last.'

Steve gathered up Gwyn's tankard, filled it, waved away his money, waited as though expecting more.

And what point saying anything. Best to leave fresh wounds to heal, leave old wounds be. The first to go was the old boy who trained him, a sarky old Trotskyist known as Alf Manifesto. A good old boy, for all his piss-and-vinegar about miners being the vanguard of the revolution. Killed when a pack hole collapsed on him, buried him chest-deep in fallen rocks. Gwyn had attacks of the shakes for months after his butty died, body sweating rivers as the cage rattled down to the pit.

Not the loss that haunted him, even so.

Steve's lips were moving. '—after what happened to your old dad.'

Gwyn didn't answer. He'd paid his dues to that bloody pit, him and his forebears.

'—then going down again tomorrow. No life for a man, that, Gwyn. No life for a beast.' Pink with emotion, Steve's face.

Gwyn touched his thumb to his one good finger. One hell of a price to pay for coal. Every piece of anthracite ripped from the earth repaid in blood. Nights like this, a man needed his butties around him. Nights like this, it was only other colliers who understood. It was alright for his men. They had each other.

Steve was still jabbering. Gwyn turned away and looked out over Ystrad again. He'd known it all his life, this little high street, as familiar as the stumps at the end of his knuckles. Blindfold him, he could make his way down from the pub to the parade of shops, past the Victorian Miners' Institute, take a sharp right-turn downhill to reach Blackthorn pit.

It was nothing special, the village, the usual shops overlooking the usual valley floor. Italian *bracchi*, unisex fashion boutique, hairdressers, butchers, bookies, funeral parlour and co-op. Behind these, up a slope fit for sledging, the usual two rows of terraced houses. And at the top, a row of semis that dwarfed the homes below, built for pit management. Superior properties on the top tier. He had barely enough puff in his old lungs to get up there, lately. Worth the effort, even so.

Footsteps approached the pub. Here they were at last: Dewi Power and that rabble from the lodge. The swing doors flew open and in they trooped, falling silent as they walked past, shooting dark looks in Gwyn's direction. Uncalled for, that. They walked through the lounge bar as usual, piled into the main bar with its jukebox and pool table and dartboard, voices muted, not a glance for the peanut girl as they crowded round the taps and waited for Steve to serve them.

Pints in hand, they gathered round the long table at the back, talking quiet, talking serious. There would be trouble in the morning, for sure. If his lads clocked in at all. Dewi Power tapped his glass. The hum of voices faded. The lodge secretary hefted himself onto the bar, face pale against coal dust-rimmed eyes, a broken-nosed little pharaoh addressing his worker hordes. His voice was low, commanding the lads' attention.

'Listen up, fellas. A sad day it's been for Blackthorn. We lost a good man today. One o' the best.' He clapped an arm around the man-mountain standing next to him. 'You do the honours, Dai.'

Gabe's butty Dai Dumbells bowed his head, launched into the Wobbly anthem sung for many a dead collier.

'I dreamed I saw Joe Hill last night
Alive as you or me
Says I, but Joe you're ten years dead.
I never died said he. I never died, said he.'

There was pathos to Dai's tuneless baritone, for once. It got the rest of the lads to their feet, voices soaring together:

'Where workers strike and organise
It's there you'll find Joe Hill
It's there you'll find Joe Hill.'

Gwyn sat, heart in his boots, willed his lads not to court trouble. Willed them not to get it wrong – so very badly wrong – yet again. Everyone knew damn well what was coming. Smith-Tudor, the area manager, had called him in at Christmas, sat him down for a chat, man to man. Promised he'd see Gwyn right if he kept his lads in line. There was a time for trouble and a time for knuckling down. Smith-Tudor spelled it out for him. It fell to Gwyn to break the lodge's grip on his lads. If he let the lodge use a man's death to stoke his lads' anger, there was only one way things would fall.

But Dewi Power wasn't done yet. 'Here's to Gabriel Parry,' he raised his glass.

Gwyn made to raise his tankard, caught Dewi's eye across the bar, thought better of it. His tankard was drunk dry in any case.

Dewi fixed him with a cold dark stare. 'Gabe's dead, and the overman's suspended two of our boys,' he said. 'Suspended two decent, hard-working colliers for going to help a fallen comrade. We won't go back to work. Not until Iwan and Scrapper Jones get reinstated.'

'Damn right,' bleach-blond Matt Price cut in.

The rest nodded agreement. Gwyn saw no point staying for

a fifth pint after that. He had no truck with the lodge's nonsense. Particularly not tonight. He might as well head off home to Carol and the girl.

Keep the boys in line, keep the coal flowing, the area manager told him. Fat chance, Smith-Tudor. Fat bloody chance.

— 2 —

Helen lay in Scrapper's arms, skin damp against his skin, carpet rough beneath her thighs. So that was it, then, the dirty deed. Nothing like she'd overheard the sixth-form girls at school whispering and giggling about. No blood, no pain. Nothing like her mam warned her about the day she started her periods, told her to keep herself nice until the day her Prince Charming walked her up the aisle. If her mam knew what she and Scrapper had done. If her dad—

Goosebumps studded her arms and legs. Scrapper's chest rose and fell against her shoulder. His eyes were closed, breath coming soft and regular. His hands and arms were scratched and bruised, the marks all too fresh. She shuddered and snuggled closer.

Next to the hearth, two mismatched, ceiling-high shelves hugged a library of books. A small television teetered on a three-legged stool. Under the window, a scuffed wooden desk held a battered typewriter, piles of newspapers and magazines and a box spilling pamphlets. Photos of Scrapper and his parents lined the mantelpiece beneath a red pennant, crossed symbols stitched in golden thread and a tinted portrait of a beardy old man with a mane of white hair. The clothes she and Scrapper tore off each other were scattered on the sofa. The faces on the mantelpiece looked none too impressed.

She tugged the hair that sprouted across Scrapper's chest. '*Scrap.*'

'Hmmm?'

'You won't tell anyone?'

'About what, *bach*?'

She tugged harder. 'About *this*, stupid.'

'Aw,' he opened one eye, smiled lazily at her. 'Reckoned I'd put an ad in *Ystrad Herald*.'

'I swear to god, Scrapper Jones – you breathe one word o' this, one word, to your creep of a butty or anyone else, I'll come after you with Dad's garden shears.'

She tried to sit up, but he yanked her down again, flipped her over and smacked her backside.

'It'll be your dad after me wi' them shears, Red.'

He got up and shrugged on his clothes, all matter-of-fact, like it was normal to strip off and make love to a girl on his parents' living room carpet. Like what happened between them was everyday business. Like a line had not been crossed.

'Get your clothes on, Red. You'll catch your death. I'll fix us some lunch.'

'But it's dark out,' she objected. 'Too late for—'

But he was gone.

She perched on the sofa, pulled on her school uniform. He was right, of course. To think of his parents coming home and catching them at it— The shame, to have fiery Angela Schiappa and bookish Iwan Jones walk in on them. She dressed, wishing she was old enough to be a proper girlfriend. Free to go on dates with Scrapper, to come home with him and stay over. To walk down the road holding hands with him. To not be the wrong side of sixteen.

Debbie Power used to stay over. Helen saw her once, on a Sunday morning, kissing Scrapper goodbye in the doorway of the ice cream parlour, his mam and dad busy behind the counter, paying them no mind. No one noticed the freckled, ginger-haired kid at the corner table, spoon dug into a forgotten sundae, gawping at Scrapper as Debbie strode across the road to the bus stop, glossy black bob and long legs in nurse's whites turning every man's head.

The sound of a car horn yanked her back from her thoughts. She twitched the curtain, saw the flashy daffodil-coloured Capri that belonged to Albright, the pit manager, stop outside The Red Lion. A man leaned into the passenger window, speaking to the driver, then the car pulled away. She would have known that tweed cap and jacket anywhere. She slid behind the curtain as the man turned, hands cupped against the wind to light his cigarette. He paused under a street lamp, raised his head. For a heart-stopping second, she thought her dad had seen her. But he was hawking and spitting a gob of phlegm into the gutter. Nasty, that collier habit of his.

She drew the curtains hurriedly and turned on the lights. Her satchel hung from the doorknob. She fished out her makeup bag and snapped open her compact. A right state on her, rats' tails for curls, mascara in flakes. She raked a comb through her hair, backcombed the front section and pinned it, quiff-style, above her forehead, dabbed her lips with a matt red shade that clashed with her hair. She squinted at herself, expecting her face to betray her crime.

'So wunnerfly, wunnerfly, wunnerfly pretty—' Scrapper was humming as he clattered around in the kitchen.

Scented steam drifted into the living room. She wondered when Iwan and Angela would get home. Scrapper had never brought her home as his girlfriend. Not once, in four months of courting. And here he was, tray loaded, two huge bowls of something pale and stringy, soaked in sauce and topped with cheese.

He set down the tray, turned on the television. 'Sorry it's only leftovers, *bach*. We're out of oysters an' champagne.'

'On a miner's wage?'

'Aye, well. But a glass o' something would be tidy.'

He slipped back into the kitchen, came back with a glass of

red wine. She took a careful sip. The one time she drank wine, she and her friends got bladdered at a party on half-drunk bottles of sour red plonk that Bethan Edwards' dad filched from his boss's restaurant.

They snuggled together on the sofa and ate their tea.

Scrapper stared at the TV with empty eyes. 'I hate that pit,' he said at last. 'It chews a man up, bleeds the strength from his bones, spits out a dried old husk.'

'So leave.'

'And do what?'

'You got to keep looking.'

His eyebrows shot up. 'What, get on my bike?'

'Even my dad says you're dead good at your job. You'll find something. My dad says—'

'Oh, right, yeah. Your dad says.'

There was an edge to his voice that shocked her. 'What about my dad?'

He looked away, didn't answer.

'What,' she repeated.

'Don't mind me. Bad day at the office.'

'I know. Poor old Gabe. And I'm sorry about Saturday.'

He shook his head.

'You know. That pathetic fight we had. About you kissing your ex.'

'What, Debbie?' Scrapper said. 'Her and Dai Dumbells got engaged. She was just telling me. Said it's an ex-boyfriend's duty to kiss the bride.'

She pinched his arm crossly. 'Why didn't you say?'

'Too busy tearing strips off me to hear it, weren't you?'

She paused, taking in the news. Debbie Power engaged, to that strapping firebrand, Dai Dobrosielski. Quite a catch, Dai, arms on him like girders, that big, solemn face splashed across the sports pages.

'And after Debbie?'

'After Debbie, what?'

'Have you had other women?'

He set down the wine glass, grabbed her in an arm-lock and ruffled her hair. Her quiff collapsed, tumbling into her eyes.

'What answer d'you want? If it's no, you'll say I'm pining after Debbie. If it's yes, you'll say I'm Casanova.'

She slapped away his hands, fixed her hair at a high, indignant angle. 'The right answer is the truth.'

'We finished long ago, me and Debbie,' he said.

But all she heard was her mam's voice: *no man wants a woman who's easy*. All she could see was Scrapper legging it, her dad limping after him with garden shears. She remembered what her dad yelled when he grounded her for being late: *you're stupid. You'll waste your life. You're a worthless little slut*. All of it came crowding in on her.

She went to the window, pushed up the sash and gulped a lungful of air. Sleet soaked the street. The cold and damp soothed her. Lights twinkled on the far side of the valley beyond the trees. She heard a crow caw and flap overhead. She shuddered. Her mam said crows were the souls of dead miners.

She pulled back and saw Scrapper's face reflected in the panes. The angled glass warped his cheekbones, the balance of forehead to chin. At last, she shut the window, drew the curtain, turned to look at him.

'It's the truth, Red,' he said.

The back door scraped open. Footsteps pattered up the stairs. Angela Schiappa-Jones burst into the room and flung herself on Scrapper, laughing and crying. At last, she let him go, studied his face.

'*Caro mio!*' She raised her hand, slapped him, then hugged him again. 'Is last time you go playing big hero, *cretino*. Understand?'

Scrapper prised her away. 'Stop fussing, Mam. It was nothing'

'Is just as well, Simon, else I'd bloody kill you.'

'Aw, Mam—'

Angela turned to Helen, kissed her on both cheeks. 'Is high time he brought you home, *bella*. Too bad it takes an accident to teach my peasant of a son some manners.'

Helen looked away, blushing. Someone else was climbing up the stairs. She prepared herself to greet Iwan Jones, thought better of it when she caught the look that crossed his face on seeing her.

'What is *she* doing in this house?' he said.

Angela frowned. 'Is no way to speak to Simon's girl.' She put a hand on Helen's arm. 'Forgotten his manners, my husband. You are welcome here, *bella*.'

'She bloody isn't,' Iwan said. 'Not after today.'

'That's not fair, Dad,' Scrapper said.

'Not fair,' Iwan echoed. 'When her old man had the pair of us suspended?'

'Suspended,' Helen said. 'What d'you mean, suspended?'

Her question hung unanswered. Iwan strode off down the corridor to the kitchen.

'Is not your fault, *bella*,' Angela said.

Helen's skin prickled with shame. 'I'd best go home.'

She shuffled her shoulders into her blazer and trudged down the stairs. Outside, the wind had picked up. The sleet had bite. She paused, half expecting Scrapper to come after her, to apologise for what his dad had said, to offer to walk her home. There was nothing doing. She let herself out and set off up the hill cursing herself.

Four pints down, Gwyn struggled to scale the hill. At last he forced open his front gate, climbed the three tall steps to the front garden, defied gale and gravity to reach his front door, taking shelter in the porch to steady himself, draw breath and slow his spinning brain. Across the valley, below the line of trees, the frosted hillsides sparkled in the darkness. Blackthorn's winding tower rose from the valley floor like the mast of a sunken ship.

The moonless sky had a yellow cast that threatened snow. He'd planned to dig his garden at the weekend, till the front borders, throw in handfuls of peat moss for his dahlias. Bishop of Llandaff dahlias, he planted. Proud red blooms on deep black stems. The Rolls-Royce of dahlias. The talk of the valleys, his summer borders.

The lace curtains were yellowing too, for want of a spring clean. Carol needed telling again. They kept a spotless house. A matter of pride. He had a home to call his own, mortgage paid on time, all the latest appliances bought on HP. The deal was that Carol kept things nice. He wouldn't have the neighbours whisper behind their hands about Gwyn Pritchard not providing. About Carol Pritchard being a slattern. They had standards to keep.

The front door was unlocked. He wiped his boots on the mat, bent to unlace them. He had tremors in his legs after the walk uphill. He stepped into his house, boots in hand, slid his feet into the slippers parked next to the grandfather clock. Carol poked her head around the kitchen door. Steam and the stench of burned meat billowed into the hall.

'Thank God, *cariad*,' she said.

He went straight into the sitting room. A good fire blazed in the grate, sprigged wallpaper wilting in the heat. He flopped down in his armchair, reached for his newspaper. Carol bustled in, wiping sticky hands on her skirt, lunged at him for a kiss.

'Stop clucking, woman,' he levered himself away from her.

She had heard the pit siren and the ambulances, knew as well as the next person what the claxon signalled. But they'd been married long enough for her to read his mood, to know when her attention was welcome and when to leave him be. She fetched his tray, perched opposite him in her armchair. Picked up her knitting and set to work on a square for a patchwork quilt. Dark red yarn flowed through her fingers but her eyes were fixed on him. She wanted to talk about it.

He looked down at his plate, at the slab of liver cooked until it croaked for mercy, lumps for gravy, peas colourless and crushed. A hunk of cauliflower, collapsed like a crushed brain. He chased a couple of peas around the plate with the tip of his fork. Set the tray on the side table.

'I'm not eating this.'

The knitting needles paused. 'It's all we got. Unless we pop up the chippy?'

'You want me to go back out to fetch grub? After the day I had?'

She lowered her knitting. Damn. He'd walked right into it.

'I tried to reach Albright all morning, *cariad*. Took hours to get through.'

'He was busy, woman. We all were.'

'But why not call, let us know you were safe?'

He closed his eyes, leaned back in his chair.

'How about I fetch you a beer, love,' she said.

The thought of drink flooded his mouth with bitter juices. One hell of a day, he'd had. First the accident, then the Jones boys defying him, then having to explain the trouble with the lodge to Albright. And now a second interrogation. In his own bloody house, from his own bloody wife.

'Where's the girl?'

'Out,' Carol said.

'What d'you mean, out?'

She shrugged. 'You don't reckon you punished her enough?'

'*Enough*? That girl got the brains to make something of her life.'

'She done well in her mock O-levels. No harm cutting her some—'

'No harm? Wait 'til she falls pregnant an' tell me no harm.'

She flinched as though he'd stung her. With luck, that would be the end of it. He looked at the mantelpiece, at the black and white photos of the two of them in their wedding suits. Carol barely nineteen, wool jacket clinging to a tiny waist, skirt four inches above the knee to show a neat pair of pins. Hair in a sleek strawberry-blonde beehive. A smart little piece, Carol, when they married. All the lads joshing him about landing himself a dolly bird ten years his junior and a dead spit for Julie Christie.

Some Julie Christie, with her stained clothes and smudged mascara, hair bleached brittle blonde.

A strapping figure he cut in his wedding suit. Brown serge that cost a whole week's wages from Howell's down in Cardiff. He had Dai Cross-Stitch the tailor let out the arms and shoulders. He'd worked fourteen years below ground by then. Twelve stones of pure muscle. Spider, they'd called him when he started, for his spindly arms and legs. He'd bulked up quick-sharp. Mining was piece work, back then: the more you worked, the more you earned. He learned to shift the load of three men, earned himself a fancy new nickname, after some Cold War worker hero. *That one'll take it for a compliment,* Gwyn heard Alf Manifesto tell the others. Damn right. Gwyn Stakhanov. It had a ring to it, that. But the men hadn't called him that in years. Captain Hook was what they called him since he lost his fingers and got promoted.

He picked up his newspaper, scanned the headlines.

Carol's eyes were fixed on his face. 'Chrissie next door said a man died. Who?'

'Gabe Parry.'

A knitting needle fell on the carpet. He shook his head, irritated now, snapped open the newspaper and raised it. Blocked out the horror in Carol's eyes, the shocked O-shape of her lips. He hid inside the newspaper and pretended to read. Started with the sports pages, worked forwards. Navigated horoscopes, motoring and women's nonsense to the news pages. Glanced at the girl on page three. Nothing special. But young and pert and silent, at least.

Carol drew breath again. He lowered the paper, glared at her. She took the hint, bent her head over her knitting, started picking out dropped stitches. The gate opened with a screech of hinges. Light footsteps clip-clopped up the path. The front door swung open and slammed shut. Already, he smelled attitude.

'That you, love?' Carol called.

'Who else, Mam?'

About bloody time the girl showed up. If she'd been anywhere near that boy again, he'd tan her hide.

Helen slung her sodden coat and bag over the banister and slunk towards the living room. She had hoped against hope to find her mam alone. Most nights, her dad stayed down the pub. Most nights, he staggered in after she was tucked up safe in bed. Rare, since the lodge banned overtime, to have him come back early. Since Christmas, he had the pub to himself, pretty much, his men skint and stopping home. But her mam wasn't watching soaps on the sly tonight. The telly was off. Her dad shot from his armchair on seeing her, a face to shatter stone.

Her mam looked pale and tense. 'Sit yourself down, love. I'll fetch your tea.'

'I got homework, Mam. I'll take the tray upstairs.'

'You sit down by there,' her dad said.

She sat. Her mam vanished into the kitchen, started rattling plates and cutlery. Took her time. A muscle twitched in her dad's cheek, ticking like a stopwatch. If that was how he handled his men, no wonder things were bad with the lodge. She curled her arms and legs around herself, rested her gaze on the carpet until the swirls of red and blue paisley bled into purple sludge.

'So where you been, young lady?'

'Round Bethan's. Geography project.'

Her dad fixed her a hard stare. Her mam came in, caught the look on his face, clattered the tea-tray in warning. Too late. The warning wouldn't save her. Not this time.

'Let's try again, shall we,' her dad said.

Her mam set down the tray. 'Tell him,' she hissed.

'I fancied a walk.'

Her dad raised his wrist, eyeballed his watch. 'Well, look at that,' he said, every word fired like a bullet. 'Already gone seven. School out at four-thirty. Walk, did you? Walk all the way to Cardiff?'

Best not to answer, when whatever she said made things worse.

'You been with that boy, haven't you?'

The room was too hot, the stench of cooked liver mixed with stale tobacco, sweat and furniture polish.

'Sorry, Mam. I'm not hungry.'

She put the tray on the side table, tucked her arms around herself. If she made herself small, maybe he would leave it. When she was small, her dad was gentle and kind, like other people's dads.

His maimed hand gripped his belt buckle, the other jabbed the air. 'What did I tell you on Saturday?'

She shrank away, muttered something vague.

'Did I or did I not say you were grounded for the rest of the month?'

'Yes,' she said.

'Yes. So I'll thank you to look me in the eye. Were you or were you not with that boy?'

She looked into his grey face, at the sagging corners of his mouth, his pouchy eyes. She saw him then. Really saw him, in all his hunched disappointment. A man, no longer young, who reached for too much, caught too little.

'Yes,' she said. 'Alright, yes. I was with Scrapper Jones. Me and him. All afternoon.'

She raised her chin, insolent. Saw shock and triumph and white-hot rage.

'Slut,' he breathed.

He unbuckled his belt, eyes fixed on her. Took time to draw

19

frayed leather under and over the buckle. To release the prong. To slide the belt, loop by loop by loop. Buckle in hand, he reached for her wrist. No grip to that maimed hand of his. No effort to twist herself free.

'No! Tell him, Mam.'

'Carol, come and hold her,' he said.

Her mam hovered in the doorway. 'Don't, Gwyn.'

'Do what I say, woman. *Now!*'

'You forgot what you promised?' she said softly.

'She's asking for it, the little whore.'

'But you're not your old man, *cariad*. You're better'n that.'

As suddenly as it started, it was over. Her dad backed away, lowered the belt, shoulders slumped in defeat.

She scampered behind the sofa, reckless with relief. 'He's been picking on Scrapper again, Mam,' she said. 'Sent him and Iwan off the job.'

A flicker in her dad's cheek showed that her blow hit home. He raised his belt, brought it down again. She felt the rush of cold air as the strap missed her cheek by inches.

'Your first punishment was being grounded,' he said. 'Defy me again, you'll regret it, young lady. See that boy again, he'll be out of a job. Go anywhere near him, and I'll skin the pair of you.'

The look in his eye told her he meant it. She backed out of the room without another word.

Gwyn shifted the belt between his hands. The scuffed black leather was fixed to a buckle of solid brass, initials etched on it. Presented to the old man to mark his twenty-fifth year at Blackthorn, that belt, only weeks before the blast that took him.

He ran his thumb and forefinger over the scratched metal. Lucky for the girl that he was slow on his feet, lately. He looped the belt around his waist and buckled it again. A dizzy spell sent him back to his chair. He'd asked the pit medic about his symptoms; the dizziness and the fighting for breath and lost appetite. He pressed his face to the bathroom mirror every morning, waited to see the anthracite bruises beneath his nails spread to his lips, for the whites of his eyes to stain blue. When coal dust showed in the face, death called within the year. Black lung. It did for his granddad and three of his uncles. Did for so many older miners. Would have done for his old man and for Gabe Parry if the darkness hadn't taken them first. Coal would come for him, too, like as not.

His arm ached, lungs threatened to choke him. The girl was with that boy all afternoon. With that firebrand, trouble-making boy. The grandfather clock chimed the hour. He set aside his newspaper, turned on the TV to watch the news. The prime minister was striding down a production line at a car plant in the Midlands. The car workers queued to be inspected, slouch-necked and awkward, dressed in spotless overalls to meet the woman taking a crowbar to the UK car industry. Britain's glorious leader, squaring up to the car unions, cwtching up to the Japanese. She glided down the line, the prime minister, hair set to concrete. Blue suit, blue shoes, blue hat, blue handbag, the better to match her politics.

Carol came padding down the stairs. He'd told her not to go after the girl. And she'd defied him, yet again.

She perched on the arm of her chair. 'Well, *cariad*?'

He fixed his eyes on the prime minister. A fine set of pins on her.

'So what happened?'

'Leave it, will you.'

'You got fresh trouble with your men?'

He sighed. 'Same old story. Nothing for you to worry about.'

Carol tilted her head, waiting. A terrier's persistence, she had.

'The roof fell in. Gabe Parry went missing. I told the men to stay put, but Iwan and Scrapper Jones defied me, went looking for the old boy. The roof fell in some more and Dai Dumbells and Iwan Jones got injured. And for nothing. Gabe was killed straight off.'

'And you punished the boy and his dad?'

'For God's sake, woman. They went against my orders. Nearly turned an accident into a disaster. It was Albright suspended them. Then the rest walked off the job.'

'But how could Albright send them home for trying to find poor Gabe?'

'Orders is orders.'

'Yes, but Gwyn—'

It was all he could do not to throw back his head and howl. As bad as that rabble from the lodge, his own wife, his own daughter. He'd had a bellyful of back-chat. His hand twitched. And he had never hit his wife.

She knelt beside his chair, took his hand.

'But you did the exact same thing yourself, *cariad*. The deputy told you not to go back for Alf Manifesto. But Alf was your butty and to hell with what the boss said – back you went.'

A low blow, that. He snatched his hand away. When he spoke, his voice was tight. 'I was young and bloody-minded. The deputy was well within his rights to tan my hide for going back for that miserable old Bolshevik.'

She sighed. 'Point is, *you* weren't disciplined. And why? Because the deputy was a former collier. He understood.'

'So?'

'So you understand and all. You could speak to Albright. Get him to reinstate the Jones lads.'

'Reinstate? They disobeyed my orders.'

'Yes, Gwyn. But you got a chance to help cool things off.'

'*Cool things off*?'

She seized his hand again. Stroked the stumps that were once his fingers. 'We both knows the price of coal, eh, *cariad*. What do they know, them managers with their clean fingernails and their number-crunching? To hell with men in suits, shuffling bits of paper from desk to desk, Gwyn. You owe nothing to them and everything to Blackthorn. To your men.'

The irony. 'To my men? It's for them to decide; are they with me or with the lodge.'

'But Gwyn—'

She was clueless, his wife. If she knew what Smith-Tudor had told him. Profitable, productive pits would live. Pits with falling yields would die. Hundreds of jobs would go. Under-performing collieries would shut. It was every man for himself now. He'd sworn him to secrecy, the coalfield boss. Pits that performed – overmen that performed – only they had a fighting chance.

He made a promise, Smith-Tudor. 'Keep the coal flowing, keep your nose clean, I'll take good care of you, Pritchard. Got a desk job with your name on it.'

A desk job. As dreams went, that wasn't much to ask.

'Are you sure it's the lodge that's the problem,' Carol said.

It took all his strength to hold back. He took in the drawn

face, the beaky nose and jowly cheeks, the permed hair thinning at the roots. Three wrinkles split her forehead like rings on a tree. One for each of her decades. A shotgun wedding, they had, Carol several weeks gone. And he'd done right by her, even so.

'Sixteen years I been married to you,' he told her. 'Put food on your table, kept a roof over your head. Are you even one bit grateful?'

She slunk back to her chair, picked up her knitting. He raised his newspaper, flicked through the pages, the columns of newsprint a blur. After a while, the needles stopped clicking.

'I'll visit Margaret in the morning,' she tried to sound casual. 'Pay our respects. Find out what she needs.'

'*What?*'

'It's the least I can do. Remember after your accident? She minded Helen while I visited the hospital. Baked casseroles—'

He hurled his newspaper at the television screen. 'You are not visiting Margaret Parry. Whose bloody side you on?'

'Gwyn, you can't be—'

'*Enough*, woman.'

Carol rummaged in the sideboard drawers, turned back, holding a yellow crocheted square, the wool faded and bobbled from years of washing. 'You remember this?'

He shrugged. 'That old thing? Used to lay it over the girl's pram.'

'And?'

He looked at the yellow wool again. A ragged old thing, it was. They used to call it Helen's *cwtch*. When the girl was a toddler, she dragged it everywhere. Loved it half to death, though it snagged and gathered stains from mud and dust and all sorts. A dirty, disgusting thing, Helen's *cwtch*. He hadn't seen the thing in years.

'Remember the day you took it off her?'

He shook his head.

'She cried her eyes out,' Carol nestled the grubby wool against her cheek. 'Bawled her head off 'til we gave it back to her. Wouldn't sleep without it. Scared silly of the *bwci-bo* under the bed without her *cwtch*.'

'What's your point?'

'Point is, Gwyn, Margaret Parry crocheted that *cwtch*. Made it for Helen's christening. Been saving it to pass on to our first grandchild. A piece of our history, that *cwtch*. A piece of Helen's history. And Margaret's a part of it.'

'Oh, for God's sake, woman.'

'When you knocked me up, Margaret Parry was the only respectable married woman in this village who'd give me time of day. The rest turned their backs and talked behind their hands.'

She put the *cwtch* back in the sideboard. Her shoulders were shaking. She turned away, grabbed the blister pack of sleeping pills from the drawer.

'I'm turning in,' she said, her voice muffled.

'Carol—'

But she was gone. He switched to the later news, watched Mrs Thatcher stride down the assembly line, smiling her shark smile at the workers. Smith-Tudor said not to worry about Mrs Thatcher. A straight fight, the area manager told him; on one side, pits with good, profitable coal and a willing workforce; on the other, troublemakers fighting a losing battle to save pits whose time had come.

His lost fingers stung like nettles. When he got stressed, the pain got worse. He hadn't used the belt, at least. He'd made a promise to himself and to his wife the first time he held his baby daughter. Held her close and swore never to hurt his little girl.

The grandfather clock ticked in the hall. The fire died down to cinders. Warmth ebbed from the room. He turned off the television and creaked up the staircase. Paused outside Helen's

25

room, heard the muffled sound of sobbing. He put his hand on the doorknob. But how could he make things right with the girl; nothing he could say or do would fix things between them. Not if what he suspected was true. Not tonight. Maybe tomorrow, if his head didn't hurt, if his hand didn't ache, he could squeeze the right words from his rotten lungs, get the girl to see sense, get his wife to back him, for once. He sighed and padded down the corridor to his room.

Scrapper took a slug of coffee. Left to cool, it had a bitter aftertaste to it. He reached for the sugar bowl, loaded a dessertspoon, forced the drink down in a gulp. His butty Matthew Price, cheeks stuffed like a hamster's, was holding court across the kitchen table, dredging over what happened when the roof caved in.

'—Then Scrapper shoved me out o' the way an' saved my life, Missus Jones.'

'Aw, come off it, Matt, I never—'

'My son, the big hero,' Angela swatted him with her teacloth. 'Take a *biscotto*, Matthew.'

Scrapper cocked an eyebrow, dared his butty to say no. He never said no. Not to anything. Sure enough, Matt helped himself again. He was happy to park his backside any place there was food and drink and an audience, Matt. He was well dug in, chair tilted on its back legs, three cups of tea and a dozen *biscotti* down his gullet, all set to make an evening of it.

'If you insist, Missus J,' Matt grabbed a couple more biscuits. 'Spoil me rotten, you do.'

'Steady on, Mam. He needs to watch his waistline, this one. Medic said he's getting a beer gut.'

Matt sucked in his stomach. 'I am not,' he said. 'Prime specimen of Welsh manhood, me, aren't I, Missus J? At the peak of my prowess.'

Iwan lowered his newspaper. 'They say a fella peaks at

eighteen. Which puts our lad a year past his prime and you a decade past your sell-by date.'

'Nonsense,' Angela said. 'Is still a catch, our Matthew. Needs the right girl to snap him up.'

Matt twisted the gold stud in his ear. 'I'm only a year back on the market; Missus J. Got some wild oats to sow before I settle.'

Scrapper sighed. If his butty started bragging about his love life, they were in for a long night. 'Anything from Albright?' he said.

Friday afternoon, there was still no news from management, production halted, the boys from all three shifts backing the lodge. It hung in the balance whether he and his dad would lose or keep their jobs. Some of the boys had a sweepstake going, money changing hands over who would crack first; the lodge, or Mr Albright.

A whole week sitting idle. Who wouldn't be worried? If the pit boss sacked him, every day would be like this, for him and for his dad. The thought of doing nothing, being nothing – it scared him witless. Scared him more, even, than the thought of getting back in the cage, swooping down through the darkness to the seam where Gabe Parry breathed his last.

The bell sounded downstairs in the *bracchi*. His mam pulled on her pinafore. Iwan gathered the ice cream scoops from the draining board and followed her downstairs. Scrapper stayed in the kitchen, wondered how to get shot of his butty in time to get up to the barn to meet Red. He carried the cups and dishes to the sink, ran the tap over them.

'You'll make some fella a lovely wife,' Matt said.

'Beats doing nothing, butty.'

'If I was seeing that little redhead, I'd find ways to pass the time.'

Scrapper steeled himself not to react; there'd be no end of ribbing if he rose to his butty's taunts. Matt reckoned himself quite the ladies' man; conquests from Monmouth to Milford Haven, so he claimed. Came strutting in on Monday mornings, full of tall tales, as smug as a panther on catnip.

'I'm only messing,' Matt said. 'Anyhow, got to see a man about a horse.'

Scrapper was glad and sorry to see his butty go. He needed to get ready, and fast. But silence brought back the warning creak of the rocks, the eerie silence that filled the chamber before the roof caved in, the memory of rubble biting his skin as he scrabbled to free himself and Matt. He couldn't sleep without the radio, found no escape in his books. Instead, he shut himself in his room, stereo a screech of guitars, his dad yelling at him to turn down that bloody racket. His dad, head full of lodge business, spent the week buried neck-deep in newspapers, scouring the business pages for portents.

Scrapper had no truck with portents. He wanted to see Red.

* * *

Time passed like the Sahara seeping through an hourglass. Joy Division, The Clash, Elvis Costello. Nothing took him out of himself. As he climbed into the bathtub, he heard footsteps thudding up the stairs.

'Iwan, you there?' Dewi Power called. 'Got good news.'

'Oh aye,' Iwan answered. 'Won the pools, have we?'

'Had a chat wi' Albright.'

'You what?'

'He stopped by ours,' Dewi said. 'Wanted to talk away from the pit—'

'You had that little English weasel *round your house?*'

Scrapper picked up his watch. Red was bunking off hockey to see him. He wrapped a towel around his waist, went to see what was afoot.

29

The lodge secretary wore a grin as wide as the Severn. 'Albright's reinstating the pair o' you from Monday.'

'What's the catch?'

If an argument kicked off now, there was no way he'd get away in time. 'Steady on, Dad. Dewi said we're reinstated.'

Iwan snorted. 'Cut a deal with Albright, did you, Dewi? Offered to drop Margaret Parry's compensation claim? Agreed a no-strike deal?'

'Look at it through Albright's eyes,' Dewi said. 'He needs local trouble like an extra hole between his eyes.'

'I hope you're putting it to the men,' Iwan said.

'That's why I've come,' Dewi said. 'We're getting together down the Stute.'

Iwan grabbed his jacket. 'Right. Get dressed and get yourself down there, son.'

Scrapper waited for the back door to close, then darted into his parents' room for a spritz of his dad's Eau Sauvage. It was a Christmas gift from his mam, the cologne; kept on her dressing table for best. He dressed, grabbed his jacket and skidded to a halt on the landing. Angela was climbing the stairs, sniffing the air.

'You heard the news, Mam? We been reinstated.'

'Is about time. A brave man, Mr Albright.'

'Brave how?'

'Is a brave man to talk to Dewi Power in his home. She's a tough lady, Mary Power. Tough and clever. Just like her *nonna*, Iron Lizzie.'

A local legend, Iron Lizzie. Famous from the lock-out of 1926, for going up to the drifts and digging coal to heat the miners' houses with her bare hands. Shifted twice the load of any man.

'Look, Mam; I got to—'

'Is always the same, son. Men talk. Women *do*.'

He stooped to kiss her forehead, dashed down the stairs.

'Give my love to Helen,' Angela grinned down at him through the banisters. 'Is very nice you smell.'

* * *

He raced up the track. Mist uncurled across the hills. Raindrops spattered as he ran past the allotments, dodged pot-holes, cleared the stile in a leap. He cursed as he landed ankle-deep in a squelch of mud. Drizzle turned to heavy rain. When he reached the barn, he was soaked and panting. He checked he was alone, then squeezed through the gap in the corrugated iron walls.

'Red?' he pulled out his pocket torch, rested the beam on hay and rusting farm machinery, clambered over sacks of feed and fertiliser. Pushed aside the wooden pallet at the back of the barn that hid their den.

The beam of light glinted on something caught on a splinter. It was a long, copper-coloured hair. A sign. Red had been and gone. He swallowed a curse, sank down on the tarpaulin laid over the straw, drew the hair across his lips. The shadows danced around him, mocking. He breathed in dried grass and cobwebs and engine oil, remembering the red curls that fell onto his face as he pulled her down on top of him.

The wind whistled through the metal sheets. He picked himself up, slid the pallet back into place.

* * *

Groups of miners were drifting out of the Stute towards The Red Lion. He trailed the boys from the afternoon shift, followed them from the lounge to the bar. Iwan, Dewi and the morning boys were gathered round their usual table.

31

Iwan waved him over. 'Where were you, son?'

'Sitting with that lot.'

'Reinstated,' Iwan grumped. 'There'll be a catch; you'll see.'

Scrapper's head itched. He raised a hand, pulled a cobweb from his fringe. His donkey jacket was flecked with dust and hay.

'I'll give Matt a hand with the drinks,' he said.

He nipped into the Gents, dusted himself down. At the bar, Matt was calling in a round. Next to him Dai Dumbells, bulk propped on a stool, hunched silently over a pint of Brains. Scrapper nodded to his butty to get one in.

'Don't bother talking to this one,' Matt said. 'He's sulking about going back.'

'I'm not bloody sulking,' Dai snapped.

'Congratulations, butty,' Matt handed Scrapper his pint. 'Get old misery guts to raise a smile, bring him over to join us.'

He raised his tray of drinks, carried it across the room to join his mates. Dai downed his pint, motioned to Steve Red Lion to pour another.

Scrapper climbed the stool next to him. 'Caning it tonight, butty?'

Dai looked past him. Scrapper followed his gaze. The morning boys were huddled around Dewi Power, talking quietly. But at the next table, Matt Price held court over a group of lads from the haulage company, a tall tale in full flow. A pause, a pay-off, peals of blue laughter, Matt tilting his chair back, knitting his fingers behind his bleach-blond head.

'Don't give a damn, do they,' Dai said.

'What d'you mean.'

'We lay Gabe to rest tomorrow. But no one bloody cares.'

'That's not f—'

'Not fair? Not fair is a man crushed to death. A disgrace, going back wi' my butty barely cold.' Dai made short work of his pint, slammed down the glass. 'Two o' the same, Steve. And whatever this one's drinking.'

'But Dai—'

Dai stood, raised his glass. 'Fellas, here's to Gabe.'

Gabe's name echoed around the pub. The men raised their glasses, turned back to their groups, voices tuned down to a hum.

'Just cos a fella don't talk about stuff, doesn't mean he doesn't care,' Scrapper said.

Dai clenched his hand around his glass, downed the third pint in one.

'Seriously, butt,' Scrapper said. 'A tough call, going back on Monday, to find your butty's not there. How about you ease up?'

Dai grunted. He grabbed his jacket, headed off without saying his goodbyes. Scrapper slumped at the bar, in no mood to join the others. He finished his pint, set to work on the second. He heard another burst of laughter from the hauliers' table. Matt was waving him over. Scrapper shook his head, ordered a whisky chaser.

'You staying or going?' Iwan walked by, coat hooked over his arm.

'I'll be along in a tick.'

The bar emptied. Few men were up for getting wazzed tonight. Scrapper took his pint and his whisky to the table near the juke box, fed fifty pee into the machine, sat back as Rod Stewart belted out *Baby Jane* in a voice that gargled razor blades, wondered how many chasers it would take to still the thoughts churning round in his skull.

He jumped as Matt piled on top of him, planted a wet, beery kiss on his cheek. 'Fuck me, butty. I'm pissed as a newt.'

'Geroffff,' Scrapper protested.

Matt pulled away. 'It's St David's Day soon,' he said. 'I'm off to find myself a nice young lady. Gonna drag her up the allotments, show her my leek.'

'Half the women seen it, butt. Seen it, and run off screaming.'

Steve Red Lion paused at their table, beer glasses stacked the length of both arms. 'Screaming wi' laughter,' he said.

'At least I'll have a bloody date,' Matt grinned. 'This lad's piece is kept in after *Young Doctors*.'

He pulled on his denim jacket and City scarf. Raised his fist in a power salute and slipped out into the night.

SPRING 1984

— 1 —

'Just do your job, eh, Pritchard. Make sure your boys do the same. That's all I'm asking.'

Gwyn clutched the telephone receiver, breath ragged, ribs closing round his lungs like a vice. Smith-Tudor had lost none of his huff and bluster, even now that the news was out. It was bad, of course – the whole country was braced for bad – but the Coal Board's announcement went way beyond even the lodge's darkest warnings. Small wonder the area manager had called him at home, at the weekend. A bloodbath was what it boiled down to.

'Five pits confirmed for accelerated closure,' Smith-Tudor said. 'A dozen under review. But don't you worry, eh, Pritchard. Nothing to do with Blackthorn, any of this. So just you keep that bunch of hotheads in line for me, eh.'

The area manager made it sound easy. But the darkness hung heavy as Gwyn trudged towards the pit, pondering Smith-Tudor's parting shot: 'There's no love for Scargill in my coalfield. Not since that business with Lewis Merthyr, eh. We play it cool, our men have no reason to trouble themselves.'

Two hours before sunrise, a sad murk of a morning. Mist slapped his face like a cold, wet towel. By the time he reached the High Street, his chest was tight, breath coming and going with the scrape of a rusty hinge. Smith-Tudor thought the pit closures would be a walkover. Madness, with the Communists well dug in at Blackthorn. Dug in as deep as maggots in a wound. He forced down a lungful of clammy air. On the road

37

below, dark figures dipped in and out of the fog like spectres. He jumped, heart lunging for his rib-cage, as something – someone – loomed out at him as he passed Schiappa's Ice Cream Parlour.

'Orright, boss. Nippy morning, eh?'

The greeting rang false. Bloody Italian boy, making an all-too-obvious effort to be civil. He must think him soft in the head, Scrapper Jones. That boy was to blame for the whispering. For the dirty laughter echoing around the pit baths and the lads' off-colour comments about the girl. If it was some other fellow's daughter the boy was chasing, he might have warmed to him. He worked hard and deferred to his elders, Scrapper Jones. Fact was, the boy was trouble. The red star pinned to his collar confirmed it.

He spotted the boy's father Iwan Jones up ahead. He strode over, clapped him on the shoulder.

'How's it hanging, butt?'

Iwan nodded a reply. Manner cool, but not hostile. That was odd. There was no question the lodge had spoken. Sheffield had ordered emergency talks. Not a flicker in those ice-grey eyes. A demon at poker, this one. Unless—

Had Smith-Tudor called it right? Had the lodge told Scargill where to stick his strike? Pride stopped Gwyn asking Iwan outright. He looked instead for Dai Dumbells. He had his heart pinned to his sleeve, that one. His heart and the rest of his innards. Dai would show him how things lay. But Dai wasn't around. Iwan it would have to be.

Gwyn braced himself. 'You heard the news? About the pit closures.'

Iwan shrugged, walked faster. Gwyn trailed after him down the High Street, past the shops, funeral parlour and miners' institute. They turned right, followed the road down the hill, under the railway that carried coal and waste material out of the pit, and emerged below the fog, near the miner's chapel, stone built and surrounded by yew hedges. At the edge of the graveyard above the road, fresh-dug earth showed dark against the frosted grass.

Dai and ferret-faced Matthew Price were up ahead.

'Poor old Gabe,' Dai's words carried on the wind. 'They might as well be burying the rest of us up by there soon enough. We're done for now, us and our pits.'

'Put a sock in it, will you,' Matt said. 'My butty's been a jitter o' nerves since the accident.'

'I have not,' Scrapper raised his voice.

'Lay off, lads,' Iwan said.

They turned into the road that led up to the pit. Gwyn stopped so fast, his feet skidded on the gravel. A dozen men lined up outside the gates, dressed in hard hats, boots and donkey jackets. They were miners, but none that he recognised, a canopy of red banners and placards flapping over their heads. A shabby entourage of men and women milled around them, flogging newspapers. As he drew closer, he spotted the usual bandwagon chasers from *Welsh Worker*, *Voice of the Proletariat* and *The Morning Star*.

An engine roared behind him. He jumped out of the way as a truck chugged past, growled up to the gates. The driver wound down his window, lobbed words at the men at the gates, who lobbed a bunch of words right back. The driver nodded, gunned his engine, swerved a neat three-point turn. A wave, a blast on the horn and the truck vanished into the tunnel.

'What was that?' Scrapper said.

'Flying pickets,' Iwan said.

'Flying what?'

'South Yorkshire men, son. Come to Blackthorn to picket. Asking us to hold the line.'

'Hold the line?' Gwyn cut in. 'Yorkshire's troubles are none of our damn business. They got no right to drag us into it. *Hold the line*? Flying pickets be buggered.'

A short, bristle-haired figure was waving them over. Dewi Power had a reporter and a camera crew in tow. Gwyn recognised the young journalist, thin vulture shoulders spoiling the line of his smart dark suit and spotless shirt. James Hackett, always hanging around like a bad smell, looking to use the South Wales coalfield to make a name for himself. A sorry state of affairs to get filmed at a picket. Gwyn ducked behind Dai Dumbells, quick-sharp. Hackett poked his microphone at Dewi, turned so that the pit gates rose behind him and addressed the camera all lah-di-dah English.

'Thanks, Nigel. Yes. As you can see, we're live today at Blackthorn Colliery, where pickets from Yorkshire are trying to block—'

At last Hackett ended his piece to camera. He clapped Dewi on the back. 'Ta, butty – bloody brilliant.'

Vanished, now, the BBC voice. Gwyn gave the reporter a hard stare. Talk down to them, would he? But he'd spotted a familiar figure, an old boy in a wheelchair, parcelled up in cardigan, coat and blankets, newsprint piled on his lap. The banner headline read *Thatcher Declares War On Britain's Miners*.

Talk about incitement to riot. He scooted over, confronted the fellow. 'Gi's a paper, Johnny Griffiths.'

The man smiled a gummy smile. 'It's twenty pee, Gwyn Pritchard. Fifty, if you're management.'

It was a cheap shot, unworthy of the old boy. Unnerving, that broken body of his. Why the pit spat out Johnny Griffiths but took his old man, Gwyn would never know. He thrust a pound note at the fellow with a muttered keep-the-change. Took cover behind Dai Dumbells before opening *Welsh Worker* to read.

'Britain's pits will stop work today, as miners walk out in protest over swingeing government cuts—'

Iwan and Dewi were huddled together, arguing in hushed voices. Gwyn edged closer, listened in.

'An impossible position we're in,' Iwan was saying. 'We've yet to put this to the vote and there's a picket already in place.'

'Aye, well,' Dewi said. 'They've driven all night down from Cortonwood, this lot. Desperate, they are.'

'Like Lewis Merthyr was desperate?'

'Fair point,' Dewi said. 'But there's a fair chance the axe'll fall on South Wales pits, and all. Not planning to cross, are you, butty?'

Iwan's eyes sparked flint. 'I never crossed a picket line in my life.'

Gwyn felt the compression in his chest ease a touch. So much the better, if the lodge was split. Maybe Smith-Tudor had called it right, after all. Maybe they had Scargill's storm-troopers on the run in South Wales.

Behind the rabble-rousing headline, *Welsh Worker* reckoned so too:

'Last night, a spokesman for the National Coal Board said fifteen South Wales delegates had voted against going on a strike, six voting for—'

Divide and rule, it would be then. Gwyn filled his lungs: there was every chance his boys would play nice, for once. See sense, keep the coal flowing, free him to save his pit from catastrophe. His lads had backed the overtime ban and for what? Every last one of them gone short over Christmas, thanks to the pig-headedness of the lodge. But now was not the time for knee-jerk games. Pits that made money would dodge the axe. Men who kept working would keep their jobs. There was every chance his lads would do the right thing, this time. Keep their noses clean and tell Sheffield to go to hell.

Trouble was, they had a fair few rabble-rousers at Blackthorn; Dewi Power, for one.

'We'll put it to the vote,' Dewi said. 'Meet in the Stute after this.'

He had the lads line up at the gates with the Cortonwood pickets. The camera crew positioned themselves as the little lodge secretary clambered onto an upturned oil drum, raised his megaphone and spoke straight to the cameras.

'The National Coal Board is taking a hatchet to Britain's mining industry,' he said. 'Twenty British pits are to close. Twenty-thousand working men will lose their jobs, starting with these lads from Cortonwood. Margaret Thatcher—'

On hearing the prime minister's name, the miners chorused pantomime boos.

'Margaret Thatcher and Ian MacGregor have vowed to smash the miners' union. Our message to Thatcher and MacGregor is, you cannot break us. We will fight to the death to defend our jobs and save our pits.'

Scrapper Jones clapped an arm around Matt Price's shoulders, olive skin glowing.

'You tell 'em, Dewi,' he yelled.

Not so respectful, was he, when push came to shove, Gwyn noted. He'd been right about that boy all along. A communist like his dad, like his forebears. High time he taught the boy a lesson or two. The miners had been here before, in the Seventies. That time, they caught the bosses and the government off guard. That time, he stood shoulder to shoulder with the lodge. But Maggie was armed and ready for a fight and he was older and wiser now. A wise man took care of his own. He knew that from bitter experience. Something Scrapper Jones would learn to his cost.

— 2 —

White placards, red banners, black donkey jackets and orange boilersuits; Scrapper had seen nothing like it. Blackthorn's winding gear rose proud and tall above them all. The line held. Not one man went in. Not even Captain Hook. He looked round but the overman was nowhere to be seen. He turned back to the pickets, felt the blood humming in his veins. A beautiful thing, solidarity. It was in the boys' power to help these Yorkshire lads to save their pit and every one of them had risen to the occasion. Pickets, miners and supporters lined up outside the gates. On a nod from Dewi, they started to march towards the village. He looked around for Iwan. He was with Johnny Griffiths, talking to some of the Yorkshire men, talking politics, no doubt, his palms slicing the air.

'You joining us, Dad?' Scrapper called.

'Too right,' Iwan's lips were a taut line of fury.

'Need a hand, Uncle Johnny?'

The man in the wheelchair grinned. 'Nothing wrong with my hands, lovely boy. Could use a leg or two, if you can spare 'em.'

'Right you are.'

He steered the wheelchair through the banners to the front of the march. The body in the chair weighed little more than a bag of feathers. He looked at the blanket wrapped over the missing legs and shuddered. The pit had done its worst with Johnny Griffiths' body, if not the old man's *hwyl*.

At last, they reached the Stute. Scrapper eased the wheelchair up the ramp and nudged it through the swing doors into the red-tiled hall. After the cold outside, the room was clammy. Steam billowed from the tea urns and noise bounced off the tall ceiling. He wheeled Johnny through the crush to a space at the front.

'Ah, there's my Susie,' the old man said.

Scrapper followed his gaze, saw a woman with a nut-brown face and a cloud of grey hair, Mary Power, commanding her troops at the tea urns. Next to her, a girl with chestnut curls was waving at him. She loaded a tray with mugs of tea and came over.

'Orright, Scrap. Thanks for bringing Gramps.'

'Sue Griffiths. Come home to slum it wi' the proles, have you?'

'Beats slumming it at college.'

Johnny beamed a gummy smile. 'Susie's heading for a First, her tutor reckons.'

'Give over, Gramps. Mary called me, Scrap. Reckons you'll need the women's help.'

'You and us, against the Coal Board, eh, Susie? Bastards got no chance.'

'Orright, gorgeous?' A hand touched his shoulder and a face drew in close: anthracite hair and eyes, lips painted candy-floss pink.

'Down, girl,' Sue said. 'You're practically a married woman.'

'Aye,' Debbie Power stamped her lips to his cheek. 'Respectable now, me.'

Mary was waving at the girls to fetch the empty mugs. Sue jumped to attention, busied herself at the tea urns but Debbie waded through the crowd, a smile or a salty word for every man who looked at her. And what man wouldn't look at her. Dai Dumbells was watching his fiancée, eyes like rivets. Scrapper gulped down the last of his tea, relieved that Debbie had moved on.

The Stute doors swung open. A TV crew stood on the threshold, wrestling with rods and cables. Dai went barrelling over, blocked their entry, told them exactly where to stick their equipment.

The reporter, a thin, long-necked man in his twenties, held out his microphone. 'James Hackett, BBC Wales. The BBC would like to know; will Blackthorn vote on strike action today, or will you wait for a national ballot?'

'Listen, mate, no union card, not welcome,' Dai shoved reporter and crew out into the street.

'What about the women,' the reporter shouted. 'Got union cards, have they?'

'Got a point, Jimmy Mosquito. About the women,' Matthew Price said.

Sue overheard him. 'You made no bloody complaint when we served your tea.'

Scrapper had never seen the Stute so packed. Not when he was tiny, playing hide-and-seek between the lines of chairs and not in four years as a collier. They were all gathered together; his butties from the morning shift and the boys who clocked in at lunchtime. Even the boys from the night shift were there, sat under the tall windows, their skin so pale they looked transparent. He walked to the front, sat down next to Johnny.

Dewi banged the podium for hush. 'Right, lads. There's a lot to talk about. First, we got the Coal Board's offer on voluntary redundancy; a thousand quid for every year's service to every miner aged twenty-one to fifty—'

'Blood money,' Dai shouted. 'They're laying off twenty thousand men in a recession. Throwing working men on the scrapheap, starting with Yorkshire. We got to stand up to them or we'll be next. You wait and see.'

Iwan lurched to his feet. 'Yorkshire did bugger-all for us when Lewis Merthyr was facing the chop.'

The crowd shivered agreement. The English and Scottish coalfields had closed their ears to South Wales' call to arms when the Coal Board closed that pit. Twelve months on, the boys were still bitter about that.

Scrapper sighed. 'Move on, Dad,' he said.

Iwan's butty Sion Jenkins stuck his hand up. His grey face was all lines and angles, but the tip of his nose had a strawberry's shape and colour and texture.

'You're fools, you young 'uns, if you reckon the Tories'll be a walkover,' he said. 'They're out to smash the unions, strongest first. They're good and ready for the NUM, fifty million tonnes of coal stashed away. They're ruddy well daring us to walk.'

There was uproar, then, every man on his feet. At the podium, Dewi was yelling at the men to sit, to let the matter rest on a show of hands. Scrapper was giving it plenty himself, when a new commotion cut through the noise. Johnny Griffiths slumped forward in his chair, face puce, body racked with tremors and fighting for breath.

Scrapper bent over the old man. Then Debbie was there, pushing him out of the way, taking charge. Soon enough, Johnny breathed normally again.

'He needs air,' Debbie said.

The crowd made way as Scrapper helped Sue to wheel Johnny outside. There was a sick, blue tinge to the old man's lips and eyeballs. Sue fussed over him, tucking woollens and blankets over him, the old man protesting that he was fine.

'But that's your second attack this month,' Debbie said.

'The second?' Sue gripped Johnny's arm. 'Gramps, you didn't—'

'Didn't want to worry you, *bach*,' Johnny barely had strength to raise his head.

Debbie buttoned her jacket. 'You're seeing Dr O'Connell, and that's the end of it.'

Johnny gazed up at Scrapper with cloudy eyes. 'Get back in there, lad. Make your vote count.'

Scrapper went back inside but he was too late. The hall was silent, Dewi busy counting hands.

'We got deadlock,' Dewi said.

There was a pause, then uproar, every man disagreeing with the man next to him, every man wanting the last word. It was deafening; Dewi waved his arms and yelled for quiet, to no avail until Mary scrambled on stage, slapped two teaspoons against her raised palm demanding hush.

'One lad hasn't voted,' she said. 'We were missing Scrapper Jones.'

The yelling stopped, then. There was no more waving of hands or stamping of feet. The room breathed a deathly hush.

'Well then, lad,' Dewi said softly.

Scrapper's feet refused to carry him forward. He stood in the doorway, legs as near as damnit turned to stone. All the boys were looking at him; his butties, the men from the other shifts who knew him by sight. It was the silence that rattled him. It was the same loaded silence that came before a blast or before a wall of rock fell in on itself. Outside, a tree swayed in the breeze, bare branches tapping the windows. Steam hissed from the tea urns. But from the men came only a faint jangle of loose change in pockets, the ragged breathing of the older boys. They were waiting for him to speak.

Iwan's eyes drilled into him. His mouth turned to sandpaper. It was obvious what his dad wanted his answer to be and the words would not come.

'Come on, Scrapper Jones, are you for striking: yes or no?'

They betrayed Lewis Merthyr, the English collieries that were now themselves facing the chop. But Dai and Dewi were bang on when they said Welsh pits might be thrown on the scrapheap too. Damned if they didn't and maybe damned if they did.

Loyalty was what it came down to. Loyalty made everything clear. He squared his shoulders; the Joneses came from rebel stock. Even so, it took all his strength to force the word out. All his strength and resolve and defiance.

'Yes.'

Iwan turned away, grey eyes dull like slate in sunlight.

'Iwan?' Dewi said.

'I been a union man twenty-seven years,' Iwan said at last. 'I'll abide by what the majority decides.'

'Abide by?' Dai said. 'We're expectin' your support.'

Iwan's steel-capped boot traced a gouged mark on the parquet floor. He twisted the chain of his pocket watch between his fingers.

'The lodge has voted to strike,' he said at last. 'So be it. I stand by that vote to the end.'

The hammering continued, insistent. Scrapper forced open an eyelid, touched the light on his watch. Quarter past five, and wasn't he on strike? He squeezed his eyelids shut, jammed the pillow over his head, but the hammering gained force. He staggered out of bed. Iwan was waiting in the hall, dressed in work boots, cap and donkey jacket.

'Shift your backside, son. We got twenty minutes to get down there.'

'Where—?'

But Iwan had stomped off to the bathroom. Scrapper heard him pee, flush, start brushing his teeth. He threw on trousers and a couple of sweaters and waited.

'You voted to strike; fine,' Iwan pushed past and lurched down the stairs. 'But if you reckon that means sitting idle, you're wrong, lad. Hard work, winning a strike.'

It took a death wish, Iwan had told him, to down tools when the bosses were organised and strong. He had figures to prove it. Figures for the millions of tonnes of coal put aside, the millions of tonnes flowing out of Polish pits, could reel off to the nearest thousand the number of UK unemployed. By the time Scrapper turned in for the night, he wanted to hack off his own ears, wished he'd not gone back into the Stute, left it to some other sorry bastard to carry the vote.

He knew better than to argue, all the same. He gave his teeth a scour, grabbed his coat and ran out after his dad. Icy wind wuthered up the High Street, shoving him backwards. He buttoned his jacket and rammed his woollen hat over his ears, cursing himself for forgetting his gloves. Despite his limping walk, Iwan was halfway down the hill. It was a struggle to catch up.

'Where we going?' Scrapper panted.

'The pit, of course.'

'What for?'

'Are you joking, lad?' Iwan said. 'You reckon Blackthorn'll stop working because you said so? You really that naïve? We need to picket. Make sure nothing and no one goes out or in.'

They walked on, steel toecaps clinking on the greasy pavement. Running footsteps rang out behind them in the darkness.

'Orright, butties?'

It was Matt. 'First time picketing, eh, Scrap?'

Scrapper grunted agreement. It was more than he could cope with, this early, to voice an opinion and give his dad something new to chew to death. Best to say as little as possible. At last they reached the Stute, to find a small crowd had gathered – perhaps fifty men, armed with printed placards. *Coal Not Dole. Save Our Pits. Support The Miners.* They looked so organised, so professional that even Iwan stopped scowling.

Dewi thrust a placard into Scrapper's hand. 'What kept you, fellas? High time we got cracking.'

* * *

It was eerie to be standing outside the pit in the dark, the gates shut, the winding gear silent. Inside the wire fence, a lump of a watchman spilled out of the tiny sentry box, opened his eyes as the men lined up outside the wire mesh, clocked the crowd and closed his eyes again. It wasn't Dai Spy, Blackthorn's usual night watchman, Scrapper noted, because Dai Spy stood out in the road with the rest of them.

An owl hooted in the trees. He huddled deeper inside his jacket, fixed his eyes on the road. No one spoke. Cold nibbled at his fingertips, ear lobes and nostrils. When he breathed out, his breath hung in the air. Some men were stamping their feet; others dragged on fags for warmth. After the thrill of assembling and marching down to the pit together, picketing turned out to be deadly dull. His stomach rumbled. He could slaughter a cooked breakfast, toast and all the trimmings.

A sudden noise splintered the darkness, a throat-splitting scream that raised hairs along his arms and legs. He damn near screamed himself.

'Bloody foxes,' Dai said.

'They're courting late this year,' Dewi said.

'That'll be the mild winter,' Iwan said pointedly.

'Give over, Dad,' Scrapper said.

Nothing moved inside the pit gates. Then, as if an alarm had sounded, the guard jerked upright. He blinked, jaws stretching a yawn. The yawn passed down the line. The guard stretched his arms, let go a loud belch and unscrewed the cap of a flask. He poured his tea, repositioned his stomach on the shelf in front of him and sparked a roll-up. As Scrapper yawned a second time, he saw a figure emerge onto the road from the tunnel beneath the railway line. The figure was short with a barrel chest. He knew who it was at once.

'Oi-oi,' Matt had spotted him too.

'What happens when Captain Hook gets here?' Scrapper said.

'You hold him down, I smack him.'

A muscle twitched in Iwan's cheek. 'You will *not*—'

'Matt's taking the piss, Dad.'

'At ease, boys,' Dewi said. 'How about we keep it civilised. Let me talk to him.'

Scrapper wriggled to the back of the line, the better not to confront Red's dad. There was no point rubbing the overman's

51

nose in it. He willed Dewi to talk sense into Captain Hook, to persuade him to turn back up the hill and not to make things worse, for Red and for the boys and for the lodge. Dewi must have a shot, at least. Scrapper remembered Gabe Parry telling them how Captain Hook stood on the line with the rest of the boys, back in the Seventies. The younger lads laughed at the notion and Captain Hook got properly riled, yelled at Gabe to shut his trap.

Poor old Gabe.

Captain Hook advanced like a tank on a battlefield, chin raised, pace steady. He rolled right up to the line, stopped in front of Dewi, stood nose to nose with him.

'Top o' the morning, lads,' he said.

A radio crackled inside the gates. The security man spoke quietly into a handset.

'This is an official NUM picket line,' Dewi said. 'We expect you to honour it, Gwyn Pritchard. This leaflet,' he thrust a flyer at Captain Hook's clawed hand, 'explains why we're out, and why we're staying out.'

Captain Hook looked at the leaflet, turned it over. For a moment, Scrapper thought he might back down. Back down and stand with the boys. Living hell for Helen and her mam if the overman stood his ground. The only thing the village despised more than a scab was the family of a scab.

Scrapper sucked in his breath, sensed the others doing the same. But Captain Hook was staring through the chicken wire at the pit. What happened next happened quickly. The guard came to the gate, keys in hand, behind him two mountains of muscle, all shoulders and no neck. The gates inched open and long arms dragged Captain Hook into the pit then the guard snapped the padlock shut again.

Captain Hook eyeballed Scrapper through the gate, smirking like a vulture eating fillet steak. 'Care to join me, Scrapper Jones?'

He turned to Dewi, held up the flyer and ripped it into shreds.

'That's what I think of your reasons. Here's how the strike'll end. For you lot and for this pit.'

Shards of paper fluttered through the wire like dark confetti. Scrapper watched, heart in his boots, as Captain Hook stomped up the path to the canteen.

No one spoke for a while.

'Should've let me smack him,' Matt said.

'Why bother,' Iwan said. 'No question he was going to cross. After all, he's not in the lodge any more. Went skipping off to join Nacods the minute he got promoted. Fat chance we'll get the pit bosses on side.'

'Oi, I'm Nacods, not NUM,' the afternoon overman Eddie Hobson said. 'I'm stopping this side o' the gate, no matter what. Pritchard didn't cross cos he's Nacods. He crossed because he's a scab.'

The line rippled agreement.

'Reckon Nacods'll come out, then?' Scrapper asked. 'Pit deputies got as much to lose as colliers if there's closures.'

'Bloody hope so,' Eddie Hobson smiled a yellow, horsey smile.

'So what if they do?' Iwan said. 'What matters is the rest of the labour movement. Won't hold my breath for Heathfield and the TUC to back us.'

Scrapper rolled his eyes. He wished his dad would stop looking for clouds in every silver lining.

'I could kill for a nip of brandy,' Matt rubbed his palms together.

But the cold was the least of their worries. A little car was speeding from the railway tunnel towards the pit. It zoomed closer, all metallic yellow paintwork and black go-faster stripes, buzzing like an angry insect.

'Is Albright Nacods?' Scrapper asked.

'You soft in the head, kid?' Matt said. 'The only union our glorious leader backs is rugby union.'

The rest of the boys burst out laughing.

'Damn right,' Dai said. 'An' the only lodge'd have 'im is the freemasons.'

The pit boss' car squealed to a halt two feet short of the line. The door snapped open and Albright leapt out.

'Morning, boys,' his voice was chipper.

He wore a suit the colour of a storm cloud, high-belt trews, matching jacket and waistcoat. A brass chain hung across his waist, dipped into a side pocket. A dashing dresser, the pit manager, but it was purely for show, that chain. It had no weight to it, Scrapper could tell. Iwan's pocket watch was passed down four generations, had weight and heft to it. That watch would belong to Scrapper one day and after him, to his own son.

'There's no need for any of this,' Albright fixed a grin to his chops. 'No one's closing *our* pit. You have my word. Come back in, boys: aren't we better than this?'

'We're better'n you, you lying rat-bag,' Dai muttered.

'Won't be your decision, will it, Edmund?' Dewi said.

Albright's cheeks clashed with his suit. 'I have assurances,' he said stiffly. 'London gave me their word.'

The boys burst out laughing.

'Ooh, London gave him their word,' Dai mimicked Albright's mimsy voice.

'Fine,' Albright snapped. 'Have it your way.'

He stalked back to his car. Revved up the engine and inched the Ford Capri into the line. Fixed his eyes on the middle distance, as though he couldn't hear them shouting, couldn't feel the fists that beat down on the bonnet. He edged the nose of the car forward until the men in the middle of the line had to move or be crushed.

The gates swung open, then the guard slammed them shut again.

— 4 —

Helen sat at the kitchen table, eyes fixed on her slice of toast. Her dad was ranting at her mam again, specialist subject, the lodge. She flinched as he slammed down his stump of a fist, the better to make his point.

'And *why*? To spite me, is why. It's sabotage, pure an' simple.'

The salt shaker fell sideways, spilling white grains. Helen licked her finger, absent-mindedly flicked salt over her shoulder, a habit learned from her mam.

'Don't bloody do that,' her dad said.

'What?'

'That thing wi' the salt. Superstitious claptrap.'

'Don't take it so personally, *cariad*,' her mam said. 'The whole coalfield's downed tools.'

'Don't blame 'em,' Helen muttered.

Her dad lurched across the table, eyes blue beams of fury. '*I beg your pardon*, missy?'

Helen bit back a yelp as her mam kicked her under the table. 'You'll be late for school, love.'

'Not so fast,' her dad said. 'I want to know what she meant, with that smart mouth of hers. Talk back to her elders, would she?'

She didn't blame the men for walking. Not if they were all as sick of her dad as she was. He had a rare gift for offending people. As for the strike. That was politics. Her mam reckoned politics was men's business, said she held no truck with it and advised Helen to follow her lead.

But her dad had fixed his eyes on her face and was waiting for her to answer. 'Fine,' he said at last. 'You'll come straight home from school, young lady. It's not safe out there now, not for either of you. You're a fool if you think you know different.'

He pulled on his tweed jacket, shuffled into his boots and walked out, shaking the door on its hinges.

As soon as he left, her mam turned on her. 'Shut your lip an' stay out of it, can't you, young lady?'

'I'm allowed an opinion.'

Her mam made a strange choking sound. 'It's not you that pays for your opinions, is it?'

Helen had heard them together, as she lay in bed, willing sleep to come, heard the hissed whispers, strange thuds and sudden silence.

'What d'you mean, Mam?'

Her mam turned away. 'Just do me a favour, Helen Margaret Pritchard. Keep your lip buttoned and stay away from that boy.'

Her dad said it was Scrapper who talked the meeting into backing the strike. Blackthorn would have told Scargill to shove his strike, he said, but for Scrapper and his dad and the lodge rabble-rousing the men to walk. Score-settling for him suspending them both over Gabe, her dad said.

Her mam was waiting for an answer.

'Don't have a bloody choice, do I, seeing as I'm grounded.'

'You keep a civil tongue in that head of yours.'

Helen pulled on her blazer, stuffed her schoolbooks in her bag and stomped off up the hill towards Bryn Tawel. The street lamps were orange eyes that watched her in the gloom. She pulled her parka tighter, walked faster. Suddenly something whizzed past her ear, passed so close that the rush of air blew her hair into her eyes.

She turned, saw an older boy from school. 'What the fuck—'

'You Red Pritchard?'

The boy fixed an eye on her. A fearsome squint on him, one eye wandering off to the left. But for the rock he held, a rock the size of a cricket ball, she would have laughed in his face.

'Get stuffed.'

The boy raised his arm. 'Your old man's a scab, Red Pritchard. A filthy scab. You better tell him to stop; else you'll get a whole lot more'n this.'

The rock was so heavy, travelled through the air so slowly, that dodging it was easy. Even so, she flinched as it crashed into the wall behind her and shattered into a dozen jagged shards.

'I'll not miss a second time,' the lad yelled. 'You tell that to—'

She didn't wait to hear the rest of it, went tearing up the hill and kept running until she reached the school gates. She crossed the yard at full pelt and yanked the doors open. Shock set in then, hands and legs turned jelly and custard. She staggered towards the lockers, panting and giddy.

A knot of girls stood huddled together. When they saw her, they turned their backs and walked off to class. She sank down on a bench, her head in her hands. The bell rang. Bodies poured from corridor to classrooms. It felt good to be alone, to sit quietly for a moment. Mr Probert the English teacher hurried past, didn't see her. After a while, she shrugged off her parka, gloves and scarf, went over to her locker. She stopped when she saw the graffiti. Written on it in thick felt-tip was the word that the boy had used.

Four letters. Scab.

Being an outcast felt to Helen like a too-tight corset, the laces getting tighter by the day. When the miners downed tools, everyone who worked at Blackthorn – even Debbie Power, the pit nurse, and Dolly Bowen who served the men their tea – came out too. Everyone came out, bar the pit manager and her dad. Albright lived up the valley, which left the Pritchards to face the wrath of Ystrad. No man, woman or child spoke to her dad from the day the men walked. Soon enough, the miners' families were dishing out the silent treatment to Helen and her mam too. As though they had a say in anything her dad did. Helen learned to walk fast, and keep her head down, learned not to talk back, not to the villagers and especially not to her dad. When he said she was grounded, he meant it.

'Don't worry,' her mam said. 'It'll all blow over soon enough. Meanwhile, we'll live with it.'

'Why should we bloody live with it?'

'He's the man of the house. What he says goes.'

At home, she tiptoed around her dad's moods. He'd stopped drinking in the pub, came straight home from his shift, carrier bag stuffed with cans, clock-watched until she came home and God help her if she walked in late. The hissed arguments shifted from the kitchen to the living room when she turned in for the night. Doors slammed when she approached. Her dad barely spoke to her directly, addressed his complaints about That Girl to her mam. Her mam was so pale she barely cast a shadow.

At home or at school, Helen felt on show, yet set apart from other people. A sad exhibit pinned and mounted and trapped behind a case of glass. March came and went and she saw Scrapper only when he came to meet her at the school gates and walk her to the bottom of her road. He seemed distant, cool. They talked politely, like adults thrown together at a children's party. They said nothing about their home lives or about the strike. She had no clue how to reach him.

The Saturday away game couldn't come soon enough. Her parents knew about the match, had overheard her, weeks earlier, talking about it on the phone to Bethan. Not that her so-called best friend was speaking to her these days.

Come Saturday, she skipped down the stairs, duffel bag spilling hockey kit, having faked twisting her ankle during hockey practice. Her dad looked up from *The Daily Express*, clocked the bag, had no questions, for once. And why wouldn't he want the house to himself after a hard week's strike-breaking, Helen thought sourly. He had his red tops spread across the table, looked unlikely to budge until her mam served his lunch.

She set off at a trot, ducked into the alley between the terraces. Damp posters draped the walls from top terrace to High Street. *All Out For The Miners. Coal Not Dole.* Scrapper and the boys had been busy. She checked no one was around, pulled out her make-up bag and set to work with mascara and lippie. As she blotted her lips, she caught a movement in the mirror. Two girls were climbing up the alley, bleach-bottle blondes with safety pins for earrings and knotty ropes for hair, one pushing a pram.

Helen knew them by sight; they were a few years ahead of her at school, although they mostly weren't at school, part of a gang of girls who hung around outside the pub, waiting for the morning shift to pass, school skirts hoiked down to show belly-buttons, up to show legs. They'd tap the single lads for booze and fags; money too, when they could. They tapped the married ones on the quiet, so rumour had it.

The taller girl blocked the alley with the pram, planted an elbow in Helen's ribs. 'Don't like scabs round yur, do we, Dawn?'

'Scum o' the earth, scabs,' her friend agreed.

Helen pushed past, kept walking with slow, bluffing steps. At the bottom of the alley someone had ripped the posters away to show a scrawl of graffiti. *Gwyn Pritchard = SCAB. Helen Pritchard = SLAG.*

* * *

Scrapper was perched on the wall next to the bus shelter, bent over a book, his skin and hair gleaming in the sunshine. Seeing him made Helen feel even grubbier. But his face split a grin when he saw her. It took guts for him to meet her on the High Street, a slap in the face to those who shunned her. She hugged him, breathing in the smell of Imperial Leather that rose through his clothes.

'What if your butties see us?'

'It's your dad that's the scab, *bach*.'

'Tell that to your dad. To the lodge.'

'Aye, well,' a flicker crossed his face. 'Dad's stopping home this afternoon. Best we go up the barn.'

'No!' she spoke more sharply than she meant to. They needed to talk. If they went to the barn, it would not be to talk.

'What's wrong?'

'Could we not do something else?'

'You don't fancy me no more, eh?'

Was that why he was seeing her, to get one over on her dad? 'It's like all you want off me is – that.'

'That's daft, Red. If I had money, I'd take you any place you wanted.'

What did money have to with it? She moved away from him,

60

vexed. He was ducking their problems yet again. Then again, so was she. A tetchy silence followed. They sat on the wall, not speaking. Thin clouds wrapped and unwrapped themselves around the sun. The mid-morning bus came coughing up the hill. The driver slowed, eyeballed them. They shook their heads and the bus trundled on towards Bryn Tawel. As it passed, Dai Dumbells and Debbie Power approached, both tall and dark, hand welded to hand.

'Aye-aye,' Scrapper said. 'How's it feel to be Mr an' Mrs Dumbells, then?'

Dai blushed. 'Very funny, butty.'

Debbie was staring at Helen's feet. 'Nice boots, them. New, are they?' She flashed a smile that showed too many teeth.

* * *

'You could make more effort, Red,' Scrapper said later. 'Debbie was trying to be nice.'

Helen lay in his arms, felt the breathless rise and fall of his chest. Daylight poured through a chink in the barn's iron roof, glinting off the dust that shimmied in the air above their heads.

'You reckon?' she suppressed a shiver, suddenly noticing the cold and the damp.

Scrapper pulled her closer, wrapped his donkey jacket over her. The woollen collar felt rough against her cheek. All the men at Blackthorn wore these Coal Board-issue jackets but her dad refused to wear his away from the pit, changed into a smart tweed jacket and matching cap to walk home, the better to set himself apart from his men.

'What my dad's doing, me and my mam disagree with it,' she burst out.

Scrapper nibbled her ear. 'You don't have to explain or make excuses for the old sod.'

'You reckon? Cos it feels like we get to carry the blame for him.'

He kissed her, pulled her closer, buried his face in her hair. It was only later, as she walked home, that it hit her. Scrapper hadn't disagreed with her.

— 6 —

The pit manager sat at his chipped Formica desk, face pale, nose twitching like a rabbit scenting a fox.

'You asked to see me, Mister Albright?'

'Yes, Gwyn. Thank you. You've heard about the vote?'

'What vote?'

Albright raised his pen and tapped his lips impatiently. It wasn't one of those fancy enamelled affairs he clipped to his top pocket for show, matching his pens to his suit. It was a yellow plastic Bic, tooth marks sunk into the end. Nine years out of college, Albright, and in charge of a pit. And not a trace of black dust beneath those neat pink fingernails.

'They've voted to come out,' he said.

'That was weeks back.'

'Not here, Gwyn,' Albright said. 'In Sheffield.'

He had no idea what the pit manager was banging on about.

'It's a disaster,' Albright continued. 'A disaster on an epic scale. Union delegates from across the country, backing the Kent miners' motion: all the UK coalfields to join the strike. All union members to respect picket lines.'

Gwyn shrugged. 'They're doing that already.'

'Yes, but this vote changes everything, Gwyn, don't you see? Head office planned to fight the union through the courts. Get an injunction, declare the strike illegal. Now Scargill can argue that the strike is legitimate.'

Albright's argument made no sense. Pit by pit, the men had voted show-of-hands on the shop floor. The shop floor delegates

63

took the lodge decision to the coalfield rep. Each coalfield sent delegates to national conference. If the strike was wrong-headed and pointless and damaging, it was wrong-headed, pointless, damaging and legitimate. Anyone who knew coal knew that. Clutching at straws to call the strike illegal and drag a case through the courts. It had nothing to do with coal; everything to do with politics. With the government squaring up to the NUM, the prime minister declaring war on organised labour. And good luck to her, Gwyn reckoned. He'd shed no tears when Thatcher smashed that bunch of no-good bolshies.

He itched to put Albright straight. What was the Coal Board thinking, hiring this boy to run his pit? Why send a prissy youngster when what was needed was a coalface man, hair on his chest and calluses for hands, a man with anthracite in his veins.

The phone shrilled.

'What is it, Sarah? Oh. Right. Just give me a minute—' Albright looked up. 'It's the area manager,' he mouthed. 'I've got to take this.'

Gwyn pretended not to understand, wandered to the open window.

'Adam,' Albright's voice turned as slick as his hair. 'How are you this morning? Good to hear—'

Beneath Albright's office, the colliery sprawled across the hillside, red brick buildings scattered as though hurled from a great height, a hotchpotch of mismatched structures spattered on the valley floor. At the bottom stood the winding house, wheels motionless, above it, the engineering sheds and workshops, canteen and bath house. All lay empty. No buzz and hum of machinery. No voices raised in laughter or dispute. Gwyn found it unsettling: his lads had been out a month and a half and already the power had drained from the place.

In the stillness, he caught the echo of footsteps. A crunch of boots on gravel. Generations of long-gone Pritchards clocking in and out. He was bound to Blackthorn by the coal that clogged his veins and by a bond of duty. The strike left him as diminished as his pit, day dragging after idle day.

'Yes, but—' Albright was trying to sweet-talk the boss.

Silly, silly boy. A straight-shooter, Smith-Tudor; expected a man to give it to him unsugared and unvarnished, to call a spade a bloody shovel. And poor little Albright wittering down the line about manual digging implements.

'Yes, Adam. In fact, I was just saying to Gwyn Pritchard—' Albright paused. Listened. Looked at Gwyn. 'Yes, he's here now. Um. Yes—' he waved the phone receiver. 'Area manager wants a word with you, Gwyn.'

He took the phone.

'Ah, Pritchard.' No mistaking Adam Smith-Tudor's fruity baritone.

'What can I do you for, boss?'

'You remember our little chat at Christmas, eh?'

'Aye.'

'Got some of the best coal reserves in South Wales at Blackthorn. But if those bastards don't go back quick-sharp, there's no way we'll convince London that the pit's worth the investment. That *you're* worth the investment. We understand each other, eh?'

'Reckon so.'

'Then you know what to do. Pinpoint the fault lines, eh, give them a little push.'

'Right you are, boss. I'll do my best.'

Gwyn handed the phone back to Albright, returned to the window. Outside, the hillsides seemed greener now, mellow April sunshine warming the brickwork. It took a collier to see beauty in this place. Generations of labour gave birth to Blackthorn, crafted it with their blood and sinew and tears and sweat. It was the colliers' not the Coal Board's pit. He'd get the coal flowing, like the man said.

Get the lads' heads down and keep their noses clean.

Scrapper paused in the entrance to the Stute, listening for the sound of voices. The hall was deserted, chairs set in crooked lines, a fug of stale fag smoke hanging in the air. Iwan told him to come over after the picket. But there was no sign of Iwan, not in the hall, or in the tiny kitchen behind it. He strode up the oak staircase, at last caught a faint rumble of voices. He followed the sound to the end of the corridor, put his head round the library door. Newspapers lay open on the table. But no one was reading *The Financial Times* or *The Observer* or browsing the dusty shelves labelled in alphabetical order: Economics, Fiction, History, Leisure, Marxism, Politics, Society and Sport. No one bent over the rack of magazines on mining, football, class politics and bird-watching. The shelf labelled Fiction called him over. He pocketed *The Plague*, and tried the room next door.

The brass plate on the door read Committee Room but some wag – Matthew Price, no doubt – had stuck a Post-it on top, printed with the words War Cabinet. The door was ajar. Through the gap, Scrapper saw Dewi at the head of the oval table, leading the area strike committee meeting. He sidled in and parked himself on a stool next to the filing cabinets.

Iwan was in full flow. 'Sorry, Dai, no. The bosses are better organised than we reckoned. Yes, we should picket Port Talbot, stop the coal imports. But we need to get Welsh steelworkers behind us and that means convincing them that we're not putting their jobs at risk.'

'Sheffield's working on a national agreement with the steel unions,' Dewi said.

'Aye,' Iwan's eyes glittered. 'Good luck to them.'

'Well, Scargill said—' Dai began.

'Stuff Scargill,' Iwan cut in. 'It's down to us to get the Welsh TUC and steel unions behind the strike. We know the boys; they know us. Sheffield can do what they like.'

'Let's just put it to the bloody vote,' Dewi said. 'Who reckons this strike committee should approach the Welsh TUC and steel unions independently?'

Hands shot up around the table. Despite himself, Scrapper was impressed: his dad had turned the meeting. Only Dai and Dewi voted no. Iwan leaned back in his chair, palms knitted, elbows to the ceiling.

Dewi sighed. 'Agreed, then. Area priorities are to stop coal unloading at Port Talbot and lobbying for solidarity from the Welsh steelworkers and TUC.'

The men rose from the table, pulled on their coats and jackets.

'Why d'you always go splitting hairs,' Scrapper said as he followed Iwan down to the hall.

'I do no such thing,' Iwan said. 'It's about strategy and tactics. You got a lot to learn about class struggle, lad. It takes brain, not brawn.'

'So, we're off to Port Talbot?'

Iwan nodded. 'Do me a favour, son. Don't get nicked.'

'As if.'

Iwan went over to the tea urns to continue the argument with Dai and Dewi. Scrapper looked at his watch. It was nearly midday; time to head up to Bryn Tawel to find Red. They hadn't spoken in a week. It was more than his life's worth to call the house and have her dad pick up the phone.

* * *

The lunch bell sounded as he reached the school gates. Kids slammed out into the yard like hosed sludge, wrapped in blazers and sweaters the colour of dung. Brown-and-yellow striped ties flapped in the breeze, but some of the boys had pierced ears and some of the girls had permed hair, their faces blank with slap. Scrapper felt old, suddenly; it would have been unthinkable, in his time, for boys to wear jewellery. For a girl to paint even her nails.

He leaned against the gate post and waited as the crush of bodies thinned but there was still no sign of Red. He was about to leave when he saw her at last. She wasn't alone, for once, but none the better for it. A sturdy fair-haired lad had wrestled her into a headlock. She wriggled and squirmed as the boy tried to drag her behind the building, two smaller boys urging the bully on. Brawn acted faster than brain. He scaled the wall, pelted across the yard and grabbed Red by the waist. He shoved his palm under the boy's chin and snapped his grip like broken elastic. Brawling was not Scrapper's strong point. He decided to make it look convincing, even so, hands against the lad's pecs, shoving him just hard enough to make a point.

'Pick on a girl, would you?'

'I—'

The lad looked familiar. A squint on him to scare the horses.

'Name?'

'Ricky Allison,' the boy mumbled.

Allison. There was a family of that name in the village. They weren't miners, though. Not in a generation. Distant relatives of Johnny and Sue.

'Well?' Scrapper said.

The boy stared at the ground, muttered something.

'What's that?'

The boy raised his head. 'She's a scab, in't she? Everyone knows that.'

Scrapper shoved the lad again. 'Listen, kid. You got a problem with her, you got a problem with me. Got a problem with me, you'll be wearing your balls for earrings. Capeeshee?'

The boy gave a faint nod.

'Right. Scram.'

He turned to the boy's two cronies, to the other kids who stood watching, open-mouthed. 'Same goes for the rest of you,' he knotted his brows for menace. 'Mess with Helen Pritchard, you mess with Scrapper Jones.'

The boys backed away. That nickname had its uses. He got saddled with it when other kids couldn't pronounce Schiappa-Jones. Luckily, he grew into the name. Got tall enough and hefty enough to not have to defend it.

He turned to Helen. 'You orright?'

'Best you go. There'll be trouble if Sir catches you.'

'Can I see you?'

'Why?'

'What d'you mean, why? I missed you, Red.'

Her face hardened. 'Missed me? I've not heard from you in two weeks.'

'Well how could—?'

'What Ricky said: you didn't deny it.'

Scrapper sucked in his breath. It was true; he hadn't. But how could he? This was how it went, when a miner sold out his butties. There were families frozen out, even now, because a grandfather or great-grandfather turned black-leg back in 1926. Most were long gone, to cities like Cardiff or Swansea, or off to England where shaking off a shady reputation came as easy as shedding a coat.

'Christ, Red. You're still my girl. But how can I make this better for you when everything your dad does makes things worse?'

Her shoulders stiffened with rage. 'No one's got the guts to come after Dad. But the women yell at my mam in the street. At Mam! Who never hurt no one.'

'I'm sorry, Red—'

'Are you? Because it looks to me like you got what you wanted and now you've dumped me. It's like you're ashamed to—'

Scrapper grabbed her, slammed her body against his, pressed his lips to her lips.

'Geroff!' she struggled to free herself, heat flooding her cheeks.

The door to the staff room squealed open. At last, Scrapper let Red go. Nothing moved in the schoolyard. Everyone was staring at them.

'You still reckon I'm ashamed of you?'

She didn't answer; too busy struggling not to smile.

'Tomorrow lunchtime,' he said. 'You know where.'

He sprinted across the yard and let himself out through the gate. When he turned back, Helen was gone. His English teacher Mr Probert, the apprentice's dad, stood in the doorway, arms wrapped around a pile of books. In that moment, Scrapper was fifteen years old again.

'Sorry, Sir,' he mouthed.

— 8 —

Which man should he get on side; which fault line would be easiest to break? Gwyn had been mulling that over for days. He lay in bed, listened to Carol bumbling around in the kitchen. Life had taken a tidy turn. A rare privilege to rise late, take a pot of tea and eat breakfast at his own table with his wife. To head down to the pit in daylight and not stumble around in the dark. All those things were everyday privileges for folk with desk jobs. He dressed slowly, went downstairs. Poured his first pint of morning tea, just the way he liked it; quarter of the mug filled with milk, two and a half sugars. A superior brew to that swill Dolly Bowen served in the canteen. He nodded a greeting to his wife and hunkered down at the table, pondering.

The strike was solid in Ystrad; not a chink in the frame. They were well dug in, Dewi Power and his acolytes. If Dewi was the guts and Dai Dumbells the heart, Iwan Jones was the brains of the outfit. He had no hope, come hell or heaven, of chipping those three from the pack.

He sliced the egg open. It took a sharp knife and a steady wrist to top a soft-boiled egg. Hold the knife unsteady, go in cack-handed, get fragments of shell all over the shop.

'You working today?' Carol asked.

'Aye. Got a survey team coming up from Cardiff.'

She looked at him pigeon-fashion.

'The longer the stoppage, the more likely the pit becomes unstable,' he said. 'Albright's getting a survey team to check that the coalface is secure. All goes well, we start maintenance work next week.'

'And who you gonna get to do the maintenance?' The girl slouched in the doorway, arms folded. She wore a baggy green sweater Gwyn hadn't seen before, skin-tight black leggings over too-skinny legs. He hadn't heard her come down. He watched what he said, lately, when his daughter was around.

'Mind your own, missy.' He sliced his toast into equal-sized rectangles.

'Bring in scab workers, will you?' Helen said.

He set down his knife. 'That's not your damn business. I'll thank you not to sneak around listening to what doesn't concern you. I catch you carrying clecs – to anyone outside this house – I'll tan your hide. You hear?'

The girl stomped off down the hall.

He turned to Carol. 'You sure she's not been seeing that boy?'

Carol shook her head. 'Says he dumped her. Wants nothing to do with her, since the strike. There's been name-calling again at school, Gwyn. She's upset.'

She gathered up his empty plate, mug and cutlery and dumped them noisily in the washing-up bowl. She'd been getting sideways comments too, from the wives, had started taking the bus to do her shopping in town, the better to avoid their neighbours.

'Sticks an' stones,' he said.

'It's sticks an' stones I'm bloody worried about.'

But the mention of school got him thinking. It was obvious. He should have thought of the teacher's little lad right away. He pushed away his chair and set off for the corner shop.

The shop bell shrilled. Geraint Mags-N-Fags looked up, saw Gwyn, fixed his gaze on his copy of *The Sun*. And there, next to the magazines, was the lad Gwyn was looking for: Alun Probert, the apprentice, skinny frame hunched like a question mark, curly head buried in *Blue Apocalypse*. Gwyn knew he'd find the boy here. The kid was obsessed with superhero magazines. *Blue Apocalypse* was his favourite. Same routine every week; rushed from his shift to the newsagents to pick up a copy ordered special. But the lad wasn't buying today, stood in the shop to read it, strapped for cash, no doubt. It was tough on the single boys, the strike; not a penny in benefit. The married lads got a tenner a week from the social, plus child benefit.

'Can I buy that for you lad?'

Alun Wet-Ears' freckled face flushed pink. He dropped the comic back on the rack. 'Only browsing,' he muttered, eyes fixed on the floor. 'Geraint said I could.'

The shopkeeper shot Gwyn a look to freeze a blast furnace. 'Orright by there, Alun?'

Alun nodded.

'Let's step outside, have a conflab,' Gwyn said.

'Best not, boss.'

'Fine,' he lowered his voice. 'Tell me, boy. How come you got an apprenticeship at a pit that stopped hiring?'

Beetroot-coloured, the lad's face.

'We both know why, eh? Mucked up your exams, didn't you? But your dad begged me to take you on. I made a special case for you with Albright. Took you when no pit in the coalfield was taking new men. Didn't I?'

'Yes,' Alun whispered.

'Yes,' Gwyn said. 'So you'll know what I'm expecting in return.'

The lad's face crumpled. Gwyn took no pleasure in bringing a grown man to tears, even a fellow barely old enough to shave. Little Probert would thank him when his job was spared. Instinct told him to leave it for now; let the lad stew, follow up with a home visit.

'If you change your mind about that rag, let me know,' he said.

The shop bell shrilled again as he shut the door. A soft spring morning, birdsong all over, the trees in bud and sunlight warming his face as he headed off to work. Beyond the village, spring cast a sheen over the hillocks of waste coal and rubble, undisturbed since the strike. But no beauty could be found in that. He'd let them green this valley over his cold, dead corpse.

Down on the High Street, he perched on the wall near the bus stop, waited for Albright to pick him up. And that's when he saw Matthew Price emerge from a flat above one of the shops. Furtive was the word that sprang to mind. Matt loped past butcher, bookies, funeral parlour and co-op, flinched and ducked his head on meeting Gwyn's eye. Come from Siggy's place, had he? So that was the lad's game. If Matt was a ladies' man, Gwyn was Shirley bloody Bassey.

Scrapper slumped on the back seat of the minibus, watched the light seep across the sky. Dawn stained the silver coast with the colours of a blast furnace, dimmed only by the smoke that belched from Port Talbot's concrete stacks. The air blown in through the open window was so gritty that his breath rasped metal filings. Each street was greyer and more drab than the last. Finally, Dewi steered into the road that led to the industrial port. A tangle of conveyor belts and hoppers and pulleys dipped and swooped overhead, a black helter-skelter from hell.

'What is this?' he said.

'It's the gateway,' Iwan said. 'The bosses shipped out all the coal and iron and steel by here, built a new industrial world—'

'Built it on sweat and blood and broken backs,' Dai said.

Scrapper shuddered. He could imagine it: the labour forged into the steel bones of this place, the bodies sunk deep beneath the blackened concrete. Even the air had the metallic taste of blood. Back then, the ships steamed in empty, loaded iron ore and coal that his grandfathers and great-grandfathers ripped from the South Wales hills, steamed out again, leaving his forebears empty-handed.

'We'll stop 'em unloading scab coal, eh, fellas?' he said.

'Damn right,' Matt said.

'How we gonna stop 'em?' Alun Probert sank deeper into his jacket.

It was Alun's first time as a flying picket, too. But while Scrapper itched to reach the port to stop the coal shipments,

Alun Wet-Ears was sucking the *hwyl* from the day. The apprentice hunched in his seat, face carefully blank, refused to sing along as Dai gave 'Part of the Union' a savaging. Dewi had driven across the valley to fetch the lad from his home. Mister Probert opened the door in his dressing gown, face like a squeezed lemon, had them wait ten minutes for Alun to come down. Which was why they were late. The kid had no heart for this. Alun's question hung, unanswered. A dark, bulky object was steaming towards the line where sky met sea; a giant ship, emptied of its Polish coal at a port built to ship coal and steel and iron around the world. Scrapper gripped the seat in front of him. Coal sent to crush Welsh miners.

'No, you gotta be bloody joking!' Dewi leaned over the steering wheel.

Up ahead, at the entrance to the British Steel docks, a line of police blocked the road. They wore padded gilets and bowling-ball helmets, carried truncheons and Perspex shields. Tooled up to stop working men defending their livelihoods.

Scrapper vowed to give it some *hwyl*, alright. Buses from across the coalfield were parked the length of the road. He helped Dai and Matt to unfurl the lodge banner and thread it onto its poles and stepped back to admire it. Magnificent, the banner. Red velvet with gold fringing, images printed on it: the brickwork of Ystrad Stute, two brass miner's lamps, a pickaxe and shovel laid crosswise. Across the top, picked out in gold stitching, *National Union of Mineworkers, Blackthorn Lodge* and a motto: *nothing to lose but our chains*.

Dai draped a long strip of black tulle between the tips of the poles, fixed it with rubber bands.

'With us in spirit, eh, Gabe?'

He picked up a pole and set off towards the line of police, moved forward so fast that Scrapper, holding the second pole, struggled to keep his footing. The others hurried behind them.

Dai went up to the tallest policeman. Behind him, against the port gates, Scrapper saw a crush of placards and banners.

'We're 'ere to join that lot by there,' Dai said.

'Right you are, mate,' the Cockney policeman waved them through without argument.

The men at the gates roared a welcome. Scrapper turned back to see the police lines close around them, pinning them against the fence, caught like mice in a trap. Why were none of the others bothered about it? His dad and Dewi went into a huddle with the lads from the area strike committee. Dai nodded to him to prop the banner against the wire fence, went over to the others. Matt, fag in hand, wandered over to some student types. He took special pleasure in winding up students; especially the ones with Marxist newspapers. He had quite a routine: opened with a joke to turn the air blue. If that failed to raise a laugh, he'd pick a fight about women's rights or the Falklands or the death penalty. The regular sellers had learned to laugh at Matt's jokes, ply him with fags and move away.

A dozen men gathered round Dai, congratulating him on his latest sporting win. Only Alun didn't mingle. He slouched on an oil drum next to the banner, scuffing the ground with the tips of his boots.

'What in hell's eating you?' Scrapper said.

Alun Wet-Ears fixed his eyes to his boots. 'Nothing.'

'Don't you get that we're fighting for our jobs?'

'By yelling at a bunch of coppers? When the folk that make them decisions are miles away in London. When them folk don't give a flying fuck.'

'So what d'you reckon we should do?'

'There's nothing we can do. No one listens to the likes of us.'

'But that's why we're here. Gonna make them listen.'

Alun sighed. 'We need to keep our heads down, cross our fingers that they leave Blackthorn be.'

'But that's—'

He never got to finish the sentence. Inside the port, a huge grey lorry was pulling up to the gates. All at once, the police charged into the crush, drove in and split the protesters down the middle. There was nowhere to run, no space to move. Bodies rammed him against the fence, chicken wire cutting into his cheek. When he pushed himself clear, Alun had vanished. A windscreen loomed over the crowd, steel mesh over the glass hiding the driver from view as the truck inched through the port gates. All around was mayhem, miners and coppers fighting hand to hand. Resin batons thudded bones, battered flesh. He heard the grunts of the hitters, the gasps of the hit, the low growl of truck engines.

Little by little, the police beat the crowd back, allowing half a dozen trucks to leave the port. He spotted Dai, half a head taller than everyone else, taking the worst of it. Truncheons slammed Dai's shoulders as he fought, head lowered, shoulders working like pistons. Scrapper saw a truncheon catch Dai across the forehead. Dai sank into the scrum of bodies and vanished.

'No!' Scrapper yelled.

He tried to push forwards, but the crush was too dense. The police paused for a beat. Then, they drove in harder, a final push driving the protesters off the road. Again, bodies pinned him against the fence. Everyone was yelling now. Scrapper raised his voice along with the rest, the words jagged in his throat.

'Scab, scab, scab!'

As the gates slammed shut, he saw Dai rise from the crush, policemen hanging off both his arms. Dai rallied his strength, shook them off like ants, but one clung on, tenacious. Dai levered his forearm against the man's chest, flexed and sent him flying. The crowd cheered. It made no difference. The brawling continued, the police batons beating the miners back. In the distance, Scrapper heard the clank of chains and pulleys. Inside the gates, outlined against a shimmering morning sea, the cranes bowed and lifted, bowed and lifted, filling yet more trucks with strikebreaking coal.

Port Talbot's proud cranes, grovelling to the bosses.

* * *

Scrapper's *hwyl* was spent as he trouped behind the others towards the car park, his face a honeycomb of gashes. He was in better shape, even so, than half the men around him, a crushed army with cut hands and black eyes and bleeding noses. Matt had to lead Dai by the arm, he'd taken such a hammering, eyes puffed up nasty, a matching pair of shiners. Iwan had turned his ankle again. Looking at them, Scrapper felt a rush of guilt; every button was ripped off his jacket, but he'd suffered no real damage. He should have fought the bastards like Dai, and to hell with what his dad said.

'All here, are we?' Dewi said.

Someone was missing. It took Scrapper a while to work out who. 'Where's Alun?'

'Christ, it would be him,' Dewi said.

The apprentice had vanished. Dewi led Iwan and the casualties back to the minibus, leaving Scrapper, Matt and Eddie Hobnob to search for the lad. Scrapper and Matt retraced their steps towards the docks. Half the police vans had followed the coke trucks out of the docks, the grim convoy heading for the town's eastern outskirts to join the motorway to Newport, making for the steelworks at Llanwern that lay beyond.

Dropped placards littered the road, smeared with footprints and tyre marks. A lone police van was parked outside the gate. Two women crouched on the tarmac, sorting piles of vests and shields. Behind them, a line of men in shirtsleeves and trousers perched like crows on a low wall, smoking and swigging cola.

Stripped of armour and weapons, they looked human again. Matt marched straight over, Scrapper dragging along behind.

'Spare us a tab, fellas?'

The man in the middle was short for a copper, but wiry. A Jack Russell type.

'Ah, what the hell,' he thrust a pack of B&H at Matt. 'Put up a good fight, your lot.'

The accents gave them away; they were local officers. Not that it made any odds to Scrapper. Pigs were pigs. Matt took a cigarette, frowned at Scrapper to do the same. Scrapper accepted a fag and a light, sucked in smoke and tried not to gag.

'Reinforcements, that lot?' Matt nodded towards the east.

'Bloody Met,' the officer shook his head. 'Loose fucking cannons.'

'You're not wrong,' Matt said.

'Scud missiles to take out a beehive,' the policeman said.

'The lads they nicked,' Matt said. 'Taken 'em to London, have they?'

The policeman clicked out a smoke ring. 'There's not been much nicking. Not today.'

'Thing is, butt, we've lost one of our lads.'

The policeman shrugged. 'Try Station Road. If not there, try Skewen or Maesteg.'

As they walked away, Scrapper flicked his cigarette into a puddle. 'How could you talk to them like we're mates?'

'None of this is personal, Scrap. It's just politics.'

'You reckon? Cos it feels fucking personal, your butties getting their heads bashed in.'

Dewi had the engine running when they reached the minibus. Eddie had no joy finding Alun either. They set off for the town centre. There was no sign of Alun at Station Road and no sign at the smaller police station in Skewen. Maesteg was several miles up the valley. At last, they pulled up at the police station.

Alun Wet-Ears stood outside, waiting in a queue of a dozen men to use the phone box. His jacket missed an arm and his nose was mashed up. He climbed in without saying a word.

'*Duw* — a boxer's job, that,' Matt was impressed.

'The mark of a man,' Dewi ran a finger along his own flattened conk. 'You're a class warrior now, kid. Got battle scars to prove it.'

Alun's eyes were red. He looked at no one, said nothing.

At last, the minibus pulled up outside the Stute. They climbed out, limping and exhausted and trooped inside, where Sion Jenkins was manning the tea urns. Scrapper was about to follow the others in when he realised Alun was slinking away by himself.

He rushed after him, grabbed his arm. 'Charge you, did they?'

Alun shook his head.

'What, then?'

'Still reckon we can make 'em listen, do you, Scrapper Jones?'

— 10 —

Cosy, that was the word that sprang to mind. Gwyn sat in Mister Probert's front room, April sunlight pouring through the windows. The schoolteacher was busy in the kitchen, preparing afternoon tea. The tang of pipe tobacco mingled with the black pepper scent of old books. It was lived-in, this room, but there was discipline too, in the batches of exam papers lined up in neat piles on the sideboard for marking.

He sank into the cracked leather armchair, eyed the bookshelves beside the chimney breast. A six-part encyclopaedia bound in faded red morocco. King James Bible. Life studies of Nye Bevan and Lloyd George. Shelf upon shelf of paperback classics, all dog-eared and thumbed. The bottom shelf piled with superhero comics. A library, this. He regretted not making time to read.

The schoolteacher had packed his oldest two off to university, got them settled in new lives in the city. Married, more was the pity, the oldest two. Either would have done nicely for the girl. This was everything Gwyn wanted for her: a cosy home filled with books, food in the cupboard, a warm hearth. Not rich, but solid, the man of the house a professional, two or three rosy-cheeked kids. A life that was secure and settled. The girl could be a modern young woman with prospects, if only she applied herself. It fell to her to seize the chance to flee the shadow of the pit.

He looked down at his hands, garden grime layered over workshop grime from the colliery, and felt a twinge of shame.

He should have dipped them in Swarfega before coming over.

The schoolteacher elbowed open the door. He carried a tray loaded with an earthenware teapot, matching mugs, milk jug and sugar bowl, and a plate with two slices of simnel cake. His hands shook as he set the tray on a leather ottoman.

'You're okay with tea, Mr Pritchard? Unless you fancy something stronger—'

Gwyn smiled. 'Tea is what's required, Mr Probert.'

The teacher poured, served him a slice of cake. Gwyn took a bite. The cake was home-made. A perfect balance of marzipan, fruit and candied peel, the sponge light and fresh. They sat back and sipped their tea. The schoolteacher seemed to be fumbling for something to say.

'You've come about our youngest, haven't you?' he said at last.

His directness surprised Gwyn. But fair dos. Better to get down to it than go wandering around the houses.

'Alun, aye. A painful state of affairs, this strike.'

'You're sacking him?'

'God, no. Why would I?'

The teacher hefted a sigh. 'I wouldn't blame you. All these weeks idle at home. Hasn't earned a penny since March. And after everything you did for him—'

Gwyn batted away the teacher's gratitude. 'He's a good little lad, Alun. Been well worth making an exception to hire him. But fact is, Mr Probert, stoppage will mean death for this pit. All of us'll be out of work soon, unless—'

Mr Probert fixed his gaze on the bookcases. 'The men would say that's why we should back the strike. Force the Coal Board to rethink their closure plans.'

There was no conviction to the words. No fire or resolve. The schoolteacher was a Labour man of the modern tendency. His grandfather put himself through night school, got promoted to pit management. Worked all God's hours to get there. His father was the first lad from Ystrad to make it from grammar school to university, got a job with the civil service. Three generations of Proberts, broken free from the pit. Ironic that little Alun had to beg to work at Blackthorn. The lad reckoned some mental block stopped him reading and writing. Lazy and slack-minded, more like.

'Listen,' Gwyn told the schoolteacher. 'I got inside information. But you got to promise not to breathe a word—'

He explained what Smith-Tudor had said about how pits that made money would make it. But now the survey results had delivered a blow. They needed Blackthorn back up and running quick-sharp, or risk subsidence after the heavy rain this spring. The race was on to contain the damage or their costs would fall through the floor.

Mr Probert listened, attentive. Nodded thoughtfully. Did not interrupt.

'We get my lads back now,' Gwyn finished, 'there's every chance we can save the pit.'

'And if you don't?'

'My lads stay out, the pit becomes less and less productive and we'll struggle to get new funds from the Coal Board. Blackthorn's costs increase, we're finished.'

'But don't you think, Mr Pritchard—'

'Gwyn,' he interrupted.

'—don't you think, Gwyn, that if the men win the strike, they can force the Coal Board to reconsider?'

'The longer they stay out, the more positions harden. On both sides.'

'And if the men go back quickly, there's hope?'

'My lads go back quickly, there's every hope in the world.'

Gwyn fell silent, sipped his tea, pondered the matter. If anyone understood what hard work brought, it was the school teacher. The girl could learn a lot from this family.

Mr Probert seemed to pick up on his train of thought.

'Helen does you proud,' he said. 'She's one of my brightest students.'

Gwyn felt colour rise beneath his skin. 'Aye, well. She's not a bad kid. Reckon she'll get good O-levels?'

'No question. If we can just resolve the problem with her attendance. But then, we all understand. The children can be vicious. Nobody blames Helen for skipping the odd class these last few weeks. No problem for her to keep up. But it's sad that she quit the hockey team. Best little sweeper we had, Mrs James said.'

Gwyn's heart slammed his ribcage. The girl had told them she was playing that afternoon. Playing away again, she said, due back on the evening bus.

He'd give her playing away, all right.

'Aye, well,' he reached for his overcoat. 'It's a rough game for young ladies. Always bruised easy, my Helen.'

Mr Probert smiled. 'In twenty years of teaching, I've found the girls a lot more combative than the boys,' he said. 'On and off the hockey field.'

Combative. Gwyn felt grudging respect for the girl when she stood her ground. But it was a whole other sorry business to tell lies and sneak around. And that boy was behind her deceit, no doubt.

'You'll think on what I told you, Mr Probert?' he offered the schoolteacher his good hand.

'It's a lot to think about. The ramifications—'

Even so, the schoolteacher's goodbye handshake had a hearty grip to it.

Gwyn set off to meet the evening bus. It was quiet, for a Saturday. The strike had been tough on the local shopkeepers. Takings down at the pub, the *bracchi*, the unisex fashion boutique, hairdressers, butchers, bookies and co-op. Belt-tightening all round.

The lights blazed in the ice cream parlour, but no customers were in. Angela Jones was busy mopping the floor. The bus stop was empty too. In his time, he'd queued for many a Saturday evening bus, gone off drinking and dancing and chasing skirt to the social club in Bryn Tawel or to the bright lights of Swansea or Cardiff. Many a night shared a taxi back to Ystrad or suffered a bleary ride home on the Sunday morning bus with all the others who got wasted or got robbed or got lucky. But there were no young folk off out on the town tonight.

Darkness gathered, damp seeping into his bones. He took cover in the pebble-dashed shelter. A wall of posters mocked him. *Maggie Out. Victory To The Miners. Coal Not Dole.* Illegal fly-posting, the length and width of the wall. Naked propaganda. He raised himself on tip-toes, grabbed a corner and pulled. The glue was still damp and the flyers overlapped. The wall of posters came away in his hand. He crumpled the papers between his hands and stamped on them. But then he saw what was hidden beneath. The girl's name in spray paint. Next to it, a scrawled stick figure with mad red swirls of hair. The stick figure was performing a sex act. On a second stick figure wearing a miner's helmet. His lungs failed him. He doubled over, clutched the wall, fighting for breath.

As he struggled, two figures walked up the road. A dark-haired lad sauntered up the *bracchi* steps. Scrapper Jones, carrying bucket and paintbrush, a roll of posters tucked under his arm. A knitted green sweater clung to his broad shoulders. The sweater looked familiar. Helen trotted along beside him, her arms filled with rolls of posters. She followed the boy into the *bracchi* and through the door that led to the flat above the shop.

11

Scrapper arrived at the picket to find Debbie sat in the moth-eaten armchair next to the brazier, sipping tea from a flask. She wore an outsized donkey jacket over her thin uniform, woollen leggings under it. She caught him looking at her legs, cocked an eyebrow at him. Those dark eyes of hers missed nothing, not when they were together and not now. Her fingers were white with cold. He remembered the touch of those fingers. Dai's gaze drove into him like a sledgehammer. Scrapper went to join his butties, his whole body twitching unease.

'What you doing here, love?' Iwan said.

'Don't you start,' Debbie said sourly. 'Had enough grief already from this one. I'm on strike an' all, aren't I? Got as much right to picket Blackthorn as you fellas.'

'It's not about—' Dai began.

'You got every right,' Dewi said. 'But we're expecting trouble, Debbie. Word is, Albright's called in a maintenance crew this morning.'

'That's why I'm here. Reinforcements.'

'It could get hairy,' Iwan said.

'So?' Debbie crossed her arms.

'So now you know.' Iwan stirred the brazier, tipped in more coal.

Dewi had dispatched some of the boys to fill a car boot with waste coal from the tip above the village. It was a happier picket with the brazier stoked good and high, still a nip in the air most mornings, even with Easter come and gone. Debbie huddled closer to the brazier as the men lined up to block the gates. She wore a wedding band now, and a second ring with a flashy blue stone. Scrapper found it strange to think of Debbie married, when not long ago they were sweethearts. She turned, caught him looking at her a second time.

'Seen something you fancy, Scrapper Jones?'

Matt snorted a laugh, dug an elbow into Scrapper's ribs.

'What's to see?' Scrapper scowled.

He knew better than to rise to Debbie's taunts. She was messing with him to needle Dai, the poor sod. Best to change the subject. He fetched a packet of digestives from the supplies box, passed the biscuits down the line.

Matt necked three digestives, one after the other. 'Women got no damn business picketing,' he spluttered. 'That one needs reminding who wears the trousers.'

Scrapper bit into his biscuit, avoided answering his butty. If anyone wore the trousers in his house, it was neither him nor his dad. His stomach grumbled. He waved at Sion Jenkins to pass the pack back down the line. He was hungry all the time, lately, his mam having cut the family food budget.

They waited and waited, the biscuits long gone and no sign of the maintenance crew. Albright drove through at his usual time, Captain Hook in the passenger seat, nose in the air, eyes fixed to the winding tower, as the guard opened the gate to let them through. Scrapper was relieved to see them gone. It was the same performance from the overman every morning, whether the pickets gave it *hwyl*, or not. Today, they were silent. Other days, they yelled and banged the car bonnet. Either way, Albright drove through and Captain Hook didn't blink.

Mid-morning, Matt raised the alert.

'Aye, aye,' he pointed towards the railway bridge.

A small figure was striding out from the tunnel, dressed in a leather jacket, a long black sweater, ripped black leggings and stompy lace-up boots. It was Sue. As she hugged Debbie, Scrapper saw that the lapels of the leather jacket were studded with button badges. *Stamp Out Racism. Victory to the NUM. A Woman's Right to Choose.*

Matt's eyes hardened; a cat sighting prey. 'Looks like we got crumpet for elevenses. Quick chorus of '*Get Yer Tits Out*', eh, lads?'

Scrapper nudged his butty to shut up but Debbie had heard him. Outrage fired her from the armchair.

'How about you show Sue some fucking respect?'

'Some kind of feminist, is it?' Matt said.

Debbie marched up to her uncle. 'D'you reckon Matt got a right to talk like that?'

Dewi blushed. 'Matthew Price, these ladies are our comrades. High time you treated them as such.'

Matt was outgunned and he knew it. Scrapper filled the tin kettle for a brew, joined Debbie and Sue next to the brazier.

'Some days, my butty's got charcoal for brains,' he said. 'You pay no mind to him. Underneath that swagger, he's good as gold.'

Debbie snorted. 'For a bloke reckons he's a ladies' man, he don't like women at all.'

'Bloke's a tosser,' Sue said. 'Brew us a cuppa, Scrap, and change the subject.'

He was about to pour their tea when he heard the engine. A van was rattling towards the pit. The men behind him drew together, formed a solid line at the gates. For one terrifying moment, Scrapper thought the van would slice right through them, but the driver slammed his brakes just in time.

He scooped up a handful of NUM leaflets and went over, chest thudding, forced himself to speak more calmly than he felt.

'Cutting it fine there, fella.'

The driver wound down his window. He was an egg of a man, stomach packed against the steering wheel, his forehead hairless and sweaty.

'Tell that lot to shift.'

Scrapper turned back to the others. There was a set speech for would-be strike breakers and generally a member of the lodge committee – Dewi, or Iwan, or old Sion Jenkins – delivered it, but the others were nodding at him to go ahead.

'This is an official NUM picket,' he began. 'This leaflet explains why—'

'I don't give a flying fuck what or why,' the driver said. 'Let us past.'

Four men in blue overalls sat in the back of the van, two others up front. Scrapper sensed his butties watching, willing him to do his best. He thrust his leaflets at the men in the back.

'This explains why we're out, why we're staying out and why we're asking you to respect this pick—'

'Respect,' the driver said. 'I'll give you respect, you little—'

Then Sue was at his side. 'A dangerous job, mine maintenance,' she said.

'You the brains o' this rabble,' the driver said.

'I know about dangerous,' Sue said. 'My granddad lost two legs to this pit.'

The driver opened his mouth to speak but Sue kept going.

'You're here because a man died below ground two months back. The bosses want you to patch up the damage, press these lads to go back.'

'So?'

'So how'd you feel if you saw a man die? Would you hurry back, risk your life to make it that little bit easier for the bosses to throw working men like you on the scrapheap?'

The men in the back seat shifted uneasily. 'Girl's got a point,' said one.

'You hired me to fetch you here an' I done my bit,' the driver said. 'Do we go in or turn back?'

'Put yourselves in these lads' shoes,' Sue's voice was almost a whisper.

'We're turning back.' The man who spoke had thinning red hair and a flat nose. He sat beside the driver and seemed to be in charge.

'You're a gentleman, sir,' Scrapper said.

The van reversed sharply, with a squeal of tyres, shot back towards the tunnel up to Ystrad.

Scrapper turned to Sue. 'Where d'you learn *that*?'

'What?'

He slung an arm over her shoulders, squeezed them. 'Blackthorn owes you a cuppa, I reckon.'

The lads cheered as he and Sue walked back to the brazier. For the rest of the morning, he had a grin across his face that wouldn't shift. He knew then that Blackthorn couldn't lose. He just wished Red had been there to see it.

12

Helen stopped writing and put down her biro with a sigh. She looked out through the open window. Morning sunshine bleached the cow parsley in the fields that stretched below the school yard. The scent of lilac rose from the tree near the gates hung heavy in the air. It made her want to gag. The heat inside the assembly hall threatened to crush her. Rows of single desks stretched in front of her. Her classmates hunched over their exam papers, most still scribbling away with hope.

Ricky Allison turned, one eye meeting her gaze. 'Scab,' he mouthed. 'We gunna get you after.'

At last, the bell rang for break. The end of the exam. The end of her O-levels. She grabbed her bag and raced down the hill towards home, before Ricky and his pathetic little mates could jump her. She couldn't care less, now, in any case. Her future, whatever it held, was out of her hands.

The house was empty, no sign of her dad pacing the hall, for once. But the back door was open. She peered out. Her mam had fetched a deckchair from the shed and was sunning herself in the garden, as though she too felt a shadow had lifted. Her eyes snapped open as she heard Helen approach, a hand raised against the midday glare.

'Your dad's away at a meeting,' she said. 'Smith-Tudor wanted him. So if you fancied heading out for a while—'

Not like her mam to encourage defiance.

'You mean it?'

Her mam fished in the pocket of her button-through skirt,

handed over a twenty. 'You deserve a break, love,' she said. 'How about you take yourself shopping. Have some fun.'

Helen planted a kiss on her mam's sticky forehead, ran up the stairs to change.

* * *

Iwan Jones sat in the window of the ice cream parlour, reading a tall pink newspaper. He lowered it as Helen burst in. No customers buying ice cream at the *bracchi*, despite the clammy heat. No sign of Angela. As Iwan folded his newspaper, Helen spotted a bandage around his wrist.

'Orright, *bach*,' he said.

'What happened to your hand?'

'Depends who you ask. Caught it on a copper, maybe. Must've done. Copper swore blind he never touched me.'

'Port Talbot again?'

Iwan nodded. 'Go straight up,' he said. 'The lad's in his room.'

That was some kind of progress. Iwan was usually stiff and formal with her. She found Scrapper alone, curtains drawn against the sun, stacks of dusty LPs piled on the floor, a tower of paperbacks teetering on the bedside table. He'd cranked up his crackly turntable, Joy Division blaring from the speakers and didn't hear her come in. He jerked, startled, when she kissed him.

'What you doing, Scrap?'

He waved at the tallest stack of vinyl. 'Selling these. Know a fella down in Barry Island might gimme a fair price.'

'But that's half your records.'

'I need the money, Red. I'll still have my books.'

'You won't change your mind?'

He shook his head.

'Let's go, then. Now. Together.'

'How? I'm broke. Got to wait 'til Friday, when the lodge gives us some cash.'

She handed him the banknote. 'We got this.'

'No we don't. Scab money, that is.'

The horror on his face. And to hell with it. She wasn't having the strike get between them yet again. Not after being holed up for weeks. If money wasn't happiness, the strike had taught her that money meant freedom, at least.

'It's not scab money,' she lied. 'I earned it babysitting at Christmas. Forgot all about it. Found it in my winter jacket just now when I went through the pockets.'

'I'm not taking your money.'

'For God's sake, Scrap,' she threw her arms around him. 'I'll hang on to the money. Now get your bloody boots on.'

13

They faced a whole heap of trouble, the Coal Board and the government. There was every risk they'd snatch defeat from the jaws of victory. That was the message Smith-Tudor delivered as he addressed his chosen few. He summoned them, a man from each of the twenty-eight South Wales pits, to a grubby Victorian hotel fallen on lean times. Each man was a key player, handpicked to attend, Smith-Tudor told Gwyn when he called to summon him. Gwyn reckoned the area manager could have spared him the flannel; he had been happy to go. The Coal Board had been as transparent as a barrel of pitch. Nothing helpful from London since the start of the strike. No point waiting for London to take the lead. It fell to coalfield men to resolve matters.

Laughter from the bar next door forced Smith-Tudor to raise his voice.

'Men from this coalfield have picketed every steelworks in the country,' he said. 'They're disrupting supplies of coal and coke, causing violence and criminal damage. We are hovering on the edge of anarchy. These people will stop at nothing to get their way, eh, gentlemen? They will destroy the coal industry and sabotage Britain's manufacturing base. And why, eh? To prove a point, is why. Their leaders are dangerous agitators whose agenda has nothing to do with coal. We must block Scargill and his followers at every turn. By whatever means.'

In the front row, a mustard-keen youngster raised a hand. 'I say we stand firm, let that rabble blink first.'

Smith-Tudor fixed the man with a cold eye. 'You need to grasp the scale of the problem, sonny. The strike is solid, across the coalfield and everywhere else bar Notts, and there's a real danger the trouble will spread. Suppose the steelworkers down tools and join the miners, eh? What about the transport unions? The port and rail unions won't handle imported coal and have their own pay claim pending. Bolshies love nothing more than a bandwagon.'

The room fell silent. Gwyn heard the man beside him breathing, the rumble of someone's stomach at the back. Smith-Tudor's little speech took some digesting, true enough. They might win yet, the hotheads. Despite the stockpiles of coal. Despite the Coal Board's contingency plans. Despite a government hell-bent on breaking the NUM. Blackthorn had been the whole of his landscape, the dispute a struggle against Dewi's lodge. Now, the walls fell away. This dispute was bigger than all of them; the men of Blackthorn Colliery as significant as ants.

The area manager stood before them, fleshy cheeks wobbling, pale eyes glassy. He seemed to gaze right through the assembled men. Seagulls screamed on the promenade outside. After a long, statesmanlike pause, Smith-Tudor served up the rest of his speech, outlined his expectations. All manner of guff about standing up to the union. About the urgent need to defend individual miners' right to work, drafting in police and troops to support them. He gave one hell of a performance. Winston bloody Churchill, fighting the miners on the beaches, selling retreat from Dunkirk as deliverance.

When the area manager finished, the room exhaled. Faint applause melted into restless silence. Tea served, Smith-Tudor worked the room, dished out smiles and nods to his disciples, come the length and breadth of the coalfield to hear his wisdom. Gwyn watched him navigate the room, a galleon in full sail.

Approached each man in turn, addressed him by name. A smile, a handshake, a lofty pat on the shoulder and off he sailed to his next target. And here he was.

Gwyn felt the room closing in on him.

'Richards,' Smith-Tudor boomed. 'You are just the man for this, eh. And trust me, you will be rewarded.'

His hand paused on Gwyn's shoulder. He was dismissed. The good ship Smith-Tudor had sailed. *Richards?* Gwyn slammed his cup and saucer on the nearest table and made a break for it, from conference room to cracked marble lobby, as fast as his coal-raddled lungs allowed. Put all the distance he could between himself and his boss. He wouldn't even notice, Smith-Tudor. Too busy dishing up his fake bonhomie. Gwyn shoved the tarnished copper door bar too hard. The revolving door creaked protest, hurled him out into the street.

He crossed the road to the promenade. The sea air lifted him a little. He filled his lungs, felt the strain of the day ebb a little. Why not profit from this miserable expedition; Albright didn't expect him back today. He needed to put several blocks between himself and Smith-Tudor, even so. He followed the promenade to the town centre, felt the magnet pull of the arcades; the jangle and buzz of fruit machines. Paused at last near the fairground and gathered a wheeze of breath. That felt better already. He bought chips wrapped in newsprint and wandered down to the water's edge. The waves crept towards him. Salt in the air. Salt on his lips. He found a quiet bench, necked his chips and watched the comings and goings of pretty girls. There was plenty to look at here, though he might as well be invisible. Just another middle-aged man with time on his hands. So many middle-aged men. So many pretty girls. He paused his gaze on one girl in particular. Skinny thighs in too-tight black leggings, red curls whipping the breeze. Helen. Hanging on to a boy with dark Italian skin. Flaunting themselves here, the pair of them, with the South Wales coalfield managers gathered two blocks away.

He hurled the chips at the seagulls and staggered away from the beach. His feet led him back to the bus station. It was time to go home. Time to put things straight. To put his own house in order.

14

The resort was loud and garish, fairground and arcades lit up to shame a Christmas tree. Helen was smitten. It was her second or third visit to the coast, but genteel Penarth was a world apart from this – brash, glamorous Barry Island, all light and speed and noise. She helped Scrapper to lug the crate of LPs off the bus. No chance she'd be spending the afternoon in some dusty, noisy record shop. She told him to find her on the seafront and skipped off towards the promenade.

She perched on the metal railings, watched the waves sidle up the pebbled beach. A curly-haired toddler ran towards the tide, a woman chasing after him. Old ladies walked small, yapping dogs. A scrum of lads strutted past, chests bare, sweaters knotted around their waists, fists clutching beer cans as they traded jokes in loud Brummie accents. Neon flashed and machinery whirred. The air smelled of fried onions and burnt sugar and sea salt. It smelled like holidays. No place was less like the grey misery of home.

At last, Scrapper appeared, his face pale and thin and tense. 'Fella gave me half of what I'd hoped.'

'Oh, Scrap.'

An impulse seized her. She grabbed his hand, dragged him down the promenade to the fairground kiosk and bought a fistful of tokens for the rides.

'This is nuts, Red. Save your money.'

'I'm taking you on the scariest, fastest ride there is, Scrapper Jones.'

He sighed, tried not to smile. 'You're nuts.'

She dragged him towards the waltzer. A fat bassline thudded from the speakers. Noise and lights pinned them to the concrete as the ride gathered speed. She watched the cars whirl round and round. The passengers gripped the safety bars, arms rigid, or clutched each other, laughing or screaming.

Scrapper watched them too, his face paper-white.

She laughed. 'Scaredy-cat, are you?'

'Course not.'

The music stopped. A group of girls hobbled off the waltzer, giggling fit to burst. Three lads followed them, smoothing their hair, patting their pockets to check their change, acting like no one had heard them squeal. She dragged Scrapper to the nearest car and waited for the fairground lad to collect the tokens. He was a skinny kid, hair cut in a wedge, had the mod look down pat; too-short trews, stripy top with collar and short sleeves. He sloped over, fag dangling from lips, took the tokens, winked at her and moved on.

The music started up, a falsetto voice above a high-energy beat. The car pitched from side to side. It twirled, hurling them left and right, the force pinning them to their seats. Faster and faster now. She clutched the bar, clutched Scrapper, lost to everything except the lights and the music and the force of the ride. She threw back her head and screamed. For the first time in months, she was free. In that moment, nothing mattered; not her dad, or her mam, or the strike and the way it had poisoned the village. She let all of it go, screamed for the joy of screaming.

Then it was over. The ride stopped. Scrapper staggered off into the crowd, teeth gritted, face tinged green. She lurched after him, drunk on sound and light and speed.

'Bloody hell. That was the best thing ever. Ever!' she planted a wet kiss on his cheek.

'Can't feel my legs, Red,' he said faintly.

101

'Again, again.'

'We're bloody well sitting down for a minute.'

'We can sit on the ghost train.'

He sighed. The carriage trundled them into darkness. They wrapped their arms around each other as the train jerked through creaking swing doors into narrow tunnels. Nylon cobwebs brushed their faces. Plastic ghouls dropped from trapdoors, lunged from dark corners. She squealed, buried her head in Scrapper's chest. The train jolted back into daylight.

'Was that it?' Scrapper said. 'See scarier stuff most days down the pit.'

He helped her off the ride with a touch of his old swagger. They walked hand in hand past the penny arcades, into the little town beyond the seafront. The sun had edged west, taking the heat of the day with it. A breeze picked up, bringing a sting of salt but the lights burned bright and the crowds kept coming. She bought herself a candyfloss and a toffee apple for Scrapper and they watched the crowds come and go from a bench on the promenade.

'Pub?' he said.

'Why not.'

She sat in the beer garden, watched him order their drinks at the bar. He looked more himself at last. Coming here had lifted him. Lifted both of them. If every day was like this – if they lived somewhere like this – did they not have a stab at being happy?

* * *

Scrapper downed his second packet of smoky bacon, drained his pint of Brains, gave a loud, contented yawn.

'Might as well get one last round in. Before we head back.'

'I wish we could stay here, Scrap.'

'You worried about your exams, *bach*?'

'An' the rest.'

'You decided what you want to do yet?'

She shrugged. Her mam and dad wanted her to stay at school, take A-levels, try for a degree.

'Why not go to college,' Scrapper said. 'You're bright enough.'

'Not for people like us, college, is it?'

He had no answer to that. She sipped her drink, gazed out across the sweep of beach, at the streaked red and gold of the sky.

'We could live here, Scrap,' she burst out. 'Imagine it; the two of us renting a little cottage, away from the slagheaps and the strife.'

He raised an eyebrow. 'There's no escaping the darkness, *bach*. It's here, too. You're just too dazzled to see it.'

Down on the shingle, a couple stood barefoot, shoes in hand at the edge of the water. The man carried a toddler on his shoulders. They stood apart, shoulders barely touching. A normal young couple, watching the sun dip below the headland. Two people who belonged to each other. Certainty bedded down like sediment: she didn't want to be *That Scab's Girl* any more. She wanted to be part of something. To belong.

She turned back to Scrapper, noticed for the first time the single grey hair in his fringe. The dying sun dripped embers on him. He was so beautiful that it hurt to look at him. She knew, then, what her future should be.

'Marry me, Scrapper.'

He paused, pint half way to his lips. 'What?'

Heat and light flooded through her, as though she was back on the waltzer, free and fearless, or soaring and swooping like a seagull above the beach.

'Let's get married.'

Something like fear flickered across his face. 'You're not—?'

Her wings buckled and folded in on themselves. 'Course not,' she said quietly.

On the beach, the couple turned back from the shallows, gathered up the toddler's beach things. The waves rushed in faster, now, dragging seaweed and bone-bleached driftwood onto the beach.

15

They sat on the bus home, not speaking. Helen gazed listlessly out of the window, watching the landscape darken, becoming bleaker and more dismal by the mile. Slag heaps loomed out of the dusk. In every mining village they passed, the shops were shut, many boarded up for sale. At last, Ystrad loomed ahead, half shrouded in a sulk of clouds. It looked smaller now, terrace hunched over terrace as though braced for attack.

The bus wheezed up the High Street, halted outside the *bracchi*. She climbed out and waited for Scrapper to say something. She knew that his answer would hurt her, wanted him to say it even so.

He sighed. 'I'm not saying no, Red. I'm saying wait.'

'Wait for what? It'll never be the right time. Not for us.'

'That's not—'

Her dad burst out of the bus shelter, came barrelling towards them. His fist caught Scrapper across the jaw. Scrapper staggered backwards, caught off guard. She winced as her dad grabbed her by the hair. He dragged her past the *bracchi* up the hill towards the house. She fought to break his grip, but he drove her on, his stump of a hand shoving the small of her back.

* * *

She staggered across the living room as he hurled her through the door, hit the mantelpiece with a crash.

Her mam dropped her knitting in shock. 'What the hell—?'

'Did you know about this, woman?'

'Know what, Gwyn? What's happened?'

'What's happened is I caught 'em together. This little slut an' that boy. Out together, bold as brass. Did you know about this?'

He grabbed Helen's wrist and cuffed her across the ear.

'No, Gwyn. I—'

'He slapped Scrapper, Mam,' Helen sobbed. 'For getting off the bus with me. He made a spectacle on the High Street.'

She realised her mistake at once. Her mam had been about to defend her. But to admit going against her dad – she had left her mam no choice but to take his side as always. Love, honour and obey. Her mam took that third vow especially seriously. All the same, she willed her to stand up to him just once. To look him in the eye and tell him he was wrong, that a girl had every right to choose who to love, just as she had defied her own dad all those years back. Defied him to make exactly that choice.

Instead, her mam covered her mouth with a shaking hand.

'Made a spectacle,' her dad said. 'I'll give you made a spectacle.'

The belt was off his waist and in his hand. She heard the leather whistle through the air. Pain rippled up her leg. Her dad raised the belt a second time, hit her again and again. His face was calm now, focused. She was invisible to him. She understood, then. This wasn't about her, not really, but about everything else that had riled her dad these last few months.

Her mam watched, eyes glittering, flinched as the belt fell.

'Make him stop, Mam.'

'You hold your tongue, woman,' her dad said. 'Else you'll feel the business end of this belt.'

The strap rose and fell, ripped Helen's leggings, tore her skin. She whimpered and stumbled backwards. As her dad raised his belt again, she heard voices in the street. She gathered all her strength and screamed.

Her dad paused, hand raised to strike again, as the front door burst open. Scrapper rushed in, Iwan behind him, and grabbed the belt. Helen broke free, ran into his arms, sobbing. He grabbed her, shoved her behind him.

'Disgraceful, this, even by your standards, Gwyn Pritchard,' Iwan said.

'Mind your own business.'

'When you hit my son, you made it my business.'

'Get out o' my house this instant.'

'Right-oh,' Iwan said. 'You coming, Helen?'

'I'm not bloody staying.'

'You guard your tongue,' her dad said.

'She's sixteen,' Iwan said. 'Old enough to curse. Old enough to have you charged with assault.'

'Assault,' her dad echoed. 'Helen Margaret Pritchard, get to your room.'

Iwan turned to her. 'Grab what you need. We'll not leave without you.'

She fled to her bedroom, yanked open the wardrobe, hurled clothing into a duffel bag. Scrapper bundled her down the hall and through the front door. Her dad tried to follow, but Iwan filled the living-room door, blocking him.

'If the girl leaves now, she's dead to me,' her dad said. 'If she walks out now, she's not coming back.'

She staggered down the garden, dizzy and breathless, turned to see her mam framed against the porch.

'Mam,' she stretched out her hand.

Her mam shook her head faintly. 'You got no right to make me choose between you, girl. I got no choice. No choice at all.'

She went inside and closed the front door behind her.

16

Scrapper braced himself as Iwan told Angela what had happened, Helen clutching his hand so hard he lost the feeling in his fingers. But the explosion never came. Angela traced a fingertip along the swirls and flourishes of the lace doily that covered the arm of her chair. At last, she looked up, face blank with defeat.

'Is decided, then; the girl is to live with us?'

'No way we'd leave her with that vicious bastard, love,' Iwan said.

'Live with us on what?'

'I'll start looking for work at once, and sign on as soon I can,' Red said. 'I'll help you in the shop, round the house.'

Even he could hear how lame that sounded. The *bracchi* had few customers these days. Who in Ystrad had money for ice cream or coffee. He and Iwan scraped together a few quid every week from the lodge to cover picketing expenses but getting saddled with another mouth to feed was the last thing his parents needed.

Angela's gaze was fixed on Iwan.

'Is OK for the girl to stay if Simon makes an honest woman of her.'

Scrapper's guts bounced like a ping-pong ball, hit ribs, hit kidneys. It was the last thing he expected her to say.

Iwan burst out laughing. 'Come off it, *cariad*. You've got no truck with all that Catholic claptrap.'

'Is not negotiable.' A hard edge crept into her voice.

Iwan stopped laughing then. Heat flooded Scrapper's cheeks. Everyone was looking at him, waiting for him to speak. Did he love Red? Yes. Did he want to marry her? At some point, why not? But not yet. And for Angela to push them into it – it was baffling.

There was a long awkward silence. It fell to him to break the deadlock.

'Right, well. I suppose we'd best get married, eh, Red?'

Angela leapt to her feet. 'Is what the hell, "*I suppose we get married*"?'

'Well, we were talking about it today and—'

'Is a peasant I raised you to be? You bloody well propose to the girl proper. Like a gentleman. As for you,' Angela wrapped her arms around Red's shoulders, 'welcome to the family, *bella*.'

Scrapper took Red to his room, cleared space for her to stow her things, fetched Germolene and plasters for the cuts on her legs. He dabbed the thick, pink ointment on her skin, the room filling with the hospital smell of carbolic.

'Rest a while,' he said.

Later, as he stood on a step-ladder, stashing his books in the attic, he overheard Iwan and Angela talking quietly in the kitchen.

'What was that about, Angie?'

'What is what?'

'You know damn well what; *make an honest woman of the girl*. They're still kids, for God's sake.'

'Is important the girl is accepted. If they marry, the DHSS'll give Simon £9.20 a week. More, if a baby comes.'

'What the hell's the DHSS or anyone else got to do with it?'

'You seen the pile of bills in the drawer. Got your heads in the clouds, you and the boy. Is gonna ruin this family, the strike.'

'Joneses take no handouts.'

'Well, is high time for Joneses to start. You got a right to

109

married man's allowance. You want to stay married, you go down the social and you claim it.'

Later, he sat on the bedroom floor with Red, listening to music, stereo cranked up to muffle the raised voices in the living room. Some welcome to the family, this. Poor Red; she'd heard enough yelling today to last a lifetime.

'You don't think he'd hit my mam, do you?' The question came from nowhere.

'Captain Hook? Why— has he hit her before?'

'I don't know. But Scrap, I never seen him that angry. It's like he wanted to kill me.'

At last, the shouting stopped. Scrapper turned off the thrashing guitars, chose something slower with a saxophone break.

'You really want to get married, *bach*?'

Red blushed. 'A girl likes to be asked, I s'pose.'

He grabbed her hand, perched next to her on both knees.

'So— I'm asking,' he felt a daft grin split his face. 'Miss Helen Margaret Pritchard, would you do me the horror of being my loyal wedded wife?'

She swatted his shoulder. '*Honour*. Not horror, pillock.'

'Honour, then. Would you?'

'You don't really want to, do you, Scrap?'

It was true and not true. But she was funny and lovely and no one ever needed him like she did. Captain Hook had made himself clear. She could never go home again. And he wanted to make a go of it. Why not? She had no one now, except him.

'It's sooner'n expected, Red. But it is what I want.'

'Alright, then. Yes.'

He dived at her, planted a smacker on her lips. Rugby-tackled her onto the bed.

— 17 —

No one came to the door when Helen knocked. It felt wrong to knock and when no one answered, she used her key to let herself in. That felt wrong, too. Everything felt wrong. But she was worried about her mam, insisted on going back. Scrapper refused to let her go alone.

'Mam,' she called.

There was no answer. She tried the living room and kitchen, but there was no sign of her mam anywhere. She went up to her room. Everything was as she left it, bed unmade, drawers and cupboard spilling clothes. She stuffed her schoolbooks into her bag, chucked boots, gym shoes, undies, parka and sweaters on top. Then, she tidied everything away, pulled the bed covers straight and closed the door behind her.

Scrapper stood at the living room window. He pulled back, startled, when she walked in.

'Let's get out of here, Red.'

'No. I got to see her.'

They sat and waited. The room was stifling hot. Sunlight flooded the window and the embers in the grate exhaled heat. Sweat beaded on her forehead. The noisy wallpaper crowded in on her, aquamarine stripes from floor level meeting sprigged navy florals from the ceiling, flowery dado strip forcing a stand-off between the two clashing prints. It was her dad's pride and joy, that wallpaper. He hired decorators to put it up. No collier hired decorators. The longer she looked at it, the sicker and more dizzy she felt.

At last, the front door opened. Her mam walked in, stopped dead on seeing them, a hand flying to her chest.

'You shouldn't be here. You heard your dad.'

'Did he take it out on you after?'

'You stupid, stupid child,' her mam whispered.

'He hit me, Mam. For seeing my boyfriend. If Dad was reasonable, I wouldn't have—'

'Reasonable—.' she broke off

Helen heard the garden gate screech open. Scrapper gripped her hand so hard that she stifled a yelp. Slow footsteps climbed up the garden path: in the hall, the grandfather clock ticked a mocking echo.

'What are them two doing in my house?' her dad demanded, accusing eyes turned on her mam.

Scrapper pushed her behind him. 'Helen wanted to see her mam,' he said. 'Me and Helen, we – I've asked her to marry me. She said yes.'

Helen breathed in sharply. Her mam gripped the sideboard to steady herself.

'I told you the little slut would get knocked up,' her dad said quietly.

'I'm not bloody knocked up,' Helen said, outraged.

'Why else do the likes of us get married?' her mam's voice was bitter.

'We're getting married because we're in love, Mrs Pritchard,' Scrapper said. 'And we'd like Mr Pritchard to give us his blessing—'

'My *blessing*? When you an' your striker butties are hell-bent on killing my pit?'

Helen took Scrapper's arm. 'We better go.'

Her dad's face had the colour and texture of coal. 'Get married, don't get married,' he said. 'I couldn't give a toss.'

'But she's a child, Gwyn,' her mam objected.

'She's a spoilt brat. Let them get married. I give it six months, tops. As for you—' he turned to Scrapper. 'Strike ends, or pit closes; either way, you'll rue the day you crossed me.'

'What's this got to do with the strike?' Helen said.

Her dad bared yellowed teeth at her. 'This one reckons he's some kind of working-class hero. But he's wrong, and you'll see you backed the wrong side, girl.'

'Can you hear yourself, Dad—?'

'You go off with him, you don't ask for money and you don't ask for help. You go off with him, Helen, I wash my hands.'

His voice had the dry rasp of ashes. But for all his fire and brimstone, he looked small now, and old. He had forced her hand and knew he'd lost.

She slipped her hand into Scrapper's hand. 'Right, we'll be off, then.'

SUMMER 1984

— 1 —

Scrapper groaned and pulled the coverlet over his head against the glare. The morning light sliced his eyeballs like a shard of glass. The stench of his own breath made him gag. He inched back out, squinted at the unfamiliar room. Dai had wrenched the curtains open and was grappling, one-handed, with the window catch. His free hand held two steaming mugs of tea, a plate of toast balanced on top. Sunshine and air flooded into the room. Scrapper was lying on a mustard velour sofa, his body wrapped in a pink satin quilt that had a faint whiff of Debbie's perfume. The wallpaper was pink and green, outsized flowers dancing on a diagonal. He closed his eyes again, feeling sick.

'*Duw*, butty, got a face on you rougher'n a badger's arse.'

Pot and kettle, that. Dai looked none too clever himself.

'Ta, butt,' Scrapper groaned. 'Why'm I here?'

Dai shoved the toast at him, took a slice himself, his face the colour of a stewed olive. 'Your mam insisted. Said it were bad luck for you'n the girl to spend the night before your wedding under the same roof.'

'Dai, love, fetch us a pint o' milk and some porridge oats, will you?' Debbie's voice floated in from the hall.

'Time's it?'

'Time we got a shift on,' Dai yawned. 'Need you spruced up and delivered to the register office within the hour.'

Spruced up? Register office? Scrapper squinted at the gilt wall clock and groaned. Helen would be dressed and waiting, bright-eyed and excited. He could barely see straight, never mind walk her down the aisle. He groaned and sank back against the cushions.

'Down to Matt Cut-Price, this,' Dai said. 'Got your dad to open a bottle o' that that nasty yellow brew your mam hides at the back o' the stock cupboard.'

A sour taste flooded his gullet. 'Oh, Christ. The limoncello. Mam fetches it out at Christmas. Not fit for cleaning tools.'

'Didn't stop us, Scrap. We finished the bottle. Then Matt fetched a bottle o' Malibu from his mam's drinks cabinet. Debbie weren't pleased when we rolled in last night. Reckoned we stank like we'd been snogging Bertie Bassett. Made me gargle before turning in.'

Scrapper pulled his t-shirt over his nose and sniffed it. 'And Matt?'

'Went off by himself. Reckoned he were meeting some bird.'

Debbie stuck her head round the door. Her hair was wet, slicked behind her ears. 'Dai, the milk. And you got to fetch the cake from Margaret Parry.'

Dai downed his tea, grabbed keys and wallet from the top of the television. 'Get some tea an' toast down this one, Debs. We need him sober and decent. Scrap, your suitcase is in the hall.'

As soon as Dai shut the front door, Debbie slid into the room. She wore a black Japanese-style dressing gown, knotted at the waist. She crossed the room and plonked herself on top of Scrapper, legs straddling pink quilt.

'Oofff. That's my stomach, woman.'

'How about it then, Scrap? One last tango, for old time's sake?'

The kimono gaped open.

'Stop messing, Debs.'

'Who's messing? Bloody obvious you want to.'

The worst thing was, part of him did want to and he felt too weak and brain-fogged to resist. He gathered his strength to wriggle away from her. She slithered off the quilt, landed in a heap on the floor, looked up at him, black mockery sparkling in her eyes.

'Why you going through wi' this wedding, Scrap?'

'Cos I want to?'

'Why would you marry that little shrimp; that scab's girl?'

'Because I love her, Debs.'

'Not the way you loved me.'

'Note the past tense.'

'Say that often enough, you'll start believing it, Scrap,' Debbie straightened her kimono. 'Lucky for you, I got to go.'

He lay back, willed his pulse to slow. He could hear Debbie padding around upstairs. After a pause, he staggered off the couch and went to fetch his suitcase. Moving stirred up the contents of his stomach. He dashed across the hall, made it to the bathroom just in time.

Bloodshot eyes bleared back at him in the shaving mirror. He turned on the taps and splashed his face, flinching as the icy water hit his skin. The shock eased the pounding in his skull. He slipped off his trews and kecks, climbed into the bath, ran the cold tap over his head and neck. After a good brisk scrub with flannel and soap, he felt better. The doorbell rang and he heard Debbie patter downstairs to answer.

Angela's voice floated in from the hall. 'Husband not home, Debbie Power?'

Footsteps clicked along the corridor and a fist rapped on the bathroom door.

'Is bad luck to keep your bride waiting, Simon. You want people to talk?'

People talk whatever, he thought sourly.

'Five minutes, Mam.'

He wrestled the brass suitcase locks, shook the wrinkles out of Matt's wedding suit – 'You're more'n welcome to it, butty.

Did me no bloody favours' – and opened the night-bag. Angela had packed his razor, shaving cream and toothbrush. His hands shook as he dragged the blade across his cheekbones. At the bottom of the case, he found Iwan's kept-for-best Eau Sauvage. Something borrowed. He smiled. Typical of his mam to cover all bases. He splashed a palmful of cologne on his cheeks, breathed out and felt as right as rainbows.

Angela had unpicked the old suit, taken in the jacket and waistband and unpicked the arms and legs. The suit was baggy, even so, legs and sleeves a good inch too short. But the shirt bought from Betty's unisex fit just right and was the exact shade of blue of his team. The problem was the tie. He tried and failed to wrestle it into something like a knot, but it defeated him. He found Iwan pacing the living room, scrubbed up tidy in his navy weddings and funerals suit, worn shiny at the knees and elbows.

'Can't be doing wi' this bloody tie, Dad.'

'You and me both, lad,' Iwan grinned. 'A badge of slavery, the tie.'

Even so, he knotted it, fixed Scrapper with ice-grey eyes. 'You sure you're ready for this, son?'

Scrapper remembered Debbie's wet hair and slick brown skin and shook himself. 'Course.'

Iwan gripped his shoulders. 'You get to do this once in your life, lad.'

'But Mam said—'

'To hell with what your mam said. The girl's young. You both are.'

If he had doubts, he beat them away. Yes, they were young but there was no question it was the right thing to do.

'She needs us, Dad.'

Helen sat in the window squirming. Her wedding frock itched something vicious. Angela found it at the back of her wardrobe, a Seventies maxi dress: fitted bodice, flared A-line skirt, spotless nylon lace over satin lining.

'But I can't take it from you, Angie.'

'Is terrible on me, white lace, *bella*. With these breasts, look like bloody milkmaid.'

It was old-fashioned, with a square neckline and puff sleeves, and three sizes too big for her. But Angela had a way with a sewing machine, tightened the sleeves and bodice, shortened the skirt to mid-thigh and fitted a satin cummerbund waistband. The result was a triumph, flirty and informal, the opposite of the show-off princess meringue her dad would have wanted. But as she waited for her bridal party to collect her, the seams bit into her skin. She ground her knuckles against her ribs, looked out at the High Street again. At last, Dewi Power pulled up in the lodge minibus, Angela next to him in the passenger seat, waving at her to come down.

Scrapper sat alone in the back seat, behind his dad and Dai Dumbells. His skin looked grey and papery. He patted the seat next to him.

'God, Scrap. You look like something dug up from the grave.'

'Matt made us drink a bottle of limoncello and half a bottle of Malibu.'

'Where *is* Matt?'

'Who knows,' Angela said. 'Is lucky this handsome gentleman offered to drive.'

Dewi's ears flushed pink. He fired up the engine, and off they set. The lodge banner hung inside the rear windscreen. Fringed gold trim flapped in the breeze. *National Union of Mineworkers, Blackthorn Lodge: nothing to lose but our chains.* Helen grinned. How she would have loved to have Dewi drive past the house, to give her dad an eyeful of her wedding carriage; have him see it and spit embers. She wished her mam was with her, even so. She snuggled up to Scrapper and watched the hedgerows slip behind them like green streamers.

At last, they were there. She jumped out, dropped Scrapper a mock curtsey. 'Well?'

'You look stunning, *bach*.'

'You look beautiful, and all.'

He did, too, for all his bleary eyes and pallid skin. He ran a shaking hand through his hair. 'We gonna do this, aren't we, Red?'

'Abso-bloody-lutely.'

Angela paused on the register office steps, hands on hips. She wore a shoulder-padded, gold buttoned, gold-belted scarlet suit, a tiny Welsh guard in scarlet pillbox hat and veil.

'Simon, where in hell is your father?'

Iwan appeared from behind the minibus looking shifty.

'Iwan Simon Peter Jones – were you smoking?' Angela shooed him inside.

'But we can't go in Mam,' Scrapper said. 'We got to wait for Matt.'

'Is too late, Simon.'

'But he's got the ring.'

Angela rolled her eyes, shoved Scrapper through the door.

* * *

The lobby had beige carpet tiles and stark white walls. A tall man with sunken cheekbones opened the door to a dark, heavy room. The bay window was swamped with heavy drapes that puddled on the parquet floor. Mr Throgmorton, the registrar, took a pen from his lapel pocket, reached for his glasses. He moved like an actor trying out a scene before stepping out on stage.

Scrapper was fidgeting now. 'Mam, the wedding ring.'

'*Lascia stare*,' Angela hissed. She grabbed her left index finger. After a brief struggle, she wrestled the gold band off her finger, thrust it at Scrapper.

'Aw, Mam—'

'Is good enough for now.'

Red blotches showed on her cheeks. Helen squeezed Scrapper's hand in warning.

They made their vows, kissed and signed the register on Throgmorton's desk. Angela's ring slipped off Helen's finger as she bent to write her name. Dewi and Dai signed as witnesses. Then it was over. Helen followed the others outside, stood blinking in the sunshine.

Angela handed her a tulle-wrapped package. 'I made confetti. Take one.'

She passed the package on to Scrapper, then to the men, paused, frowning. 'Is bad luck, having one left over.' She vanished back inside.

Helen looked at the sugared almond nestling in her palm, nudged Scrapper.

He sighed. 'Mam and her traditions.'

She popped the almond into her mouth, bit down hard. The sugar coating exploded into fragments. Shards of almond and sugar lodged in her throat.

She squeezed Scrapper's hand, tried not to choke. 'My husband?'

'Aye, *bach*. For better and for worse.'

'So now what?'

'We've organised a reception down the Stute,' Dai said.

'Down the Stute?'

She had never set foot in the Miners' Institute. Enemy territory, her dad called it.

'You're a union wife now, eh, love,' Dewi said.

Angela came barrelling out of the register office and heard him. 'Don't you listen to this one, *bella*. A naughty tease, Dewi Power. You are a Jones. Union wife is optional.'

＊　＊　＊

The road from Bryn Tawel to Ystrad wound through woodland. As they emerged above the village, sunlight struck the minibus like lightning. Scrapper groaned.

'That'll teach you to get caned,' Helen said.

'I'll never drink again. Not ever.'

'Until Matt Price shows up with the next bottle.'

'I could throttle him. Gets all of us pissed as newts, misses the bloody wedding.'

'It's alright—'

'It's not bloody alright. We pawned Dad's pocket watch to buy that ring.'

'Oh, Scrap. No,' she gripped his hand.

Dewi screeched to a halt outside the *bracchi*.

'Gonna carry the missus over the threshold, then?' Dai grinned.

'There's no—' Helen began.

But Scrapper grabbed her, hoiked her over his shoulder, hefted her into the shop, up the stairs and flung her on the bed. They were both giggling and breathless as he kicked shut the door and unzipped her itchy, beautiful dress.

— 3 —

Scrapper walked into the Stute to loud cheers, Red clinging to his arm. All the boys from his shift were there, a couple of dozen fellows from the lodge, the married men had brought their wives and kids. All gathered to see him and Red walk out as man and wife. Someone had dusted off the lodge's Christmas streamers, slung them from wall to wall. Gold and silver tinsel shivered from the beams. The toffee-apple scent of home-brew scrumpy filled the air. A trestle table ran the length of the room, piled with sandwiches, sausage rolls and crisps, in the middle, a two-tier iced cake. Loaves and fishes and water into wine; his butties had pulled off a miracle.

'Aw, boys—' words failed him.

Red's hands were trembling.

Dai noticed too, squeezed her shoulders. 'Margaret Parry made the cake,' he said. 'An' the boys had a whip-round, wanted to lay on a bit of a spread.'

It took an effort for Scrapper to steady his voice. 'It's a tidy spread. So what'll you lot be having?'

Angela pushed past him. 'Speeches before food, Simon.'

Eddie Hobnob busied himself at his kegs, his wife Chrissie loading tin mugs filled with cider onto trays. The boys had the eyes of ravenous beasts; they no more wanted speeches than Scrapper did. And Red looked horrified.

'Listen, love,' Dewi pulled Angela aside. 'There'll be a riot if this lot don't get fed.'

Scrapper shot him a grateful look. 'Food then speeches, Mam.'

Dewi bounded on stage. 'Right, brothers and sisters. We're here today to celebrate the marriage of Scrapper Jones and Helen Pritchard—'

A low murmur rose from the back of the room. Red went rigid. Her cheeks flushed pink. For an awful moment, Scrapper thought Captain Hook had turned up like the evil fairy at the christening, but he saw no one except his butties and their women. Nothing that ought to upset her.

'—so let's hear it for the beautiful bride and groom: to Scrapper and Helen.'

The boys cheered fit to raise the rafters.

'Now Scrapper an' Helen invite you all to tuck in.'

Pandemonium broke out. Their guests fell like pack animals on the sandwiches and sausage rolls. Scrapper wandered among them, a bowl in each hand, inviting the little ones to grab fistfuls of crisps. At last, everyone was seated, food piled on tin plates. Eddie kept pumping out his mugs of scrumpy. Steam hissed from the tea urns. Scrapper filled two plates and went to join Red, but Angela grabbed her arm and dragged her off to join the women. Red turned back to him, eyes frantic and pleading but Dai steered him towards the boys. Soon, Scrapper's belly stretched tight with food and drink. He watched the women, Angela as chatty as Red was silent. A second miracle. That fit young girl with endless legs and mad red curls — that was his wife.

'Another one bites the dust, eh, Scrap?'

It was Alun Probert. His nose had healed up tidy, although it angled east now, not due south. Something else had shifted in the kid since Port Talbot. Matt reckoned so and all. Went on and on about it at the stag do, threatened to open a sweepstake on changing Alun Wet-Ears' nickname to Alun Black-Ice.

'Invisible but treacherous, that kid, you mark my words.'

Dai passed Alun a scrumpy. 'Best thing in the world, getting hitched,' he said. 'Next best, a babby. Wonder who'll hear the patter of tiny feet first, Scrap; yous or us?'

'You two go right ahead,' Scrapper grinned. 'We're planning to put in some practice first.'

'Good on you, Scrapper Jones,' a voice cut in. 'A regular seeing-to *and* a tenner a week off the DHSS—'

Scrapper scowled. 'You've got some front, Matthew Cut-Price. Miss the wedding, bang on time for the food.'

'Don't be like that—' Matt's face was yellow, his skin waxy.

Despite the heat, he wore a peaked cap pulled low over the bridge of his nose. He twisted and untwisted his hands, pinched a hangnail between a shaking thumb and forefinger and tugged it. It came away, leaving a strip of raw flesh. He flicked the skin on the floor, did not lift his gaze.

'I'm mortified, Scrap,' he said at last.

The hat hid his eyes. Scrapper yanked it off his head, gasped. Matt's left eye was half closed by a deep purple bruise.

Matt raised a shaking finger to his cheekbone. 'The other fella's none too pretty neither, mind.'

'Who the hell done this?' Dai demanded.

'Fella didn't give a name,' Matt said. 'Didn't waste breath on niceties.'

Scrapper gawped at his butty. It didn't make sense. Matt reckoned himself more a lover than a fighter, first sign of trouble he'd take shelter behind Dai or whatever other solid object came to hand.

Matt nailed his gaze to the floor. 'I'm sorry, Scrap. I was out cold. Woke up in a ditch.'

He really did look a mess, hands bloodied and unsteady, denim jacket muddy and grass-stained. He peered at Scrapper with a pleading, bloodshot eye, like a puppy facing the business end of a slipper.

'You got the ring?'

'I'm an arsewipe, Scrap' Matt murmured. 'I lost it.'

Scrapper felt the ground give beneath him. How could Matt lose the ring? Angela would skin him for this. Matt dipped his head, gave a loud sniff. Scrapper sighed. What point having a go at Matt, when his butty knew full well he'd screwed up royally.

'Jesus, Matt. Explain yourself to my mam and my missus. They forgive you, you stay.'

He watched Matt slink across the hall, shoulders around his ears. A mocking cackle rose from the women's side of the hall. Matt's head hung lower. Finally, Angela handed him a plate and led him to the buffet.

Iwan was watching too, a look on his face that Scrapper couldn't read.

'Lost it,' he murmured. ' D'you believe a word o' that?'

'My butty wouldn't lie to me, Dad.'

'You reckon? Things are getting tougher by the week and that one's stone broke.'

'He wouldn't bloody steal from me, alright.'

A collier defended his butty, no matter what, as a matter of honour. No matter that his butty's story was as lame as a three-legged pit pony. No matter that he no more believed Matt's story than Iwan did.

* * *

He was half-asleep by the time Angela dragged Red into the middle of the room and waved at him to join them. The sun had moved beyond the windows and Angela had Dewi snap on the strip lights. Scrapper stumbled as he crossed the floor, half-dazzled. When he got there, Red leapt into his arms.

'Sorry 'bout the ring *bach*,' he murmured.

'Sod the ring. Can we go?'

'Go? But why?'

'Get me out of here, I'll let you do anything you want.'

He hugged her, puzzled. 'But why? It's our wedding, you daft ha'porth.'

'Is time to cut the cake,' Angela announced.

He laid his hands on Red's. It took their four hands and plenty of welly to crack the knife through the icing. When it splintered, finally, everyone cheered.

Dewi raised his mug. 'Here's to the happy couple and a long and happy life together, Helen and Scrapper Jones.'

The toasts were drunk and speeches made, the cake sliced up and shared. Someone wired a tinny Walkman to the Stute's outsized speakers. Red begged him to dance, but his belly was too full, his head too fogged.

The door creaked open and a small figure walked in, leaning on walking sticks. She wore a grass-green skirt suit, matching hat perched on her lacquered black up-do.

Margaret Parry returned Red's kiss. 'A ruddy shame Carol's missing this.'

'Too bad, yeah,' Red smiled thinly. 'She'd be having a blast.'

'She'd feel proud of you, love. Glowing, you are. And so's the fine young lad who tried to save my Gabriel—'

Scrapper's stomach lurched. There it was, again. The torn, dead face. The helmet knocked backwards. Mrs P seemed to read his thoughts. She squeezed his hand.

'Now's not the time or place,' she said. 'But I'll not forget what you done, Simon Jones. And you,' she turned to Red. 'Don't you be hard on your mam. Your dad's all she got.'

'She chose him over me, Auntie Margaret.'

'Aye, stick wi' her man or do what everyone else wants? Peas in a ruddy pod, the pair o' you.'

Red had no answer to that.

'Tuck in, folks,' Dewi lurched over, plate of cake slices

unsteady in his hands. 'As handsome as the woman who made it, this wedding cake.'

'You can cut out your silver-tongue nonsense, Dewi Power,' Mrs P said.

'Now then,' Iwan grinned. 'Can't blame the old boy for trying. You still turn a man's head, Margaret Parry.'

'Trying; that's the word. Speaking o' which,' Mrs P turned to Matt. 'You're not looking too clever, love. Been fighting lamp-posts, have we?'

'Something like that,' Matt mumbled.

'You're wasting away, *bach*,' Mrs P said.

Scrapper grabbed two handfuls of Matt's belly. 'He's been following the MacGregor Weight Loss Plan, Mrs P. Reckon we'll get him down to a size ten?'

'Well, 'e wasn't bloody huge to begin with,' Mrs P said. 'You come round mine tomorrow, Matthew Price, I'll fix you a nice Sunday lunch.'

'Aw, you don't—'

'I'll expect you at twelve-thirty sharp,' Mrs P said. 'Bring little Probert, an' all. A crime, that bloody woman trying to starve the single boys back to work.'

She picked up her canes and tapped across the hall to join the women.

Scrapper frowned at Matt, questioning. His butty's *hwyl* had deserted him altogether if the promise of food failed to raise a smile. Matt wasn't his usual chesty self, despite the women forgiving him, despite the boys cracking jokes about the state of his face. There was something shifty about him, something more than guilt about losing the ring. He cornered Matt, tried to ask him, but Matt ducked beneath his arm and slunk away.

In any case, Red wanted his attention. He flung his arms around her, planted a kiss on her forehead. The heat of her body burned through the thin lace dress. She tugged at his earring with her teeth, firing a depth-charge in the pit of his stomach.

'Easy, Red,' he whispered. You know that drives me nuts.'

'C'mon, Scrap. Let's make it an early night.'

4

Gwyn breathed in the heady scent of may thorn. It was shaping up to be a fine evening, his laburnum dripping golden chains on the lawn. His borders blazed yellow and orange, late tulips clashing with early carnations. He straightened his back, shouldered his hoe, took stock of his labour. A hard day's weeding and pruning and tilling of soil. Made a damn good job of it. He returned his tools to the shed, each piece in its rightful place, and was about to close the door when he spotted the deckchairs piled at the back. Used for high days and holidays, those deckchairs. A rotten shame to save them for best, when it was warm enough and enough daylight left to sit outdoors for another hour. Why not? He dragged one of the chairs out to the patio, placed it facing away from the house to give a clear view to the top of the garden, to the tangle of honeysuckle and clematis that hid the stumps of the apple trees that he tore down when they moved in.

Birdsong shrilled in the fields beyond. He slipped off his wellies, padded into the kitchen to fetch a bevvy. What the hell. He'd earned it. It was a struggle to open the tab, a fiddly business with thumb and finger. Carol was somewhere upstairs, slow to get started on his tea. The house was big and empty since the girl left. Evenings stretched long silences. He pushed the thought away; a lovely evening, his daughter and his wife be damned.

He wrestled the tab open at last. Lager fizz soaked his fingers. Barely half made it into the glass. Better half than none. He took a long, cool slurp and carried the glass outside, sat down, beer in hand, feeling a touch light-headed. It passed soon enough. A fine day. A tidy view. It took little things to lift the spirits.

A robin hopped from branch to branch in the hornbeam hedge. It tilted its head to look at him. Territorial little bastards, robins. Hostile black-bead eyes. He'd had a gutsful of hostility, lately. He flapped his arms, watched the bird flutter down onto the path, then vanish.

He sensed something move on the other side of the hedge. Eddie Hobson, no doubt, or worse, Chrissie, Eddie's sullen piece of a wife.

'Aye-aye,' he announced his presence.

'Evening, Gwyn Pritchard,' Eddie's horse-like face peered over the hedge.

Gwyn raised his glass. 'You'll be in on Monday, then?'

'Why would you think that?'

'The judges said, didn't they; strike's illegal.'

Eddie snorted. 'Can't wait to hear you tell that to the lads.'

'Christ, Eddie. We're not in the lodge. Strike's got nothing to do with overmen.'

'That's as maybe, but a picket line is a picket line.'

'Come off it, man. We got to respect the law.'

Eddie leaned into the hedge, fists gripping tufts of hornbeam. When he spoke, Gwyn caught a waft of cider.

'When the ruling class wields the law to break a working man, the law becomes an ass, Gwyn Pritchard.'

'*Ed*-WARD!'

A woman's voice cut through the air. Chrissie Hobson, lungs like the pit claxon. Horse-face Eddie ducked down behind the hedge and vanished indoors.

'Edward Hobson – what did we agree about talking to that scab?' Chrissie's voice was slurred. She'd been on the sauce, too, from the sound of her.

Eddie's voice floated out of the kitchen. 'You got to feel sorry for him, all the same. Think what he missed today. There's nothing left for him here, whatever way this ends.'

The door closed, but Chrissie's reply came loud and clear. 'He got no one to blame but himself.'

* * *

It took one snippy comment to ruin a perfect day. Gwyn downed his lager in a gulp, folded the deckchair and slung it into the shed. He headed indoors, legs wobbly. And no wonder. He was ravenous. But the kitchen was still empty, Carol nowhere to be seen. His tea nowhere to be seen. Lazier by the day, his wife. He paused, listened. Was that her voice in the front room? She was tittle-tattling on the phone to her sister in Wolverhampton, no doubt. He stomped into the hall, pulled up outside the living room. Not one voice, but two. His wife had company. They'd had no company in months. He paused his hand on the door knob. It had better not be the girl. He'd made himself clear. The girl wasn't welcome. Not if she came crawling back. No welcome for the girl, as long as she was with that boy. He put his ear against the door. A woman's voice, not the girl's. A jab of disappointment. He paused, brushed mucky hands on mucky trousers and swung open the door.

A tiny figure sat parked in his armchair, a pair of walking sticks hooked over the arm. Despite the heat, she was bundled up in a suit and coat, a hat the colour of bile perched on her head. All the rage in the Fifties, those hats. It made him think of the time when the lodge hired charabancs to take the whole village to the Festival of Britain. His mam and her friends piled into the back of the coach, all dressed for best in their little hats, flasks of sherry passed round surreptitious, their gossip louder and more lurid by the mile.

It was Margaret Parry. Gabe's widow. The last person he'd expect in his house. Carol sat in her armchair, face pale, eyes bright with tears. Margaret bloody Parry; what the hell had she said to upset his wife?

'I'm sorry for your loss,' he said at last. 'Gabe was—'

'Save it,' Margaret grabbed her walking-sticks. A frail figure, she cut, the weight fallen off her since Christmas. 'Like I said, Carol. *You're* welcome at mine any time.'

She patted Carol on the shoulder, pushed past Gwyn and hobbled into the hall. He followed, still at a loss.

She opened the door, turned to face him. 'You reckon you're the big man round by 'ere, Gwyn Pritchard, but someone got to set you straight—'

'Spare me the homily.'

Margaret laughed. 'I remember you as a snotty-nose kid. Acting the big I am cuts no ice wi' me. You want to sell this community down the river? Fine. But don't you care what this is doin' to your daughter – and worse, to your wife?'

He gripped the door, itching to kick the interfering little woman down the steps. 'Appreciate your concern, Margaret Parry. But you got no business with my wife. As for the girl, she's dead to us.'

Her hand paused on his arm. Liver-spotted, that hand. A tremor to it.

'You'll make a bitter, lonely old man. Terrible, it is, to be alone.'

He swatted her hand away. 'I'll do just fine.'

* * *

Gwyn found Carol slumped in her armchair, dabbing her nose with a grubby tissue.

'Well,' he demanded.

'You bastard.'

'What now, woman?'

'Helen. She got married.'

'She *what?*'

'Got married. This morning. Without her mam. There's a party down the Stute, half the bloody village there. But not the bride's parents.'

'You're not going.'

Carol laughed a hacking laugh. 'Oh, aye, there'd be one hell of a welcome down the Stute for a scab's missus.'

'Don't call—'

'It's what I am, Gwyn. Thanks to you.'

The last straw, that. He grabbed his coat, stuffed his feet into his boots and hurried outside, almost slamming the door off its hinges. He set off up the hill at a trot. There'd be no one to trouble him up The Mountain Ash. No hostile stares. No gossiping neighbours. No widows to rub his face in it. No wife with accusing eyes.

5

Helen hovered in the doorway of the Stute, feeling like a spare cog at her own wedding. She waited for Scrapper to say his goodbyes, slid Angela's too-big wedding ring around the base of her thumb. The plates of food were empty, vats of home-brew scrumpy drunk dry. Scrapper had wandered off again. At last, he reappeared, only for Dewi Power to ambush him again. It had been a long afternoon with the union wives. She had no idea what to say to these women. Luckily Angela, tipsy with relief that the wedding had gone ahead with only minor disasters, talked for both of them.

Darkness was falling. The women lolled on the shabby velour banquettes like big cats unwinding after a hard day's hunt. They batted jokes between each other, smoked roll-ups and shared the last of the sandwiches. Were these the battle-axe women who blanked her mam in the Co-op? An uncomfortable thought. She willed Scrapper to hurry.

The door swung open. 'Well fancy seeing Helen Pritchard in the Stute,' Debbie Power smirked. 'Just cos Scrapper's dumb enough to marry you, you reckon you belong here?'

She smoothed her glossy hair, flashed a smile that showed too many teeth. Everyone in the room, male and female, was watching Debbie and didn't she know it.

'Just one thing, Debbie,' Helen said.

'What's that, then?'

'It's Jones now. Helen Jones.'

Debbie's smile stretched wider. 'You wish, kid. You'll always be a Pritchard to the rest of us.'

She strutted across the hall, white court shoes clack-clacking on the parquet, satin jumpsuit swishing, and stamped the Black Cherry outline of her lips on Scrapper's cheek. One of her spaghetti straps slipped, accidentally-on-purpose. She slid it up with a flick of her shiny bob, said something that made Scrapper lean in closer. Helen glared at Debbie's tanned back, wished she had a fistful of darts. Too late, she realised Scrapper had caught the look on her face. She flapped her hands, frantic now. He took the hint at last.

'Sure you can tear yourself away, Scrap?'

His cheeks were flushed. 'Had to thank Dai's missus for helping wi' that spread.'

Debbie joined the women, said something that made the whole table turn to look at them. Helen grabbed Scrapper's arm and bundled him through the swing doors onto the street. Outside, she rubbed the lipstick off his cheek, hurried him up the deserted High Street.

'Why the rush, Red?'

'Your mam an' dad; they staying?'

Scrapper shook his head. 'Said they'd be along in a jiffy.'

She slipped her hand inside his waistband. 'Let's go up the barn.'

'What, why?'

'You know why, Scrap.'

'But we're married now.'

'We'd be all alone up there. We could make all the noise we wanted.'

His kiss tasted of scrumpy. 'I'm knackered, Red. Let's crash at home.'

They trudged up the street to the ice cream parlour. Scrapper tumbled into their bedroom. She slipped into the bathroom. It was heaven to shed the itchy dress. The seams had raised welts along her ribs and shoulders. In the bath, she soaped herself and rinsed her sores with tepid water, washed off the concealer she used to camouflage the scars on her legs. Towel over damp skin, she burst into the bedroom.

'Ladies and gentlemen: the one, the only — Missus Helen Schiappa-Jones!'

But Scrapper didn't answer. The room was dark. In the light that spilled in from the hallway, she saw he was naked, head thrown back and snoring. She shut the door, dropped clothes and towel on the floor and picked her way across the room, still uncertain of her bearings.

'Scrapper?'

He rolled over onto his side, pulled her towards him and wrapped his arms and legs around her. His breathing slowed. For the first time all day, she felt safe.

* * *

When she woke, Scrapper was pacing the room, searching for something. He rummaged on shelves and in drawers, patted the pockets of his clothes. Helen lay still, eyeing the crease between the pads of muscle on his shoulder blades, his narrow waist and the apple swell of his butt.

He turned, caught her watching him. His face split in a grin. 'There's something I want you to have.'

He landed on her with a flying leap, one hand hidden behind his back.

'Show me, show me!'

He uncurled his fingers. A dark shape nestled in his palm, three-cornered and smaller than an egg. It was a lump of coal, but glossier, heavier and more dense than regular coal. It felt cool to touch, but caught the light like molten tar.

'What is it?'

'Anthracite,' Scrapper said. 'Top-grade coal. They found it in my granddad's pocket when he died. Now it's yours.'

'Mine, why?'

'Closest thing I got to a diamond. Keep it safe. We win the strike, I'll trade you my granddad's anthracite for a diamond and gold band. Deal?'

'Deal.'

She kissed him until their bodies melted together. They moved slowly, fingers lighting fires, lips shooting sparks. She cried out, heard something clatter in the kitchen down the hall, the sound of a kettle being filled. She lay still, certain that the whole village could hear her pounding blood. Scrapper wriggled into his kecks, padded off to the bathroom. She pulled the duvet up to her chin, listened to the cistern gurgle, to the creaking of floorboards and the voices drifting in from the kitchen. She closed her fingers around the lump of anthracite, felt it warm to the touch. She was dozing off when a knock on the door woke her. Angela walked in, set a tray on the bedside table. She perched on the bed, ruffled Helen's hair.

'Angie, you didn't have to.'

'Is a little something to say welcome to the family, *bella*.'

The tray held a plate of heart-shaped biscuits and two steaming cups of coffee the colour of gravy browning. Angela took one cup herself and offered Helen the other. She took a sip and nearly dropped the cup. Heat and bitterness singed her taste buds. She longed, then, for her mam's tea, served lukewarm the way her dad liked it; too much milk and stiff with sugar. The thought surprised her. She hated her mam's tea, but maybe nothing else tasted like home.

6

Scrapper woke with a jolt as Dewi halted the minibus in a narrow country lane. He climbed out after the others, stretched his spine and yawned. Lately, he and the boys seemed to be picketing other pits most days, setting off hours before dawn. Barely three hours' kip and off to Yorkshire, arriving in time to see a lazy sun haul itself towards the horizon. The breeze raised a meaty scent from the blossom that spattered the hedgerows. Other minibuses were pulling into the lane. It was shaping to be a tidy crowd, the men around him sparking up their first smokes of the day, trading bleary-eyed jokes and wrestling poles and canvas to raise their banners.

Iwan handed him a placard. 'Listen, son. It said on the news there's coppers drafted in from all over. Reckon it may get hairy today. Stick with your butties and stay out of trouble.'

'Aw, change the record, Dad.'

'I'm not bloody joking, Simon.'

'What happened to Matt?'

Dai, Dewi and all the boys were here, but not his butty. Scrapper hadn't seen him since the wedding. No sign of Matt on the picket, not in two weeks. He'd phoned Dewi, given him some half-baked tale about his mam falling sick. None of the boys believed a word of it. Dewi had read Scrapper the riot act, ordered him to visit Matt, set things straight with him for the good of the lodge. Scrapper felt a twinge of guilt. He'd made excuse after excuse not to go. And now, with all the boys dispatched to Yorkshire, Matt's absence was obvious. He vowed to track him down that night. What kind of man fell out with his butty over a stupid piece of gold?

They gathered under the Blackthorn banner, waited for the signal to set off. At last a group of policemen approached, an officer in the lead.

The officer raised his megaphone. 'Move off the road. You're blocking the lane. Move away from the road.'

Scrapper fell in with Iwan and Dai Dumbells, followed the bodies and banners through a gap between the hedgerows that opened into a vast field. Up ahead, beyond the trees, he spotted the coking plant's square quenching tower and sooty chimneys. It was as dark and forbidding as a fortress. He rolled his sweater over his elbows, caught the scent of Helen on his fingers, wondered what kind of prat went tramping across a Yorkshire field at stupid o'clock, rather than stopping in bed with his wife.

The field filled with people. They weren't just the usual NUM die-hards and the grey brigade with their communist newspapers. He spotted banners from France and Belgium and Italy, slogans in other languages. And between the banners, there were kids of his age, done up all alternative, ripped black jeans or khaki fatigues, regulation exotic hair. Students, hundreds of them, waving placards printed by the Socialist Workers or the Revolutionary Communists or Militant. There were no boys and girls like these in Ystrad. He wished he had Sue and Debbie with him. They knew how to talk to students. Students left him feeling stupid and ignorant and shy.

Dai nudged him, pointed at a skinny lad, thin, hook-nosed face under a crest of multi-coloured spikes.

'State on that,' he murmured.

But Scrapper couldn't fault the lad; a parrot in a flock of sparrows.

The field stretched across a hillside, looking down on the coke plant. Below them, a line of police stood ten deep, long shields glittering coldly. Scrapper shuddered. The couple of thousand miners and supporters were well outnumbered by the boys in blue. Behind the shields, he saw dog handlers, muscular Alsatians straining at the leash, and other officers on horseback. Time passed and heat rose as the sun hardened in the sky. At the top of the field, some boys from Kent kicked a ball between them. Scrapper stripped down to his vest, tied the arms of his sweater around his waist, tried not to stare at a group of knotty-haired students sprawled against a tree trunk, breathing clouds of pungent smoke. A girl with pink hair, long legs in torn fishnets, marched up to Dai, hustled him to sign a petition for free abortion on demand. She smiled, thanked him, moved on. Scrapper wished desperately that Matt was there. He could see it; his butty chasing after the girl, demanding to know about men's rights.

The lines of police and dogs and horses drew closer together, shifted into a solid mass. The miners did the same. Scrapper sensed both sides waiting for some kind of signal. Then he heard it – the far-off growl of engines. On the road beyond the hedgerows, a lorry was approaching the plant. The mood darkened so fast, he thought clouds had closed around the sun. All at once, his boys were shouting, bodies crushed against him, carrying him forwards. A slow, heavy beat rose from behind the line of long shields, batons thudding on Perspex, daring the miners to come down.

The cry went up: '*The workers. United. Will never be defeated.*'

Goosebumps studded Scrapper's arms and legs. He and his butties, stood shoulder to shoulder with men from the other coalfields, with trade unionists and newspaper sellers and students. Tears pricked his eyes. He was proud – so fucking proud – to be a part of it. He grabbed Dai's belt with one hand, Iwan's arm with the other. His toes snagged molehills and rabbit holes, but the scrum was so tight he couldn't fall. He kept moving forward, breath forced from his lungs, the roar of the crowd hurting his ears. He flinched as a brick flew over his head. They were close now. Close enough to hear the brick thud against the wall of shields. As suddenly as they had surged forwards, the crowd slammed to a halt. Panic rippled through the crowd. Howls of pain rose from the men at the front of the crush. He heard the muffled thud of batons on flesh; the grunts of the hitters and yelps of the hit.

Dai, jammed against him, had a good few inches' advantage.

'What's happening?'

'Bastards are going in,' Dai said. 'Giving the front line a pasting.'

He ducked as bricks, stones and bottles whizzed overhead. Scrapper heard the thuds and grunts and yelps more clearly now. He found himself getting sucked forwards, the crush in front of him thinning as men fell or were dragged through the police lines. His boot caught something on the ground. He looked down and saw a man of Iwan's age curled up in a ball, dark blood oozing from his ear. He tried to reach down to the man but the crowd drove him on.

Rage kicked in, then. This was a massacre. The police lines loomed yards in front. Behind the shields, he saw blue helmets, round and dense and shiny like bowling balls, their visors lowered, steel rivets glinting in the sunshine. He squinted, tried to see the riot policemen's faces. But the light bounced off the Perspex, dazzling him. He saw nothing beneath those helmets. The enemy was faceless. Masked like executioners.

The wall of long shields parted. Horses charged at the crowd, flailing hooves and tails, so close that Scrapper could smell them. A truncheon grazed his shoulder.

Dai dragged him clear. 'The bastards are trying to kill us,' he gasped.

Scrapper was too furious now to feel scared. The blood juddered in his veins. He braced to push forwards, and to hell with his dad's warning. But where was his dad? Dai was mouthing something, pointing towards the lane. Beyond the banners and placards, Scrapper saw the shuttered roof of a coke lorry approach the plant. The gates inched open. Dai flexed his massive shoulders, started wading through the crush towards the riot shields. Scrapper grabbed Dai's belt and went after him. The crush tightened again, as the other men pressed forwards too, fists raised. The men at the front raised a yell of triumph as a clutch of miners crashed through the police lines. But to no avail. Cheers turned to boos and whistles as the coke truck slid through the gates.

They had failed.

The cry went up. 'Move back, lads. Move back!'

The horses were coming back in. Scrapper grabbed Dai, pointed, yelled at him to turn and run. Everyone seemed to realise the danger at the same time. The crowd thinned and dissolved and everyone was running. Hooves thudded in pursuit. Batons fell on bone and flesh. The cries of the injured men filled the air. He felt heat singe the back of his neck as a horse bore down on him. Something hard and heavy caught him across the back of his skull.

He went down.

* * *

He opened his eyes to find his dad, Dai and Dewi bent over him, taking cover under a hedge. The back of his head pulsed pain. When he touched the spot, his fingers came away red and sticky.

Dai looked close to tears. 'They could've bloody killed you, Scrapper Jones.'

Dewi held up his hand. 'How many fingers, lad?'

'Give over,' Scrapper struggled up onto his elbows. 'Still got my fucking marbles.'

'Language,' Iwan scolded.

Scrapper peered out from under the hedge. What he saw made him suck in his breath. Groups of police roamed the hillside, beating any man they could catch. Fallen bodies littered the field, horses charging past and over them. The walking wounded dragged their comrades to safety. At the top of the field a group of men, faces bloodied, clothes ripped, were staging a half-hearted fightback, but they were outnumbered and out-armed, bare limbs no defence against batons and horses and dogs.

'The pigs are out o' control,' Dai whispered.

'Are you soft in the head?' Iwan rounded on him. 'They're teaching us a lesson.'

Then Scrapper spotted the kid, the one with multi-coloured spikes for hair. He was standing alone on the field, a squad of short-shield officers pelting towards him. The kid held out his arms to them, as though in surrender. The batons fell on him. Scrapper heard the crunch of resin on bone, saw the kid spit broken teeth. Two pickets ran to help, but the police beat them down and dragged them away. The kid crumpled on the ground.

Beyond the field, the coking plant gates opened and the coke trucks slipped away.

'What the fuck is this?'

Scrapper realised he had spoken the words aloud.

'It's war,' Iwan said.

* * *

Dewi gathered the boys for a headcount. By some miracle they were all present and correct, only the banner missing. Dai and Eddie slipped away, returned triumphant. The banner had survived the worst of it, only the gold trim torn and flapping in the breeze. Scrapper helped Dai to fold the cloth and dismantle the poles. They waited for a signal from Iwan, who was watching the field, to let them know when it was safe to move. When Iwan gave the signal, Dai led the way. He burst out of the undergrowth and charged across the field like a bullock.

'Where we going?' Scrapper said.

Dai pointed at a gap in the hedgerow on the far side of the field. 'Reckon there's a way out by there, across the railway. Reach the other side, we're home an' dry.'

They were nearly at the hedge when Scrapper heard footsteps. He turned to see half a dozen short-shield officers closing in on them.

'Run, lads,' he yelled.

He picked up pace, too scared to look back. He could hear the coppers' ragged breath, the crackle of radios and the jangling of metal cuffs. Dai reached the wire fence first. They could go no further. The fence blocked a steep embankment, beyond it the railway line.

'Christ,' Iwan said. 'We'll get ourselves killed.'

'We got no choice, Dad.'

Scrapper placed fingers and thumbs between the metal barbs, lifted the wire for the others to pass underneath, shouted at the boys to move it. He hefted himself after them, kept running. Half way down the embankment, he lost his footing. He fell a good twenty feet, rolling over stones and rubble, coming to a stop beside the track. Then he was up and running again, no chance to check for trains, towards a cluster of industrial units.

He turned to see the policemen grab two miners who were half way through the fence. They dragged the men back, no thought to the wire barbs that raked their skin, gloved fists smashing into faces and torsos.

* * *

He chased the others up the far embankment. They found themselves in a kind of scrap yard, pieces of steel and aluminium strewn all over, rusting iron sheets piled against the walls. Students were hefting lumps and sheets of metal towards the gates, setting fire to tyres to hold off the police. The air stank of oil and burning rubber and fear. It smelled like his rage. He picked up a rusty bumper.

Iwan wrenched it from his hands. 'No you bloody don't.'

Out on the road, a long-shield squad was chasing a group of pickets. Dai found a gap in the bushes at the back of the yard and signalled for them to follow him. They skirted a wall, sprinted across a patch of wasteland that split the industrial estate and ducked behind buildings, crouching to pass under office windows, to creep around waiting trucks. At last, they got back to the minibus. Scrapper collapsed in his seat, panting, feeling the adrenalin ebb away. His head hurt and there was a heaviness to his chest that wouldn't shift.

* * *

No one spoke as the minibus sped south. Somewhere outside Birmingham, Dewi switched on the radio.

'...*Violent clashes have been reported in South Yorkshire this morning after miners surrounded a coking plant at Orgreave near Sheffield. Police came under fire from bottles, stones and other missiles. There are reports of heavy casualties, at least seventy-two policemen injured in the clash...*'

'Seventy-two fucking policemen,' Dai thumped the dashboard.

Dewi snapped the radio off.

At last, they pulled up outside The Red Lion. No one spoke.

'Look, I could murder a bloody pint,' Scrapper said.

He was in no rush to head home. Red would get upset about the lump on his head. Worse, Angela would have listened to the news on her tinny shop radio, heard it and feared the worst, her rage gathering force all afternoon, a scolding to come for the pair of them.

He led the others into the bar. The pub was busy, for once, and the regulars raised a cheer on seeing them.

'First round on the house, lads,' Steve Red Lion grinned. 'Yous've earned it.'

They gathered round their usual table.

'Heroes' welcome, this,' said Eddie Hobnob.

'Feel like a hero, do you?' Dai said.

'Steady on,' Iwan said. 'Not one of us threw a stone. Not one hit a copper.'

'A bitter thing, to be brutalised in your own country,' Dai said.

'What the hell d'you expect from the police?' Iwan said. 'Flowers? Dancing girls?'

The door opened and a small figure shuffled in wheezing.

'A pint on the house for Sion Jenkins, for holding the fort at Blackthorn,' Steve proclaimed.

Sion sank onto a stool, fighting for breath. There was something shrunken about his posture, the light gone from his eyes.

'Cheer up, butty, we all made it back,' Iwan said. 'Eyes, teeth, arms and legs all present and correct.'

Sion was struggling to speak. 'We got scabs,' he said at last.

Someone dropped a pint. Glass shattered on the floor. No one moved.

Dewi gripped the table. 'Who?'

'Matt Price an' Alun Probert. The pair o' them sat behind Gwyn Pritchard in Albright's car. Captain Hook smirkin' like he's won the pools.'

'Matt would never do that,' Scrapper said.

'Strike's been hardest on the single lads,' Iwan said. 'No benefit. Not a penny, in fourteen weeks.'

It was bullshit. All of it was bullshit. Scrapper snatched up his stool and lobbed it across the room. It slammed into the pool table, two legs snapping clean away. He went to pick up a second stool, but Dai grabbed him, pinned his arms to his sides. Held on to him, speaking softly, until Scrapper stopped struggling, flopped limply against his chest.

7

Helen struggled to settle at her in-laws'. It was no fault of Angela and Iwan, who treated her like family, encouraged her to muck in around the house and in the coffeeshop. But she struggled to shake dark thoughts about her mam and dad. The village had a hundred theories about how her dad had talked two good men into breaking the strike. Down the shops and in the *bracchi*, everyone had an opinion. Everyone, bar Scrapper. Scrapper said nothing. Not about her dad and not about his butty, Matthew Price. Helen felt she had to make good her dad's sins. Angela agreed to let her mind the *bracchi*: she had work to do in her garden. As summer peaked, Angela thinned and weeded, mulched and harvested. Staked and fed, pruned and hefted, gathered and composted, as though it fell to her, single-handed, to keep the family from ruin.

Helen helped her mam-in-law to preserve and store the day's harvest. She was a willing but hopeless apprentice. Her mam's practical skills stretched no further than knitting quilt squares. It fell to her mam-in-law to teach her to braid onions, dry tomatoes in a low oven, top and tail bucketloads of fresh-picked beans to stow in the *bracchi* freezer. Her mam-in-law was a stickler for instructions; no truck with improvising. It took a long time before she trusted Helen to stir the boiling vats of spiced vinegar and to clean and chop the beetroot and baby onions for pickling.

Helen was washing the men's breakfast mugs, when her mam-in-law appeared later than usual, skin creased with sleep, wrapped despite the heat in a heavy dressing gown.

'Have the men gone, *bella*?'

'Two hours back.'

Angela peeled off her robe. She was dressed up proper smart, in her favourite mauve silk blouse and a taupe skirt suit.

'You're off out?'

'Is nothing.'

It was a proper effort for nothing. Angela was powdered and lipsticked and trailed a scent of crushed flowers. She slipped into the patent heels she kept for best and pulled a cardboard folder from the drawer in the kitchen table.

Seeing Helen's face, she flapped her hands. 'Is no big deal. Is meeting with bank.'

'That's not nothing.'

'Listen, *bella*, didn't want to worry Iwan, is all. You'll open up for me?'

After her mam-in-law left, Helen put away the dishes, wandered downstairs to get the *bracchi* ready. There was no rush, with business slower by the day. She lifted the chairs off the tables, set up the coffee machine and emptied crumbs from the huge toaster. It was her first time to open shop unsupervised. Not that there was anything to it. She piled home-made Welsh cakes under a cloche and placed tubs of vanilla, strawberry and chocolate in the ice cream counter. Before the strike, the *bracchi* stocked eight flavours of ice cream, sold three large cakes a day. They'd eat leftover Welsh cakes for tea that night.

It was dead quiet all morning. Helen was pouring tea for her elevenses, when the bell jangled and the vicar and his wife walked in with their twin grandsons. They ordered the works; two coffees, two portions of Welsh cakes, a plate of sandwiches, two banana splits and two milkshakes. The vicar patted her hand on the way out, told her to keep the change. Later, a road-building crew stopped by, ordered cheese rolls to take away. At lunchtime, Dr O'Connell's nurse and receptionist sat in the window sharing a sundae and moaning about their men.

After they left, no one else turned up and the afternoon began to drag. Helen watched the clock. No sign of Angela. She was wondering whether to pack up for the day when the bell jangled. The man looked familiar; large square spectacles, a snooty tilt to his large square head.

'Table for two, sweetheart.'

She blinked at him, confused, waved him to Iwan's favourite table in the corner and went over to take his order.

'No Angela? Still, you'll look after me, eh?'

'What can I get you?'

'Hmm,' his eyes travelled along her legs. 'How about a coffee. To start with.'

A right sleaze, this one. She wanted to run back to the counter. A man of his age. Disgusting. He was at least as old as her dad. The doorbell jangled again. James Hackett walked straight past her. She knew him from the news. Scrapper had thrown his newspaper at the screen when Hackett said something about the lodge being Scargill's boot boys, said the men went to Yorkshire looking for a fight. Said they deserved the bashing they got.

Jimmy Mosquito, Iwan called him. 'Always buzzing around, looking for blood.'

'Harry – great to see you again!'

Helen recognised the older man then. Harry Cross, member of parliament for Bryn Tawel and Ystrad. Always being interviewed on the telly, more often than not by Jimmy Mosquito. The reporter barked an order for tea and a cheese sandwich and pulled a pen and notebook from his jacket, eyes fixed on Harry Cross.

'Off the record, eh, boyo?'

The reporter nodded.

'The branch would lynch me if I said this publicly,' Cross said. 'Denounce the strike, they'll deselect me. But they've got the party over a barrel, Jim. The miners win, we'll lose the entire labour movement to the hard left.'

The reporter was twitching like a flea. 'Can't allow them to win; can't be seen to hope they lose?'

'Quite.'

She served the reporter his tea and sandwiches. The cutlery clattered more loudly than she meant it to. 'You'll need to make it quick, gentlemen. We're about to close.'

Harry Cross grabbed her hand, trapped it between two damp palms. 'You'll be glad to see the strike end, won't you, sweetheart?' He shot the reporter a meaningful look. 'These are the people we need to reach, Jim. The little people. The small, hard-working businesses that the unions threaten to destroy.' He gripped Helen's hand, tugged it. 'The strike's been a disaster for this cafe, hasn't it, girlie?'

She pulled her hand free, closed her fingers on the lump of anthracite in her pocket. It was warm, reassuring, gave her strength to square up to Harry Cross.

'A bigger disaster if we lose the pit.'

* * *

The MP and the reporter dragged out her afternoon. On and on they talked, even after she started stacking the chairs. She was sorely tempted to drop the shutters, lock up and leave them to it, but they took the hint at last, paid and left her to close up. She gathered the day's post and went upstairs, spread the envelopes on the kitchen table. Five brown envelopes: two addressed to The Occupier, no doubt from one of the loan companies come skittering out of the woodwork since the strike. The third was a telephone bill, printed in red ink; the fourth a bill for the electric. The fifth was addressed to her, typed address crossed out and redirected in her dad's jagged handwriting. Her exam results. She ripped the envelope open. Four passes; four fails.

* * *

The knock on the back door startled her. The kitchen was thick with steam, the kettle boiled nearly dry. She turned off the hot plate, shoved the letter in her pocket. Why would her mam-in-law knock? But it wasn't Angela. She opened the door to a tall woman with tanned skin and a dandelion shock of grey-blonde hair. It was Mary, Dewi Power's wife.

'I was lookin' for your mam-in-law. Shut shop early, has she?'

'She's—'

'Not a problem. Wanted to give her this, is all.'

Mary handed her a carrier bag filled with tins, cardboard packages and vegetables.

'What's this?'

'Food parcel. First o' many, we hope. Compliments of Ystrad Women Against Pit Closures.'

Helen looked at the bag. Was this to be her life, then? A train wreck for O-levels, a drain on her in-laws, Angela hauled up to the bank to explain their money troubles, the family forced to live on handouts. Shame flooded her cheeks. Her dad had drummed it into her long and loud that hard work brought reward, that no Pritchard accepted charity.

'No,' she said.

'What d'you mean, no?'

'Nice of you to offer. We'll not be needing handouts.'

Mary batted a hand at her. She had a kitten's spiky playfulness. 'Bollocks to handouts. Worked hard to raise the money, we did. Solidarity, this is. Not bloody famine relief!'

Helen set the bag down, feeling churlish. 'Fancy a tea?'

Mary shook her head. 'Got half a dozen deliveries before dark, *cariad*.'

'So, the food parcel—?'

'Us women got organised,' Mary said. 'Needed to, what wi' the big freeze.'

'The what?'

'Courts seized South Wales NUM's bank accounts. Squeezing us every which way, the bastards. So we been rattling cans outside the shops in Bryn Tawel. Collected way more'n expected. We're starting a soup kitchen down the Stute. Got big plans: jumble sales, fundraiser shows. You'd be welcome to help out.'

She made it sound normal. As though the Stute wasn't hostile turf. As though Debbie and her cronies kept a welcome for the scab's girl. And yet – was this her chance to show them, to prove to all of them, and to herself, that she belonged?

Mary watched her closely. 'You're one of us, now, *bach*. Angie made sure of it, insisting on you an' Scrapper getting married. Knows her onions, that one. Anyone gives you chops, you send 'em to Mary Power. I'll set the buggers straight. That goes for our Debbie, an' all.'

She was so riled up that Helen had to laugh.

'I'll think about it.'

* * *

Scrapper reacted better than she expected. She told him as they were walking up the track above the village towards the barn. A breeze rustled through the clumps of hogweed, sun-bleached seed heads whispering as they passed.

'It's only exams,' Scrapper kicked a loose stone up the path.

'I've stuffed up, Scrap.'

He kicked the stone a second time. 'We'll be fine.'

The barn loomed ahead, long shadow puddled on the patchy grass. Slashes of paint scarred its corrugated iron walls. The graffiti read *Death To Scabs*. Helen shuddered. But the barn was not their hideaway now. Other people came here. She was married now, had a room of her own. There was no need for them to sneak up here, lay their jackets on the dusty, vicious hay and breathe in cobwebs and mice droppings and engine lube. Part of her missed those days, even so. Despite the trouble from her dad, things felt simpler back then.

Scrapper clambered onto the stone drinking trough set into the brow of the hill. The basin was empty, water dried away, leaving a powdery green stain. She perched next to him and watched the swallows wheel and turn, black outlines against a sky in flames. Seen from above, Ystrad looked tired and used. The brick terraces were smudged with coal dust, back lawns brown from too much sun.

Below the village, the colliery buildings stood out like scar tissue against the valley floor. The land around the pit was ripped and torn, rail tracks like catgut on a wound. Ystrad was so small beneath that blazing sky. A pinprick of a place. She leaned her head against Scrapper's shoulder and gazed down at the winding tower. So still. So silent. As though the huge wheels would never turn again.

'If you weren't a miner, Scrap, what would you do?'

He paused. 'You'll think it's daft.'

'I won't.'

'Mr Probert said I oughta write.'

'What d'you mean, *write*?'

No one made a living writing. No one from the coalfield. One more thing that wasn't for the likes of them, if only for want of proof that such a thing was possible.

He blushed. 'I know it's daft. But years back, Probert sent a poem I wrote to the *Herald*. Won a Valentine's Day competition, got it published.'

A Valentine. To Debbie Power, no doubt. Bloody woman.

'Will you write a poem about us, Scrap?'

He planted a kiss on her cheekbone.

'One day, sure. Why not?'

8

Gwyn came down to breakfast to find Carol pressed up against the front door, one eye fixed to the spyhole he had fitted at the weekend.

'Back, are they, the coven?'

But Carol didn't answer. She fled into the kitchen, shutting the door behind her. He took her place at the door. One of his better ideas, putting in a spyhole. His family couldn't be too careful. He squinted, adjusting his gaze to the fisheye view of the road. Sure enough, there they were; his fan club. Four grim-faced women, dressed in black like witches. Trouble, Stubble, Goyle and Bubble, he called them: Dewi's wife Mary, the vicar's whiskery missus Shirley, hatchet-faced Chrissie Hobson and a pretty young thing with chestnut curls. He wouldn't kick the girl out of bed. Too bad about the rest. There every day, lately, the women in black, stood in haloes of morning sunlight. They started coming after Orgreave, after he convinced his two lads to come back in. Two so far, but time would tell. The women knew that too. Small wonder they were riled.

They waited for him every weekday morning, stood outside his gate with their arms crossed, until he left the house. Carol had him call the police that first morning. Had him summon poor old Johnny Boots. Fair play to the village bobby, he came straight up. Huffed and puffed up the hill to speak to the women.

A fat lot of good that did.

'There's no law stops a woman standing outside her house, passing time of day with her neighbours,' the copper said.

'No law to stop a bunch of women intimidating an honest citizen?'

Johnny turned back to the women. 'You been intimidating Gwyn Pritchard, ladies?'

The young girl spoke for the group. 'Some of the lads were talking about taking a pop at him,' she said. 'But we've told them no one's to touch the scabs, or harass their families or wreck their property. The strike is a political dispute. Picketing is how we protest.'

The brass-neck of the girl.

'D'you hear that? She called me a scab. That's slander, for starters.'

Johnny pulled him aside, his tubby face slick with sweat. 'Sounds to me like these women are the reason you've not had rocks through your windows or been given a good seeing-to. Reckon you should be grateful. There's scabs in South Wales not been so lucky.'

Gwyn glared at the bobby. 'Who the fuck you calling a scab?'

And there they were, yet again. He turned the key in the new five-lever mortice lock, yanked open the door.

'Morning, you lot,' he called. 'Lovely day for it. Fetch you a cuppa?'

The women glared at him, didn't answer.

'Yell if you change your minds, ladies.'

He shut the door, pleased with himself. That was them told. Ladies. If that rabble were ladies, he was Dennis Thatcher. Getting too assertive by half, the country's females. The strike must be struggling if the lodge had to send out the wives and daughters to play rent-a-mob outside decent people's houses. To corner a man in his own home.

Carol sat at the kitchen table slouched over a mug of tea. Her pink dressing gown highlighted the shadows around her eyes. His tea and toast were ready, for once, but his wife's hunched misery put him right off food.

He took his mug out to the back garden. Stood on the patio, let the morning air cool his cheeks. The scent of his sweet peas floated on the breeze. He breathed deeper, tried to ease the knots in his lungs. Something caught. Some kind of blockage that threatened to choke him. He doubled over, dizzy and wheezing. Set down his mug and waited for it pass. By the time he returned to the kitchen, his wife was gone. Gone back to bed, knowing her. She did that often, lately. It struck him that she hadn't spoken to him. She had nothing much to say for herself at all, lately, his wife. She'd been sulking since that business up at Orgreave. Sat rigid in her armchair as they watched the fighting replayed on the evening news, Scargill's stormtroopers taking the hiding they deserved. She watched the whole thing, fists clenched. Flinched a little, every time a truncheon fell.

'But it's that rabble that started it,' he scolded her. 'Go looking for trouble, trouble's what you get.'

* * *

The women moved aside as he pushed through his front gate. Their faces were pale, lips tight with disapproval.

'Lovely to see you, ladies. It's business as usual at the pit this morning, if your fellas'd care to stop by—'

Chrissie Hobnob lurched forwards, as if to slap him. Gwyn flinched. A nifty right hook on Chrissie. He heard her through the walls, dishing out clips around the ear to her sons.

'What d'you say to them two lads?' she demanded. 'How'd you drive 'em to turn scab?'

'Remember what we agreed, Chrissie,' Mary said.

Chrissie pulled back, face like ash against too-black hair. 'Enough is enough,' she said. 'I say let the lads do their worst.'

* * *

In the corner shop, Geraint Mags-N-Fags took Gwyn's five-pound note, slammed twenty Embassy on the counter. Handed him his change without a word.

Gwyn rolled his *Daily Express* under his arm. 'A bloody fine morning to you, and all.'

He waited outside the shop for the pit manager. At last, Albright pulled up in the hired Land Rover, Alun Probert and Matthew Price slumped on the back seat. He climbed into the passenger seat, pasted a smile to his face to greet his boss.

'Orright, Mr Albright, boys?'

Albright fired up the engine. The Land Rover pelted past the shops. Gwyn gripped his seat belt. As nervy as a cat on a fish tank, the pit boss. Same performance every morning, speeding through Ystrad like the devil was giving chase.

He turned to Albright, thinking to distract him. 'Got a game at the weekend, then?'

'We're playing Liverpool.'

'The Reds'll struggle to beat Everton at home,' Alun Wet-Ears said.

Gwyn shot the lad a sour look. Since when did the apprentice give two figs for football?

'Bridgend are playing, and all,' he said.

Albright yawned. 'Maybe you boys can take me to a game some time. These little local games must be fascinating.'

Gwyn felt his missing fingers prickle but decided not to rise to it in front of his lads. He ferreted around for something else to say.

'Lady wife doing alright?'

'I've bought tickets to see David Bowie for her birthday next month.'

Matt breathed in sharply. 'Bowie? He's not coming to Wales?'

Albright nodded. 'Only St David's Hall, of course. But still.'

'Loves Bowie, I do.'

Gwyn lowered his sunshield, used the mirror to turn a hard stare on Matthew Price.

'Really?' Albright said.

'Aye. Got every single one of his albums.'

Albright beamed at him. 'Well, I'm becoming quite a fan. That new duet with Tina Turner – marvellous.'

'More a Ziggy man, me,' Matt said.

'Aren't you just,' Gwyn muttered.

'There are tickets left, apparently,' Albright said. 'If I see you there, I'll stand you a drink. You and your girlfriend.'

In the mirror, Gwyn watched Matt blush and button his lip.

* * *

Smoke rose as usual from the braziers outside the pit gates. But as the Land Rover sped closer, Gwyn saw something had changed. The usual line of pickets had vanished. The men had not reached the gates. Tooled-up policemen had shoved them to the side of the road, where quite a crowd had gathered. A couple of hundred men were penned in behind a line of shields and helmets. As Albright sped past, Gwyn saw most were strangers. Flying pickets pitched against riot police, both sides drafting outsiders into Blackthorn. He turned and grinned at the lads.

'Looks like Scargill sent you a welcoming party. Took him a while, didn't it?'

The little apprentice was shaking. Matt pulled his denim jacket over his head, slumped lower in his seat. As they drew closer, a roar burst from the crowd. Bodies thudded against the shields, tried to break through to the road. Albright leaned on the horn and accelerated towards the gates. Gwyn raised his good hand, flashed two fingers to the pickets. At the front, he spotted the hotheads from the lodge: Scrapper and Iwan Jones, Dewi Power, Dai Dumbells. Matt buried himself deeper beneath his jacket. Gwyn pressed his face against the mesh that covered the windscreen, locked eyes with the girl's husband.

'Fuck you,' he mouthed.

Something thudded against the boot of the car. In the wing mirror, Gwyn saw Dai Dumbells launch himself at the Land Rover, grab the metal grille on the rear windscreen, lose his grip. Dai fell back into the road, writhing on the ground. Two policemen leapt on Dai, went in heavy with their truncheons.

Matt turned and saw it too, sucked in his breath.

Albright put his foot to the floor. The Land Rover sped through the gates.

'Shit!' the pit manager's soft white hands gripped the steering wheel, veins showing blue beneath his skin. 'We'll get a bus and driver to bring us in. I won't be held responsible for some idiot getting himself killed.'

The jeep squealed to a halt outside the management offices. Albright turned off the engine and leaned back in his seat, face pale and clammy. He pulled a purple handkerchief from his breast pocket and mopped his brow.

'No concern for safety,' he said. 'Not theirs or ours. You'd think they were desperate.'

He wrenched open the car door and vanished into his office. Gwyn levered himself out of the car and waited for Matt Price.

'*Ooh, I loves David Bowie,*' he mocked.

Matt curled in on himself, said nothing.

'You'd rather scab on your butties than tell the truth, eh, lad?'

Matt slunk away, went to join Alun Wet-Ears in the cafeteria.

The men had nothing to do most days. Gwyn kept them busy, even so. A matter of pride, that. He might have them sweep out the lamp room again. No point getting them started too soon, though. He'd let them fix themselves a tea, give them time to cool their heels. He leaned against the car bonnet, dizzy suddenly, breath coming ragged. His second attack in a week. He vowed to see Dr O'Connell, get himself checked over. It would take all his strength to see this through to the end. But he had two lads back at work, even so. Two, against the odds.

9

Angela had shut the *bracchi* early again, went off to sweet talk a supplier demanding payment, leaving Helen to tend to the garden, with a long list of dos and don'ts. Helen was setting about Angela's herbs with secateurs, beheading chives, oregano and fennel to stop them running to seed, when Mary Power showed up at the garden gate.

She brought a second food parcel. A box of eggs, a tin of corned beef, a cabbage, packets of rice, white beans and kidney beans, a tub of margarine, two packets of digestive biscuits and a carton of powdered tomato soup. Angela got sniffy about packaged food, especially the powdered stuff, and they had more tomatoes than they knew what to do with. Even so, Helen thanked Mary warmly, grateful to take a pause from gardening. She ignored Mary's protests and went to brew up a fresh pot of tea.

'Tidy crop you got by there,' Mary plonked herself on the wall with her mug. 'Fruit trees, an' all.'

Helen nodded. It was more than they could do to keep up with it all. The plum trees were shedding fruit faster than she could pick it. Iwan and Scrapper could only help out at the weekend. They had gathered bucket-loads of plums for Angela to fill a dozen glass jars with home-made jam. Now, they were out of containers. Fallen plums lay on the lawn, raising clouds of fruit flies. Meanwhile, she had onions, courgettes and runner beans to pick, and gooseberry and blackcurrant bushes about to ripen.

'My mam-in-law's got green fingers.'

Mary nodded thoughtfully. 'A lot o' work for you both, the lads out picketing all week. Reckon we might help each other out?'

'Help each other out how?'

'Soup kitchen's got a hundred families to feed. We could help you harvest, take what you can't use to the Stute.'

It sounded fair enough but Helen didn't fancy Mary's chances. Angela was as tetchy as a teased cat since the meeting at the bank.

'Best you ask my in-laws.'

Iwan and Scrapper walked in then, clothes streaked brown and green, hair flecked with bracken and stick-a-back leaves, as though someone had bounced them down a hill.

'The pigs chased us cross-country,' Scrapper said.

'Ask the in-laws what?' Iwan said.

'I was looking at Angela's fruit and veg,' Mary said. 'Wondered if we could help you wi' harvesting. Take whatever's spare for the soup kitchen.'

'That's a superb idea,' Scrapper said.

Helen dug her elbow in his ribs. 'We'll ask your mam, won't we.'

* * *

Later, Helen showed Angela Mary's gifts. Her mam-in-law still felt affronted to receive food parcels, although she didn't say so to the men. Angela held a lot back, lately.

She picked up a square tin, narrowed her eyes to read the label. 'Is what, corn beef: meat or vegetable?'

Helen shuddered. 'Corn*ed* beef. My mam uses it for sandwiches. Cooked and mashed meat; looks and smells like dog food.'

Angela clapped her hands to her cheeks. 'Twenty years I lived in South Wales. Still shocked by what people eat.'

'I love corned beef,' Iwan said. 'Reckon we should give it a try.'

'You want it, bloody cook it yourself,' Angela said.

Helen left them to it. By the time Scrapper came out of the bathroom, scrubbed and clean, the smell of fried onions wafted from the kitchen. He turned on the evening news. Iwan appeared from the kitchen, proudly carrying three plates piled with corned beef hash. Angela stomped in behind him with a plate of toast and sliced tomatoes.

'Go on, *cariad*; just try it,' Iwan said.

Angela ignored him. 'You are right, *bella*. Smells like dog meat.'

Helen hadn't eaten all day. The gloopy mess of onion, potato and meat smelled better than it looked. She took a cautious taste.

'Oh wow, Iwan— that's dead good, that is.'

Iwan beamed. 'Just fried it up with potatoes, chucked in a heap of garlic, chilli powder and onions.'

They ate in silence, eyes on the television, waiting for the newsreader to mention the miners hurt at the picket at Didcot. But the reports moved from politics to international affairs to sport.

Scrapper shook his head. 'Seven men in hospital and not one bloody word.'

'Anyone from Ystrad?' Helen said.

'Bloody lucky Dai Dumbells wasn't one of them,' Iwan said. 'He nearly fell under a truck. Police were straight on him. We fetched him from the cop shop on the way back. They've charged him with affray.'

'Dai was gutted,' Scrapper said. 'Said Debbie'd tan his hide.'

'No question she'll do that,' Iwan said.

'Which reminds me,' Scrapper said. 'Mam, Mary wanted to know if you could spare some fruit an' veg from out back.'

Angela dropped her toast. 'She wanted *what*?'

Helen glared a warning at Scrapper, put down her fork. 'Mary asked if she could help,' she said. 'Noticed we been struggling to harvest. Said she and the other women could lend us a hand, maybe take the leftovers to the Stute.'

'Fair dos,' Scrapper said. 'We got more than enough for ourselves.'

'More than enough?' Angela echoed. 'I worked these fingers to the bone.'

'C'mon, Mam. We're sick of runner beans and courgettes and plum jam. If Mary wants some, why not?'

'It's for feeding the lads and their families,' Iwan said.

Angela slammed her plate down on the coffee table. 'You are not serious. Is five months I put up with this strike. No money coming in. Not from son, not from husband. Schiappa's *bracchi* survived the general bloody strike. There's every chance it won't survive this. And now those women after my garden? My garden! No – *basta*. Is final straw.'

Iwan put out a hand to ruffle her hair, drew back thinking better of it. He switched off the television.

'What's this about, Angie?'

Angela stacked the plates. Forks clattered angrily. Knives tumbled onto the carpet. She dumped the plates with a crash in the kitchen, blasted back into the front room.

'Is about the fact that you were wrong, Iwan Jones. Wrong to defy Gwyn Pritchard and get suspended. Wrong to fall in behind a strike you cannot win. Five bloody months, the village on its knees and no one backing down. Is madness. All of it.'

'You don't mean that,' Iwan said.

'I do mean it. Is too much. I'm sick of no money. Sick of bills.

Sick of politics an' picketing. And now those bloody women after my vegetables.'

'It's only runner beans and courgettes, Mam,' Scrapper said.

'*Non solo fagioli e zucchine*, Simon Jones. Is about feeding a family. About owing the bank five hundred pounds. Is about putting this family first.'

10

Summer dragged on, hotter and more oppressive by the day.
Scrapper felt sluggish, weighed down by the stalemate, by the
bills that piled up. His arms and back were stiff from under-use,
muscles melting to reveal his bones. Even his body betrayed
him. Red's face was paler and thinner than before. Iwan's hair
had thicker streaks of grey. Angela walked as though wading
through quicksand. He couldn't forget her words: *you were
wrong to stand up to your bosses, wrong to back a strike you
cannot win*. Truth was, they had to win. Had no option but to
keep going.

The more he thought about it, the more rage seeped from his
pores. All of it came back to his butty. Of the many wrongs the
boys had faced, that betrayal hurt him most. He made up his
mind, at last, to find Matt, to talk to him. He needed to hear from
his butty's own lips what turned a solid class fighter into a scab.

Come Saturday night, the clock crawling towards closing
time, he set off down the High Street on his bike. He rested his
feet on the pedals and cruised down the road that wound below
the coal tip, braking only when he reached the settlement below
Ystrad. It was a ghost town, now, built for a coal seam long dug
dry. There was nothing to keep anyone here. The lone terrace
of two-up, two-down miners' cottages was all but derelict, most
of the dwellings boarded up and left to rot. In the middle was
Matt's house, lights off, curtains drawn upstairs and downstairs.
Scrapper leaned his bike against the lamp-post across the street
and parked his backside on the pavement to wait.

An owl hooted portents up in the fields, unnerving in a night as thick and warm as soup. He was dozing off when he heard footsteps running towards him. Hands slammed his shoulders, shoved him backwards.

'Come to dish out more, have you?' Matt loomed over him. 'Despicable, holding an old woman prisoner at home.'

'I wasn't—'

'Bad enough getting shunned and picketed, but Mam's had a guts-full of the graffiti and silent phone calls.'

Matt stank of ale and sweat and fear, his eyes were sunken and rimmed red. Scrapper almost felt sorry for his butty. Everything he knew about mining, he had learned from Matt Price: the difference between the moaning of rocks settling into position and the rumble of rocks about to drop. How to hold a pickaxe and hold his drink.

He stood, rubbing the elbow that broke his fall. 'I need to know why, Matt.'

'Aye, cos you'll understand.'

'How the fuck can I, if you won't say?'

Matt didn't answer.

'You've not got the balls to explain, have you, Matthew Price? You got no balls, no backbone, no loyalty to your butties.'

'Loyalty,' Matt echoed.

'Yes, loyalty. All of us looked out for you. Fed you, stood you drinks. You've thrown all of it back in our faces.'

Matt balled his fists. Scrapper braced himself to get hit a second time. Maybe he'd hit back, just this once, since Iwan wasn't here to stop him. Or maybe he'd hang his hands by his sides, let his butty do his worst. No pasting could hurt more than the dull ache sunk deep beneath his skin. But Matt held back, a look on his face that Scrapper couldn't read.

'I'm fucking sick of it all. Sick of pointing fingers, of walking around with my head bowed.'

His self-pity robbed Scrapper of breath. 'Then get the fuck back behind the strike,' he struggled to get the words out. 'Every last one of the boys would welcome you back with open arms. It's not too late, Matt.'

Matt laughed bitterly. 'Are you stupid or deluded, kid?'

'We stick together, we can win this.'

'You seriously believe that, with the bosses using force to smash the strike? With the labour movement hanging the miners out to dry? Look behind you, Scrapper Jones. There's no one there.'

'*That's* why you shafted us? Pull the other one, Matt.'

But Matt was no longer looking at him. He was staring at the house, at a figure hammering on the upstairs window. Her hair was pale against the orange glow of the street lamp. An old woman, with mad terror in her eyes. Matt's mam struggled to open a security catch.

'It's fine, Mam,' Matt shouted. 'I'm fine.'

The woman vanished, reappeared with a telephone, the receiver wedged between her shoulder and her ear as she dialled with unsteady fingers.

'Great,' Matt said. 'You'd better go, Scrapper Jones. Fuck off and don't come back. We got nothing to say to each other.'

11

Helen woke to the sound of rain thrumming on the slates on the roof, to the rumble of thunder and voices raised in the bedroom next door. Better the raised voices of Scrapper's parents than the poisoned silences she remembered from home. The sound unsettled her, even so. The rain drummed on and on. Eventually, the voices stopped. At last, the downpour ended.

The men left to go picketing in Nottinghamshire and her mam-in-law announced that the *bracchi* needed a spring clean. The shop was spotless. Helen was cleaning the grout between the tiles with an old toothbrush when the doorbell jangled and Mary Power trotted in, followed by Chrissie Hobnob and a woman who looked about Scrapper's age, who had long brown curls.

Her mam-in-law greeted the Women Against Pit Closures delegation like long-lost friends, kisses all round, sat down with them, had Helen fetch coffees and ice cream sundaes.

'On the house, *bella*,' she said, with a complicit nod.

When Helen brought the order, Angela had her pull up a chair.

'Is like this,' she was saying. 'You ladies got your local jumble sales and street collections. Sue here and Debbie go to meetings up and down the country. I say we make the fruit and veg pay. You help us harvest, I fill your jars and bottles with secret-recipe Schiappa chutneys and jams. Sell them at jumble sales, street collections and meetings. Split the profits, everyone wins.'

Helen gawped at her mam-in-law, surprised and impressed.

Angela had clawed back her fighting spirit, armed herself with an idea, gone out to battle for it.

Mary's eyes narrowed on hearing the word profit. Her friends sat, spoons poised, considering.

'The lads can sell too,' Sue said. 'I'll get labels printed: *buy me to back the miners.*'

Mary shot Angela a sidelong glance. 'So when you say profit—?'

'Sixty-forty, to me,' Angela said.

There was a shocked pause. Then Mary broke into a deep, earthy chuckle. Angela's eyes darkened. Helen braced herself. But then her mam-in-law was laughing too, and so were the others.

'Damn it, Angie,' Mary wiped her eyes. 'If we had you negotiating for the lodge, we'd win the bloody strike in a week.'

'Is what, your offer?'

'Our labour, our jars, our leg-work doing the selling,' Sue said. 'Make it twenty-eighty in our favour. Payment on sale.'

Angela sighed. 'Twenty-five, seventy-five, we got a deal.'

'Done,' Mary said. 'A pleasure doing business wi' you.'

They raised their coffee cups and clinked them together.

After the women left, Helen and Angela went back to spring-cleaning. Angela climbed onto a chair and unhooked the covers of the strip lights, tipped the bodies of dead insects into the bin. Looking up, Helen saw her mam-in-law's hips had lost their fullness, the softness firmed to sinew.

She finished stacking the dishes, wiped damp hands on leggings.

'You reckon we'll make enough to get the bank off our backs?'

Angela sloshed soapy water into the light casings. 'Don't be daft, *bella*. Not if we kept all the profit. Things gone way too far.'

* * *

On Sunday morning, Mary Power and half a dozen members of Ystrad Women Against Pit Closures came trooping into the back garden, armed with gardening tools and pails. Sue drove up in her battered Ford Anglia, boot loaded with jars and preserving bottles, gallon containers of vinegar and a sack of sugar. Helen helped her to carry it all up to the kitchen, where Angela had her first vat of pickle on the boil.

Helen had seen most of the women around the village, apart from Sue. She was an old school friend of Debbie Power's. Just when Helen had decided that the women weren't at all scary or unfriendly, Debbie herself wafted through the garden on a drift of Poison, all cheekbones and bile-green eyeliner, dressed for gardening in snake-print leggings and a one-shoulder top.

Scrapper leaned out of the kitchen window. 'Morning, ladies.'

Debbie grinned up at him, a hand shielding her eyes, bobbed hair shimmering like jet in the sunshine. She looked as sleek as a model from a pop video. Little wonder Scrapper was gawping at his ex-girlfriend.

Helen stalked off to join Iwan, who was showing the women round the garden. When her in-laws married, Angela had Iwan dig up her late uncle's rose beds and replace them with fruit and vegetables – her dowry, she liked to joke. The plum and pear trees hung heavy with fruit. Beetroot leaves and cabbages burst from the earth. Butterflies flitted between tins and pots crammed with herbs. At the end of the garden, half a dozen stocky gooseberry bushes lined up like sentries at the borders.

'Right,' Mary said. 'Sue's got gloves. She'll pick goosegogs. Debbie, you sort out the runner beans. Shirley an' Chrissie will pick courgettes an' tomatoes. Rest of us'll sort out these trees.'

'Me and Simon can help too,' Iwan said.

Mary rapped his knuckles lightly. 'You done enough letting us loose by here.'

'No trouble,' Iwan said. 'Game's not on until two.'

'What about me?' Helen asked.

Debbie shot her a sideways look. 'Don't you trouble yourself, Helen Pritchard. I'm sure we'll—'

'Excellent, Red,' Mary said. 'Debbie could use a hand picking beans.'

Of all the bad luck. Helen grabbed a wicker basket, stalked off towards the canes, not caring whether Debbie followed her.

Sunlight beat down on the garden. The other women cracked jokes, swapped gossip. Helen and Debbie had nothing to say to each other. Pain scorched the tendons in Helen's shoulders and fingers. She lowered her arms, tried to find shade beneath the canes. Debbie laboured on, back turned, hands a blur of fingers and thumbs as she twisted the beans from their stalks. She seemed to sense Helen stop. Her hands slowed.

'Given up already, Helen Pritchard?'

Helen swallowed a sigh, raised her basket again. 'Not by a long shot, Debbie Power.'

As time creaked by, the other women fell silent too. The sun beat down on them, relentless. By lunchtime, Helen and Debbie had picked all the beans, topped and tailed them, and bagged them for storage in Angela's freezer. Helen went upstairs to see how her mam-in-law was getting on. Angela was busy in the kitchen, face glowing with steam, two huge batches of chutney cooling on the windowsill, a vat of sugared plums boiled up for jam.

Helen brewed a fresh pot of tea, took it down to the garden. Scrapper was perched on a stepladder among the plum trees, Iwan below him, both using rakes to comb the tree of its fruit. Plums thudded onto the lawn as fast as Mary, Chrissie and Shirley could gather them. When Helen called them over, they downed tools, grabbed a mug and perched on the wall sipping tea.

Only Sue kept going, battling the gooseberry bushes at the far end of the garden, a battered raffia hat tilted over her eyes, man-sized industrial gloves covering her arms from fingertips to elbow.

Helen filled a mug for her, took it over. 'Proper collier's gloves, those.'

'Borrowed 'em off Gramps. He worked at Blackthorn, until his accident. Owes his hands to these gloves. Too bad he didn't have them for his feet.'

Helen shuddered. Her own granddad died in that blast and her dad had lost his fingers to the pit some years later.

'Blackthorn's got a taste for human flesh,' she said.

'I used to think that,' Sue said. 'Gave me nightmares.'

'So why fight to save it?'

Sue shoved her hat out of her eyes. 'It's all we've got, isn't it. Close Blackthorn, Ystrad's finished. There'll be nothing for the boys and nothing for the rest of us.'

* * *

By mid-afternoon, they had loaded Sue's car with bottles and jars of pickles and jams to be labelled and stored at the Stute. Scrapper brewed up a last round of tea. Helen picked up a knife and went to help Sue top and tail goosegogs. She watched Scrapper talking to Debbie, two dark heads bent over the teapot. Scrapper said something that made Debbie flick her curtain of hair and give a showy laugh.

'How come I've not seen you around before this summer,' she asked Sue.

'I'm at college. Got digs on campus. But then Gramps got poorly. Since there's no one else to care for him, I deferred two terms and came home.'

'D'you come home most summers?'

Sue shook her head. 'Last year, I went to Greenham.'

'What, the peace camp?'

Helen was shocked. Her dad went on and on about the Greenham Common women whenever he saw them on the news. No-good trouble making lesbians, the Greenham Common women, her dad reckoned. Harridans and hoydens, he called them.

'One time, we used wire-cutters to get through the fence. Climbed onto the missile silos. Had a song and a dance before getting nicked.'

'Nicked, seriously? Oh my God.'

'Occupational hazard,' Sue shrugged.

A shadow fell across them. Scrapper topped up their mugs, plonked himself on the grass next to them and set to topping and tailing gooseberries with his pocket knife, working at breakneck speed.

'You seen Matt?' Sue asked. 'Since—'

'Oh, I seen him,' Scrapper said. 'Swanning past in the boss's car.'

'Poor, deluded bastard,' Sue said.

'Treacherous bastard,' Scrapper said.

'Matt showed up down the pub the other night,' Sue said. 'The men put down their pints and walked out. Then Steve Red Lion refused to serve him.'

Despite the heat, Helen felt crystals of ice form along her spine. It was no small thing to be shunned in this village. She could see it all too well: Matthew Price, waiting at the bar, naked in his bravado. Ferrety face crumpling as his former butties showed him their backs. Matt lived to impress the boys. Without them, he was— what?

'Poor Matt,' she said, not thinking.

'Don't waste your pity on that one,' Scrapper snapped.

* * *

That night, despite her aching arms, sleep would not come. She rolled from side to side. Nothing helped. At last, daylight stuck grey fingers through the curtains. The dim glow fell on Scrapper's sleeping face. She propped herself up on one arm and lay there, looking at him. It was strange, even now, to wake up next to him. It felt exciting but wrong, somehow. As though she had stolen something and sooner or later would get caught.

His face, neck and arms were tanned from his hours on the picket line. His hair, uncut since the start of the strike, spilled over the pillow. His skin looked properly Italian now. When he worked below ground, he looked half-baked. But his cheekbones were sharper, lately. He was thinner now. A lot thinner since Orgreave. She leaned closer, tried to count his flickering eyelashes. He muttered something she didn't catch.

'Scrap?'

'Hunhhh?'

'Do you love me?'

'Mmm.'

'And Debbie?'

He looked at her through half-closed eyes. 'Huh?'

'Debbie. Is there something between you still?'

He rolled towards her, trapped her in his arms. 'Don't talk daft, woman.'

AUTUMN 1984

— 1 —

When Helen sat her mock O-levels, the school brought in a careers adviser to talk to the class. The lady stood at the blackboard wearing a nice beige twinset and a tiny pearl crucifix and pecked their illusions apart. Hundreds of unemployed chasing every job, no-experience school-leavers last in the queue. She handed out brochures for the new youth-training scheme. Get trained, she said, the opportunities would flow, leaving the untrained by the wayside to scrounge on the dole.

When Helen repeated to her in-laws what the careers lady had told the class, Iwan was outraged. '*Scrounge*, with two million unemployed? Don't you dare give your labour for free, love. The likes of us can't afford to work for nothing. Stuff the YTS.'

Her in-laws wanted her to stay at school, resit her exams, take A-levels. She disagreed. Surely something would come along. But summer was over and now was her last chance before term started to prove to her in-laws and everyone else that she wasn't planning to scrounge. If Angela was fighting to save their little family, she wanted to help out too.

The careers lady had talked about grooming, about dressing as the person you wanted to be. Helen sighed and reached for her wedding dress. Her skin prickled as she zipped it up. She scraped her hair into a bun, pulled on her black leggings and a cardigan and slipped her feet into her boots. The box file was under the bed. It was crammed with carbon copies of application letters bashed out on Iwan's battered Brother, most stapled to a typed reply. Fifty three replies, all short and to the point. Words flickered before her eyes: enthusiastic; keen to learn; not afraid of hard work.

Scrapper walked in, laughed at the sight of her. 'Nice outfit, *bach*.'

'Thanks a bloody bunch.'

She stomped off to the kitchen. Angela, pouring tea, looked as grumpy as Helen felt. Her mam-in-law was missing her morning coffees.

'You don't have to do this, *bella*.'

'I got to get a job, Angela; high time I paid my way.'

'Is ridiculous, Helen. Get A-levels, is lots more opportunities. I'll speak to Mr Probert.'

Helen grunted. She kissed her mam-in-law on the cheek and headed out to the High Street. Should she try the pub again? Last time she asked Steve Red Lion for work, he said he wasn't hiring. Offered her a shot of Irish Cream, tried to pat her bum. Definitely not the pub. That left Betty's Unisex, the hairdressers, the butcher, the bookies, the funeral parlour and the Co-op.

Betty Bowen was alone, flame-red helmet of hair bent over a rack of nylon blouses. She didn't hear Helen walk in, looked up when she sensed her presence. Her face cobwebbed into a smile, orange lipstick oozing into the cracks around her mouth.

'Where you been, *bach*? Got the perfect top for you. Kept it back for you, special. Now where'd I put the ruddy thing?'

She ducked into the stock room, reappeared with a square of stiff fabric. Heat flooded Helen's cheeks. She wouldn't be buying, no matter what treasure Mrs B produced. She unfolded the fabric. It was a black, fitted waistcoat with jet-look buttons, a halter back that left the shoulders bare. The girl from The Pretenders, the coolest chick that ever walked, wore something like it on Top of the Pops. Mrs B had found the perfect thing. She always did.

'I reckoned Gwyn Pritchard's girl would still be buying.'

There it was again, that shrinking sense of shame. But pride was another thing Helen couldn't afford.

'I left home, Mrs B. I've not seen Dad in months. I'm looking for work.'

The old lady turned back to her blouses. 'I've already let the Saturday girl go.'

'You're managing okay?'

'Oh, aye. Right as ruddy rain, me.'

'Save that top for me, Mrs B. Soon as I'm earning, I'll treat myself.'

The old lady laughed; a bitter edge to it.

The next shop was Split-Enz Salon. Helen hadn't cut her hair in years, had her mam take a scissors to her curls twice a year. But she fixed a smile to her face, pushed the door open. Her boot caught the mat. She staggered and nearly fell. The hairdresser was lowering a dryer over a customer's head. He jerked round, raised his scissors like a weapon. The customer lurched forward, banged her forehead against the dryer.

'My God,' the hairdresser said.

'Sorry, Mr Sigmund,' Helen gasped.

The hairdresser patted the elderly lady's arm, eased her back in the chair. He strolled towards Helen with a rolling, mocking gait, stern gaze trawling from her boots to her hair. His eyes had a sapphire glint that matched the threads woven through the scarf draped across his chest. His dark blond hair was short at the sides, crowned with highlighted curls. Helen drew back, feeling shabby.

'What then, sweetie? Flood? Fire? Red hair alert?'

'I— um—'

'Sit. I must finish Mrs Price.'

He went back to the customer, pushed the dryer against the wall, unpinned the woman's rollers. Violet curls sprang up between his fingers. As he worked, the old lady eyed Helen in the mirror. Mrs Price, he'd called her. Of course: Matt Price's mam. There was a strong family likeness. The old lady raised a shaking hand to her face, blinked at the hairdresser with anxious eyes. There was a mouse-like look to her round forehead and turned-in teeth. If Helen moved too quickly, the old lady might leap from the chair and slip between the floorboards. Again, that shrinking feeling. People saw her either as Gwyn Pritchard's daughter or as Scrapper Jones's wife; on the wrong side, whichever.

Hair set, the old lady nodded her thanks, shed her polyester gown and scuttled out without paying.

The hairdresser turned to Helen. 'So what then?'

'I came to see if you got any work going.'

Mr Sigmund didn't answer.

'I could sweep the floors. Wash customers' hair and take appointments. My teachers said I'm hard work and not afraid of enthusiastic—'

The hairdresser twitched an eyebrow.

'Please, Mr Sigmund?'

'Siggy. And you are the fourth girl to ask this week. Sorry, but no.'

She sagged against the counter. 'Really no?'

Siggy eyed her. 'Not even to get my mitts on that pretty hair, more's the pity.'

Same answer from Johnny Scrag the butcher and Dai Punt at the bookies. After that, Helen lost her nerve. She loitered outside the funeral parlour. Dusty curtains lined the double windows, framed a blank slate headstone. Next to it, two lacquered urns and a brass lamp, etched with the names of the men lost to the Blackthorn Disaster of 1960, her granddad among them. Yellowed net curtains lined the funeral parlour door. She thought about the dead who passed through that door: the old and exhausted, the young and maimed. Try as she might, she could not go in.

She moved on to the Co-op. Narrow aisles ran between shelves bowed under cans, cartons and packets. Nothing was sold fresh. At the back of the shop, a woman bent over the chill cabinet, loading her wire basket with frozen pancakes. Her toddler sat on the floor, sucking a crisp the size and shape of his fist. In the next aisle, two pensioners bickered over packet soups. At the till, a pasty brunette checked her ponytail for split ends. Helen searched the aisles for Mr Daniels, the manager, knocked on the office door. No one answered. The checkout girl confirmed it; Dan the Can wasn't in.

'What d'you think you're doing?' The young mum charged across, basket on one arm, toddler on the other, safety-pin earrings and knotty bleach-blonde hair all too familiar.

'Looking for Mr Daniels.'

'Why d'you want 'im?'

'What's it got to do with—?'

'He promised me first dibs if a job came up. Queue-jumping, are you?'

'No, I—'

'Once a scab always a scab, eh, Helen Pritchard? It's in your blood.'

'You what?'

The woman smiled nastily. 'We won't forgive what your dad done to this village.'

'What my dad does is his business,' Helen said. 'I don't—'

But the woman wasn't listening. 'You're the same, you Proberts and Pritchards. Alun's great-granddad scabbed on the Great Strike. Small wonder the lad's turned scab now. And you're the same. Blood will out, Helen Pritchard. I fucking hope you never have kids!'

The words stung like the business end of a wasp. Helen backed away, turned and ran from the shop.

187

* * *

At the *bracchi* Angela, slate-faced, was serving tea and Welsh cakes to Jimmy Mosquito. Last week's Welsh cakes, but even so.

'Iwan said we weren't to serve that one,' Helen whispered.

'Beggars and choosers, *bella*.'

Her mam-in-law had a point.

'What's he after now?'

'Is TUC meeting down in Brighton. Electricians' union want to cross picket lines. He's chasing Dewi for a quote.'

'Pay danger money, do they, BBC Wales?'

'Bloody hope not. How did you get on?'

'Nothing so far.'

'Ah well, *bella*. Is simple, then. Back to school and make the best of it.'

'Angie, no—'

'Is nothing to stop you applying for jobs when you're back at school.'

Helen knew better than to argue with her mam-in-law. She set to work on the washing up. At last, Jimmy Mosquito paid up and buzzed off into the twilight.

'Angie, did Alun Probert's great-granddad scab on the General Strike?'

'No idea. Why?'

'Something someone said.'

'These people,' Angela shrugged. 'Like Mafiosi for nursing a grudge.'

2

Scrapper sat at the kitchen table, twitching unease. His mam stood at the draining board, grinding together two teaspoons to squeeze the last drop of flavour from a teabag. At last she sat, tugged her cardigan around herself for warmth.

'Is beyond us to pay gas and electric and now the nights become so cold.'

Iwan sighed. 'I'll fetch more coal from the drifts. The lad'll help.'

'Course I will,' Scrapper said.

Angela was in no mood to be humoured. 'Is dangerous up by there. What point risking life to gather coal, if not for a living wage?'

They sipped their tea in silence. Angela's lips were as tight as the family purse strings. Iwan slipped his hands inside his sweater, patted his ribs to try to lighten the mood.

'I've not been this slim since I walked you up the aisle, eh, love?'

She shot him a dark look.

'Spoke to Mary before,' he kept on. 'We'll have a food parcel tonight. Plenty of apples and onions and potatoes in the shed.'

'Is not enough,' Angela snapped. 'Not if strike lasts to spring, like Dewi reckons.'

Red came back from school in time to finish off the tea. She slung her satchel on her chair and sank down with a sigh. Her face was pale, cheekbones too sharp, as delicate and fragile as an icicle.

'I seen more meat on a lamb cutlet than on you, *bach*,' Scrapper said, not thinking.

Red eyeballed him over the rim of her mug. 'That a compliment, Scrap?'

But Iwan and Angela were looking at her too.

'We'll fetch that coal tonight,' Iwan said.

'I'll help,' Red said.

'No you don't,' Iwan said. 'It's filthy, dangerous work. Men's work, carrying coal.'

Angela served up ladlefuls of *cawl*, beef bones cadged from Johnny Scrag, bulked up with onion, potato and cabbage from out back. Scrapper finished two bowlfuls, pushed his chair back, enjoying the glow that spread from his stomach to his arms and legs.

Later, Red bent over her books. Dark circles shadowed her eyes. An age seemed to pass before she looked up, yawned and stretched.

'You done, *bach*?'

She nodded.

'You been working too hard. Let's take a walk. How about you make yourself presentable?'

She grinned. 'You saying I've let myself go, Scrapper Jones?'

'My son, the gentleman,' Angela tutted.

'Touch o' lippie wouldn't hurt.'

He helped Red into her jacket and they left the house hand in hand, following the trail to the top of the fields. Dusk was closing in. He wrapped his arms around her and they stood, looking down over the village as the sun flayed streaks of red and orange across the sky. Then, with the Pole Star high above their heads, he pulled her into the barn.

* * *

He woke to the sound of shouting. Red turned over, pulled the bed covers over her head. He dressed quickly and rushed into the living room to see what had happened. Angela was dragging cushions off the sofa and armchairs, tossing them on the floor. Iwan stood over her, trying to reason with her.

'Mam?'

'Is down the back, you mark my words.'

'Stop it, Angie, you're being ridiculous.'

She ignored them both, carried on searching down the back of the sofa. At last, she held out her palm; a bottle top, a nail cutting, a fifty pence piece, three pennies and an amethyst earring. She pocketed the coppers, handed Scrapper the silver coin.

'Go down the shops, buy the girl a chop, or some sausages. Whatever Johnny Scrag got for the price.'

'But Mam—'

'Is no *but*. You said yourself how thin she is.'

Iwan's eyebrows twitched fury. 'And the earring?'

'Is twenty-two carats. Now I found it, pawn the pair.'

'You'll do no such thing – that's my gift to mark our tenth anniversary.'

'Is too late now to get sentimental, Iwan Simon Peter Jones.'

'They cost a month's bloody wages,' Iwan exploded.

'Is good for a tidy few bob, then. Strike ends, buy them back.'

Off she stalked to get dressed. Iwan glared after her, worn too ragged to try to jolly her along. He'd lost his *hwyl*. Since Orgreave.

'She don't mean it, Dad.'

'You reckon?'

Iwan's vest showed the muscles across his chest had softened, like clay heated too quickly. His skin was stripped of colour. Scrapper thought of Captain Hook, suddenly. But Captain Hook was further along the journey back to coal, surely?

'Are you sick, Dad?'

Iwan snorted. 'Sick an' tired.'

'What is it?'

'Suppose we hadn't come out on strike, son. Suppose I'd stuck to my guns, told Dewi Power and the lodge and Sheffield to get stuffed?'

'We had no choice,' Scrapper said. 'Once they start cutting jobs and closing pits, who knows where they'll stop.'

'So where's Heathfield's TUC? Where's Kinnock and the Labour Party? They've got plenty to say about picket-line violence, about why we should hold a bloody ballot. Nothing to say about working men losing their livelihoods, getting beaten by the police. Open your eyes, lad. It's a sell-out.'

'But there's thousands of people like us, who—'

'We came out on strike to look out for our own. But look at Red and your mam. Look at any of the lads' wives and kids. All of them cold and tired and hungry. Fact is, the only man caring for his own is Gwyn Pritchard.'

'*Caring for his own*?' Scrapper said. 'Caring for himself. All Captain Hook cares about is crushing the lodge and pocketing his pay-off. You saw what he did to Red.'

He couldn't let Iwan slide into despair. If they caved in now, Red and Angela would fold too. Everything rested on the pair of them holding their nerve. 'Gwyn Pritchard can rot in hell, Dad. We're gonna prove the bastard wrong.'

He turned to see Red standing in the door. He saw from her face that she had heard him.

3

Time was, Gwyn spent his evenings down the pub, sank seven or eight jars with his lads, felt all the better for it. But these days Steve Red Lion kept no welcome for a working miner. So he wound up drinking alone at The Mountain Ash – four pints down, strung tight as a winding rope. A disaster of a day, the pit deputies voting to strike. Bad news and too-cold beer weighed heavy on him. His chest whistled distress. By the time he sank his fifth pint, he felt ready to march down to The Red Lion, put that rabble from the lodge straight on a few points. Instead, a good hour before closing time, he set aside his drink and headed home.

A long walk from Bryn Tawel to Ystrad, all the longer for being sober, steel-capped boots lobbing stones at the road. He unlocked the front door, boots still on. The house was silent, but for the ticking grandfather clock. He double-locked the door, pulled up short in the living room. The room was dark but thick with heat, the fire burned low in the grate. In the dim glow, he saw a figure crouching on the floor.

He snapped on the lights. 'Why you sitting down there, in the dark?'

Carol wiped a hand over her face. Her skin was blotchy, eyes red. 'I had dinner ready hours ago,' she mumbled.

'You're crying over a missed dinner?'

'I wasn't crying.'

He grabbed the TV remote and sat down. 'Could've fooled me.'

Carol stayed where she was, huddled by the fireplace. He swallowed a sigh. Unnerving, this behaviour of hers. He looked at her again. She was bent over a card, a white horse on it, galloping through a field of poppies, the number thirty-five embossed in glitter. Shit.

'You thought I forgot,' he blustered. 'I never forget. Planned to take you out at the weekend. Planned to surprise you.'

'Nothing about you surprises me.'

'Well that's where you're wrong, woman. I booked us a table up the Harvesters.'

'We've wasted enough good food—'

'What you talking about, wasted?'

'Bought a ham, didn't I.'

'So? We'll eat it cold.'

She pulled a tissue from the sleeve of her cardigan, blew her nose. 'I chucked it over the fence. Max couldn't believe his luck.'

'You fed a ham to Eddie Hobson's stupid dachshund?'

She was lying. She had to be.

She flashed him a nasty smile. 'Had it all to himself. When there's families in this village near starving.'

'Nobody needs to starve,' he said. 'Everyone got a choice.'

He flicked from chat show to snooker. There was nothing worth watching. Carol was swaying from side to side now, bobbing in front of the screen.

'For God's sake, woman. Give it a rest.'

Her lips puckered as though tasting something bitter. 'You think it's enough, don't you?'

'What?'

'You think it's enough that I got a home, an' a husband making money.'

'It's more'n some people got.'

She made a sound half way between a laugh and a sob. 'Well, take my word for it. It's not enough. Not when my daughter's gone. When our neighbours turn their backs on me.'

'Carol—'

'Don't touch me. I've had it with you, Gwyn. I've had enough.' She pushed past him, grabbed her sleeping pills off the nest of tables and lurched up the stairs.

He turned back to the television, stared at it without seeing. They had an arrangement. It worked. She gave him two week's warning about her birthday; he got her a gift and a card. Had no one to blame but herself for this mess. It was her own stupid fault he forgot. The clock ticked, another hour passed. Sleep was nowhere to be had. The heat leached from the room. He switched off the television and padded up the stairs to find that she'd locked him out. He leaned against the doorframe, defeated. Time was, he'd have put his shoulder to the door. But even that felt beyond him. If his wife wouldn't sleep with him, to hell with her. In any case, those damn pills left her for dead.

The girl's room was as she left it. Posters pinned to the ceiling, knick-knacks scattered on her dressing table. A brush shedding long, red hairs. He rubbed his sleeve over the scuffed wooden surface to clear it of dust, sank down on the bed. Her pillow smelled of apple shampoo. He stretched out on the bed, but sleep wouldn't come. His belt buckle dug into his abdomen. He shifted his weight, unbuckled the belt.

The old man was wearing that belt the day he died. Gwyn dug out the corpse himself, brought the old man up to the top, the broken body already stiff and cold. Sorry old bastard. His earliest memory was of the old man filling the kitchen doorway, yelling seven shades of murder as he and his kid brother cowered under the table. Anything set the old man off. Trouble at work or trouble at home. One too many payday drinks or stony sober for want of a bob; the same outcome. Him or the kid feeling the business end of that belt. No wonder the kid left

Ystrad as soon as he could. Ran off to Manitoba, didn't once look back.

He wore the belt like an amulet, to remind himself what it meant to be powerless. A pledge that no one would make him powerless again. Yet he'd vowed never to raise the belt against the girl, broke that vow and now the girl was gone. Just like his brother. He sat up. There was no peace to be had here. He headed back downstairs, grabbed his jacket, stepped into his boots, shut the front door and set off down the hill.

* * *

He had no clue where to go. It was gone midnight, a star hanging solo in a sky gathering clouds. The High Street was deserted. He paused at the ice cream parlour. The curtained windows above the shop revealed no secrets. The girl was somewhere behind them. Was she sleeping like an innocent, or awake and tormented by regret like him?

If he raised his voice to call her, would she hear him? He shook himself. If he raised his voice, the whole village would come out to laugh and jeer. He moved on, cold air like a knife in his lungs. As he crossed the road, dizziness slammed him sideways. He staggered to the bus shelter, collapsed on the bench fighting for breath.

'Please, mister, you got two quid for a taxi?'

As his eyes adjusted to the gloom, he saw a pair of skinny legs, a stretch of naked thigh. An indecent skirt and a puffy jacket nipped tight at the waist. Hair like bleached pipe-cleaners. Safety pins for earrings. Black makeup smeared across sunken cheeks.

'Why you wanting a taxi?'

'I got to get to my mam's. Went an' missed the last bus.'

'So get your boyfriend to take you.'

'We 'ad a fight. Owes me money, 'e does. Actin' like it's my fault. Not my fault 'e's flat broke.'

'Why's he broke, then?'

The girl narrowed her eyes. 'You takin' the piss?'

'No, love. I'm genuinely interested.'

'How many miners are makin' money right now?'

'Ah. Blackthorn man, is he?'

The girl wiped her nose on the back of her hand. 'Please, mister. Lend us five quid to get off 'ome.'

Made him smile, that. She was after two quid a minute ago, and no mention of it being a loan.

'And what's in it for me?'

The girl falls quiet. 'Orright,' she said at last.

'Alright, what?'

'How much would you pay me to—?'

He gawped at her. He meant the question as a joke. She must be desperate, this girl. He shot her a sideways look. She was young, for all the muck on her face. Barely older than the girl. Unsettled him, that. The girl was nothing – nothing – like this drunken slut. It was a fair while since he'd had an offer, even so. Nothing doing with Carol. Not in months.

He leaned across and whispered.

'You'll give me 'ow much?'

'Five,' he repeated.

The girl staggered to her feet. 'You filthy old—'

He put a hand on her arm to silence her. 'Alright, ten.'

The girl scowled.

'Listen sweetheart,' he told her. 'Ten quid, you get home tonight with change left over for booze, or smack, or glue, or whatever it is you're on.'

'Twenty,' the girl said.

'Last offer: fifteen. Take it or leave it.'

The girl slumped against the wall. 'Money first.'

'Don't push your luck, missy.'

The street was silent. He peered up and down to check that no one was around. He thought of Iwan Jones and his family asleep across the road. To hell with them. To hell with them all. He slipped back into the shadows, stood in front of the girl, unzipped his flies.

'How about you gimme a kiss, then?'

The girl raised listless, lager-scented lips. That wouldn't do at all. He grabbed her shoulders and shook her. 'I said, kiss me. Properly.'

He prised his tongue inside her mouth, pushed her fingers inside his trousers. Her hand connected with a touch like ice. Far from hardening, he shrank away. That never happened. Not to him. He pushed the girl down onto her knees, thought back to when Carol was young and pretty and panting for it. But memory and imagination defied him too. He shoved the girl aside, zipped himself up. The shame of it. It took all his strength not to burst into tears.

He fumbled in his jacket pocket, thrust the money at her. The notes scattered limply on the ground.

— 4 —

Helen was trudging up the hill towards school when she heard footsteps behind her. Someone close and coming closer. She turned to see Ricky Allison and Seamus Hobson.

'What?'

'You up the duff yet, then?'

'You what?'

'Told you she was,' Seamus said.

'Piss off, the pair of you.'

She walked faster. The clear blue sky blackened, cast down bursts of sheeting rain. She had no umbrella, no parka to protect her. She broke into a trot, her shoes and blazer sodden, her hair plastered her cheeks. Her socks squeaked wetly with every step, the rain pelting her sideways.

'D'you reckon her tits got bigger?' Seamus chased after her, craned over her shoulder.

Ricky rammed her other shoulder. 'Nah, she got bee stings for tits.'

She broke into a trot, the boys racing after her, sniggering.

'Oi – Ricky Allison! What d'you think you're doing?' A battered blue car pulled up beside her. The two boys fell back.

'Nothing,' Ricky said, face puce.

'Don't look like nothing,' Sue's brown curls popped out of the driver's window. 'Reckon I should talk to Ricky's dad, Red?'

'We wasn't doing nothin', Auntie Susan.'

'Apologise, or I'm calling your dad, Ricky.'

'Sorry,' Ricky mumbled.

Sue nodded. 'Right. Scoot. Hop in, Red. I'll give you a lift.'

Ricky and Seamus scuttled up the hill without looking back. Helen climbed into the passenger seat, wet clothes squelching dry plastic. The back seat of the Anglia was piled with boxes of printed pamphlets.

'Cheeky little buggers,' Sue said.

'They're a pain.'

'Well, that pain's my cousin's lad. Don't stand for any nonsense.'

'I'd never have guessed.'

'Here—' Sue reached onto the back seat and handed her a towel. 'We'll stop off at mine, I'll lend you a jacket.'

'You don't have to.'

'It's no bother,' Sue said. 'Me an' Gramps live across from the school.'

She fired up the engine and they set off up the hill. But as the car turned a corner, they hit traffic. The car rattled to a halt. Sue cursed under her breath. The streaking rain blurred the vehicles up ahead. Blue lights showed a police car blocking the road. A uniformed officer stood over the crushed wheels of a motorbike, held an umbrella over the body of a man in leathers.

'Looks nasty,' Sue said.

She flicked on the radio. Hi-NRG music faded into pips for the news. The announcer was breathless.

'*Prime Minister Margaret Thatcher has escaped unhurt after a massive blast ripped through Brighton's Grand Hotel in the early hours of this morning—*'

'Bloody hell!' Sue and Helen spoke together.

'*—At least two people are confirmed dead in a suspected bomb blast. Scores of others have been injured. Despite the attack, the prime minister is expected to address the Conservative Party Conference later this morning—*'

Helen grabbed Sue's arm. 'You don't think— it wasn't us?'

'Good God, no,' Sue said. 'It's terrorism, this, *bach*.'

'Who, then?'

'Provos, maybe. Argies. Reckon they'll know soon enough.'

'What's a Provo?'

Sue explained the Irish Question. They listened to the news. The traffic did not move. Finally, an ambulance bellowed past, pulled up next to the motorbike. Men in green scooped the motorcyclist onto a stretcher. The ambulance bore him away in a glare of lights and blare of sirens. At last, the traffic began to edge up the hill.

Sue drove a block past the school and turned into a terraced street. 'Come on in.'

The hall was dark and scruffy and smelled of Germolene and burnt toast.

'Susan? Su-u-uuuusaaaaaan!'

'Coming, Gramps,' Sue called.

She led Helen through the hall, past the front room and down a ramp, through a door that opened into a large kitchen. A bay window flooded watery light. One side of the room wrapped around stove, sink and kitchen units. The other stretched around a bay window and a wide hearth. Two scuffed velour sofas flopped next to the fireplace, around a vast coffee table piled with papers, pamphlets and magazines.

'Sit yourself here and warm up,' Sue tipped coal onto the grate.

Helen peeled off her blazer and sweater and draped them over the clothes horse next to the hearth, slid her shoes near the grate, jumped as the door burst open. A wheelchair bowled down the ramp at speed. In it sat a hunched old man. Sue grabbed hold of the chair, stopped it before it hit the stove. The man's arms and shoulders were wiry, but he had stumps for legs, pyjama bottoms folded under his thighs.

Helen knew Johnny Griffiths by sight. He had lost his legs to the pit. A miracle that he survived his injuries, people said. Her dad reckoned it was pure cussedness pulled the old boy through.

'Turn the radio on, girlie,' the old man said. 'You won't believe what's happened.'

Sue kissed his forehead. 'We just heard,' she said. 'Gramps, this is Helen, Scrapper's wife.'

The old man shot her a gummy smile. 'Orright, love?'

Looking at him made Helen feel shy. Johnny Griffiths had been a strapping collier in his day. Now his body was a dried-out shell. She had seen him out and about with Debbie Power, Debbie in her uniform, wheeling the old boy around the shops. It unsettled her. Debbie, tall and strong and vital, chattering like a parakeet to a broken husk of a man. But Johnny didn't look broken, up close. The thin light revealed a lively, sinewy face, brown eyes glittering with curiosity.

'They've made a right bloody hash of it, the Provos, eh, girls?'

Sue tutted at him and went to fix the tea.

'They'll be busy with their enquiries, the police,' Johnny continued. 'Fifty million of us wanted shot of the old coot.' He wheeled his chair closer to the fireplace. 'You a fan o' Mrs T, girlie?'

'Course not,' Helen said.

'Atta girl,' he grinned. 'Not like your old dad, then.'

Sue set the teapot down. 'Don't let him wind you up, Red.'

Johnny held Helen's gaze. 'He changed, your dad,' he said. 'Changed after he carried your granddad out of the pit. Eats away at a man, a thing like that. Forces him to make tough choices. Sometimes, a man chooses wrong. You follow, girlie?'

Helen nodded.

'See death, everything's different,' Johnny said. 'I lay trapped there for hours, the only man to make it out of that seam alive. I lay there in the dark, your granddad dead beside me, swore if ever I made it out, I'd fight to make life better for our boys.

When your dad got to us, he knelt in the dark, cursed the pit and the village and the coal business. Swore nothing would matter from then on. Nothing but himself and his own.'

She felt a lump in her throat that hot tea wouldn't shift. She saw it. Her dad's terror and fury. Darkness with its leeching grip.

She wiped her eyes angrily. 'There's people will never forgive my dad.'

Johnny grabbed her hand. His grip was strong, despite the clubbed nails and liver spots. Hands like shovels.

'You're not to blame for the sins of your father, girlie. He made his choice. You'll make yours.'

'You reckon?'

'I knows it, *bach*.'

Low sunlight filled the surgery windows, lighting up the hairs that framed Dr O'Connell's pate and sprouted from his ear lobes and nostrils. The little doctor peered at Gwyn over his spectacles, tucked away his stethoscope and scribbled into his notepad.

'And you say you've never collapsed before?'

'Collapsed? Well, no—'

'Any dizzy spells?'

Gwyn hesitated, struggled to a sitting position, started to button up his shirt. It had scared him silly, the blackout. One minute, giving Alun Wet-Ears a dressing-down about his shoddy attempt to sweep out the wheelhouse, the next sparked out cold on the floor. Woke to find his workmates gathered round. At his feet, Alun Wet-Ears, pale and twitching like a rabbit. Albright on the wheelhouse phone, calling an ambulance.

At his side, Matthew Cut-Price, bucket of water in his hand, a nasty gleam in his eye. 'He'd have woke a damn sight quicker if you'd let me splash him, Mister Albright.'

An ambulance ride to the hospital in Bryn Tawel, came over woozy in the waiting room. A rainbow of coloured uniforms. Men in green. Men in white. Girls in pink and yellow and pastel blue. Small hands touching him. Perfume masking the jagged smell of antiseptic.

'Brought 'im up from Blackthorn,' the paramedic said.

'Another miner?'

'Mus' be. Jus' look at that hand.'

'That's six this week.'

'A disgrace, coppers beating a working man for defending 'is livelihood.'

Gwyn raised his head. 'Not police – not on strike – working miner – proud of it.'

The nurses busied themselves with other patients, left him to sleep it off. Later, Carol sat by his bedside. Then came more white coats and questions and tests and chest x-rays. He ended up sedated, kept in overnight. For observation, the consultant said. He found out next morning that Carol had made a pest of herself, ringing the duty desk all night. They sent him home after lunch, under strict orders to rest.

'Dizzy spells,' Dr O'Connell repeated. 'Have you had any? It's important, Gwyn.'

'One or two.'

'And you've had that bronchial cough a couple of years now.'

Gwyn shrugged.

'Gwyn, you remember what we discussed about your smoking?'

Got him riled, that. A man deserved a few small pleasures. A smoke or two couldn't hurt. Not with his lungs already shot to pieces.

'Aye, well. That was before the strike. It's been a tough few months.'

A muscle flickered in Dr O'Connell's cheek. His Adam's apple bobbed and ducked. Working up to bad news, the doctor.

'Spit it out, doc.'

'Progressive massive fibrosis. The x-rays show a dark mass across your upper lung. Shortness of breath and a chronic cough is just the start of it.'

The words washed over Gwyn. 'It's black lung?'

'The tests indicate an increase in blood pressure in the pulmonary circuit. That explains the dizziness, fainting spells, breathlessness. Your lungs are seizing up, Gwyn. Heavy physical labour and stress will only make things worse.'

'But you'll fix it. Give me pills or something.'

Dr O'Connell took off his spectacles, rubbed them on his lapel. 'Nothing can fix PMF,' he said at last. 'The best we can do is ease the symptoms. That means no more physical labour, no more exposure to stress. We'll sign you off work for starters.'

Gwyn staggered to his feet. 'No you bloody won't.'

Obvious what the tests would find, of course. Every miner knew the signs. First, the fighting for breath, the cough that would not shift. Skin tinged blue beneath the fingernails, colour spreading to lips then the whites of the eyes. After that – silently, invisibly – your innards swelled and failed.

The coal dust, come to claim him.

'How long do I have?'

'There's no point guessing. We must focus on easing your symptoms. You need to rest.'

'Is it months?' Gwyn persisted. 'Weeks?'

Dr O'Connell straightened his notes, cleared his throat. The low autumn sunlight melted into a bank of cloud.

— 6 —

Come December, Helen sensed something amiss, couldn't remember having had a period. She and Scrapper had decided not to try for a baby straight away. Not that she didn't want to start a family, but they were young, their lives crammed to bursting with what-ifs, and what point rushing into things? They had plenty of time, they agreed.

Angela was less than impressed when they told her.

'Listen, Mam, we're not having a babby so the family can claim seven quid a week extra off the social,' Scrapper snapped.

Angela stopped talking about grandchildren after that. She marched Helen down to the surgery, had Dr O'Connell talk to her about contraception. The village doctor refused Helen the pill. Not with the Pritchard family history of high blood pressure and heart disease, he said. Not with her being so young. It was news to Helen that she had a family medical history. She'd assumed it was the pit, mostly, that did for Pritchards. But he was adamant, Dr O'Connell. Offered her a choice: condoms or the cap.

Angela, tight-lipped, said there was no more money for condoms.

Dr O'Connell peered, mole-like, over his spectacles. 'Ah, yes. And since the strike, we've run out of free supplies.'

The discussion was closed. Helen left the surgery with a little rubber bowl in a little plastic case and a large tube of spermicide. Hellish fiddly, all that faffing around with case and cream. Six months married, half the time they forgot to bother with it all. And now her breasts were sore and tender. She said nothing to Scrapper, dithered and hoped and prayed for blood.

Finally, she dropped by the surgery after school.

'You'll be keeping it, of course.' Dr O'Connell busied himself with pen and notepad.

Of course? There was no of course, with the men out eight long months and with the *bracchi* on its knees. She left the surgery on shaky legs, sank down on the bench outside. Fallen leaves swirled around her feet. The wind whipped her hair into her eyes. Lucky for her, the village was empty. After a while, she gathered strength enough to stand. She zipped her parka, trudged up the High Street, paused outside the *bracchi*. She was tempted for a moment to keep walking up the hill, to pocket her pride and run to her mam and beg her to tell her what to do. Instead, she went up to the flat, pondering how to break the news to her in-laws. She found them in the kitchen, Angela, Iwan and Scrapper, wearing extra sweaters against the cold, hands clamped around their mugs of tea.

'Where you been, Red?' Scrapper sounded tetchy.

'I—'

'Never mind,' Angela said. 'She's here now. All of us are here.'

'What's going on?'

'Is family meeting.'

When Angela called a family summit, it meant Iwan or Scrapper had displeased her. Now was not the time to speak up. Helen sat next to Scrapper, waited for Angela to begin.

Spots of colour mottled her mam-in-law's cheeks. 'I'm closing the business.'

Iwan's hands tightened around his mug. 'Don't be daft, Angie.'

'Daft?' Angela echoed. 'Two paying customers last week. Two. No one buying ice cream. No one drinking coffee. Is no money for gas, for electric. Got suppliers banging on the door with their bills. And now Christmas coming.'

'Must be something we can do,' Scrapper said. 'Something short of closing.'

'Is costing money to stay open. Money we do not have.'

'But how much do we owe?' Helen asked.

'Well,' Iwan counted on his fingers. 'We're three months behind with the rates and the electric, two months behind payments for the chest freezer on the never-never. Got the phone bill outstanding for the quarter. We're looking at seven hundred quid.'

'Is like we are criminals,' Angela said. 'Never owed debt to no one.'

A shocked silence followed.

'There's no point giving up yet,' Iwan said at last. 'By all means close for winter. We'll give it another go, come the spring.'

'*Come the spring?*' Angela said. 'Short of a fucking miracle, Iwan Simon Peter Jones, is what will be different, come the spring?'

Iwan and Scrapper flinched. Helen felt in her pocket, squeezed the lump of anthracite for reassurance. No one knew what to say.

A knock on the door broke the deadlock. A voice called up a greeting, then heavy footsteps tramped up the stairs. At last, Dewi Power appeared on the landing, breathing heavily.

Angela folded her lips into a man-stopping smile. 'And now this handsome face to complete our evening. Cuppa tea, Dewi Power?'

The little union boss doffed his cap, flustered. 'Don't you go to no bother, Angie,' he said. 'Something came up. Need to talk it over with Iwan.'

'Nonsense,' Angela fired up the kettle. 'Sit.'

Iwan hefted a sigh. 'Whatever it is, spit it out. There's no bloody secrets in this house.'

Helen's stomach knotted, unknotted. But no one noticed her discomfort. They were waiting to hear what Dewi had to say.

'Sheffield just called,' he said. 'Coal Board's offering a bonus. A lump sum to every man who goes back before Christmas.'

'How much?' Angela said.

'Couple o' hundred apiece, the convenor reckoned.'

'Bastards,' Iwan breathed.

Angela leaned against the work-top, gaze fixed on Dewi's face. The kettle boiled, but she ignored it. Helen turned off the heat and fixed Dewi a mug of tea, added milk, found barely a teaspoon of sugar in the caddy. She swallowed a sigh, tipped the last of the week's ration into the mug.

'A lot of lads could use that kind of money,' Scrapper said.

Dewi took for his tea, nodded his thanks. 'Question is, how many will crack?'

'I reckon the boys are solid,' Scrapper said.

'We thought Matt and Alun were rock solid six months ago,' Iwan said.

Dewi hunched in his seat as though he carried the weight of the coalfield on his shoulders.

'Dewi reckons someone'll crack,' Helen said quietly.

He looked at her, surprised. Held up his hands. 'It's our Debbie's lad.'

'Dai? Be serious,' Scrapper said.

Dewi shook his head. 'I would've said the same, an' all. But our Debbie's up the duff.'

Scrapper let out a long, low whistle.

'Congratulations, Dewi,' Angela said.

Iwan clapped him on the shoulders. 'Your first great niece or nephew, eh?'

But to Helen's ears, the good wishes sounded forced.

'They told us last week,' Dewi said. 'Dai stayed back, wanted a quiet word. Said they're badly behind wi' the rent.'

'All the same,' Iwan said. 'He's sound as a pound, Dai Dumbells. Body of a bull, heart of a lion—'

'Head of a mule. Like the rest of you,' Angela snapped.

Dewi burst out laughing. Slapped the table. Stopped when he realised no one was laughing with him. 'Angie?'

She waved a dismissive hand.

'She's joking. Aren't you, Mam?' Scrapper said tightly.

Iwan's eyes hardened. Angela had pushed him too far now, Helen could tell. He wanted Dewi out of the way, and fast.

'Let's call the lads down the Stute,' Iwan said. 'It's best they hear it from the lodge. That way, we see their reaction. See who might be tempted.'

Dewi bolted his tea. 'I'll go spread the word.'

As soon as the back door closed, Iwan turned on Angela. 'The answer's no. Forget it.'

'Is a couple of hundred quid each.'

'Mam!' Scrapper was outraged.

'No,' Iwan repeated.

'Not for a couple of million,' Scrapper said.

Iwan turned to him. 'Between me and your mam, this.'

'No, isn't. Not when it's about selling out the bloody strike, Dad,' Scrapper picked up his mug and hurled it across the kitchen.

The mug crashed into the wall above the stove, shattered into a dozen jagged shards. Helen flinched. She had never seen this side to Scrapper, this white-hot fury.

She put a hand on his arm. 'Let's go next door, Scrap.'

He swatted her away. 'We don't sell out our pit, our butties, our community. Not for any price.'

He never snapped at her before. Had never raised his voice, not in twelve months courting. She went to the stove, gathered the broken crockery, unsure, suddenly, where she stood.

'Is not about you, Simon Jones,' Angela said.

'Yes, but Mam—'

'You heard your wife, Simon,' Iwan said. 'Scram.'

Scrapper stormed out of the kitchen, slammed the living room door behind him.

* * *

He stood at the window, slumped against the frame, gazing through the curtains at the street, Helen moulded her body against his, leaned her cheek against his shoulder blade. Slipped her arms around his waist. The tighter she held on, the more scared and alone she felt.

'Sorry, Red,' he said at last. 'Shouldn't have blown a gasket by there.'

'I'm pregnant and all, Scrap.'

His body stiffened. He pulled away, eyes the colour of ash. 'Oh God, Red. No.'

'I'm sorry.'

The word hovered between them. Helen sank down on the sofa.

'Sorry?' he said at last. 'After all, it takes two.'

'What should we do?'

He perched next to her, didn't touch her. 'Are we ready to do this?'

'No.'

'D'you want to get rid of it?'

'No. Maybe? I don't know.'

'How far gone are you?'

'Five weeks, the doctor reckoned.'

'We got time, then. To think it over.'

The argument continued in the kitchen. Iwan's voice was low, insistent. Helen knew she had chosen the worst of times to deliver this news.

'You're not to tell them, Scrap. Not today.'

'Damn right. You know what Mam's like. We'll decide first, tell 'em after. Agreed?'

'Agreed,' she breathed.

The argument became louder, more heated. Angela was yelling now. Then a loud crack rang out, the sound of flesh striking flesh. The yelling stopped.

'C'mon,' Scrapper pulled Helen to her feet. 'Let's go.'

'But Scrap, shouldn't we—?'

'It's not dad did the hitting, *bach*.'

7

Winter loomed. The trees shed their leaves as though laying them down in surrender. Scrapper threw himself into picketing. Whatever he and Red decided, everything had a new urgency. Come rain or sun or bawling gale, he stood on the line with his pamphlets and his placards and stoked the brazier higher and gave it some *hwyl*. But nothing stopped Albright and Captain Hook and his two one-time butties speeding through. Albright gave up driving when the flying pickets showed up. He hired a scab driver and a scab minibus to fetch the four of them to and from work. Albright cared more about the state of his car than for the livelihoods of his men or the future of his pit.

It was scant consolation that no one joined Matt and Alun in the back of that bus. All the same, Scrapper found himself counting the lads in as they gathered every morning before dawn. And that's how, one wet Friday, he spotted that Dai was missing.

'We'd best go round,' he told Iwan.

Dai and Debbie's two up, two down was scruffier than ever, the pavement and doorstep smeared with mud. A cobweb covered the front window, a tiny spider twirling in the breeze.

Scrapper had overheard the women teasing Debbie about her poor housekeeping.

'So,' Debbie snapped. 'How I keep a fella happy got nothing to do with housework.'

Debbie was away, off raising funds in the West Country with Sue. All the same, Scrapper felt a jolt of fear when no one answered his knock.

The door was unlocked. 'Dai, you home?'

They found Dai slumped in his armchair, his bulk almost dwarfed by the outsized flowers that danced across the living room walls, two empty bottles of Thunderbird chucked on the floor. Dai was snoring like a tractor. Scrapper put a hand on his arm, shook him awake.

'Huh? Gabe?'

'It's us, you daft sod,' Iwan said. 'High time you eased up on the liquor.'

Dai squinted up at them, cheeks flushed purple. Bits of paper were scattered all around him. Unopened brown envelopes; unpaid bills. He gathered up the papers and shoved them under the cushion.

'How much?' Scrapper said.

Dai shot him a look as prickly as his chin. 'Dunno what you mean,' he answered, his voice a little too slurred, the better to dodge the question.

'We're strapped for cash too,' Iwan said. 'How bad's it got, butty?'

Dai's fist landed heavy on the cushion. He didn't speak.

'We're short at least seven hundred,' Scrapper tried to lighten the mood. 'C'mon butty, bet you can't top that.'

Dai raised a dark eyebrow. When he spoke, his voice was clear. 'At least you own your fucking home. At least you got a roof above your women's heads.'

But for how long. Scrapper shuddered. 'Bank on your tail again?'

'Landlord,' Dai said. 'He's given us a fortnight to stump up five months' rent or out on our ears.'

What could Scrapper say? There was nothing he could do to ease the pressure on Dai. None of them could. All of them had gone month after month without a wage packet and no end in sight.

'What does Debbie say?' he said at last.

Dai shrugged. 'Fuck the landlord, an' fuck the banks, she said. Gone off giving speeches when the world's caving in on us. As helpful as a rubber chainsaw, my missus.'

Scrapper laughed, saw the look on Dai's face, stopped.

Iwan grabbed Dai by the shoulders, shook him lightly. 'You're not considering the Christmas bribe?'

Scrapper braced himself for rage, for indignation. Dai said nothing. There was a long, awkward silence.

The tension was shattered by a racket in the street outside. He heard the growl of an engine, shouts and then a short, sharp scream.

* * *

Mary Power lay in the road next to the lodge minibus, bags of groceries scattered around her. Scrapper ran out in time to see a van clear the corner at speed, tyres screeching on the tarmac. He caught a flash of white panelling before it vanished. He ran over to Mary. She was struggling to get up, her face blank with shock.

'Did the bastards hit you?'

Mary shook her head. 'I tripped. They tried to scare me, is all.

'Scare you – but who?' Iwan demanded.

'Buggered if I know,' Mary's voice was unsteady. 'They drove right at me, yelling, *die, commie bitch*.'

'Must be NF,' Iwan said.

'Nazis, squaddies, off-duty coppers, same difference,' Mary said.

Scrapper gathered the scattered groceries, followed Iwan and Mary back to safety on the pavement. Dai stood framed in his front door, a hand on each wall to steady himself.

'Scumbags,' he said. 'They come at us with truncheons. They starve us and beat us and lie to us. Now they're attacking our women. Reckon the fucking Provos had a point.'

'You don't mean that,' Iwan said.

'You reckon,' Dai's face was dark with fury. 'An eye for an eye. It's what that Tory bitch believes.'

'We'll not stoop to her level, love,' Mary said.

'Stoop to her level? She won't stop – the bosses won't stop. Not until they finished us off. Like they finished off poor Gabe.' Dai lurched back indoors, slamming the door behind him.

'I told you not to worry about Dai, Dad,' Scrapper said. 'He's solid. He'll never scab.'

Iwan and Mary exchanged a look.

'He's taken Gabe's death way too much to heart,' Iwan said.

'Debbie's struggling with him,' Mary said. 'Says he's forever finding fault with her. Small wonder she's gone off fundraising, when she's having it tough at home. But she needs to keep an eye on that one. We all do.'

* * *

Scrapper insisted they drove Mary down to the Stute. She was too shaken to get back behind the wheel. By the time they got home, dusk was bedding in. Rain drifted sideways. At the top of the High Street, the *bracchi* was ablaze with light. Angela stood at the window, arms folded. On seeing them, she burst out into the street, a flurry of hands and bosom and hair. 'Is Helen not with you?'

He shook his head. 'We've been down the Stute. Mary Power got attacked.'

'Is why I'm bloody worried. Madmen driving round and the girl not home from school.'

Ice crackled the length of Scrapper's spine. Where could Red be? He looked up and down the road, expecting to see her walk towards him. But the street was empty, the silence broken only by the hiss of rain on slate roofs. It was tea-time. If Red hadn't phoned, something must be very wrong; something to do with the baby, or with the thugs in the white van.

'Wait by the phone, Mam. Dad, go back down the Stute, ask the women if they seen Red. I'll try the school.'

He set off up the hill. The skies split open, rods of rain soaking his jacket. He scaled the school gates and jogged around the building but the doors were locked, classrooms dark and empty. He headed back to the High Street. The shops would be shut and shuttered. Even the doctor's surgery would be closed. A thought struck him. Should he take the bus to Bryn Tawel, ask for Red at the hospital? He shook himself; no point panicking. Not yet. Not before he'd tried everywhere else first.

The Co-op was open. He peeked through the window. A figure was walking towards the cashier, wire basket piled with cans of beer. It was Matthew Price. Their eyes met. Matt shot him a half-arsed smile; less a smile than a smirk. Rage hurled Scrapper into the shop. He grabbed Matt, shoved him backwards.

'Attacking women now, are you?'

He slammed Matt against a shelf. Cartons of breakfast cereal, powdered desserts and instant mash crashed onto the floor. Then Iwan was there, pulling him away. The checkout girls huddled in a corner, hands raised to shocked mouths.

Iwan turned to Matt. 'Bunch of blokes went for Mary Power. Know anything about that?'

Matt shook his head. His bleach-blond hair had grown out, half an inch of black roots matching the bags beneath his eyes.

'We can't believe a word this lying toe-rag says,' Scrapper burst out.

'You seen our Helen today?'

'No,' Matt said.

Iwan shoved Scrapper towards the door. 'We'd best keep looking.'

Scrapper was still fired up to give Matt a smack. But he knew Iwan was right; the thugs in the van were out there somewhere. They had to find Red, and fast. The rain had stopped. Across the road, Johnny Scrag was loading his van with trays of unsold meat.

'She went by about an hour ago,' Johnny said. 'You tried Siggy's? I'm sure I heard a woman's voice by—'

Scrapper rushed to the hairdresser's, burst in, the doorbell clanging protest. Siggy was bending over a customer, his back turned to the street. He snapped upright.

'Have you seen—?' Scrapper broke off, thrown by the sight that greeted him.

Siggy looked him up and down, stepped aside with a flourish. 'And here he is, your gorgeous husband.'

Helen sat in the slouchy leather swivel chair, waist-length curls sheared into a glossy, chin-length bob. Scrapper glared at her, relieved and wrong-footed and annoyed.

'You like?' Siggy purred.

'What in hell's going on, Red?'

'I got my hair cut—'

'Bloody obvious you got your hair cut,' his voice was harsh with relief. 'But why not tell Mam where you were? Why waste money we haven't got on getting your hair fixed?'

'A woman's beauty is not a waste. Not ever,' Siggy said, affronted.

Helen smiled up at him. 'Siggy bought my hair, Scrap. I've earned us five quid. Enough to buy a Sunday roast.'

'Siggy did *what*?' Iwan's face turned pale with shock.

Siggy held up a long red plait and stroked it. 'My friend is making hairpieces for theatre. Rare to find hair this beautiful.'

The shame of it. 'Red, how could you sell your hair?' Scrapper demanded.

Hurt chased confusion across her face. 'I wanted to treat us to a roast dinner. I wanted to cook for you, just this once.'

'That's a lovely thought, *bach*,' Iwan said. 'But you shouldn't have. It's not like it's a special occasion.'

Scrapper frowned at her in warning.

'We don't need no occasion,' she murmured.

Siggy fussed around, chasing stray hairs from her face and neck with an outsized brush.

'*So schön*,' he said. 'Maybe you can model for me, test some new styles?'

'What, me?' Red blushed.

'Of course you,' he handed her a five-pound note and kissed her on both cheeks. 'These two could not carry it off, I think.'

They crossed the road to Johnny Scrag's van, where Iwan picked out a shoulder of lamb.

Scrapper pulled Red aside. 'We agreed, didn't we? Not one word. Not 'til we decided.'

'We agreed.'

She paid the butcher, tucked the parcel under her arm. Scrapper hung back, watched her walk up the street, her hair the only spark of light and colour against the monochrome landscape. It called to mind the old days, when she first caught his eye. When everything he did was to try to impress her. When he wasn't broke and exhausted and worried.

Angela was waiting, face pressed up against the *bracchi* window. She rushed out, threw her arms around Red, pulled back, shocked.

'Is what, this hair? Look just like that Debbie Power.'

Red flinched.

Iwan handed Angela the parcel of meat. 'The girl swapped it. For this.'

Angela eyed the meat, then Helen. 'Is some kind of barter deal? This whole bloody country gone back to Dark Ages.'

* * *

That night, Scrapper lay in bed, belly full, for once, skin slick with heat. But the feast had brought him no peace.

'Red?'

'What?'

'We can't do it. It's no world for a child, this.'

'We can try, Scrap. I'll do my bit, you'll see.'

Knowing that was what troubled him most. 'Red?'

'What?'

'Maybe it's time you went home.'

'What?'

'I got no right to keep you hungry. To risk the roof over your head. I got no right to be a dad if I can't support my wife and kid—'

She sat bolt upright. 'Scrapper Jones!'

He couldn't look at her. 'What choice we got, *bach*? Got nothing to live on. Scares me stupid, to think of the alternative.'

'What alternative?'

'Don't you get it?' he burst out. 'I'm not a man if I can't feed and provide for my wife and babby and lower than a beast if I go crawling back.'

8

Helen stood outside the Stute, shaky from cold, stomach in knots. It felt like crossing enemy lines every time she walked in there. Some of the men and women in the Stute still saw her as the scab's girl, would never change their minds. It made her uneasy, too, to be courting the women who stonewalled her mam in the Co-op. Whose kids scribbled graffiti about the Pritchards in the alleyways and in the toilets at school. But she had no choice. She had a solid reason, now, to help the women. Help them she would.

She took a breath, squeezed the lump of anthracite in her pocket and went inside. Chatter and the rattle of cutlery bounced off the rafters. Half a dozen women were unfolding trestle tables and setting places for supper. Others were shaking out snagged bunting and knotted tinsel. Chrissie Hobnob smiled, waved Helen over to the kitchen.

Steam pillowed through the serving hatch. Mary Power stood at the stove, face pink, hair net restraining her dandelion curls. She raised her ladle in greeting.

'Orright, *bach*?' she said. 'Come to give us a hand again, eh?'

Helen nodded.

'Excellent. Let's start you off by here.'

'Christmas decorations, already?' she asked.

'Why not?' Mary said. 'It'll be here soon enough. We're makin' *cawl* for tea today. Butcher donated a huge bag o' bones. Nothing more festive'n a bowl o' hot soup.'

'So where d'you want me?'

Shirley, the vicar's wife sat at the kitchen table, knife in hand, in front of her a hillock of unpeeled carrots, turnips and potatoes. She handed Helen a peeler.

'You can help with this little lot for starters.'

Helen swallowed a sigh and set to work on the vegetables.

The vicar's wife was staring at her. 'So what do Iwan and Simon think about the Coal Board's Christmas incentives?'

'The bribes?' Helen said.

'Atta girl,' Mary grinned. 'Always best to call a spade a bloody shovel.'

'Just wondered who'll fall for it,' Shirley said.

'Buck up, Shirl,' Mary said. 'The lads stuck it out this long.'

At rest, Mary's face was weary, her eyes sunken and shadowed. But when she smiled, she buzzed energy and strength. Helen felt a rush of warmth for the union boss's wife. Of course the lads would stick it out. They had to. If they fell short, God help them. Mary and her troops would hold them to account.

Shirley was waiting for an answer. 'Ice cream parlour's not open much, lately. Everything alright at home, Helen?'

The glint in her eye said the question carried more than its weight.

'We're fine,' Helen said. 'And to answer your other question, they're solid behind the strike, my in-laws. And if it's what you're really asking, so am I.'

Shirley's grey lips tightened. 'I didn't mean— I just wondered how Angela would manage without her business. What with the language problem—'

The doors burst open. Debbie and Sue staggered in, arms around bulging bin bags. Helen went to help, but Debbie dodged her, dumped her bags on a banquette.

'There's two dozen bags in the car,' she announced.

'Oh great,' Mary said. 'Bloody jumble day tomorrow. I clean forgot.'

'Orright, Red,' Sue said. 'Got you slaving away, have they?'

Debbie's smile glinted daggers. 'Her ladyship's honouring us with her company, is she?'

'Lay off, Debs,' Sue said.

* * *

In the time it took the women to unload Sue's car, set chairs, plates and cutlery for a hundred people and deck the Stute with dusty bunting, Helen barely dented her mound of vegetables. Sue mixed oat crumble topping, scattered it over half a dozen trays of defrosted gooseberries and hefted the first batch into the oven, then grabbed a knife and sat down next to her.

'A waste to peel carrots and potatoes,' Sue grumped. 'All the vitamins are under the skin. At Greenham, we scrubbed them and ate them whole.'

'Well we're not at Greenham now,' Shirley picked up a strip of potato peel and held it to the light. 'Can you please peel more thinly, Helen.'

She picked up the bucket of scraps and went to empty it.

Sue twitched an eyebrow. 'Who put Amazing-bloody-Grace in charge?'

'We're not at Greenham now, Missy,' Helen mocked. 'We'll have none of your fancy-pants ideas round here.'

Sue laughed. 'D'you reckon you'll leave Wales one day, go see the world?'

The question caught Helen by surprise. 'Depends what happens, I suppose. Scrapper's job and the *bracchi* are here.'

'If you had the choice?'

Helen sighed. 'I'd like to see the world. I've never even been to England. But—'

But where did choice come into it? Where else could she raise a child? There was no one to help if they left, but work was hard to find if they stayed, especially if jobs went at the pit. Could she trust Sue, confide in her? Sue would listen and consider, not scold her and wring her hands like her mam or tell her what to do like Angela. But Sue was up and off again, gathering vegetable peel, stirring the *cawl*, sharing a joke with Mary, and the moment was lost.

9

Another visit to Dr O'Connell brought Gwyn no better news.

'The results are clear; there's no point running any more tests,' the doctor said.

He started on at Gwyn about why he should sign off work, why he needed to talk to Carol. The final straw, that. Why add to his wife's worries, with Carol already in bits about the treachery of the girl. Gwyn made his excuses and left. Outside, the cold air brought on another dizzy turn. He leaned against the gate post to gather breath, continued up the hill on shaking legs. The weather had turned, air heavy with the scent of rain, the sky buckling under clouds as menacing as the x-ray shadows on his lungs.

The wind gathered force as he reached the High Street. It seized the For Sale hoardings and tugged at the plywood nailed over derelict shop fronts. The din made him think of marching footsteps. But there was no one buying at the *bracchi* or the butchers. No one upturning the odds in the bookies, or getting the hairdresser to gild where nature fell short. A deathly hush on the funeral parlour. Unisex fashion fallen out of style, Betty's shop closed, the For Sale board hidden by fly posters' *Coal Not Dole* defiance.

Light spilled from the *bracchi* onto the pavement. No customers supped coffee and cake and ice cream. The chairs were stacked on empty tables. Angela Two-Scoops sat alone in the corner, a ledger and a pile of papers in front of her. Her hair hung midnight loose, slim legs crossed at the ankle. One hell of a woman. A lucky bastard, Iwan Jones. Gwyn hefted himself up the steps, collapsed into the seat opposite her.

She looked up, startled. 'What you after, Gwyn Pritchard?'

'Can't a fella pass time of day with a neighbour?'

'Neighbour, is it?' A smile served with a sliver of ice.

He opened his mouth to answer, but a fit of coughing bent him double. She fetched a glass of water, set it down, stood over him, hands on hips.

'Is terrible you look.'

'I been better.'

'You sick?'

'Course not. I'm right as rubies.'

'You here to see Helen?'

How tempting to say yes. Could it really be that simple? Six little words: *I want to see my daughter*. Could it really be that hard? Say it, and get to see her, give the girl a chance to right her wrongs. Time was running out for the girl to apologise.

'What if I did?'

'Try the Stute. Is where you'll find her most evenings. With that lot from Women Against Pit Closures.'

'Not a fan?'

Her face told him the answer. Interesting. It wasn't all happy families, then. Comeuppance for the Jones boys, for poisoning the girl's mind and dragging her into this sorry mess. And now the cracks were showing.

'Is none of your business.'

Angela picked up her papers, stuffed them into the ledger. Official-looking, the papers. Several printed in red ink. 'Had it tough these last months, eh, Angie?'

'Not as tough as some.'

'Aye, but you never signed up for this, did you? One thing to have your menfolk on strike. A whole other to have your business hit the skids.'

'Sooner they win, sooner we get back in shape.'

She'd told herself that for months, he reckoned. She might even have fooled her son and her husband. But Angela was a businesswoman from her eyelashes to those dainty ankles. A tough woman and loyal, but not stupid. No more likely to trail the pack than he was.

'We're not like the rest, you and me. We see the bigger picture, don't we? Got the kids to think of. They're married now. Soon enough, they'll start a family. Then what? Bring a babby into this world to starve?'

'No one starves under my roof.'

'And if the *bracchi* goes bust?'

Angela strode to the door, yanked it open. 'Is time you left, Gwyn Pritchard.'

He tried to stand but his legs defied his orders. Angela yanked the door a second time. Spots of colour marked her cheeks, black eyes sparked fury.

'You think I don't love the girl an' you're wrong,' he told her. 'I loved that girl like you love your son. If she'd let me, I'd have stopped at nothing to look out for her.'

Angela looked away. 'Sell the rest of us down the river?'

His legs recovered power of movement. He stumbled to the door. Leaned in close to answer. Her hair had the coconut smell of summer gorse.

'Cut from the same cloth, you and me,' he said. 'We both do what we do to look out for our own.'

He staggered outside, breath coming ragged. He'd said more to Angela than he ever said, to Carol or to the girl. So now what? He decided to wait. Angela would tell the girl what he said, that he'd swallowed his pride to come see her. She'd meet him half way, help him set things straight before he went. He'd forgive her, for her mam's sake, once the girl admitted to her errors. Wipe clean the slate before he went.

— 10 —

The shorter the days became, the more Helen yearned to see her mam. It wasn't help she wanted; more another point of view. She and Scrapper could not agree about the baby. More than two months gone and she was desperate for a third opinion. Couldn't her mam, against the odds, rise to the occasion for once? She worried about her mam, too. Chrissie Hobnob had pulled her aside at the Stute, said she hadn't seen Carol in weeks. That clinched it. Helen vowed to catch her mam alone at home.

The house looked sad, squalid. Someone had sprayed SCAB in red letters across the garden wall. Someone else – her dad, no doubt – tried to paint over it. But the whitewash was smeared pink, the letters visible underneath it. Her dad's beloved lawn was threaded with moss and dock leaves. The gutters above the windows were bowed with dead leaves.

Scrapper had phoned from outside the pit to report that her dad had gone in. That gave her until lunchtime. She hitched her satchel onto her shoulder, knocked warily on the door. No answer. Inside, she heard the ticking of the grandfather clock. Her mam had to be home. Where else would she be? She knocked a second time, but nothing moved inside the house.

She fumbled in her pocket for the key. It turned, but the door didn't budge. That was when she noticed the second, larger lock. She slumped on the doorstep, defeated. After some time, she heard a rattle of chains and a scrape of metal. The door swung open. Her mam stood in the doorway, hair unbrushed, the whites of her eyes matching the pink of her dressing gown.

'What d'you want?'

Helen pushed past her into the house. They were not doing this in front of the neighbours. A sharp, sour smell filled her nostrils. That threw her, too. The house she remembered smelled of burned food and Dettol and furniture polish. The stench seemed to come from the living room. She stopped in the doorway. The sideboard and coffee table were piled with papers and food wrappers and unwashed dishes. A full ashtray spilled onto the hearth. The fireplace was coated with coal dust and ash. It was all too much. She wanted to gag. Wanted to hurl open the windows, to let in light and air. Her dad's iron control had cracked, at last. Outside, their troubles painted over; inside, raw chaos.

'What's wrong with you, Mam?'

Her mam fussed with her dressing gown, tucked the folds around herself with unsteady hands. 'Nothing.'

'Nothing? C'mon, Mam. Look at yourself. Look at this bloody place.'

'Mind your language.' The only force to her words was force of habit.

'Are you sick?'

No answer.

'It's the pills, then?'

Her mam's pallid face darkened.

'How many you been taking?'

'Enough to take the edge off things. Make things fuzzy, get a full night's sleep.'

She sank into her armchair, gazed up at Helen as though struggling to focus. Helen swallowed a sigh, went to the kitchen. She brewed her mam a strong cup of tea, then set to work with bin bags and dustpan. She worked from living room to kitchen, gathered papers and wrappers and fag ends, swept out the hearth and vacuumed front to back. Filled the sink with suds and put the dishes to soak.

* * *

Her mam had not moved. Her tea had cooled, untouched.

'Listen, Mam: I'm pregnant.'

Her mam blinked, said nothing.

'D'you understand what I said, Mam?'

No reaction. It floored Helen, this blankness. She'd expected her mam to slam the door in her face. To cry or yell or order her to leave. She'd considered all those possible reactions. She'd not considered— indifference.

'I'm expecting Scrapper's baby. What d'you think about that?'

Her mam sighed, closed her eyes.

The clock ticked down the minutes. It would soon be lunchtime. Helen's fury collapsed into defeat. It was a mistake to have come here. Her mam was closed off to everything but her pills. She shrugged on her parka, fumbled with the zipper. It snagged, stiff with damp. She'd been too busy to notice that the house was heart-stoppingly cold, the fire long dead in the hearth.

How could she leave her mam like this?

'Mam, you got to lay off the pills. Talk to the bloody doctor. Promise me?'

She knelt at the grate, tipped coal from the scuttle and fumbled with the matchbox. Her hands were shaking. She tossed match after spent match at the fireplace. Nothing took. Finally, down to the last match, she struck a light, tucked the matchbox into the pile of coal, held the spark to the cardboard and breathed relief as it caught.

'Don't—' her mam's voice was as feeble as the flame in the grate.

'What?'

'Don't do it.'

Helen waited for her to continue. But her mam shut her eyes as though the subject was closed.

'What d'you mean?' Helen repeated.

There was a long pause.

'Don't do it,' her mam whispered. 'You want to end up like me? Get rid of it.'

'But Mam, I—'

'You got a chance to break free. Take it. If you got half a brain, girl, you take it. Leave, get away from here. Go and don't ever look back.'

11

Dai and Debbie had stacks of furniture and belongings to shift, for newlyweds. It took Scrapper and the boys three trips to empty the little house, working through the night to clear it before the bailiffs showed next morning. It was dawn by the time he and Iwan lugged the last case out of the minibus. They hefted it through Dewi and Mary's hall and up the narrow staircase to the tiny attic bedroom at the top of the house. Debbie and Dai perched on the narrow bed, as though clinging to a life-raft. Dai nodded his thanks, dark eyes glittering pain and anger and shame.

He slung a heavy arm across Debbie's neck. 'That's our lot, then, love.'

'Well, best get ourselves straight.'

To Scrapper's ears, the chirpy note in Debbie's voice rang false.

Dai tightened his grip on Debbie's shoulders. 'I'm sorry, Debs, alright.'

She shrugged off his arm, leaped off the bed and began stuffing tops and undies into the scuffed chest of drawers.

Iwan set off down the stairs. 'C'mon, lad. Let these two get themselves sorted.'

'You stay right there, Scrap,' Debbie ordered. 'Dai needs a hand stacking that lot.'

A row was brewing; the little room hummed with tension. Scrapper decided that the sooner he got them straight, the quicker he'd get out. He set to work, helped Dai to pile the boxes against the two longer walls, cleared a path from door to bed that opened space enough for two people to sit on the floor.

Debbie watched them, kept up a barbed silence.

'You know I done my best,' Dai spoke to her as though Scrapper wasn't there.

'Sure,' Debbie's voice was bone dry and brittle. 'Done the right things, said the right things. All the while, believing in none of it.'

'What in hell d'you mean by that?'

'You're not man enough – not for any of this, are you?'

Dai raised a shaking hand to his face. She meant to hurt him. And she had.

'That's not fair, Debbie,' Scrapper said. 'Dai's solid. He's been a rock. To all of us.'

For a pretty girl, Debbie could look properly ugly when riled. 'Solid?' she snarled. 'He wanted us to take the Christmas bribe.'

'I got desperate—'

'You think I'm not desperate, and all? I'd still sooner starve than board the scab bus.'

'That's—'

Debbie turned to Scrapper. 'It's true,' she said. 'I said I'd rather sleep naked under a bridge than stay with a man who'd betray his butties.'

Dai leapt up. A pile of boxes teetered, crashed down onto the floor. 'It's not about you, this,' he yelled. 'Not about me, neither. It's about the child you're carrying in your belly. About givin' some kind o' future to our babby.'

'What bloody future?' Debbie said.

Dai's strength seemed to fail him then. He backed out of the little attic, staggered blindly down the stairs. The front door opened and closed behind him.

Debbie was hell-bent on having the last word, even then. She yanked open the window, leaned out over the sill 'Some things matter more, Dai Dumbells. Principles and loyalty, for starters.'

Scrapper kept his head down and his hands busy. He sorted out the spilled boxes, stacked them as neatly as he could. Debbie watched him, arms folded, all the while.

'You reckon I'm a bitch too, don't you, Scrap.'

'That's an ugly word.'

She sighed. 'So what would you do? In my position?'

But they were in that position, him and Red.

'Fucked if I know, Debs. Shouldn't the pair of you sort it out together?'

12

Days and weeks passed. Gwyn waited for the girl to come to him, but in vain. A hard-hearted creature she'd become. All the more reason not to tell his wife about his x-ray results. Pointless getting her upset, when she'd tried so hard to rally herself lately. She'd eased off the pills, these last weeks, cleaned the house at last, even made a couple of trips into town. Christmas loomed; thoughts of family hung heavy on him. He considered a second trip to the *bracchi* then batted the thought away. A man had his pride. It fell to the girl to meet him half way.

He opened the front gate, wrestled the fir tree up the garden, needles dropping as he dragged it up the path. A deep green scent filled his nostrils. He breathed in. Cold air and exertion were a lethal mix for his clapped-out lungs. He doubled up coughing at the door. After taking a moment to clear his dizzy brain and calm his racing pulse, he dragged the tree indoors.

The house was silent, the hallway damp and cold. 'Carol?'

No answer. He hauled the Christmas tree into the living room. No sign of her. He propped the tree against door frame, popped his head round the kitchen door. The kitchen clock showed half past six. Nothing for his tea on the stove, nothing ready for him in the fridge. Maybe she was heading back from the shops. Best to start without her. Make it a surprise and maybe put a smile on that sad face of hers.

He crunched across the frosted lawn to his shed. All his tools and equipment were lined up neat and proper, every piece in its place, as Alf Manifesto taught him all those years back. Work smart, live smart, Alf used to say. True at home and true below ground. Gwyn had no trouble laying his hands on the pail filled with sand. He gathered half a dozen stones from the rockery and hefted the lot inside.

Musty and dank, the living room. But the grate was stacked with coal, at least. He set to work with matches and firelighters, got the embers going, set the pail of sand below the window and sank the tree into it. He took his penknife to the lower branches, piled stones into the pail to position the tree, pulled it this way and that to set it straight. He stood back, admired his work. All it needed now was lights and tinsel, a signal to that rabble from the lodge that it was Christmas as usual in Gwyn Pritchard's house and to hell with the rest.

Maybe not exactly as usual but they'd give it a damn good stab. He looked at the tree again and sighed. It was the girl's job to dress the tree. She spent hours positioning lights and baubles and tinsel just so, often changed her mind and started over. But Carol would be pleased he'd given it a stab. He trudged upstairs to fetch the decorations from the top of the wardrobe, flicked on the bedroom light, jerked backwards in surprise.

His wife was curled up beneath the blankets.

'You poorly?'

She rolled away, turned her face to the wall.

He raised his voice. 'I said, are you poorly?'

'Go 'way,' she whispered.

'What's wrong wi' you now, woman?'

It threw him, this setback. He thought she'd seen sense, at last. His best intentions scuppered by her moods, yet again.

'Jus' leave me alone.'

'But I bought you a tree—'

'What bloody point's a tree?'

'It's Christmas in a couple o' weeks. We always have a tree in this house.'

He stared down at her, defeated. She was too wrapped up in herself to see the effort he was making. He wrestled the urge to blurt out the truth about his test results. Anything to shock her into thinking about someone other than herself, for once.

'Christmas is for family, Gwyn. Not much of a family, are we?'

She was looking at the dressing table, at the framed photographs of grandparents, parents, uncles and cousins. At the front, Helen's primary school photograph. A freckled little girl with copper-coloured ringlets and a gap-toothed smile. Gwyn snatched it up, opened a drawer and slammed the photograph inside.

'No!'

React to that, would she? He ripped the blankets off the bed. She lay there, not moving.

'Christ, Carol. We're still a family, you and me. And if you give a stuff about that at all, you'll shift your lazy arse and help me dress that bloody tree.'

* * *

Where to start? Armfuls of silver, gold and red tinsel spilled out of the box, snagged together and bristling hooks. He pulled out a string of bell-shaped fairy lights, several bells missing. Loose baubles rolled under the sofa, some without their wire hangers, others rubbed bare of colour. Glitter and pine needles studded the carpet. At the bottom of the box, he found three crosses made of cinnamon sticks, tied with green and red tartan ribbon and a Christmas angel.

He raised a cross to his nose and sniffed, but the scent had long ago dried to a rasp of dust. It was Christmas 1976. He still had his fingers. Helen would have been eight. She came rushing home from school, home-made crosses in one hand, the angel in the other, first prize for the best home-made Christmas decoration. She loved that angel with its golden hair and cherry lips and gauze wings. He lifted the girl so she could stick the angel on the crown of the tree. She danced around after, face flushed, clapping her hands with delight. The same ceremony to crown the tree every Christmas after that. Even when she got too big to lift. Even when he lost his fingers and everything fell from his grasp. Even these last years, when she shrank away from him, fetched herself a chair.

Time had not been kind to the angel; the halo was cracked, gauze wings streaked grey. He scooped it up with the cinnamon crosses, hurled them into the waste paper bin. He turned to see Carol in the doorway.

'Don't sneak up on me like that woman.'

He set to work on the fairy lights. Tightened the bulbs and fiddled with the plug, cursed as the glass bells blazed then died. He scrabbled in the sideboard for spare fuses. A hell of a job this had become. The simplest task was a struggle since he lost his fingers. He clutched plug between thumb and forefinger, fumbled with his knife to loosen the screws. At last he fixed the lights and strung them across the tree so that most of the tiny bulbs faced the window, pinprick lights fighting a losing battle against the darkness that flooded in from the street.

Then Carol was next to him, her movements shaky and unfocused. Despite the pills, she gave it a go, strung up a length of tinsel, placed the crosses between the branches and hooked baubles from the ends. Gwyn stood back to assess her work, wondered whether to laugh or cry. None of it looked right. He pushed Carol out of the way, shifted the baubles, stood back, only to find the tree looking even more forlorn. Carol slipped from the room, a face on her like a kicked puppy. He lost patience, then, hurled the rest of the tinsel at the branches, hung the least shabby baubles in between.

* * *

In the kitchen, Carol slumped at the table, turning the broken angel between her hands. He grabbed it from her. 'You fixing supper, or what?'

She didn't answer.

'Fine,' he said. 'I'll fetch me some fish an' chips.'

He reached in the larder for the cocoa tin and prised off the lid. It was empty.

'Where's the housekeeping?'

Carol wrapped her arms around herself, didn't answer.

'I gave you an extra twenty this week,' he yelled. 'Should be fifty quid by here. What you done with it?'

She raised her head, looked him straight in the eye. 'Spent it.'

She hardly ever looked at him at lately. It was baffling, her behaviour.

'But the fridge – it's bloody empty. Nothing to feed a mouse.'

'Fancied myself a mink coat.'

Unbecoming on a woman, sarcasm. He decided not to rise to it, too tired and hungry to begin to know what to do with her. He reached into his pocket, found a fiver and some loose change. Enough for a fair few pints, cod and chips on the way home. He slammed out of the kitchen and set off for The Mountain Ash.

* * *

The bedroom was dark, no sign yet of daybreak. His mouth was dry and scratchy, heart beating a flutter. It did that often, lately, when he'd had a drink. He reached out to Carol. Her breath was raspy and shallow. She lay as far from him as the bed allowed, body pressed against the wall. If he wanted to, he could reach over and drag her towards him. She wouldn't know

240

or feel a thing, senseless from those bloody pills. But no. He turned away. There was too much distance between them, now, for that, awake or asleep.

The letterbox clattered. Light footsteps retreated down the garden path. It was too early for the postman. Gwyn reached for slippers and dressing gown and went down to investigate. A dim glow of fairy lights spilled into the hall. A pink envelope lay on the doormat. He picked it up and turned it over. Addressed to Mrs Carol Pritchard. Unevenly printed capitals, no stamp. Hand-delivered. And who would hand-deliver a letter to his wife. He sat on the stairs, tore open the envelope.

A couple of hours later, Carol shuffled downstairs, wearing a shapeless jumper to match her pallor and stained nylon slacks. She moved heavily, as though wading through deep water, as she filled the kettle, dropped a teabag into her mug. The letterbox clattered again. She drifted down the hall, returned with a fistful of envelopes.

'Anything of interest?' He struggled to keep his voice level.

She thrust the post across the table. A brown envelope addressed to Mr Gwyn Pritchard. Three white envelopes for Mrs Gwyn Pritchard.

'Expecting anything special?'

She said nothing, took the bread knife to the envelopes.

'Well?'

'They're from my sister, her eldest an' Margaret Parry.'

'Margaret Parry? We didn't send her a card.'

The look on her face told him otherwise.

'Expecting anything else?' he leaned in closer.

'Why would I? Few enough friends before. None, now.'

He shoved the pink envelope at her. 'So what's this, then?'

Her back and shoulders went rigid. 'You tell me. You went and opened it.'

He reached into the envelope, pulled out the sheet of

notepaper, the sheaf of ten-pound notes, spread the money on the table.

'"*Dear Mam*,"' he read. '"*I hope you are OK. I'm sorry I missed you. Angela said you were too upset to stop and talk. I know you're not well. I'll come and see you again soon but I don't want you getting in trouble.*

'"*Mam, I know why you left the money, but I've asked Angela to give it back to you. Dad earned it from the Coal Board. And that makes it scab money. And I've made my decision, so I don't need it. I know you meant well. But me and Scrapper will do OK.*

'"*I miss you and I'm grateful you wanted to help.*

'"*Lots of love, Helen.*"'

Carol's face was clammy, her eyes and cheeks tinged pink. The morning light showed no mercy to her sallow skin, to the shadows around her eyes.

'*Scab money*?' He slammed his fist on the table, made the pile of notes jump. 'How dare she? How dare you? Did I or did I not tell you to leave her be – her and that boy?'

'I wanted to see her.'

'And I said not to.'

She raised her chin. 'Who gave you the right? To tell me not to?'

'Who gave me—? *This* is my house, *that* is my money, *you* are my wife.'

She squared her shoulders. 'So?'

Knocked the breath from his lungs, that did. 'So you should be grateful,' he said at last.

'*Grateful?*'

'Look at you. Can't keep house or put dinner on your man's table. Nothing doing in the bedroom. Not for months.'

He decided to ignore the grimace that crossed her face.

'Only married you to save your reputation,' he said.

'My—?'

There was a name for girls who got knocked up out of wedlock. Stood by her, he had, when a lesser man would have legged it. Some thanks, this.

'You married me,' her voice was icy. 'Because my dad went to the lodge, had them remind you of your responsibilities.'

'My—?'

'You want grateful? Let's see,' she counted on her fingers. 'I married you. Kept house for you. Kept my mouth shut about the drinking and mad rages—'

'The mad—?'

'A stranger you been since you lost your fingers. Angry and hard and closed in. Like you lost whatever part of you was good and kind and loving with 'em.'

'That's crap.'

'It's when you turned vicious towards me an' the girl—'

His fist slammed into her ear. She lurched sideways, crashed into the fridge. Gwyn pushed her down on the floor, aimed a kick at her ribs. She curled away from him, hands raised to protect herself. Rage crashed over him in waves. He seized his slipper, brought it down with all his strength. Hit her again and again.

It was no good. He felt his strength ebbing away. As he slowed, she twisted out of reach, aimed a sharp upward kick that caught him square in the groin. As he doubled over, she staggered to her feet, wrenched open the cutlery drawer. Turned to face him, rolling pin in one hand, bread knife in the other. Her ear dripped blood.

'I never cared how you treated me,' she panted. 'But I'm pig-sick that you cast out my daughter. And for what? For loving a lad the way I loved you.'

He tried to stand, but his chest was in spasm. She wriggled into coat and shoes, stuffed the money into her pocket and walked out of the house, the door shut quietly behind her.

13

Carol would come shuffling through that front door any day now, Gwyn knew. Where else could she go, his wife? In the meantime, he made the best of it. Ate better, for one thing; fish and chips, saveloy and chips, sweet-n-sour Chinese. One night, he even fetched an Indian takeaway on the way down from The Mountain Ash. A rum business, the Indian; chicken the colour of dried blood, nuts and raisins and whatnot mixed into the rice. Kitchen bin overflowed tin foil trays and plastic bags and greasy newsprint. The sink filled with smeared dishes. He wouldn't touch them, on point of principle. He'd have Carol clean it up. Her penance for taking his money. For defying his orders and seeing the girl.

He should never have raised his hand to her, fair dos. Her fault for pushing him to the limit, that. Both of them equally to blame. A trial, the waiting, even so. Some nights, he sat in the bus shelter, watched the flat above the ice cream parlour. She might be with her daughter. Might have sheltered, the better to punish him, with his nemesis, Iwan Jones.

One night, he saw the girl at last. She emerged into the street, wrapped up in hat and scarf. He caught a drift of raised voices before she shut the door. Angie and her husband were fighting cats and dogs, from the sound of it. The girl set off up the hill. He waited a moment, then followed at a distance. Hope eased his wheezing chest. Maybe she was on her way to see him. Off to visit her old dad, at last. Instead, she turned into the lowest street of terraces, crossed the road towards a door with peeling red paint. Number fourteen, it was. His chest tightened. A familiar look to that little house. A long time since his family lived in this street of two-up, two-down collier's houses.

He fell back as the door opened. Of course. Where else would his wife have gone? Helen stooped to kiss the little widow, vanished inside the house. He strode across the road. Margaret Parry, about to pull the door shut, saw him, paused with a hand on the latch, mastered her tremors just long enough to slam the door in his face.

* * *

It was an odd start to Christmas Day. He woke in the front room, curtains drawn, fairy lights dim pinpricks. They called to mind the twinkle of his men's headlamps. It was comforting to sit in the dark and ponder. Below ground, a man's thoughts were stronger, more lucid for being wrapped in darkness. Even now, he carried that darkness inside him, fused into his cells, like the coal dust sunk deep beneath his skin.

His stomach growled. He searched his jacket pocket for the pasties bought from the Co-op. A sorry excuse for a Christmas breakfast. He made short work of them, all the same, crumbs and packaging brushed onto the floor. She'd left one hell of a mess, his wife. Had him worried for a while. But he'd found her now. High time she stopped her nonsense and came home.

Minutes ticked into hours, his chest grew ever tighter. The walls pressed in on him. At last the garden gate squealed. He staggered up, edged around the stupid Christmas tree. Cursed the needles that fell into his slippers, as he twitched the curtain. He was too slow. Already, her key grated in the lock and the front door swung open. As he pushed past the tree to confront his wife, the fairy lights snagged on his cardigan button. For a dangerous moment, six feet of knobbled pine wobbled, threatened to crash down on him.

He struggled to free himself, turned to see the girl framed in the doorway. She wore a floor-length, green velvet gown with a fitted bodice and flared Seventies-style sleeves. It wasn't the outlandish clothes that threw him. She was here, after all the weeks of waiting and hoping. He forgot what he'd planned to say. His mouth opened and closed. She looked fine, pale skin glowing, hair cut short, worn loose and glossy. Put on a few pounds, too, from the look of her. But he saw no softness in the girl's blue eyes. She came no closer, hung in the doorway and glared at him.

'I've come for Mam's stuff.'

'You've what—?'

A figure appeared behind the girl, put a hand on her shoulder. 'We're not looking for trouble, Mr Pritchard. Helen's fetching some things for her mam.'

That boy. That bloody boy. Joy and relief ebbed away. 'You got a nerve—'

'Go, Red. For God's sake, make it quick.'

The boy shoved the girl towards the stairs, blocked the doorway, trapped Gwyn in his own living room. The boy wore jeans and a green sweater, a strange dishcloth affair slung over it. Two rectangles of pool table baize, stitched together at the shoulders. The same green as the girl's gown.

'Maid Marian and Robin-bloody-Hood?' Gwyn asked, incredulous. 'You dressed up to rob my house?'

Scrapper shifted from one foot to the other. 'It's the lodge Christmas party. And no one's robbing your house.'

'It's exactly what you're doing. Robbery and trespass and false imprisonment, this. I'm calling the police.'

Gwyn tucked his arms against his chest, barged the lad with his shoulder. But the lad had lost none of his strength. Gwyn staggered backwards, light-headed from exertion.

'Don't make this worse for Red, Mr Pritchard.'

'You don't—'

'She misses her dad, you know. Broke her heart when you kicked her out.'

A low blow, that. The nerve of it, bursting into his house, taking his property and now emotional blackmail to boot. He barged Scrapper a second time, his good fist landing one where it hurt. Pure luck, that glancing blow. The boy doubled over. Gwyn dashed into the hall, grabbed the phone and dialled.

The boy recovered breath enough to shout a warning. 'Red – we got to go. *Now.*'

The girl dashed down the stairs, duffel bag over her shoulder, a suitcase in her hand as the telephone operator gabbled questions into Gwyn's ear.

'Fetch me the police,' he turned to the girl. 'You stop right there, young lady.'

The girl slammed her hand down, tried to cut the phone. But the operator kept twittering away.

'I said, *stop.*'

The girl went rigid, coldness melting into fury. She looked ready to slap him. Instead, she dropped something on the telephone book.

'All you care about's your property, eh, Dad? Well, this is yours. Keep it, Mam says.'

She grabbed the boy's hand and dragged him down the garden. Gwyn went after them, but they were tearing round the corner by the time he reached the gate. He staggered back indoors, picked up the phone.

'Send your men to the Miners' Institute, number one Ystrad High Street. My name's Pritchard. I'll meet them there, show 'em the lad that robbed me.'

He dropped the receiver, fighting for breath. That boy had pushed him too far this time. This time, he'd have him. And who would the police believe: a dying man, disturbed at home on Christmas Day, or a striking miner strapped for cash two Christmases on the trot?

He looked down to see what Helen had left for him. A small, gold object glinted feebly in the half-light.

* * *

Half the village was outside the Stute. Gwyn watched the comings and goings from his hiding place inside the telephone box. The stench of urine and stale fags made him gag. He sank lower inside his jacket, took in air through the fabric, pulled his cap down further over his eyes. Mary Power stood on the steps meeting and greeting, wearing a red coat with white fur trim, cotton wool for a beard. Behind her, holding the doors, Dai Dumbells and his glamorous missus wore leather-look togas, a pair of bickering gladiators.

The Stute blazed light under a glowering sky. Miners and their families streamed inside. Gwyn spotted a tiny female Elvis, a burly Shirley Bassey, a Snow White, a Cinderella with designer stubble. A group of pirates of various ages and sizes walked in behind a Captain Hook, sack slung over his shoulder, the word *Plunder* spray-stencilled on it.

Captain Hook sloped over to the bus stop to cadge a smoke off Margaret Thatcher – joke-shop mask and navy suit and hairy rugby-player calves. A placard round her neck read *Wanted for Murder*. He heard jeers and catcalls from a bunch of spike-hair teenagers wearing ripped bin-liners and safety pins. They circled Mrs Thatcher, fascinated and appalled.

'I still might, if yous lot bet me enough,' said one boy.

Mrs Thatcher chuckled a forty-a-day chuckle. 'I'm the one does the screwing, boys.'

Mary Power waved them into the building. The doors shut

and the street fell silent. Gwyn wrenched the door open, gulped down clean air. He didn't fancy the policemen's chances of entering the Stute to nick the boy. Not unless they wanted a repeat of the Rebecca riots. And where in hell were the police?

He heard footsteps at the top of the High Street, shut the door and turned his back as the girl walked past with the boy, both still dressed in Sherwood green, the boy lugging the duffel bag and suitcase.

'They're late,' the girl was saying.

They sat on the steps of the Stute. They seemed to be waiting for something. After a while, Gwyn heard the puttering of an engine. A car squealed to a halt outside the Stute. But it wasn't a police car. It was Idris No-Handbrake, the local cabbie. The boy ran over, dumped the bags in the boot. Helen leaned into the front window, speaking to someone. Idris gunned his engine again. As the girl stepped back, Gwyn saw Carol in the passenger seat. But before he could act, Idris had sputtered off in a blur of thick exhaust fumes. His wife was gone.

He slumped against the putrid glass, watched the girl fall sobbing on the boy. At last he heard the clinking of steel toecaps, spotted local bobby Peter Plod turn the corner onto the High Street.

'At bloody last,' he burst out of the phone box. 'There's the lad you want, officer.'

'Right you are,' the policeman palmed his handcuffs, marched smartly across the road.

The boy and girl clung on to each other, sensed nothing of the danger they faced. The policeman grabbed the boy by the wrist, yanked him off the pavement.

'So what's he done this time, Gwyn Pritchard?'

'He broke into my house, knocked me about, walked out with my stuff—'

'He never,' Helen burst out. 'My mam sent me round to pick up her stuff. My dad went mental, gave Scrapper a shove and—'

'Do I look like I could shove a six-foot collier,' Gwyn cut in. 'The lad's twice my height and not half my age.'

The policeman snapped a handcuff on Scrapper's wrists. 'Right, Simon Jones. You're arrested on suspicion of burglary and assault.'

'You can't do that,' the girl sobbed.

But Peter Plod was already dragging the boy down the street, to the police car waiting on the corner.

'Right, then,' Gwyn turned on the girl. 'There's no point crying about that boy. He's trouble, that one, through and through. Ridiculous, carrying on like that in public. And high time you came home.'

She backed away from him, tears glittering in her eyes; gave him a look that felt like a jackhammer hitting glass. He felt the air punched from his lungs, the blood drain from his veins. She turned without a word, strode off in the direction of the police car.

'Helen Margaret Pritchard – you get back here right this minute!'

But the girl did not turn back. As she walked away, the sky darkened, the wind took on a razor's bite. Gwyn felt sleet claw at his cheeks. A peal of laughter burst out from behind the closed doors of the Stute.

He stared down at his shaking hands, helpless to stop loneliness closing in over him.

Helen was at a loss to know what to do. Instinct drove her up the hill, towards the police station. But what the hell would she do when she got there? She stopped, reconsidered. The police would laugh in her face if she demanded to see Scrapper. But there'd be outrage and mayhem if she burst into the Stute, told everyone what her dad had done. The shame floored her; and why let her dad ruin everyone's Christmas? She ducked into the alley, the better to avoid running into the old man again, and paused to regroup her thoughts. When she emerged onto the High Street, her dad had gone.

As she reached the Stute, the door swung open. Iwan stood at the top of the steps, smiling down at her.

'Ah, good. You're here,' he said. 'Get in quick, love, for God's sake. There's a bunch of locusts got designs on your dinner. I can't hold them off much longer. Where's Simon?'

'He got nicked.'

'Nicked? For what?'

'Dad called the coppers, said Scrapper robbed the house.'

Iwan shot a furtive look over his shoulder, shut the Stute door behind him and lowered his voice. 'You told them different?'

'They wouldn't listen.'

'Jesus,' he buttoned his jacket. 'We'll fetch your mam, have her make a statement. High time she had the bastard for assault.'

'Mam just left. Sue found a refuge to take her.'

The Stute blazed light. Loud music drifted through the open

251

windows with the smell of roast dinner and burned brandy and cigarette smoke. The music stopped. Helen heard chair legs screech on the wooden floor, a burst of laughter.

'Right,' Iwan said at last. 'Guess we'd best say nothing to that lot, get ourselves up the cop shop.'

'What do we tell Angela? It'll ruin her Christmas, this.'

'And the rest of them. Best we say nothing. Not yet.'

They set off up the hill to the police station. It loomed above them, blocks of dark stone glowering across the village. The tall, helmet-shaped gable raised a weather vane like a truncheon. Helen followed Iwan up the shallow steps. He flung open the door, charged over to the desk sergeant.

'I'm here to fetch my son.'

The policeman fixed his eyes on his magazine, on a photo of a golf course. 'And you are?'

'Iwan Jones, father of Simon Jones.'

'Take a seat,' the officer said. 'We'll deal with this presently.'

'You'll deal with me now, thank you. You got him or not?'

'Take a seat. We'll deal with you in our own time.'

'Now look here,' Iwan said. 'The lad's got rights. Number one, the right to let his next of kin know he's been arrested.'

'I said *wait*.'

Iwan hefted an impatient sigh. 'The boy's done nothing wrong,' he said. 'My daughter-in-law can vouch for him.'

The officer raised a mocking eyebrow, moved his spectacles an inch lower down his nose. Iwan stiffened.

Helen put a hand on his arm. 'My dad had Simon arrested, officer. Said Simon broke into our house. It's not true. He was helping me fetch my mam's stuff.'

'That's as maybe. You still have to wait.'

A row of cracked and stained plastic chairs backed up against the far wall. She led Iwan towards them.

'Officious bastard,' he spoke so that the desk officer would hear. 'Knows damn well why we're here. Knows we know our rights.'

'So now what?'

Iwan lowered his voice. 'I'll try and call our brief. But the fellow's down in Cardiff and there's not a snowball's chance we'll get him up here on Christmas Day.'

He fumbled in his jacket for his wallet, pulled out a scrap of paper with a number scrawled on it. Scrabbled in his pockets for change. Helen fished in her parka, brought out three ten pence pieces.

Iwan took the coins. 'I'll nip down the hill. The walls got ears here. Might fetch Dewi too. You alright to wait?'

I nodded. 'You gonna tell Angela?'

'Not if I can help it, *bach*. Not 'til we get this mess sorted. If Angie shows up, she'll hang that jobs-worth from the light fittings.'

* * *

Time passed. Nothing moved inside the station. Iwan did not return.

'Can you at least say if he's here or not?'

The desk officer lowered his magazine, looked up at her, unfolded himself into standing position. He was a beanstalk of a man, with the high shoulders of someone who had to stoop to be heard. 'We have procedures.'

'On Christmas Day?'

'Nice try, girlie.'

'Don't you have a family of your own?'

The man grinned, showed slab-like teeth. 'With the overtime I get to tell the likes of you to sit down and shut up, I'll have the money to get away from them come new year, catch me some sun.'

She slouched back to the waiting area. Dusk had fallen. Orange light burned through the warped glass. She leaned her head against the wall. There was no way to get comfortable. Her stomach growled. She hadn't eaten all day. Too busy trying to fix things for her mam. And what was her mam doing now? A grim Christmas, settling in for the night at a refuge, away from everyone she loved. Popping pills to shut herself down, no doubt. She wished Scrapper would come out. All she wanted now was to get him home, take off her stupid fancy-dress costume, drink hot, sweet tea and turn in for the night.

She was drifting off to sleep, when the wooden door swung open. A figure walked out. He was short and barrel-chested, dressed in tweed jacket and cap. Her dad. Seeing her, his face showed surprise, anger, dimmed into something like defeat. The strip lights cut him down to size. He looked small here, and old. He paused, as though he expected her to speak.

Then the door to the street opened. Dewi and Iwan rushed in. Her dad walked past them without speaking and melted into the night.

'What the fuck's Captain Hook doing here?' Dewi said. He saw Helen, rubbed his nose. 'Sorry, love. What was he after, your dad?'

'He came from by there,' she pointed.

Iwan and Dewi held a muttered conflab.

'Did you speak to the lawyer,' she asked.

Iwan shook his head. 'Reckon they'll keep Simon overnight because they can.'

They sat and waited. At last, the heavy door opened again. Scrapper shuffled out into the waiting room. He looked pale and tense and exhausted. Helen flung herself at him.

'Did they hurt you?'

'Did they charge you?'

Iwan and Dewi spoke across each other.

'Burglary and assault,' Scrapper said.

Iwan sucked in his breath.

'Bastards,' Dewi said. 'First offence, but still. Find you guilty, it's at least a fine—'

'A fine?' Scrapper said. 'How can they fine me, when I'm broke?'

'That's if you're lucky,' Iwan said. 'Gwyn Pritchard puts on a good show in court, you're looking at a prison term, son.'

Helen clung to Scrapper, not believing what she'd heard. It couldn't happen. Not to him. Not to them.

WINTER 1985

— 1 —

Scrapper pulled his donkey jacket closer. Overnight sleet had hardened into sheet ice. The street glittered glass. Even the air had an icy bite. He paused outside the *bracchi*. The cafe was shuttered and locked, a heap of bills and flyers piled inside the door. Iwan looked away, pretending not to see. Scrapper made a mental note to clear them away when he got back. Mist draped the hillsides. The High Street, once bustling on Saturdays, was silent, Betty's Unisex Boutique boarded up, cracked plywood pasted with layers of posters. *Victory to the Miners. Maggie Out.* But Maggie was still in charge and ten months in victory was no closer than the moon.

He slipped and slid down the High Street, past hairdressers and butchers and funeral parlour. His plastic buckets glowed yellow in the gloom.

'You should have stayed home,' Iwan said. 'You need to keep your nose clean these next few weeks.'

'Give over, Dad. There's no harm picking coal waste.'

The track up to the tip was six inches deep in half-frozen mud, the crown of the hill masked in swirling mist. Scrapper soon felt breathless; lately, his strength and stamina were quickly spent. The fog thinned, revealing a man slumped on the stile up ahead, dressed in so many layers he looked as wide as he was tall. As the man doubled over coughing, Scrapper recognised him at once. Sion Jenkins was a martyr to his chest.

He hurried over. 'You alright?'

'Came over all peculiar.'

Two empty buckets lay at Sion's feet.

'Aw, butty; should've called us. We'll fetch your coal.'

Sion tried to protest, but his chest was having none of it. He collapsed in a spluttering, coughing heap.

'Go home, Sion,' Iwan said. 'We'll stop by when we've filled your pails.'

The old boy staggered back down the track. Scrapper picked up his buckets. As they climbed higher, weak sun dissolved the fog. A hefty figure was outlined against the sky, bare hands plunging into the snow, hurling coal at two outsized buckets, huge arms like pistons. Not one lump of coal fell short or too far.

'Orright, Dai,' Scrapper called.

Dai snapped upright, a hand flying to his chest. 'You scared me outta my skin, Scrapper Jones.' He bent down again, started picking coal even faster than before.

Scrapper filled Sion's pails first. The coal was brittle with cold. Wind hissed in his ears. Soon, his gloves were sodden, a chill sunk deep into his bones. Gusts of wind shook the trees below, shaking off day-old snow. His fingers ached, but a beat in his head kept him going. *Small Town Boy*. It made him think of the funfair at Barry Island, the waltzer ride with Red. He'd felt free for the first time in months, that day. Now, they were cash-strapped and cold, a baby due and a court case to come.

He turned to Dai. 'How are you and Debbie getting on at Dewi's?'

'She's never there.'

'You'll have more time together, once the baby comes,' Iwan said.

'What babby?' Dai started hurling coal with raw fury.

'But—'

'There's no babby,' Dai snapped.

Scrapper frowned at Iwan to lay off the questions. Dai would explain, if he wanted to. Best to leave it if he didn't. A collier knew not to push his luck. It was the code they all lived by. Downright dangerous, below ground, to poke a man until he snapped.

The three of them laboured steadily, not speaking. The sky gathered darkness, clouds heavy with snow. Soon, Sion's pails were full. Scrapper carried them down from the tip and tucked them in a clump of bracken, sheltered from the wind and the wet. He climbed back up, started to fill his own buckets. Below, in the trees, a magpie cawed, cross and insistent. The bird spooked him. One for sorrow. He grabbed a lump of coal, lobbed it towards the trees. The magpie cackled and fled on glossy wings.

He straightened his back, rolled his shoulders. 'Strange how quick you get out of shape. Used to shovel on hands and knees for hours and not get knackered.'

Iwan pulled his tobacco pouch from the lining of his jacket pocket where he hid it from the pit searcher and from Angela. He twirled a sliver of a roll-up, passed the tin to Dai.

Dai took it with a thin smile. 'Didn't mean to bite your head off.'

'Forgotten already, lad.'

For all Dai's heft, Scrapper sensed something shrunken in him, the light gone from his eyes. So Debbie had done it, then. It took guts to make that choice, to go through with it; a damn sight more guts than he had.

Eerie purple light washed over the valley. Dad and Dai finished their roll-ups. They gathered up their buckets and set off down the slope. But as they clambered over the stile, Scrapper heard footsteps squelching through the mud.

Peter Plod was steaming up the track, his tubby colleague Johnny Boots panting along behind.

'Fuck,' Iwan pushed Scrapper behind him.

Penny-sized lumps of sleet began to spatter the hedgerows.

'You know it's against the law scavenging coal, boys,' Peter Plod called. 'You're trespassing on National Coal Board property.'

Dai drew himself up to full height. 'Local bobbies property of the National Coal Board and all, are they?'

'I don't like your tone, Dai Dobrosielski,' Peter Plod said. 'Step away from the buckets.'

Scrapper opened his mouth but Iwan got in first. 'There's families cold and hungry across this valley. You boys got nothing better to do than guard a coal tip?'

Johnny Boots stared at the ground, round face dripping embarrassment. 'Orders is orders.'

'Orders is orders?' Dai echoed. 'Reckon the guards said that at Auschwitz.'

Peter Plod moved closer, jabbed a finger on Dai's chest. 'Set down your buckets *now* or I'll arrest all three of you and it won't look good for Scrapper Jones when his case comes to court.'

'Do it, Dai,' Iwan murmured.

Dai set down his pails, slammed the policeman with the flat of his hand. 'Orders is orders? Next you'll be saying this got nothing to do with politics.'

The policeman reached for his radio. 'Fancy a night in the cells, do you?'

There was no way Scrapper could let that happen.

He handed Johnny Boots his two pails. 'That won't be necessary.'

Peter Plod paused, radio in hand. He was itching to book all three of them. Sleet pelted Scrapper's face as he handed over Iwan's pails, yanked the last two pails from Dai's clenched fists.

Peter Plod picked up a bucket, eyes still fixed on Dai, tipped the coal over the fence into the brambles.

All the pails emptied, he stacked them, tucked them under his arm. 'I'll keep hold of these, thanks, lads.'

He strode off down the track. Johnny Boots staggered after him.

Dai's fists balled rage. 'Why the fuck d'you back down?'

'Gwyn Pritchard's hauled me up in front of the beak.'

Scrapper explained what had happened at Christmas. Dai's jaw worked as he listened, as though he was chewing over the information.

'You're looking at time in jail?'

'Anything to line up three square meals a day, butt.' His attempt at a joke rang sour.

Dai's face darkened. 'Bastards. Bleeding all of us dry.'

'We still got Sion's buckets,' Iwan tried to lighten the mood.

Scrapper felt his exhaustion turn to glee. One of them would have a toasty warm house tonight, at least. He would see to it personally. Screw the pigs.

'I'll come back for them when night falls,' he said.

* * *

Scrapper peered through the curtain. The High Street slumbered. Across the valley, the evening star lit a sky the colour of anthracite. He pulled on boots, scarf, gloves and jacket. Red looked up from the telly, her breath rising like steam. She was wrapped in more layers than an onion. He tucked the blanket tighter over her shoulders. She was far too pale and thin, arms and legs like matchsticks. But under her clothes, she had a little belly. A chill blessing, the cold; so far no one had guessed.

The wind howled, vicious, as he shut the back door and picked up the pails Steve Red Lion had lent him. Iwan trotted behind him, lugging an armful of hessian sacking. There'd be no freezing in their beds tonight. Scrapper turned into the track, checked there were no policemen. He was sure they would be safe, now. The plods had gone home to their toasty living rooms, cooked dinners heating their bellies, central heating on full whack. He shook himself. A miner's life was too short for bitterness.

Up ahead, he heard rustling in the undergrowth. Foxes, perhaps. He picked up pace, toes numb in his steel-capped boots, frozen sleet crunching underfoot like *biscotti*. He found Sion's pails where he'd left them. Iwan walked on towards the tip. Scrapper grabbed the pails and set off back to the village. It was a battle to climb the terraces, wind gusting knots, his boots sliding on the ice, forcing him to double his steps. By the time he reached Sion's terrace, he was breathless. It would surely be the death of the old boy, that climb.

He turned into number twenty-one and stopped. The house was dark, upstairs and down. A carrier bag – the day's food parcel – was parked on the doorstep, uncollected. Where could Sion and his missus be on such a curse of a night? He rattled the letterbox but no one came.

The latch clicked open when he pushed.

'Sion?' His voice echoed in the empty hallway.

He set the buckets on the tiled floor, dragged the carrier bag inside. Nothing stirred. He headed for the kitchen, pushed the door open. Dying embers glowed in the grate but gave off no heat. He pushed the light switch but the room remained stubbornly dark.

'Who's there?' The voice came from a low sofa near the fireplace. Two figures were huddled together under a quilt.

'That you, Sion?'

The figure shifted. Scrapper moved closer, saw Sion and his wife Mavis, their eyes hollow, faces grey with cold. Mavis was shaking, her breath coming shallow and slow.

'What happened to the electric?'

'Meter ran out,' Sion's voice was barely a croak.

The coal was so damp, it hissed when Scrapper tipped it into the grate. He fished in his pocket, found a fifty-pence piece. It was all he had left from the week's picketing expenses. He opened the cupboard under the stairs, fed the coin into the meter. As it clattered into the slot, the hall lights blazed. He turned them off, went back to the old people. The fire was taking time to catch. He jabbed the coals with the poker until sparks shot up the chimney.

'Thanks, lad,' Sion's face was pale, his breathing as fast as Mavis' breath came slow.

'How long you two been like this?'

'Couple of days.'

'You called Dr O'Connell?'

'Seeing him next week.'

'Christ,' Scrapper grabbed his shoulder. 'You'll see him tonight. Where's your phone?'

'Cut off,' Sion's voice was ragged.

Scrapper filled the kettle and went through the carrier bag. He found tins and dried goods, a sliced loaf, frozen almost solid, and a slab of cheddar. He fed the bread into the toaster, sliced the cheese and handed the old people tea and a plate of sandwiches.

'Eat,' he said. 'I'm off to fetch the doctor.'

* * *

Hypothermia, Dr O'Connell said. It was late by the time the ambulance took the Jenkinses off to hospital. Scrapper slipped and slid down the hill to the coal tip to fetch the sacks that Iwan had filled and left for him to collect. As he trudged through the sleet towards home, doubt hardened into certainty. There was no way back from this, now, all of them cold and sick and hungry. They were trapped, left facing a bleak choice: cave in now, admit all was lost, or fight on in the slim hope the pit had some kind of future. But what kind of future would that be?

Red was sound asleep when he climbed into bed, still wearing socks, vest and underwear. He snuggled closer, sinking into her warmth, heating his chill hands on her belly.

'We got no right,' he murmured. 'It's no world for a child, this, *bach*.'

Helen climbed off the chair, looked up at her handiwork. Sheets of pasta hung from kitchen maid and curtain pole. Pasta ribbons trailed over the backs of the chairs. The kitchen looked like an Egyptian mummy's dressing room, bandaged with pasta and powdered with flour. It was her mam-in-law's new business venture; she'd cut a deal with Bethan Edwards' dad to supply his restaurant in Cardiff. Angela reckoned she'd undercut his regular supplier by a third. She had Iwan pawn his brothers' davy lamps, took delivery of two sacks of plain and semolina flour and a dozen trays of eggs. Helen had helped to make the trial batch. If it all went well, Mr Edwards had promised them two orders a week.

She jotted notes as her mam-in-law mixed the dough and helped her to pass it through the rollers and to hang the sheets to dry. Two orders a week would keep their little family ticking over until late spring, Angela reckoned.

Late spring. Helen touched her belly. She'd nearly be due by then.

They had tidied the kitchen by the time the men staggered in from the picket.

'How'd you get on?' Iwan's voice was hoarse.

Angela waved at the ceiling. 'Is not bad. The girl's first try, after all.'

'Fantastic. Done well, haven't they, Simon?'

Scrapper grunted, vanished into the bathroom. Judging by the yelps and gasps, Helen guessed the water was freezing.

'He's been like a bear with toothache all day,' Iwan said. 'You two had words, *bach*?'

'No,' Helen lied.

Scrapper said they couldn't keep the baby. He said they should see Dr O'Connell, said they were running out of time. But her mam walking out made Helen all the more certain. She and Scrapper were nothing like her mam and dad. They and the baby would do just fine.

But when she told Scrapper her decision, he froze.

'We'll manage,' she persisted.

'No, Red. Fact is, we won't,' he said coldly. 'Can you not look beyond yourself, for once. Things are bad enough without a baby to worry about.'

Something had changed in him these last weeks. As though he blamed her for landing him with a court case. She felt guilty about that. But if she hurt the baby, she'd feel worse. Her only choice, she reckoned, was to stop arguing and play for time.

Angela took the pasta machine out to the shed, came back with Sue Griffiths.

'You got a visitor, *bella*.'

Sue gazed up at the ceiling, puzzled. 'What's this; medical supplies?'

'*Tagliatelle* and *lasagne*,' Angela said.

Sue looked none the wiser.

'Home-made pasta,' Helen said.

'*Duw*, there's impressive,' Sue said. 'Always thought that stuff grew on trees. You free tomorrow, Red? The girls are picketing the pit.'

'A women's picket?' Iwan said.

'Thanks for the enthusiasm,' Sue said. 'Dewi bust a gasket. Said there's no place for women on the line.'

'He might have a point,' Iwan said. 'Been hairy out there,

268

lately. Coppers bussed in from all over. They're handy with their truncheons, the big-city pigs.'

'We're keeping it peaceful,' Sue said. 'There'll be no argy-bargy.'

'Might not be down to you, *bach*.'

Helen had no enthusiasm about joining the picket. But if she went, she'd make her point. Scrapper would have to see that she was serious. That she was willing to do her bit for the cause.

'I'm in,' she said.

'No you don't,' Iwan said. 'Dai Dumbells took a truncheon across the face last week. We're packing lads off to hospital every day.'

Sue shuddered. Helen grabbed her hand and squeezed it. 'We'll look out for each other,' she said.

She turned to see Scrapper in the kitchen doorway, eyes on him like flints.

* * *

He sat on the bedroom floor, wearing three sweaters, rifling through his leftover LPs. Joy Division blared from the stereo.

'You're not going, an' that's an end to it.'

He wouldn't look at her. He was acting like a Victorian husband. It was unconvincing, sat like an outsized suit on his skinny frame.

'I want to do my bit, Scrap.'

He turned the music up to drown out the sound of their voices. 'You're not to go, Red. Not in your condition. The last thing I need is you getting nicked.'

It was the final straw. For weeks, he'd acted as though the baby didn't exist. Now he was using it against her. Every way she turned, he had her trapped. All the more reason to break free for a few hours. It was a chance to speak to Sue; she would know what to do.

269

'Like you care about my condition,' she said. 'You want our baby dead.'

He got up, grabbed his jacket. 'That's low, Red.'

The back door slammed behind him.

* * *

She woke to the creaking of floorboards, to the icicle nudge of toes. Scrapper's hair was thick with tobacco smoke, his breath sticky with cider. She lay still, wondered what to say to him. But he rolled away from her, already snoring. Next time she woke, he was creeping around the bedroom, getting ready to go out. She heard him shuffle arms and legs into clothes, scrape a comb through his hair. The bedroom door opened, closed. A mutter of voices. Then two pairs of boots clomped across the landing and down the stairs. She waited until she heard the back door close, then snapped on the bedside light and pulled on her clothes.

Her mam-in-law was standing on a kitchen chair, turning the sheets of pasta. Her hair hung down her back like seaweed, her face creased from sleep and worry.

'How can I change your mind?'

'You can't.'

'Is trouble today for sure.'

'We're not out for trouble. We're showing that we support the lads.'

She downed her tea, went to the bathroom. What she saw wasn't pretty: freckles dark against blue-white skin. Eyes shadowed purple. She patted on base and blusher, fixed her hair in a knot, on impulse, added a slap of red lipstick.

Her mam-in-law bit back a smile when she emerged. 'Is a while since you put on your warpaint, *bella*.'

* * *

At ten to six, Mary Power pulled up in a scruffy VW camper. Her grey-blonde hair fluffed damply around her ears. Helen climbed in, greeted the dozen women inside, sat next to Sue. Mary fired up the engine, and they juddered down the High Street with a crunch of brakes and gears. The road was lined with parked cars, vans and minibuses, windows draped with union banners, placards and hand-drawn posters. Mary leaned on her horn. As they passed, the vehicles pulled out behind. Every car, van and bus had a woman behind the wheel. It was unusual, in Ystrad, to see a woman in the driving seat.

'Bloody hell,' Mary said. 'Not bad for three days' notice.'

The convoy stretched the length of the village as the minibus turned off the High Street. Helen squeezed her hands inside her gloves. Her parka, jumper and leggings offered scant protection against a morning that had teeth. Debbie sat alone, cheek pressed against the window. Her face was clammy. Helen felt sad for her, suddenly. She hadn't found being pregnant hard, at least physically. Debbie looked to be struggling.

'Heard about the baby,' she said quietly. 'Congratulations.'

Debbie flinched as though she'd been slapped. 'You spiteful little bitch.'

'Let's raise us a tune, ladies,' Sue's voice was unexpectedly loud. 'How about a blast of 'Build A Bonfire' to get us in the mood?'

'Let's not,' Mary said.

No one took up the call to sing. Helen turned to Debbie again, but Sue tugged on her arm, started talking about Angela's pasta. The bus emerged from the railway tunnel. Up ahead, a line of blue uniforms stretched across the pit gates. As they drew closer, Helen saw armoured bodies, standing three deep. Police vans lined the slope above, glinting in the half-light like rows of teeth.

'Well, girls,' Mary wrenched the handbrake. 'Reckon they been expecting us.'

They climbed out of the van. Helen pulled her parka closer. The thin cotton was flimsy, her boots drank in mud and morning dew.

Sue pulled her aside. 'What was that, with Debbie?'

'Didn't mean to upset her. Dewi said she's expecting. Told us before Christmas. Is she not telling people yet?'

Sue sighed. 'I could throttle Dewi Power. Look, Red; Debbie's not pregnant.'

'But we heard it from Dewi. He said—'

'Debbie decided not to have it, Red. And Dai's taken it bad.'

Helen clutched Sue, horrified. No wonder Debbie was so quiet. So cold.

'Shit. I never meant—'

'Leave it. I'll explain to her.'

Now was the time to talk to Sue. This was her chance. But before she could begin, Mary had shouldered her megaphone.

'Comrades, sisters,' she shouted. 'This is a non-violent picket. We're here to show solidarity with the lads. Link arms, an' follow me.'

The women drew together. Sue pulled Helen to the front to join Mary, behind them a dozen lines of women, everyone chanting.

'Here we go, here we go, here we go. Here we go, here we go, here we go-o-oooo!'

Ahead of them, Helen saw the police line harden into a barricade of bodies and shields. Resin batons thudded on Perspex shields; slow, thuggish, brutal. Goosebumps studded her arms and legs. Her pace slowed to the truncheons' beat. Mary halted a yard from the riot shields, raised her megaphone.

'We are women from Ystrad an' from all over Wales,' she

said. 'We are here to make peaceful protest. Here in solidarity with the men.'

The drumming quickened.

A hoarse voice answered from inside the police lines. 'You do not have permission to protest here. Your presence outside this pit is illegal. You must leave immediately, or we will arrest you for obstruction.'

Mary stretched on tip-toe, tried to look the speaker in the eye. 'Blackthorn is our pit. We're here to defend our pit and our community. We got every right to be here. Every right to protest. Ladies, make some noise.'

The chanting started up again; louder, more defiant. But the batons beat louder too, and faster. Helen stared up at the policemen, saw narrowed eyes, faces creased from the weight of helmets and the tug of chin straps. The many pairs of visored eyes seemed to look right through her.

A light flared. Someone was filming the protesters from deep inside the line. As Helen blinked, dazzled, the riot shields slammed forwards. Bodies packed around her, crushing her ribs.

'Ladies,' the hoarse voice mocked. 'You call yourselves ladies?'

'They're sluts,' came another voice. 'Scargill's sluts. They think they got the balls to take us. Bunch of fuckin' lezzies.'

A bellow of outrage rose from the brazier, where the men were gathered. Their placards bristled with outrage. The blue line stirred, bubbled, broke loose. Beyond the crush of bodies, Helen heard the sound of running feet, the thwack of truncheons, the shouts of the men. The sound echoed across the valley; cries of pain and fury, chanting, shouting. And she was caught in the middle of it all, crushed and trapped and scared.

As she squinted into the light, she heard the growl of an engine.

'Shift girls,' Sue yelled. 'It's the scabs.'

273

The police line softened for a moment; paused, hardened and drove forwards. The shields attacked in a v-formation. Helen lost her footing. As she struggled, a shuttered windscreen loomed over her. The cry went up.

'Scab, scab, scab!'

As the bus drew closer, the police lines split for a second. She saw Scrapper on the far side of the road, a riot shield rammed into his face.

'Red,' he yelled. 'Go home, for fuck's sake.'

'I'm fine,' she shouted, but she could tell he hadn't heard her.

The pit gates swung open. Helen looked up, saw a baton rise above her head. Instinct kicked in. She ducked as it slammed down. The woman behind her screamed a wounded animal scream. Terror kicked in then, for the baby, if not for herself. As the crush surged again, she clawed her way to the back of the crowd, her breath tearing at her lungs.

The scab minibus slipped through the crowd. Next to the driver sat Mr Albright, the pit manager, his face hidden behind a copy of *The Times*. Behind him, she made out two bodies huddled under blankets. As the gates slammed shut she saw the face pressed up against the back windscreen, mouthing insults through the glass. Stones and cans and bottles bounced off the grilles that covered the windscreen, thudded onto the roof, but her dad didn't flinch.

Mary bobbed out of the crush, saw the look on her face. 'You got us, now, Red.'

The bus vanished into the darkness that swirled out of the pit.

'Watch out, girls,' Sue yelled. 'They're coming in.'

Deep inside the police lines, Helen spotted dozens of officers tightening their chin straps. The front line of shields swung open. Dark shapes darted out, grabbed women from the edges of the group. Three leapt on Shirley, the vicar's wife. Two others dragged Chrissie to a waiting Black Maria.

Sue gripped Helen's arm. 'When they come for you, go soft and limp like you're dead,' she said. 'Don't fight. You'll get hurt, and the bastards get off on it.'

Shields slammed into the crowd like bulldozers. Helen looked up through the warp and bend of Perspex into a suntanned, snarling face.

'Aren't you ashamed, attacking women?'

The policeman smiled. 'We're getting ninety quid overtime for this, you silly bitch. No shame in that.'

She couldn't help herself. 'No shame in blood money?'

'I'm doin' my job, darling. Shame your men won't do theirs.'

He dragged her to the line of police vans. She relaxed her muscles, let her body sag. It made no difference. The policeman picked her up and lugged her through the doors like a builder tossing bagged cement. She fell heavily, jarring her spine. Flashes of colour exploded behind her eyes. She lay where she landed.

* * *

By the time the doors of the van opened again, morning had ripped a gash in the darkness. Helen lay, not moving, blinking against the light. Long blue arms reached for her, dragged her out into a car park beneath a busy flyover. They were not in Ystrad any more. Two policewomen dragged her into a tall, pebble-dashed building, pulled and pushed her down a long corridor, past dazed-looking protesters.

Time passed. She sat alone in a locked cell. Something wasn't right. She felt cold to the bones, but her clothes dripped sweat. Her heart thudded to the remembered beat of the police batons. Women's voices seeped through thin walls. She wished she had company. Wished she could call her mam. For a long time, no one came. At last, the door creaked open. She had never been so relieved to see anyone. But when she tried to stand, her legs were having none of it.

'Sue!' It came out strangled.

'Christ, Red,' Sue rushed over. 'Are you sick?'

'Don't feel too clever.'

'Put this on.'

Sue took off her donkey jacket, tucked it around Helen's shoulders, ran back to the door and hammered on it, yelling for help. The heavy miner's jacket made no odds, nor did the yelling. Eventually, Sue gave up. Midday passed. No one came. Helen curled up on the bench, knees curled towards her chin, Sue slumped on the floor nearby. Suddenly, a sharp pain tore through Helen's abdomen. She writhed and shrieked in agony. Cramps juddered up her body.

Sue grabbed her. 'What is it?'

But Helen couldn't gather breath enough to answer. She tried to stand, but dizziness laid her flat. Sue threw aside the jacket, gasped. Helen looked down at herself. The bench was pooled with thick, dark blood.

— 3 —

Gwyn waited and waited, but the girl did not come. Weeks passed and she had yet to come to thank him. Even though he put a good word in for that boy with the police, offered to drop the burglary and assault case, refused to leave the cop shop until the sergeant agreed to free the boy on police-to-court bail. And to see her now, turning up on the line, howling like a harridan. Disgraceful behaviour. Some thanks for trying to care for his family and save his pit, for speaking up, against his better judgement, for that rabble-rousing boy.

He peered at himself in the living room mirror, comb in hand. Rearranged his hair, first this way, then that. He was greyer than ever, these last months. He squared his shoulders, called up his old bravado. Still a good head of hair on him, even so: in good nick for a fellow who'd spent half a life below ground. He'd already notched up more years than the old man. He breathed out sharply, chest grating a metallic rasp. He dusted his shoulders. His best suit, bought from C&A in Cardiff. He slipped his feet into his best brogues and set off past the women – 'Do you *not* look lovely this morning, ladies.' – and waited at the end of the road for Albright.

He boarded the minibus, nodded his good mornings, sat himself down in the back. Metal-shuttered windows shattered the landscape into a thousand tiny squares. He gazed through the naked trees at the winding gear. The twisted skeleton was coated with a fine red layer of rust. He sighed, pressed his spine into the plastic seat cover, pondered what he needed to do.

Albright had some big-shot Coal Board managers coming up to Blackthorn from London this morning, asked Gwyn to sit in with them. He sensed an ill wind.

The minibus split the ranks of pickets, like an ocean liner through rough seas, roared through the gates. Matt Price and Alun Probert climbed out, wandered down to the workshop. Gwyn went to the canteen, fixed himself a tea, nipped out to the courtyard for a smoke in time to see the pit gates swing open and a chauffeur-driven black Rover purr into the yard.

* * *

The big shots went straight to the boardroom. Low winter light flooded through the windows, bounced off beech veneer. At one end of the table sat Adam Smith-Tudor. At the other stood Albright. Between them sat the two senior managers, dressed like undertakers in fine dark wool suits. Gwyn shuffled in, took a chair opposite them, feeling shabby. The men raised their eyes briefly, turned back to their documents. He felt judged and found wanting. Albright flitted round the room, poured coffees, distributed papers, showily eager to please.

Turnbull, the younger, brasher senior manager tugged his platinum cufflinks, consulted an outsized platinum watch. 'Right, gentlemen. When you're ready.'

Henshall, his colleague, nodded. 'We're due at the next pit on the list at eleven.'

Albright cleared his throat. 'Right. Thanks for allowing me to put my case to you. Simply put, as the survey reports I sent you show, there is no good reason – economic or practical – to shut down Blackthorn.'

Gwyn jerked to attention. Shut it down? The words sank in like rocks hitting water. He fired a shocked glance at Smith-Tudor. But the area boss had his eyes fixed on Albright, now positioned at the whiteboard, where he'd taped a map of the mine.

The little pit boss took a dark red fountain pen from his pocket. It matched, exactly, the colour of his suit.

'As you know, we had some flooding after heavy rainfall last month. The survey shows the coalface to be unstable here, near seam two,' he jabbed the pen. 'We need to shore up the tunnels that lead to seam three. We also need to prop up the roof here, in the main seam, after an incident eleven months ago when a man was killed.'

He paused, bowed his head. Smooth English hypocrite. All the while Blackthorn's lawyers fighting Margaret Parry's compensation claim.

'All in all, the survey found that nearly a third of the mine's working area fails to meet the minimum safety standard,' Albright said. 'We need to address this before we reopen the coalface.'

Henshall and Turnbull put their heads together, held a muttered discussion.

'And your projections for securing the mine to standard?' Turnbull said.

'A hundred and twenty grand, tops, to secure the work areas, ready to resume full operations.'

Henshall shook his head. 'Money we don't have.'

The bravado seeped from Albright's smug little face. Not the answer he'd expected. Not what Gwyn expected. It would fall to Smith-Tudor to sort out these jumped-up English paper-shifters. He promised, Smith-Tudor; said Blackthorn would be fine. Said it was pits with falling yields that faced the chop.

Gwyn waited for the coalfield boss to tell Henshall and Turnbull to get stuffed. A long silence followed.

'With respect,' Albright started up again. 'Did you look at my calculations? Based on the Coal Board's own price forecasts, invest now and you're looking at a return of more than seventy-five percent within five years. Secure the mine now, the strike should be over by the time we've finished.'

Gwyn's missing fingers throbbed murder. Highfaluting talk of forecasts and figures defeated him. Bottom line was, when the men come back to work Blackthorn would turn a profit; there was damn good coal – and plenty of it – to be mined at his pit.

Red-faced now, Albright kept going, 'My figures show that Blackthorn is not – I repeat, not – an uneconomic pit,' he said. 'With adequate investment, it would be highly profitable. It employs a hundred and fifty men, sustains a community of twelve hundred souls—'

'That's neither here nor there,' Henshall cut in.

'I disagree,' Albright practically hissed the word. 'One of the militants' most powerful arguments is that the Coal Board is taking a hatchet to traditional mining communities. Ystrad is as traditional as it comes,' he waved a hand at Gwyn. 'Let's prove the hardliners wrong.'

Smith-Tudor rolled Albright's survey report into a baton, fixed the pit manager a patronising smile. 'That argument is bullshit, dear boy.'

Gwyn jerked to attention. Why in hell was the area manager siding with the toffs from head office – toffs who wanted to take a hatchet to his pit? Smith-Tudor had promised to see Blackthorn through the bloodshed.

'No it isn't,' Albright said. 'Not when all I need is a hundred and twenty grand and six weeks to get the pit moving.'

'Now you listen to me, eh, sonny,' an ice-pick for a voice, Smith-Tudor. 'I have twenty-eight pits to consider. My budget is tight. You expect me to throw that kind of money at one pit, eh, for sentimental reasons?'

'Sentimental? Close the pit, and you dump this community

on the scrapheap,' Albright said. 'You agree, don't you, Gwyn?'

'Ah yes,' Smith-Tudor smiled through bared teeth. 'Our proud local warrior. What d'you say, eh, Richards?'

'Pritchard,' Gwyn said.

'Come on, then,' Smith-Tudor said. 'Suppose we did pour money into Blackthorn. Reckon that rabble would be grateful, eh? Reckon you could talk them into coming back to work?'

Gwyn pushed his chair away and stood, all four bosses staring him down like a firing-squad. He gripped the table until his missing fingers ached for mercy.

'Sod the lodge,' he said. 'We got 'em on the ropes. There's only one way the strike will end. They'll lose, we'll win and they'll come back to work on our terms. The lodge is finished. It'd be a crime to close this pit.'

A wolfish smile spread across Smith-Tudor's face. 'You realise the implications of what you're saying, eh, Pritchard?'

'I do, aye.'

Smith-Tudor turned to the London men. 'Well I've heard nothing in this room to change my mind,' he said. 'Fact is, gentlemen, closure is the quickest, least painful option for Blackthorn.'

Gwyn's stomach went into free-fall. He lied then, Smith-Tudor. Lied when he said the pit would be safe. When he said they had to smash the lodge to let Blackthorn get on with making coal. Lied from start to finish.

Henshall was addressing himself to Albright. 'Make no mistake, Edmund,' he said. 'Your efforts will not go unrewarded. The NCB is committed to progressing young talent. This decision bears no reflection on your management skills.'

Turnbull cleared his throat. 'Our decision is confidential until the Coal Board announces it. Any leak, whether to the miners or to the media, will have severe repercussions.'

'You're not telling the men?' Gwyn said flatly.

Henshall, the more senior manager, eyeballed him. 'Our number one priority – and the decision has been made at government level – is that the union must not win this strike,' he said. 'We expect a national return to work. On our terms.'

'Can't have individual pit closures cloud the issue, eh,' Smith-Tudor said.

Henshall clicked shut his briefcase. 'If we announce that Blackthorn is to close, support for the strike will harden. The union is buckling; the labour movement is on its knees. We are *this close* to winning. We can't let the loony left regroup around a fight to save named pits.'

Albright slammed his fist on the table. 'Have them limp back to be sacked?'

'A conscience, eh, Albright?' Smith-Tudor smiled cyanide at him.

'Won't be you doling out P45s,' Gwyn muttered.

The thought of it. Of looking two hundred men in the eye and handing them their marching orders. Albright stood, folded his papers, followed Henshall and Turnbull out to the corridor.

That left Gwyn alone with Smith-Tudor. He was tempted to grab the area boss by the lapels and shake him until his chins rattled.

'You said if we kept the coal flowing there'd be a future for this pit. Said you'd look after me.'

'You've let me down, Richards. Too bad you aren't up to scratch, eh. Would have suited you, a desk job. Given you the chance to wear them kecks—' he switched to mocking Wenglish '—more reg'lar, like.'

He closed his briefcase and left the room, a jaunty bounce to his gait.

* * *

By the time Gwyn staggered outside, the Rover had left the courtyard. The wind was biting cold, gusting a force that hurled him sideways. He steadied himself, struggled to fill his lungs with air, tasted wood smoke blown from the braziers beyond the gate. The winding gear was still. He closed his eyes. When the wind dropped, he could have sworn he heard footsteps. Far echoes of the many men that Blackthorn had chewed up and spat out over the years. Alf Manifesto, the fifty souls lost to the firedamp blast of 1960, Gabriel Parry, his old man.

What would he have to say for himself, the old man? No point thinking that way. The old man never had a good word to say about anything. In that instant Gwyn saw him, squatting in the shadows of the winding house, a roll-up between his lips. Vivid as the day, he was: black moustache bristling, blue eyes slitted against the light.

'Maybe one of us'll outlive this pit, eh, Dad?'

4

Day after day, Helen lay in bed. The blankets weighed down on her. She didn't leave the bedroom, lay barely moving, said not a word. Life went on as usual, for the men, at least, off every morning to picket, plodding back in the afternoons. But for Helen life did not go on. How could it? Her mam-in-law whirled around mopping and dusting and clearing cupboards, as noisy as everyone else was silent.

Sometimes she came to sit with Helen, tried to get her to talk, to eat.

'Is crazy you didn't tell us. Why?'

Because your precious son wanted rid of it.

'At least try to eat, *bella*.'

But she couldn't. She couldn't.

She had even less to say to Scrapper. When he came to bed at night, she moved away from him, feet hooked over mattress. They lay awake, not touching, not speaking. Laid out next to each other like the dead.

His words – stupid, empty words – drove more distance between them.

'You're wrong to think I didn't want the baby, Red.'

But you didn't, did you?

'We should sue the police. The lads reckon we got a case.'

Bring our baby back, will it?

'Won't you hold me, at least? It's not only you that hurts.'

She lay like a boulder in his arms, pulled away as soon as she could. Some nights, she drifted off to sleep for an hour or two.

Slept and heard a baby cry, the sound drowned out by the thudding of batons on Perspex, by the juddering pulse in her head. She woke up every time bathed in sweat. When she slept, the dream replayed itself. She tried her best not to sleep.

Scrapper came home later and later, stayed in the living room, spent the night there, more often than not. When he did climb into bed, his skin smelled of sweat and booze and rage. On one of those nights, he reached for her, laid cold hands on her arms, her legs, her breasts. She said nothing, felt nothing, lay still and let it happen. When he finished, his tears fell hot and salty on her face. She rolled away from him. After that, he didn't touch her at all.

Finally, her mam-in-law summoned Dr O'Connell again. Helen heard him creaking up the stairs, the squeak of leather shoes on floorboards.

Whispers floated in from the kitchen. 'Is natural, the grieving. Destroyed all of us, this. But she's a ghost, doctor. Won't talk to us. Can't eat. Can't look at us.'

The cold whisper of a stethoscope.

More questions. 'You're in good shape physically, Helen, if too thin. Let's talk about how you feel.'

Ta very much, Doctor. Let's not.

'Okay, fine. I'll prescribe you antidepressants. See how you go.'

An image of a grubby dressing gown. Of empty, red-rimmed eyes.

No.

'The pills will take the edge of it, my dear.'

'I said, *no*.' The words exploded from her chest.

'Well, we have to do something,' the doctor said, exasperated.

'It's all my fault,' she whispered.

'Don't be ridiculous. How is a miscarriage anyone's fault?'

He didn't understand. None of them did. The baby was gone.

Her mam's words came back to her. The irony. To end up like her, anyway, and with no baby to show for it.

The doctor scribbled into his notebook, packed stethoscope and thermometer into leather briefcase and left. She waited until she heard the kitchen door close, threw on some clothes and grabbed her parka. She crept down the stairs, daps in hand, set off into the cold. It was only when she turned onto the High Street that it struck her she had nowhere to go.

A couple stood on the porch of the pub, yelling at each other. It was the girl with bleach-blonde dreadlocks. Her boyfriend had a smacked-up nose and flattened cheekbones, arms bare despite the cold in a sleeveless t-shirt, biceps like pale balloons. The girl was giving it plenty, face pushed into his face, screaming at him. Helen watched them, felt something like envy. Only people who had feelings for each other could fight like that.

She slipped away into the dusk, followed the track past the allotments to the fields. Something drove her towards the barn. Wind whistled across the hillside. As she staggered through a gap in the hedgerow, she saw a figure up ahead on the track. A man of medium height, styled like a Russian spy in waisted, wide-shouldered felt. Only one man in Ystrad could wear such a coat. Siggy Split-Enz. It had to be.

She moved closer. Siggy was heading straight for the barn. She and Scrapper had guessed that other couples met at the barn. Who might Siggy's lucky lady be? He cleared the stile in a leap. She chased after him, panting, saw him reach the barn and take his lover in his arms. When they came up for air, the shock knocked her sideways. No lucky lady, that. It was Matthew Price.

* * *

She staggered away, crashing downhill through the mud and dried bracken. Two men together. In Ystrad? Was that possible? And those two, of all people. Glamorous, strapping Siggy. Ferrety divorcé Matthew Price. A ladies' man, Matthew Price, everyone said. A string of conquests from Milford Haven to Monmouth. So he said. So Scrapper said. Scrapper: did he know about this?

The night closed over her, a drawstring bag pulled tight. Patches of light splattered across the valley. She had only one place to go. She staggered back across the fields. As she emerged above the allotments, she saw Angela and Iwan in the kitchen window, arms wrapped around each other. Despite everything, they kept going, her in-laws.

She opened the back door, fumbled with her shoelaces.

Voices drifted down the stairs. 'Talk to her, and say what?'

'Is not important what you say, Simon. Get her to talk to you.'

'It won't work, Mam. We're strangers now.'

'She's not a stranger, son. She's your wife. Not helpful, you going out every night. You need to stop home, for once. Fix this mess.'

'I've tried, Dad. She won't look at me. Won't touch me. Like she's the only one that hurts.'

'Please, *caro mio*. Try one more time.'

'Can't you butt out, the pair of you? It's not down to me, this. Red don't want me no more.'

The hall light snapped on. Clumsy footsteps clattered downstairs. Scrapper paused when he saw her, but didn't stop.

He pushed past, grabbed his coat, vanished into the night.

If he came home, she didn't hear him. When she woke alone, she knew a void had opened between them too wide and too deep to cross.

* * *

Some days later, she woke to find Sue next to her bed.

'Did Angela send for you?'

'Shaping up to be a gorgeous day, *cariad*. Fancy a walk?'

Outside, sunlight splintered the February clouds. The hillsides breathed a faint green scent of spring. A robin dipped and bobbed under Iwan's fruit trees. Crocus buds and nodding snowdrops broke through the black earth. On the High Street, the pavement glistened from overnight rain. Everything had a newborn shine to it. Helen clutched Sue's arm, blood roaring in her ears. They headed downhill, past shops that were shuttered and vacant. Outside the Stute, figures loomed at her. Faces smiled and nodded hello. They kept walking, ducked beneath the railway bridge, emerged below the stone-built miners' chapel.

Sue looked tired and stressed.

'You been working too hard.'

She gave a laugh that was more a yelp. 'Busier than ever, with the rumours about the pit, Red.'

'What rumours?'

Sue gripped her arm. 'Scrapper didn't say?'

'Me an' Scrapper don't talk much, lately.'

They trudged past the chapel, paused at the fork in the road. Up ahead, a listless plume of smoke rose from the picketline braziers. Sue steered Helen the other way, following the black, slow-flowing stream that wound beneath the slagheaps to a cracked bench, green with algae, placed at the water's edge.

Helen flopped down, exhausted. 'What rumours?'

'Word is, the pit needs serious repairs. Lodge reckons the bosses would sooner shut down than shell out.'

'D'you believe that?'

'Who knows? Gramps says not to worry about what ifs. Win the strike, he reckons, Blackthorn's future'll take care of itself.'

Sue lobbed a stone at the brackish water. It bounced twice. Blackness closed over it. There was something more, Helen could tell.

'What else?'

'Debbie's gone.'

'Left Dai, you mean?'

'Yup. Gone to stay at her sister's.'

'Because of the abortion?'

'Who knows. A few marriages hit the rocks, lately. Money troubles, mostly. Or the husbands getting antsy about their women being too busy fighting to put dinner on the table. Some of the girls got badges made: *My Marriage Survived The Miner's Strike*.'

Helen snorted. 'Won't be ordering mine.'

Sue bounced another stone across the water. 'How about we take a drive this weekend? Get away from this dump.'

'Could we visit my mam?'

'Only if she sends for you. Sorry, *bach*.'

Helen sagged against Sue. God only knew what state her mam was in. She'd made no phone calls, sent no letters since the day she fled to the refuge. She picked up a stone, lobbed it at the still, dark water. It sank without bouncing. The world was a cold, hard place. No one looked out for anyone. Not really. She was completely and utterly alone.

5

Scrapper knew he should never have let Red picket. The silence between them was an accusation. As with his other crimes, he had no clue how to plead.

'Talk to the girl,' Angela kept saying.

And he tried to talk, but Red stared at him with empty eyes. He spent more and more time on the line or down the Stute or speaking at fundraisers. Throwing himself into things made sense, at least. No one asked painful questions at the solidarity groups. The gatherings, held in pub back rooms and public libraries, raised much simpler debates. Reform or revolution? Do men benefit from women's oppression? Which way forward for the Welsh working class? And everyone had plenty to say. He felt safer, more sure of himself at the meetings than at home with Red's hurt silence, with Angela's fermenting rage. And for the strike to lose was not an option now, when all of them had lost so much.

Meanwhile, the women kept raising hell, as passionate and full of *hwyl* as the men were burned out and defeated. Mary announced a Valentine's Day fundraiser, invited the boys, the rest of the village, the solidarity groups and supporters from across South Wales.

'Come with me, Red,' he tried to take her in his arms.

But she turned her face to the wall.

* * *

The Stute was in near-darkness. Strings of fairy lights hung from the rafters. The lamps were draped with sheer red scarves.

Debbie was taking money on the door. She waved at the room. 'What d'you reckon?'

'You're asking the wrong fella.'

'I reckon it looks romantic.'

'Set the mood for you and Dai to patch things up, eh?'

'Stuff Dai.'

The man in question perched on the edge of the stage, clutching a pint of ale, eyes fixed on his estranged wife. Unsettling, the look on his face. Not affection, not sadness; rage, barely held in check. Scrapper spotted some of the other boys, went over to join them. If there was trouble brewing between Dai and Debbie, he wanted none of it.

A heavy, yeasty smell filled the room. The boys were clutching plastic mugs. Eddie Hobnob said Bryn Tawel home brew club had donated the bevvies. Scrapper showed his lodge card at the bar, brought away a free pint. It was pay-what-you-can for all the others and the cash kept rolling in. Someone fetched him a second beer; someone else a third. The brew had a kick to it.

A band got up on the stage, played protest songs. The women sang along and some got up and danced. That reminded him how Red loved to dance. Then Mary dragged Angela on stage to sing 'Bella Ciao', which got everyone on their feet to shout out the chorus. Scrapper watched, his throat tight with sorrow. The words of loss cut too deep. And no amount of ale in the world would dull the pain he felt.

After came the speeches, Mary wrestling a whistling microphone, Dewi next. Then several trade union types; a nurse from Bryn Tawel hospital, a couple of lads from the railways, a blonde firefighter – whoops and catcalls from the lads when she finished. The final speaker was someone Sue had brought from the university. An old boy, short but vigorous, hair rising from his crown in snowy tufts.

The room fell silent as the man thundered about the power of the proletariat, and seizing the means of production and the false dichotomy of Thatcherism and how the miners, undefeated would be the gravediggers of British capitalism. The boys hung on the man's every word, heads cocked, some nodding agreement, some shaking their heads. He gave it *hwyl*, the speaker. Fired them up to fight the good fight. When he finished, the boys were cheering.

Scrapper watched the others crowd around the old boy. He grabbed another bevvy and hung back. Debbie was talking to a man with tanned skin and chin-length white hair, chunky silver bangles on his sinewy brown arm. He'd turned up with the old Marxist. Debbie talked and the man smiled and nodded intently. Scrapper watched sleepily as Dai pushed through the crowd, snapped awake when he realised what was afoot.

He bowled after him, got there just as Dai yanked the man away from Debbie, arm raised to strike. Someone seized Dai's wrist, Scrapper grabbed his other arm and helped to shove him to the far side of the hall, to cool him off. It didn't work. Debbie chased after them, hell-bent on giving Dai a tongue-lashing. They were both angry and the worse for drink. After a struggle, two hauliers pinned Dai against the wall, as he fought and bellowed like an ox.

'Get Debbie out of here, Simon,' Iwan yelled.

'C'mon,' Scrapper clamped an arm around her waist.

'I'll go when I'm bloody well ready.'

The white-haired man followed them out, a bottle in his bangled hand. Scrapper had a sense that the man was studying them both. Analysing the chaos.

'That man didn't hurt you, comrade?' the man said.

'I'd like to see the bastard try.'

Scrapper gripped her again. 'C'mon Debs. Show's over. I'm walking you home.'

'Says who?'

'You want to stay?' he hissed. 'With that ponce?'

'Jealous, are you?' She turned to the man. 'Gi's a sip, eh, comrade?'

The man handed her the bottle. 'Keep it. We'll continue that discussion some other time.' He raised a fist by way of a salute and slid back inside the Stute.

Scrapper grabbed Debbie, dragged her down the steps onto the street. She staggered against him, laughing. Just how drunk she was, he couldn't tell. He was struggling himself, the cold, damp air filling his head with clouds.

'Let's go to the gatehouse,' she slung an arm around his waist.

'No, I—'

'Drink,' she ordered.

He took a gulp, choked as bubbles filled his throat, burst as they hit his gullet. 'Jeezus—'

'You not had champagne before?'

'Is that what you call that crap?'

He wiped his lips on the back of his hand. His mouth tasted dry and sour. Part of him wanted Debbie to get him wasted and part wanted to be safe at home, snuggled up with Red. But Red didn't want him and Debbie was deaf to the word no.

He let her drag him under the railway bridge and up the steps to the lych gate of the miners' chapel. It was where they came to be alone, when they were courting. Debbie collapsed, laughing, on the stone bench inside, pulled him down next to her.

'Does a tidy job getting a girl pissed, this stuff.'

He took a couple more glugs from the bottle. His arms and legs turned numb. He leaned against Debbie, head full of bubbles. 'Why do we lose the things we love?'

She rested her cheek against his cheek. 'Love? I'm done with it. Gets you nothing but grief.'

'Me and Red—'

'I'm gonna start enjoying life. I'm sick of being trapped.'

'So that's your game, *comrade*? But that bloke's a tosser. Don't blame Dai for trying to smack 'im.'

'Don't you know who he is?'

'I don't give a stuff. He's not one of us.'

Debbie sucked the bottle thoughtfully. 'The be all and end all, is it?'

'What?'

'Belonging. To Ystrad. To Wales. What if we didn't? What if we went different places, met new people? Belonged any place we damn well pleased.'

Scrapper snorted. 'Lose the pit, we'll have no damn choice but to go.'

Debbie made it sound exciting. But Angela didn't belong, not really. Not even after twenty-odd years in Ystrad. It was no fun being the Johnny Foreigner at school, the teachers calling him Scrapper because they couldn't say Schiappa. The other kids calling him Iti or Wop. There was nothing stupid about wanting to belong, the way he saw it. He'd never belonged, before meeting Red.

'Saul's a fourth internationalist,' Debbie said. 'Permanent revolution, and all that. Wants me to speak to his students about the strike. Said I could stay over.'

'*Ych y fi*, Debs. You know what he wants.'

'Maybe it's what I want.'

'There's nothing to say about the strike. We're halfway to hell in a handcart.'

'Don't be like that, Scrap. It's changed us, and for the better. We never knew our own strength, before.'

'Aye. And where's it got us?'

'It's been the making of us,' Debbie said. 'And when we win, thousands of men and women and children'll rest easy in their beds knowing they got a future.'

'And if we don't win?'

She flung her arms around his neck. 'There's no fucking if, Scrapper. Win, or lose everything.'

She clamped her lips to his lips. Her tongue fizzed like champagne against his tongue. They clung together. She opened her jacket, shoved his hand inside. The shock brought him to his senses. He pulled away. Debbie's body went rigid. She buttoned up her blouse, face hidden beneath her curtain of hair.

'It's not that I don't want to—' It sounded lame, even as he said it.

'How do I get myself a real man?' Debbie said. 'A man fit to be my equal? Cos I'm fucking sick of being strong. You're the same, you and Dai. You're all the same. Women got all the strength. And that scares you.'

'Debs, me and Red need to sort things out.'

'You're wasting your time on that daddy's girl, Scrap. She's got no guts for this. You need to let her go. We were good together, you and me.'

Was it guts, or was it choices, he wondered. Red started out with options. He and Debbie and the rest of the boys had none. Red could have chosen not to be cold and hungry and defeated, could have walked away undamaged. Instead she chose him over her family. The strike had asked too much of her. But he was trapped and maybe she wasn't. And perhaps Debbie had a point.

Perhaps he had no right to make Red stay.

6

A car pulled up outside the ice cream parlour. The driver beeped the horn three times. Helen peered down, saw Sue's battered Ford Anglia. She shrugged on her parka, turned to see Angela in the doorway.

'Is good to see you up and about, *bella*.'

Her mam-in-law was pale. Not easy for her either, these last few weeks. Helen threw her arms around Angela's waist.

'I'm sorry, Angela. For all of it. We should have told you. I don't know why we didn't.'

'Is alright.'

'But it's not alright, is it?'

'It will be, *bella*. If you and Simon talk.'

'Tonight. I promise I'll try tonight.'

She meant it, too. If everything went to plan today, perhaps she and Scrapper could start over, talk over their differences, find a way to put their losses behind them, to drop her defences and let him back in.

She climbed into the passenger seat, gave Sue a peck on the cheek.

'So. Where to?'

'Cwm Gwragedd.'

'The magic forest?'

Helen nodded.

'Well, I'm not scared of tree spirits. But why?'

'We're gonna say goodbye to my babby.'

Ystrad blurred as the car picked up speed. They rattled across the valley past a cluster of low-rise concrete buildings inside a barbed-wire fence.

'What's that?'

'New industrial estate,' Sue said. 'There's a Japanese firm making components. And a factory's opening soon to process chickens.'

They sped through a village of detached houses, tricycles and space hoppers parked on huge front lawns. Sue pointed out the pit manager's house. Pots of cyclamen peeped through gleaming lace curtains. Parallel box hedges led to his door. As the road wound higher, there were no more front lawns. Each terrace village was more derelict than the last, houses opening onto thin pavements. Streets empty, only the old and infirm staggering along with canes. Whole parades of shops were boarded up and abandoned, only bookies open for business.

At last, the desolation was behind them. Fields became woodland. They crossed a stone-built bridge, pulled into a copse of silver birch. As Helen stepped out of the car door, two things hit her: the thin, sharp scent of pine trees and the silence.

Sue squeezed her arm. 'You're sure we shouldn't drive to the top?'

'I want to walk.'

The road slipped under a canopy of foliage. Squirrels skittered in the leaf mold, tails twitching. As she watched them, she heard a shrill of bells, jumped aside as a dozen racing bikes sped towards her. Middle-aged men in neon Lycra that jarred against the February landscape. The last cyclist turned as he passed, waggled his eyebrows, wolf-whistled.

'Prat,' she muttered.

She followed Sue up the road. Blackbirds hopped among roots that rose from the soil like outstretched hands. Two magpie couples traded insults from the tops of the trees. *One for sorrow, two for joy. Three for a girl, four for a—*

Sue waited for her to catch up. 'You're sure you're okay?'

'We need flowers.'

'Early in the year for flowers, *bach*.'

'We gotta find something. Where should we look?'

'Try where the light hits the soil, I guess. Nothing grows in darkness.'

They combed the verges but found nothing. But as they rounded a corner, Sue cried out. Up ahead, vivid against dark tree trunks, a flowering cherry blazed with white blossom. Helen pulled off half a dozen small branches then Sue pulled a loop of string from one of the many pockets in her dungarees, tied them into a makeshift bouquet.

'How's that?'

'It's perfect,' Helen said.

She plunged into the woods, following the sound of running water. Her feet sank into leaf mulch as she pushed through low-slung branches.

'We need to find the stream, Sue.'

'I hear it up by there.'

An eerie screeching sound split the undergrowth. Helen saw a flash of pink and blue as a jay fluttered past her. She followed the bird, saw it settle on a tree stump. She pushed after it and found herself in a tiny clearing, split by a stream. Splintered sunlight turned the water into a ribbon of sequins.

'This is the place.'

Sue looked at her.

'I just need a minute.'

Sue clambered up the bank, perched on a flat-topped boulder under the straggly pine trees. She pulled out her tobacco tin. Helen scrambled up next to her. They sat together, watched the smoke melt into the sharp, cold air.

'I came here once,' Sue said. 'After my mam died.'

'So that's why you understand.'

Sue squished her cigarette stub into the earth, rolled another.

At the water's edge, Helen breathed in the sawdust scent of ferns. Watched the crystal water tumble between the rocks.

'Will you sing something, Sue?'

'Like what?'

'I dunno. A song to say goodbye.'

'Like 'Joe Hill'?'

It was the song the men sang for the dead and the fallen on the line and at lodge funerals. Sue took a deep breath.

> *'I dreamed I saw Joe Hill last night*
> *Alive as you or me*
> *Says I, but Joe you're ten years dead.*
> *I never died, said he. I never died, said he.*
> *'In Salt Lake, Joe, I said to him,*
> *Him standing by my bed.*
> *They framed you on a murder charge*
> *Says Joe, but I ain't dead—'*

They sang the final verse together, voices soaring into the trees.

> *'Joe Hill ain't dead, he said to me.*
> *Joe Hill ain't never died.*
> *Where working men are out on strike,*
> *Joe Hill is by their side. Joe Hill is by their side.'*

Helen gripped the bouquet, touched her lips to it and breathed in the scent of winter. Time to let go and find a way to live. She hurled the bouquet into the stream, watched the current bear it away.

* * *

They drove back to Ystrad in the rain, passing retired miners, heading home from their allotments, backs bent against the downpour. Children chased each other through puddles. Soon, the triangle of metal that marked Blackthorn loomed above the trees. The village and the colliery looked peaceful, from above, beautiful, even, the winding gear silent and gathering rust.

Helen turned to Sue. 'Do we have to go back so soon?'

'Red Lion?'

'Can't face people just yet.'

'How about The Mountain Ash? There'll be no one we know up by there.'

* * *

The rain had stopped by the time they pulled up. Sunshine leaked through cracks in the slate-coloured clouds, cast an eerie orange light. Ivy clung to the pub's stone walls. Helen stooped under the lintel, entered an old-fashioned room with low, deep-set windows that let in a trickle of daylight. Dried flowers and copper kitchenware hung from the beams. A real wood fire sucked the air from the room. They ordered two halves of bitter, walked through the lounge bar towards the rose garden terrace outside.

Sue, walking ahead, pulled up abruptly.

'What is it?' Helen pushed past, stopped too.

Scrapper stood on the stone balustrade, gazing out across the valley. He had his arms around Debbie Power, his cheek pressed against her cheek. Helen put out a hand to steady herself. The sky darkened as a cloud chased its shadow across the sun.

Scrapper seemed to sense he was being watched. He turned, startled.

'Red?'

A flicker crossed Debbie's dark, pretty face. 'Well, now. Look who's here.'

300

But they didn't move away from each other. Debbie wasn't the intruder here, Helen realised.

'Why?' she croaked.

'We were talking,' Scrapper said.

Two glasses stood on the balustrade. A pint glass, nearly empty, a wine glass stained with lipstick the colour of strawberry milkshake.

'All the way up here, to *talk*,' she said flatly.

Debbie picked up her glass, touched Scrapper's arm and walked with a swagger back to the bar.

'I'll be in the car park,' Sue said.

Helen put a hand on the balustrade to steady herself. 'I always knew you'd go back to her. In the end.'

'Go back? That's nuts, Red. There's nothing going on with Debbie. But I can talk to her, about anything, and not feel like I'm trampling on eggshells.'

'You're throwing this back at me?'

'Let's keep this simple; d'you trust me; yes, or no?'

'No,' she said.

7

Scrapper's thoughts were muzzy from the drinks he'd scored at the solidarity meeting. He'd stayed on after giving his talk, let the trade unionists and newspaper sellers and pick-and-mix lefties stand him round after round, the better to avoid that cold house and colder bed, the loss and disappointment in his parents' eyes and that same conversation, rewound over and over.

But here it came again. This time, it was Iwan who'd waited up for him.

'There's nothing between me an' Dai's missus,' he said again.

Iwan breathed an angry sigh. 'You're not stupid, son. Why seek any kind of comfort from a woman other than your wife? You got no chance to make things right if you can't see why that's wrong.'

Make things right. With Red gone to live at Sue's. After Iwan turned in, he slumped on the sofa, watched the fire in the grate flicker and die. Everything was lost. What hope did he have of winning back his wife? What right did he have to try? There was nothing for her here, except cold and hunger and misery. But without her, he was— what? There was nothing ahead for him but emptiness, a yawning void.

He picked up the phone and dialled.

'He-e-ey,' Debbie spoke in her huskiest voice.

He realised his mistake at once. 'Orright,' he mumbled.

'I dropped by the Stute earlier.'

'How come?'

'Came looking for Dai. To talk about the divorce.'

He sucked in his breath. He might not be an innocent bystander, not exactly, but what happened between Dai and Debbie had nothing to do with him. No matter how anyone else tried to frame it.

There was a long, awkward silence.

'But he loves you,' he said at last.

Debbie's breath hissed down the line. 'You alone?'

'Aye.'

'You know what we could be doing, you and me, alone together, right now?'

An image assaulted him. Not an image; a memory. Debbie opening her blouse. Undoing the tiny buttons, one by one by one. Eyes fixed on his face. A black lacy bra. Hard little breasts.

'Don't.' It came out like a groan.

'You're missing it just like me, eh, Scrap?'

'Stop it,' his voice shook. 'Look at us; both married. Both a complete mess.'

'And?'

'And talking like that just fucks things up more.'

'So-o-ooo?'

'So I can't do this. Maybe you've given up on Dai but I've not given up on Red. Not yet.'

The receiver clicked. The line hummed. Debbie was gone. Suddenly his thoughts were sharp and clear. He'd done it. Here was proof how much he loved his wife. He needed Red to know that one of them, at least, still believed in their marriage. He went to the kitchen, gulped down a mug of water. It was icy cold, made his forehead ache, sobered him a little. He fetched boots and jacket and set off out. If Red wouldn't talk to him, she had to hear him out, at least.

It was mild outside, for February. The steel toecaps of his boots clinked on the pavement as he paced up and down, pondering what to say to make Red see sense.

As he passed the bus stop, a figure peeled out of the shadows, silent but at speed.

'Nowhere to go, Scrapper Jones?'

'Mind your fucking business, Captain Hook.'

'I'll give you Captain Hook, insolent boy,' Red's dad was swaying, his eyes glassy. 'Word is, my daughter's gone and left you. I knew it wouldn't last. Knew she'd come crawling back.'

Hearing the overman say it made Scrapper realise how laughable that was.

'She'll never go back to you. Not walking, crawling or on wings,' he said. 'You've done your worst with me but you're the one who's lost, Gwyn Pritchard. You've lost everything.'

The overman caught Scrapper by surprise, grabbed his collar and slammed him against the wall.

'You got a nerve, Scrapper Jones. You put your stupid, wrong-headed principles before my daughter's well-being. Some husband.'

'You don't know shit about—'

'I know you're too proud and lazy to take care of your own.'

Scrapper's legs buckled. The words struck home. Was that how Red saw it? When he looked into those eyes that were so much like Helen's eyes, he saw that he and Captain Hook were the same; rigid and angry and pathetic. But there was no sympathy on that tough, grey face, only Captain Hook's certainty that he was right. That everyone else, who fought so hard and gained so little, was stupid and short-sighted and wrong.

He gathered up his strength and slammed Captain Hook into the bus shelter until the overman doubled over, coughing.

'Speak to me like that again, I'll fucking kill you.'

Gwyn stopped coughing then, barked out a laugh. 'Stupid boy. You'd struggle to manage even that.'

Scrapper backed away. Was the overman daring him –

goading him – to do his worst? He was angry enough to oblige him. He grabbed Captain Hook by the collar, flexed his arm to strike.

Footsteps ran towards him. 'No, Scrap. He's not worth it.'

It was Matthew Price. He had filled out since Christmas. His skin was clear and scrubbed, hair freshly bleached. No black roots now. No roots to him at all.

'Typical scabs, sticking together.'

Matt ignored the comment. 'Don't get yourself nicked a second time. Not on account of this scumbag.'

Captain Hook stopped coughing, smirked at Matt. 'Tell him, shall I?'

'Tell me what? What in God's name does he have on you?'

Their eyes locked. Matt looked away first.

'You'll never understand, Scrap,' he said quietly.

'Does it bloody matter? Whatever it is, it's not too late, Matt. Come back out, and you'll see.'

'*Come out?*' Captain Hook scoffed. 'Welcome him with open arms, would you?'

'Why not?'

'Why not? If you believe a word this one says, you got coal dust for brains, Matthew Price.'

Matt slumped as though his bones had come unglued. He backed away. Shuffled down the street without a second glance.

'Nice one, lad,' Captain Hook said. 'You've lost your butty, lost your wife. You're hell-bent on losing your job and your livelihood. Well done, lad. It's over now. For all of us.'

8

'You reckon that chicken factory might be hiring?' Helen asked.

Sue blinked at her. She looked like a child in the mornings, in her outsized, mannish pyjamas, curls falling into her eyes as she fixed their tea and toast.

'You said when we drove past,' Helen persisted. 'Near that Japanese components place. Said there'd be a chicken factory soon.'

Johnny Griffiths was sorting leaflets. His deft fingers shuffled three stacks into single batches to hand out with his newspapers. Slogans in heavy type. *A Day's Pay For The Miners. No Benefit Cuts. Free the Guildford Four.*

'They got no unions,' he said. 'Bloody dodgy, them new industrial estates.'

'I got to start earning,' Helen said.

'Stick with school, Red,' Sue yawned. 'Get A-levels, you'll have more choices. Get a better job, or get a grant and go to college. Do anything you want.'

'I can't sponge off you forever.'

Johnny stopped sorting, rapped her on the hand.

'You're helping take care o' me,' he said. 'An' we like your company.'

'Damn right,' Sue said.

But it wasn't right, scrounging from her friends. Helen went up to the bedroom that belonged to the old man until his accident. It was crammed with too-large furniture, a foot of paisley carpet between the solid, dark wardrobe and the carved wooden bed. The heaviness that pressed her wouldn't shift. She pulled on the black jeans and matching polo neck borrowed from Sue. The outfit might just pass for businesslike.

The phone shrilled in the hall. 'Red, it's for you,' Sue called.

She caught her breath. There was no chance she'd hear back from Bryn Tawel Hospital this soon. Not with twenty people chasing every vacancy at nursing school. Most likely it was Scrapper. But Sue was under orders not to put Scrapper through.

'Hiya, *bach*. How you keeping?' it was an older voice, warm and concerned. 'I know it's hard. But we miss you, all of us.'

'Iwan I—'

'I'm not calling to put pressure on you, *cariad*. Just to say, we'd love to see you. When you're ready. Take care, lovely.'

She could see them both, Iwan in his armchair, grey eyes narrowed in concentration, lost in his tall, pink newspaper or some tome from the library at the Stute. Angela in her kitchen, dark ponytail swishing as she cranked out armfuls of pasta, something tasty bubbling on the stove. She could see both of them, but not Scrapper. When she tried to picture Scrapper, Debbie Power blocked her view.

* * *

The ice cream parlour was shuttered, lights blazed above it. She was tempted to slip round to the back door, let herself in, go up to the kitchen to sit with her mam-in-law. But she wasn't ready. Not yet. Betty's boutique was boarded up, planks nailed across the door, the flat above deserted. She would never keep her promise to buy that waistcoat with her first wage packet.

She jumped as a figure emerged into the half-light, donkey jacket buttoned, head hidden under a flying helmet with sheepskin flaps. Part fighter pilot; past ghost-of-miners-past. She laughed, relieved. Siggy Split-Enz. It had to be.

'What?' He took her relief for mockery.

'I thought you were a *bwci-bo*, come to drag me into the fog.'

His eyes crinkled. 'You wish, sweetie. Heard you left the *bracchi*. Fancy a brew?'

He unlocked the metal shop grilles, snapped on the salon lights. Fluorescent strips blazed white. He pulled up a chair for her, fussed with kettle and tea bags as she told him about leaving home and looking for work. He poured the tea, parked himself in front of the mirror, removed his hat and reset his flattened hair with wax. His upper lip sprouted a new pencil moustache. He'd turn heads in any town, Siggy. A diamond on a coal tip.

Helen couldn't stop herself. 'I saw you,' she burst out.

'What?'

'You and Matt Price. Up at the barn.'

'And what did you see?'

'You and him. Together. Like boyfriend and girlfriend.'

Siggy gave a low chuckle. 'Like boyfriend and girlfriend. Who did you tell?'

'No one. I never breathed a word.'

'Well, you had better not. Matthew does not tell the truth about himself.'

'Ashamed of you, but not ashamed to scab?'

Siggy dabbed wax on moustache and eyebrows. 'Your dad found out. Used that information to bully Matthew back to work.'

Helen took a gulp of too-hot tea. A piece of work, her dad. She could imagine his glee unmasking Matthew Price. It made sense at last. Why else would Matt turn scab?

'Siggy, I'm so sorry.'

Sorry was too small a word for the shame she felt.

Siggy picked up a hairbrush, advanced on her. 'Did you walk through a hedge this morning? This needs a trim.'

'Can't afford it.'

'You are not looking for a job with this hair. You will ruin my reputation.'

He set to work with clips, comb and scissors, stepped back with a flourish. 'Now you can say to people, Siggy cuts my hair.'

She turned from side to side, admiring his handiwork. 'What would you do if you caught Matt with someone else.'

'Who cares, if it is just sex.'

'But if he loved you, why go somewhere else?'

'Women,' he sighed. 'I hear the same thing, all day long. *If he loved me, he would. If he loved me, he wouldn't.* Men are simple creatures, *schatzi*. It is never as complicated as you think.'

'You reckon I should give Scrapper another chance?'

'Not if you do not want to. But why not let him explain himself?'

9

Another night, another solidarity meeting. Scrapper downed several pints for courage before getting up to speak. The student comrades seemed to find him exotic, somehow, which made them less exotic to him. Afterwards, he let them take him out for a curry. They ordered bottle after bottle of sour red wine and the girls asked wide-eyed questions about working below ground. Wine was no friend to him, he found. It got him properly maudlin for missing his wife. He wound up too wazzed to cycle and had to wheel his bike home. Sleet and wind battered him as he staggered across the valley. By the time he passed the pit, the sky was edged with light.

The security man dozed in his box, radio clutched in mittened hand. What point going home, Scrapper thought. Why give his parents fresh cause to have a go at him. But it was raining now and he didn't fancy waiting around outdoors. He paused below the chapel. The wind whistled through the railway tunnel. He leaned his bike against the hedge, climbed up to the lych gate.

Above him, the terraces of Ystrad stared blindly across the valley. A boxy tomb towered above the slate headstones, green-stained marble angels topping the plinth, one on each corner. It was the family crypt of the coal barons who owned Blackthorn and a dozen other South Wales pits before nationalisation. Their names were chiselled in chipped gilt: Humphrey Humphrey, buried aged eighty, his son Edward and grandson Henry, both in their mid-seventies. There were no Humphreys around these parts now. They died out or moved on, having squandered their wealth on a stately pile – now The Mountain Ash Hotel – and laying themselves to rest in white marble.

He moved on to a cluster of slate headstones near the road. Simon Peter Jones, 1917 – 1960, Mary-Anne Jones, 1920 – 1978, his gran and granddad. Next to them, his uncles. Dafydd Jones, 1943 – 1960, and Idris Jones, 1945 – 1960. His gran lost three of her men in one day. This was what coal cost: torn bodies, wrecked lives.

He peeled a patch of algae off his uncles' headstone, feeling sick. It was fate that Iwan had been off work that day, laid up with a sprained wrist, that he survived, went on to marry and have a son of his own. A miner paid his dues over and over. It was true in the Humphreys' time, true today. A year had passed, yet Gabe's grave was not grown over. It hurt to see that rectangle of bare earth. Hurt more to remember the other lost soul who was not yet here. He paused at his grandmother's grave, made her a quiet promise that one day, as soon as he had the money, he'd lay a headstone for the baby next to hers.

Nearby, another grave: Jahaziel Price, 1928 – 1960. An inscription: *Without the shedding of blood, there is no forgiveness of sins*. Matt's granddad. The wind howled through the trees. Scrapper shuddered, pictured old Jahaziel rising from his grave, sleepless for knowing that his grandson was a scab.

Rain pelted down in sheets. Scrapper ran to the chapel, yanked the door open. The smell of cobwebs and floor polish tickled his nostrils. He peeled off his sodden jacket, piled two pew cushions on top of each other, stretched himself out for a kip. He lay still, as the wind bellowed murder and the rain whipped the tiled roof and let the storm howl him to sleep.

* * *

When he woke, his spine was knotted. He heard the door open and close, the scratch of dead leaves on flagstones. Footsteps tip-tapped past, halted beneath the pulpit. He peered over the pews. The room was almost dark. A large man slumped on the front pew, shoulders bent, hands clasped and head bowed.

At last, the man stood, breathed out loudly. 'May God forgive me.'

Scrapper ducked down. The door opened again, filling the chapel with the scent of rain. The man's footsteps tapped across the porch, then faded. Scrapper peered out. Grey mist stretched lazily across the sky. The man crossed the cemetery, stopped next to Gabriel Parry's grave.

It was Dai Dumbells. He gripped the headstone and heaved, but the stone was wedged solid. He moved on to the next grave, with no success. Scrapper could tell from the set of Dai's shoulders, from the tremors that shook his thick arms, that something was wrong. Dai moved forward, dipped out of view. Scrapper heard a loud scraping sound. He stepped outside, saw Dai stagger across the graveyard, a heavy object hefted on his shoulders. It was one of the Humphreys' marble angels, its wings brushing raindrops from the yew hedge.

Dai would never steal for stealing's sake.

Scrapper set off after him. 'Dai,' he yelled. 'Dai Dumbells.'

Dai turned, saw him, picked up speed. Scrapper caught up with him at the bottom of the bank that led up to the railway track. The ground was soft and Dai lost his footing. The angel landed in the mud with a squelch.

He hefted the angel back onto his shoulder. Its face was smeared with earth. 'Don't try an' stop me, Scrapper Jones.'

'What the hell's going on, Dai?'

'Nothing to concern you, butty. Fuck off home.'

'But what you doing with—?'

Dai's ham-sized fist slammed into Scrapper's jaw. He

sprawled in the mud, branches blurring above his head. He heard a grunt and a grating sound. Dai hefted the angel onto the bridge and climbed onto the track. Scrapper staggered after him, rolled over the wall onto the railway track. Dai stood on the parapet above the tunnel, gazing up the road towards Ystrad, the angel propped next to him on the wall.

'Dai?'

'Stay back. Don't move another step.'

'But—'

'Piss off.'

Scrapper inched closer. 'No trains since the strike, butty. Wrong bloody place for killing yourself.'

Dai gawped at him, seemed to register, threw back his head and laughed. The angel teetered on the edge of the wall.

Scrapper understood at last. 'The scabs?'

'Bastards got it coming.'

Blood roared in Scrapper's ears. He gripped the wall to support himself. 'Don't be daft, Dai. Form a queue to kill Captain Hook, I'd be first in line if I thought it'd make a jot of difference. But it won't.'

Dai dabbed loose earth off the angel's marble cheeks, a tenderness to his massive paws. 'That the best you got, butt?'

'The best?' Scrapper said. 'You and Debbie'll get back together, try for another baby. Things'll get better, Dai, you'll see.'

Dai chuckled softly. 'Things never get better for the likes of us. An' Debbie's a lying slut.'

'But—'

'But nothing. I lost my butty, my baby, my woman and my home. Soon enough, we'll lose the pit. It's over, Scrap. All of it.'

Scrapper edged closer, steel toecap clinking on metal rail.

'I said, stay back.'

But Scrapper inched forwards. He could hear voices at the

top of the slope. The boys were coming down to picket. He'd get them come up and sort this. He only had to call out to them. But Dai had heard them too. He launched himself across the track, all seventeen stone of him knocking the air from Scrapper's lungs. He planted his paw over Scrapper's mouth.

'One peep, and I'll break your neck.'

The men's voices drew closer. Footsteps passed under the bridge, amplified by the tunnel walls, emerged on the other side. The sound of steel-capped boots faded. Dai heaved himself to his feet, went back to the angel.

Scrapper doubled over, retching. After a while, he drew breath enough to stagger across the track.

'Where d'you think you're going?'

'You're a spanner short of a toolkit, butty. I'm fetching Dad and Dewi.'

Scrapper swung his legs over the wall, but Dai crossed the tracks in three long strides and yanked him back. He used his bulk to pin Scrapper against the bridge, one hand on the angel, his gaze fixed on the road.

At last, Scrapper heard the growl of an engine; saw a white minivan at the top of the hill.

'Bingo,' Dai said softly.

'No,' Scrapper forced the words out. 'That's the boys from Maerdy.'

He lunged for the angel. The statue wobbled. His throat tightened as the van came splashing through the potholes towards the tunnel. Lodge banners flapped in its windows. Dai's shoulders relaxed. The minibus hurtled beneath them and passed into the tunnel, unharmed.

Scrapper wiped a hand over his sweating forehead. 'Bloody ridiculous, this, Dai.'

'Never asked you to come, did I.'

'So you kill Captain Hook. Then what? You gonna kill all the

NCB bosses, all the bankers, all the coppers, all the journalists? Kill every last fucking Tory, will you? Beyond even the bloody Provos, that.'

'Spare me the beginner's guide to revolutionary socialism, Scrapper Jones.'

'Fuck's sake, Dai. You're better'n this.'

There was a pause. Scrapper thought he'd got through to him at last. But the sound of an engine shattered the moment. He saw something flash beyond the trees, then a police car appeared, behind it a minibus, windscreens and windows shuttered under metal grilles.

'Here we go,' Dai shifted his weight, flung both arms around the marble angel as the vehicles raced towards the bridge. Scrapper wriggled away from him. He leaped onto the wall, arms flapping windmills.

'Stop,' he yelled. 'You got to stop.'

The police car accelerated, flashed under the bridge. Scrapper's arms flailed faster. Looking down, he saw faces peering up through the minibus windscreen. Dai bellowed triumph, gave the angel a mighty shove. Time bent and warped into freeze frame. Scrapper turned, hid his eyes, heard and felt the thud of stone on metal. The bridge shuddered.

As Scrapper lowered his hands, a crow burst out of the hedgerow, cawing fury. Black wings flapped inches from his face. He caught a glint of sharp blue eyes as the bird rose squawking and vanished beyond the trees.

10

Was this his hand over his mouth, his heart hammering the back of his throat? Were these his feet lurching away from the wall? Was this his body, legs leaden, spine rigid with shock? Was this the sky above Ystrad, that dark triangle his pit? Was the railroad calling him towards it, urging him to flee? Or was this where it ended, on this bridge?

He heard shouts floating up from beyond the tunnel, footsteps thudding up the embankment. Instinct seized him. There was a ditch up ahead. He dragged himself towards it and leapt in. The ditch was deeper than it looked. He peered out. Dai had clambered onto the wall, huge body braced to jump. Scrapper pulled the bracken over his head, waited to hear the thud of a body hitting the road.

* * *

Dai howled in protest. Scrapper heard a high-pitched scream of pain then a second thud, a third, a fourth. Each blow was studded with sharp, grunted breaths. He heard the chink of toecaps on metal track, then something heavy dragged across the stones.

The voices were harsh with anger. They belonged to Peter Plod, Johnny Boots, others he didn't recognise.

'Grab his feet, mate. We'll need to heft the bastard over.'

* * *

Sirens blared down the hill, shut off at the foot of the bridge. He heard a babble of raised voices. The shriek of cutting equipment. The squeal of metal on metal. A sudden silence.

'What's the fella's name?' A stranger spoke at last.

Matt sounded shaky. 'That's the overman. Name's Gwyn Pritchard.'

'Skull cracked like a walnut. Poor fucking sod.'

Matt's voice was amplified by the tunnel roof. 'D'you mean he's—?'

'It's best you boys don't look.'

'Dead? But he can't be dead,' a shrill edge to the apprentice's voice.

'Damn right,' Matt said. 'Bullet-proof, Gwyn fucking Pritchard. Everyone knows that.'

* * *

Red. She was all that mattered. Scrapper listened to the footsteps leave the tunnel, heard doors slam and engines rev. The sirens started up again, whether to carry Dai to the nick or the others to hospital, he didn't know or care. It wasn't his business. None of it was.

He heard footsteps scrabbling back up the embankment, ducked down, listening.

'Kid must've legged it when they dropped the thing,' Johnny Boots, breathless.

'We'll catch the bastard,' the stranger said. 'Reckon the lodge was in cahoots?'

'I don't know about that,' Peter Plod answered. 'The kid had several run-ins with the deceased. Reckon he did this to settle some scores.'

The footsteps faded. There was a long pause, as though the valley was too scared to breathe. Scrapper peered out. No one.

He hauled himself onto the track, crept back onto the bridge, peered over the wall. Two black helmets, faces hidden from view, a white hand scribbling notes, next to them, a mangled minibus. A stone object poked, pale and obscene, from a gash in the roof.

* * *

He followed the railway as far as he could. But the loading shed was locked, the pit secure inside its belt of chicken wire, under a crown of metal barbs. He skirted the perimeter fence, set off up the hill through the fields, and the long, stiff climb to Bryn Tawel. He ploughed on as though the ghost of Captain Hook was on his tail. He found a call box at the edge of the village, a piece of silver dropped outside it. One piece of luck, at last. A second piece of luck if Red took his call, for once.

* * *

He wasn't sure Johnny would put him through, unless it was out of pity, hearing the terror and panic in his voice. He wasn't sure Red would come, unless it was to finish things between them once and for all. As he waited in the dusty blackness of the barn, doubt weighed heavy on him. At last, the metal sheet scraped sideways. A blast of air and light. She was there, her face lighting the gloom. He ran to her and grabbed her. Pulled her down on top of him onto the oily, dusty floor.

12

The wind raised and dropped the barn's corrugated iron roof. Sunlight leaked through the gaps between the sheets, through rusted nail holes, forming spotlights in the darkness. Helen raked cold fingers through her hair, brought away dust and shards of hay. Scrapper's words hung in the air between them He slumped against her, pale and lost and broken, as brittle and fragile as the cobweb wrapped around her finger. The wind raised and slammed the roof again. The metal walls shuddered. She imagined the barn collapsing inwards, crushing the breath from their lungs. Just like her dad had been crushed.

'It wasn't me, Red. You got to believe me.'

How could she tell him what he needed to hear. She believed none of it.

'Tell me what happened. Start at the start.'

He fixed his eyes on a patch of oil that slicked the dusty floor. Told her what happened. The barn moaned and shivered. She moved closer to hear him, his voice fallen to a whisper.

'But the police are after *you*?' she said at last.

Her dad or her husband; all her choices seemed to come to this. But she knew what she had to do. She leaped up, started pulling on her clothes. Scrapper watched her, as though paralysed. She picked up his jeans and jumper, hurled them at him.

'Best they don't find you, then. Get dressed.' She dragged him to his feet, surprised by her strength, by his weightlessness. 'Bastards want you, they'll have to find you.'

'Red, that's insane—'

'Completely insane,' she grabbed his shoulders and shook him. 'I went for a job at the chicken factory. The manager liked me. I'll earn money, Scrap. Not much, but some. We'll find some place to hide you. And one day— One day we'll get away from here. Rent a little place by the seaside—'

But it was hopeless. He no more believed that than she did. He dressed as though the effort would break him. Outrage flared through her veins. Was he not the man? Should he not be stronger? It was too much for him, all of this. His fire burned down to ashes.

Somewhere near – too near – she heard a dog bark. Footsteps approached the barn. They stood inches apart, barely breathing. The metal doors burst open. The barn filled with the shouts of policemen, the snapping and growling of dogs and the crackle of radios. A huge black and tan dog launched itself at Scrapper. He shrieked with pain. At last, a policeman got between Scrapper and the dog, wrenched Scrapper's hands behind his back, slammed his face against the wall.

'No,' she screamed.

All of it stopped.

The dog showed the whites of its eyes at her. The radios fell silent. Even the wind dropped. Weak daylight flooded the barn, revealed a million tiny specks of dust. They rose, those many tiny specks; rose and soared. Whirled in mid-air. Slowly, softly fell back into the dirt and vanished.

She looked up into the bug-eyed gaze of Peter Plod, one hand inside his lapel, feeling for his notebook.

'This piece of scum killed your father, Helen Pritchard.'

A broken sound escaped from Scrapper's throat. 'I never. She knows it. You knows it, don't you, Red?'

Then he was gone, dragged out into the feeble morning, feet

scuffing hayseeds and dust and spilled oil. Peter Plod loomed over her, a jackal with a pad and pen.

'Scrapper says he didn't do it,' she said.

The policeman snorted. 'Like he didn't break into your father's house at Christmas. Like he never blockaded the pit. Never stopped decent folk doing a decent day's work. Never went up the tip thieving coal. Never joined the rabble in the streets and on the docks. Never told a bunch of students to overthrow a democratically elected government.'

Helen stood and faced the policeman. 'What would you do, in his shoes? Go down without a fight?'

'There are laws—'

'Rich men's laws: Maggie fights the Argies for some island no one gives a stuff about, she's a hero. But when miners fight for their livelihoods, they're criminals.'

The policeman pocketed his notebook, turned, walked away.

Outside, the wind had dropped. The weak sunlight was as warm as milky tea. Blossom flickered on the apple trees in the allotment gardens below the fields, where a woman in headscarf and wellingtons was gathering daffodils for St David's Day. The dog handler strode past, metal leash slung over his shoulder. Helen turned, expecting to see the Alsatian snarling at her. But the huge, ragged dog was running along the top of the field, tail wagging as it tracked rabbit trails from burrow to burrow.

Its work here was done.

13

Angela and Iwan sat at Sue's kitchen table. Tension etched lines and shadows on their faces. They were too upset to answer Helen's question.

'What did they charge him with?' she repeated.

'Murder,' Iwan said weakly.

Angela shuddered.

Sue brought tea, put the sugar bowl in front of Angela. 'Take some; it'll help with the shock,' she said.

They sat, hands cupping their mugs. Helen wondered what to say, what to feel. Her gaze wandered to the pictures and flyers Sue had Blu-tacked to the fridge doors. Cartoons from *Coalfield Woman*, a slogan postcard: *A Woman Needs A Man Like A Fish Needs A Bicycle*. On the wall, Picasso's *Blue Nude* hid her face and wept.

'*Lui non è un assassino*,' Angela burst out. '*Bella*, the boy made stupid, stupid mistakes these last weeks. But a killer? Never. No.'

'I want to believe that—'

'We've got to be practical,' Sue said. 'I'll call the support group in Cardiff, have them find us a criminal lawyer. They'll know what to do about the press, and all.'

Helen grabbed her hand. 'What d'you mean, the press—?'

'Mary called. Jimmy Mosquito's outside the Stute with his crew. Circling like starving foxes, she said. Dewi sent them packing.'

'This'll be on the news?'

'What time's it?' Sue scarpered upstairs, came back with the box television from her bedroom.

She perched it on the scuffed dresser, fiddled with the aerial. The set crackled as she turned the wire loop backwards and forwards, tried to get the flickering images to settle. The newsreader emerged from a blur of grey static.

'A South Wales miner was killed this morning, attacked as he travelled to work at Blackthorn Colliery. Police say striking miners dropped a heavy object on a vehicle carrying working men into the pit. Medics treated three people at the scene for shock and non life-threatening injuries. Police have arrested two men, said to be striking miners from the nearby village of Ystrad. Both have been charged with murder—'

The newsreader paused to draw breath.

Helen gripped the table. Her father's fate and Scrapper's. This was real, then. It had to be, if she heard it on the television.

'Prime Minister Margaret Thatcher, speaking exclusively to the BBC this lunchtime, condemned the killing as "a strike at the heart of British democracy". A statement from the TUC echoed the prime minister's words, calling the attack "vicious and—"'

Iwan clamped his hands over his ears.

The scene switched to an outside location. The camera panned over a minivan – windscreen shattered, tarmac glittering anthracite under a dusting of broken glass – came to rest on a nervy, twitchy little man. Blackthorn's winding gear soared behind him.

'Local journalist James Hackett is live at the scene. What more can you tell us, James?'

The camera zoomed over the reporter's shoulder, came to rest on a pale, solid object rising like a sail from the wreckage, returned to the reporter, who was waving a piece of paper at the camera.

'Got a scoop for you, Nigel. A written statement from Adam Smith-Tudor, the Coal Board's most senior man in South Wales. In it, he tells the BBC: *"Gwyn Richards was a loyal worker. A solid family man who died defending his right to go to work at the pit he loved. We owe it to Gwyn's memory to stand firm against the hired thugs of the National Union of Mineworkers"*.'

Sue strode across the kitchen, snapped off the television. 'Bastards couldn't even get your dad's name right.'

'Hired thugs,' Iwan echoed.

Helen said nothing, robbed of speech by the sight of the wreckage. By the thought of her dad, beneath that mangled metal, a pale object sticking out of it like the wing of some flesh-eating bird. She thought about Scrapper pleading with her: *it wasn't me, Red. You got to believe me.*

'You'll make that call, Sue?' Iwan said.

'Right away.'

He nodded his thanks. 'I got to see Dewi. Then get back up the cop shop.'

Angela didn't move. Fixed her eyes on Helen. 'Is no point talking to Dewi. Not when Simon's own wife thinks he's guilty.'

'It's not that—'

'He loves you, *bella*. He needs you. We need you.'

After Iwan and Angela left, Sue fetched a bottle from the top of the dresser. Put a tumbler on the table and poured.

'Southern Comfort.'

The drink had the colour and stickiness of treacle. Helen slammed the liquid down her gullet. It warmed her a little.

'D'you reckon Scrapper done it, Sue?'

'Not in a million years, *bach*.'

'So many times I wished my dad was dead.'

'None of this is your fault.'

'You sure about that?'

Sue poured her another drink. 'I'd best make that call.'

As she stood, a quavering voice echoed down the hall.

Helen downed the Southern Comfort, rinsed her glass under the tap. 'Go. I'll look after Johnny.'

She knocked on the door to the front room, now Johnny Griffiths' bedroom. A draft blew through the open window. The curtains rose and fell. An old miner's quirk, to sleep with the window open, believing that fresh air sooner cured than killed. The gaunt old man was sitting up in bed.

'Slept late today, Uncle Johnny.'

'Lay awake half the night. Couldn't sleep for the pins an' needles in my legs.'

'Your legs?' That made no sense.

The old man's face split into an impish grin. 'Lose one leg down the pit, that's an accident: lose two, it's bloody careless. Know who wrote that, girlie?'

She shook her head.

'Oscar-bloody-Wilde. Or very nearly. A fine writer, Wilde. Almost a patch on Dylan Thomas. You know, *bach*, even something long gone can hurt like fresh.'

He threw aside the quilt. She grabbed the handles of the wheelchair, positioned the seat below the bed and helped the frail body into the chair. In the hall, Sue was giving it plenty on the phone. She steered the old man to the bathroom, went to fix his tea and breakfast. By the time Johnny called her to fetch him, Sue had dashed out.

Helen wheeled Johnny to the table, served him toast and scrambled eggs.

'So,' he said. 'The way our Susie's carrying on, sommat's afoot today. Won the strike, have we?'

The question caught her off-guard. She burst into tears.

Johnny sipped his tea and munched his crusts, waited for her to dry her eyes. Listened without speaking as she told him about her dad and Scrapper. When she finished, he breathed out a whistle.

'*Duw*. Bloody mess, eh?'

'The worst is not knowing what to believe.'

When Uncle Johnny smiled, his years and infirmities fell away from him. 'You know what I tell my Susie? When you can't fathom right from wrong, trust your gut.'

'It's that easy? Yeah, right.'

The old man removed his top row of false teeth, chipped away with a yellow fingernail at a stray crumb of toast. Slid his teeth back in, eyed her gravely.

'You're bloody joking, girlie. It's the hardest thing in the world. It's not easy, learning to trust yourself. Don't let no one tell you different.'

14

Helen paused outside the Stute. The last time she saw her dad was here, on Christmas Day, yelling at her in the road. It felt disloyal to his memory to enter the building. But Sue had summoned her. She raised her head, called up her old defiance and walked in. The meeting was already underway. Dewi stopped mid-sentence as she wheeled Johnny through the crush to the front of the room. People moved aside for her. Heads turned. Johnny pointed to a spot at the front. She parked his wheelchair, slid away to join the women behind the tea urns, away from the staring eyes.

After a pause, Dewi started speaking again. The men listened, barely breathing, as still and frozen as fossilised trees.

'And as you'll know,' he wound up, 'Dai Dumbells an' Scrapper Jones were charged this morning. Police are saying it's murder.'

'A travesty,' Johnny shouted.

Some of the men murmured agreement.

Dewi patted the air for hush. 'The lodge'll do what it can to help the two lads. We got a lawyer—'

'Bollocks!' Mary Power exploded as though fired from the tea urns. 'The lodge has been squawking like a bunch of headless chickens all morning. It's Sue called the brief.'

Dewi ignored her. 'The killing of Gwyn Pritchard marks a low point. We done our best, lads, held out nearly a year, but here's where it stops.'

A tremor rippled through the crowd. Helen felt the women

327

breathe in sharply. There was a pause, then uproar. Voices demanding to be heard.

'*You're selling out*?' Mary's white hair quivered.

Dewi addressed himself to the men. 'We can't do it, lads. All the other coalfields have had folk drift back to work since Christmas. We've had nothing from the TUC. The best hope for this pit – our only hope – is to go back to work united. Regroup to fight the closure.'

'That's suicide,' Johnny's voice came back sharp as a whip. 'Go back defeated, you'll give the bosses free rein to shut the pit.'

'We can't back down,' Mary said. 'We said all along, it's a fight to the death.'

'We held out a year,' Eddie Hobnob said. 'We did our best.'

The meeting was split, Helen saw; the men defeated and tired, the women fired up to fight on. But how could their best be good enough, if it left her dad dead, her mam homeless, Scrapper charged with murder and every man in the room heading for the dole queue?

Mary was watching her. 'You tell 'em, Red.'

'Me? But—'

'Mary's right,' Sue said. 'They'll listen to you.'

Arms pushed her forwards. She stumbled to the front of the room, dug deep, mined a thin seam of resolve. 'You all know me,' she began. 'My name is Helen—'

A burst of white light dazzled her. She paused, shielded her eyes. The arc lights of a television camera blazed from the doorway. Jimmy Mosquito was pushing through the crowd.

'Get that bastard journalist out of here,' someone growled.

'No,' Helen said. 'Reckon the bastard journalist should hear this.'

A ripple of laughter boosted her nerve.

'Gwyn Pritchard was my dad. But Scrapper Jones is my

husband. Scrapper was on that bridge trying to stop Dai Dumbells attacking the bus. He did what any one of us would have done. He's no murderer, my husband; it's down to us to clear his name. Go back now, it's like you've tried and found him guilty.'

As she staggered back towards the women, Uncle Johnny nodded to say she'd done alright. But the men stood in silence, their faces masks of defeat and exhaustion and shame. And Dewi was shaking his head.

Someone launched himself at her, gripped her hand between clammy palms. 'James Hackett, freelance journalist.'

She backed away from him.

'Helen said what she wanted to say,' Sue told him. 'We'll be watching to see if you use it. Bet it don't fit your script.'

15

The smell of mothballs hung in the half-light. The old boys from Blackthorn Colliery Band had dusted down their red serge uniforms and were tuning up their trumpets, trombones and tubas. Staccato toots and beeps echoed along the High Street as a crowd gathered. Dewi Power stood in front of The Red Lion, donkey jacket over orange boilersuit, helmet under his arm. All the men were dressed for work for the first time in a year. The red banner of Blackthorn lodge billowed and flapped above them.

Helen watched them sadly, shivering in her white t-shirt. Around her, the other women wore white t-shirts too. On each, a slogan: *Justice for Scrapper Jones*. Were they her friends, these women? Getting there, maybe. They were bound together now, an uneasy sisterhood.

A bizarre gathering was taking shape. She saw students from the solidarity groups in Swansea and Cardiff, a ragged army in dreadlocks and khaki and denim, come out for one last defiant march. Among them stood Margaret Parry, done up in her Sunday best, smart eau de nil coat and a little hat to match. She was leaning on the arm of her eldest, come home to the village with a busload of car workers from the Midlands, all dressed in blue boiler suits, rising sun logo stitched on the breast. Small figures darted in and out of the crowd, the children of Ystrad, wearing outsized white t-shirts over their clothes.

There were dozens of red banners for the railway workers and the printers, the nurses and the civil servants. But there were banners of many other colours too. Pink flags and purple; banners with rainbow stripes. Black flags for anarchists. Green for the ones Mary called lentil botherers. And Mary, where was she?

Tension rippled through the crowd. Helen climbed the *bracchi* steps, saw a well-padded man wearing a double-breasted navy suit, a camera crew pushing after him through the crush.

Sue clambered up behind her. 'Our so-called local MP,' she said sourly.

The cameraman lined up a gang of students to wave placards behind Harry Cross. The MP pulled a comb from his pocket, folded his hair across his scalp. His cheeks puffed importance, as the sound girl fussed around him.

'Got a nerve, that one,' Sue said. 'He's not spoken to the men in twelve months.'

The MP's words floated towards them. '—a slap in the face for the Tory government. Today's return to work is a triumph for common sense. It's a moral victory. For the miners and for the Labour Party in Wales.'

Helen had to hold Sue back. Physically restrain her.

'Don't worry,' she said. 'They want to interview me later about Scrapper. I'll make sure you get your say, and all.'

Iwan and Angela climbed the steps to join them.

'Good of old Double-Cross to show his face,' Iwan cast a scowl over his shoulder at the MP.

'Where's Mary?' Angela asked.

'Not coming,' Sue said.

'What d'you mean?' It was the first Helen had heard of it.

'She's packing to leave.'

That was unthinkable. Mary couldn't leave. How could they fight to free Scrapper without her? Helen marched over to the film crew, cadged ten pence from the producer who wanted to interview her. The phone box outside the pub was empty. She dialled Mary's number and waited.

'Orright, love,' Mary's voice was thin and tired.

'We're about to move. When you coming?'

There was a long pause. The telephone line clicked and whirred. 'I'm not coming.'

'But we need you, Mary. I need you.'

'I'm sorry, Red. I'm off to Manchester to stay with my eldest for a while.'

'You and Dewi, an' all?'

Mary's laugh had the dry rasp of coal dust. 'I'll leave you my badge, love. Your marriage has a shot, at least.'

'You reckon?'

'I knows it. Damn proud of you, girl.'

The coin clattered to the bottom of the slot. Helen replaced the receiver, leaned against the grubby glass. Something round and solid dug into her thigh. She reached into her pocket and touched the lump of anthracite. It was as warm as her skin. Scrapper's words came back to her: *I'll trade you this lump of anthracite for a diamond and gold band.*

She wouldn't hold him to it

* * *

The colliery band struck up a marching tune. The crowd oozed down the hill. The shops and businesses that had survived, from The Red Lion down to the Co-op, had closed for the morning. Customers and shopkeepers lined the pavement as the march surged past. A lone figure in a tweed great coat stood outside the salon. It was Siggy Split-Enz.

He waved Helen over. 'I'm so sorry about your husband, *schatzi*. Matt saw what happened. We know it wasn't Simon.'

The shock sent tremors up her legs. She grabbed Siggy's arm.

The police said there were no witnesses, said it was Scrapper's word against theirs. Dai Dumbells had fallen apart like a worn-out sack of coal in custody, couldn't or wouldn't answer questions. Debbie refused to visit him. He wasn't fit to stand trial, his lawyer said.

'Matt is not a villain,' Siggy said. 'Just scared to tell the truth about himself.'

'Would he tell the truth in court. About Scrapper, I mean?'

'I will ask him,' Siggy said. 'It is a small way to make amends before we go.'

'Go where?'

'Somewhere no one knows us. A new town. A new life.'

'But I'll miss you, Sig.'

'Steady on,' he held her at arm's length and studied her. 'I saw your picture in the papers: *Red Helen says No*. The hair was half tidy, if I say so myself.'

She said goodbye to Siggy, ran to tell Sue and Angela the news. She found them with the other women, at the front of the march. They passed the Stute, turned down the hill towards the pit. Thin daylight picked out a green haze on the slag heaps. When they reached the railway bridge, the band stopped playing. Helen gripped Sue's hand. The verges were scarred with tyre marks. Chipped brickwork marked the spot where the minibus had hit the wall. The marchers entered the tunnel in silence, heads lowered, emerging below the chapel gates. She looked up and saw the mound of earth that marked the grave dug for her dad, his body returning to coal. She hoped she could persuade her mam to come back to lay him to rest, at least.

At last, the lodge banner reached the pit gates. It took a while for the hundreds of marchers to assemble. Iwan waited with his butties, stoic in his donkey jacket and helmet. The men dragged deep on roll-up cigarettes, traded blue jokes and hollow banter, the better to hide their feelings from the cameras. At last, the stragglers reached the gates. Dewi clambered onto an oil drum and cleared his throat.

'Today is a sad day and a proud day for Britain's miners, out on strike for two days short of a year. It's a sad and proud day for Blackthorn, for the community, for the women who fought beside us. We go back with our heads held high. The struggle continues.'

The women moved aside as the pit gates swung open. All the men, dressed in donkey jackets, boilersuits and hard hats, lined up behind Dewi in their working pairs. When he gave the word, they trudged behind him through the gates. All of them, hardened colliers to the death, nailed their eyes to middle distance, marched in on heavy feet, towards a future no more solid than the clouds above their heads.

Helen felt a hand on her arm. It was the old boy, Sion Jenkins, already breathless and wheezing, face tinged blue.

'You lasses,' he said. 'More balls, more brains, more guts than any of us.'

He shook his head, shuffled off to catch up with Iwan. The gates slammed shut behind him. Steel-capped footsteps echoed across the hillsides.

The crowd thinned. People began to drift away, some towards waiting cars and vans, others on foot, heading back to the tunnel for the long climb back up to the village. Helen helped Angela, Sue and the other women to roll up the lodge banner and load dropped placards into the minibus and said their goodbyes to the nurses and printers, the civil servants and the railway workers.

'You coming?' Sue held the minibus door open.

Helen nodded towards the camera crew. 'I still got to speak to that lot. They want to film it outside the pit. Want to give them a few words, and all?'

Sue grinned, shook her head. 'You'll do fine. Come and find us after in the pub.'

She climbed in next to Chrissie Hobnob. All the women were waving as the minibus sped away.

Interview finished, Helen perched on one of the oil drums and watched the camera crew pack their things. She narrowed her eyes, tried to make out signs of movement beyond the gates. But all the men had vanished. A breeze picked up, studding goosebumps along her arms and legs. But she wasn't ready to go home. Not yet. She needed to see for herself how this would end. At last, the winding ropes tightened. She heard the faint rumble of the winding drum starting to unspool. There was a pause, then the pit's iron wheel shrieked like a speared animal. The sound made the hillsides tremble. Flocks of crows fired themselves squawking from the trees. Helen had never seen so many crows, dozens on dozens of them. They drew together, those thin, dark birds, rose so that they blotted out the thin grey sky. Then, they turned and flapped towards the sun. She stood and watched them until they disappeared.

The valley fell silent.

Acknowledgements

In the book the song 'Joe Hill' is from the 1930 poem by Alfred Hayes titled 'I Dreamed I Saw Joe Hill Last Night', later turned into a song in 1936 by Earl Robinson and recorded (MCA Music). The book also quotes from Idris Davies' debut collection *Gwalia Deserta* (Dent, 1938).

Although every effort has been made to secure permissions prior to printing this has not always been possible. The publisher apologises for any errors or omissions but if contacted will rectify these at the earliest opportunity.

Further acknowledgements

Kit would like to thank ...

Iris Ansell, Hilary Bailey, Dave Cohen, Agnieszka Dale, Yaz Djebbour, Martina Evans, Sophie Hignett, Amanda Hodgkinson, Dorothy Kreinders, Sophie Lambert, Kim Morrissey, Gail Robinson, Jacob Ross, Tribe Thomas and Nick Wray, the inmates at online creative colonies the Writers Asylum, You Write On and The Book Shed and fellow travellers from Centerprise, Mary Ward and City Lit.

Special thanks also to South Wales Miners' Library at Swansea University, the British Library, Colindale Newspaper Library and Big Pit.

Last and not least, Richard Davies, Susie Wild, Claire Houguez and all the wonderful team at Parthian Books for backing this novel.

Awakening
Stevie Davies

THE VISITOR
KATHERINE STANSFIELD

THE SCRAP BOOK
CARLY HOLMES

PARTHIAN

NEW FICTION

'Carries an impressive deal of intensive research lightly ... the portraiture throughout is graphic, richly detailed and subtly shaded'
New Welsh Review

Dream On
Dai Smith

PARTHIAN

WHILE NO ONE WAS WATCHING

DEBZ HOBBS-WYATT